APACHE SNOW

By William Casselman

APACHE SNOW

By William Casselman

©2015 By William Casselman

Front Cover Artwork by Elizabeth Holloway

Edited by Susan Smith

Operation Apache Snow, though an actual operational military code name used for the 11-day Battle for Hill # 937 in the Vietnam War, which history records the epic struggle under a more memorable title-- "Hamburger Hill". This story is a work of fiction.

Names and characters are a creation of the author, having no resemblance to actual persons, living or dead, except in the case where family members and dear friend's names were used in appreciation. Locations in the United States and in Vietnam listed in this book do exist, or possibly still exist in the case of Vietnam.

It was the author's intent to place a fictitious rifle squad into an actual platoon and show what occurred leading up to, during and after Operation Apache Snow. The North Vietnamese medic character is also fictitious.

Published by:
Alaska Dreams Publishing
www.alaskadp.com

Revised Editon July 2016
ISBN numbers:
ISBN-13: 978-0-9903454-1-1
ISBN 10: 0990345416
E-Book versions available.
Please visit www.alaskadp.com for links.

Contents

DEDICATION iv

AUTHORS NOTES 5

FOREWARD: 7

1 – A Brothers Love 27

2 - Going Where the Action Is 35

3 - The Screaming Eagles of the 101st...........................57

4 – Innocence Lost 79

5 – The Dear John Letter 109

6 – New Friends and Enemy's..123

7 – Into the Valley of Death Rode the 600 133

8 – Lions, Tigers and Bears – Oh My! 149

9 – Promotions Come Fast in War.................................163

10 – Who's Counting?...187

11 – Cannon Fodder..203

12 – I Need More Men...217

13 – Trapped in Hell 237

14 – And the Rains Came 265

15 - Renamed it Hamburger Hill..................................285

16 – At All Costs…Again! 297

17 – In the Company of Friends 313

18 – Counterattack! 325

19 – Leaving Paradise Without Buying Even a Post Card 343

20 – Acceptance Doesn't Come Easy 359

Epilogue: Old Acquaintances and Unveilings 379

About the Author..393

DEDICATION

Mona, my wife of 34 years, my love and best friend; to all of my children, grandchildren and first great-grandchild for their patience in watching the old man spend many a long hour in pounding away at the computer; to the Lord Jesus for carrying me through the rough spots in 10 years of military and 20 years of police work; to my fellow Vietnam Veterans, to highlight the POWs and remember the MIAs who are still unaccounted for from the Viet Nam War; to the men of 3rd Battalion who made this historic climb up Hill # 937, while facing insurmountable odds to defeat the 29th North Vietnamese Regiment after 11 days of battle; especially to those 70 brave US soldiers who lost their lives in this battle, their families and finally to the 420 American soldiers who were wounded to secure what was to be called Hamburger Hill.

AUTHORS NOTES

When I retired from police work in 1994, Apache Snow became my first completed manuscript in my attempts to become a published writer. Over the years I have dragged it out of the file cabinet for additional fine tuning; shortening or adding a page or two. As a Vietnam veteran and a Christian, my drive behind writing this story was to tell a story about many of the young Christian men who came to this vile war to serve their country, only to become disillusioned with the cause behind why the US was even involved in Southeast Asia. Many suffered a loss of faith in their Lord; if only for a time. Eighteen and 19 year olds, faced their own moral battles when that crucial moment came and a trigger was pulled in the heat of battle. Innocence lost, never to be regained and the nightmares soon to follow. For some, the servicemen remain on base as support personnel, but here, too they become targets for enemy mortars and rockets. There was no safe place in Vietnam. Children sell bottles of Coke with crushed glass in them and the old people carry satchel bombs.

I was not a believer during my time in Vietnam, that came many years later, but I saw several young men of faith reach those crucial moments when they questioned their beliefs. The horrors of war can easily force 18 or 19 year olds to wonder if God really cares, or if he truly exists, when he sees what an enemy rocket do to a barracks full of troops, or veiw the outcome of a firefight in a sweltering jungle. The stench always there, a constant reminder of one's days and nights in Hell.

But not only in battle did these young men stumble or fall. No, even on base or post, the liquor ran freely, the dope was available and the South Vietnamese women were very pretty. No, here too, many a young Christian youth lost his innocence in life, to return home a different person with his mind now filled with a sinful past he must account for and seek forgiveness, or turn away from the Lord.

Writing this story was a healing experience for me and this was apparently noticeable by my wife, Mona. It is my hope this story will bring healing to others and acquaint parents, sons and daughters, and friends of veterans with a snap-shot view of this perverse war. I use the word perverse because it was never fought as a war, only a political display of might for the Russians and Chinese to view. It began on a falsehood and ended in deceit, clearly not our country's most shining moment.

5

The most difficult time I had in writing this story was remembering this was a Christian tale of fiction and having to keep the profanity out. For this was a very profane war, where officers and enlisted commonly used four-letter outbursts to relay their feelings about current and past goings-on. Trash talk was common, but amazingly racism was barely noticeable. Vietnam was the one single place in the world where Americans stuck together and watched each other's back. Color didn't seem to matter when the bullets started flying.

FOREWARD:

SONG BO RIVER CAMP, SOUTH VIET NAM, MAY 12, 1968

A blackened kerosene lantern hung from the bunker's ceiling by a bent wire, casting eerie shadows upon leaky sandbag walls. The humidity inside this small fortress kept pace with the rising temperature which created a smell reminiscent of a high school gym boy's locker room--three-day old smelly socks, week old jocks and white t-shirts you were afraid to take home to mom because of the blood and grass stains.

He sat behind a makeshift table, constructed from discarded ammo crates, checking his wristwatch-again. This nervous act had been repeated five times in the last fourteen minutes. Sgt. Luke Kendal could feel the pressure in the air and on late nights like this, where a jungle's silence was an omen of foreseeable enemy attack, stress and a man's imagination, kept a heightened level of woe and a shaky body stuffed with nervous energy.

Luke pulled radio duty on the midnight to 6 a.m. watch. This amounted to security checks for the perimeter posts at fluctuating times to prevent the enemy from knowing when those checks might come. His major battle was to fight off sleep and to do this he would work on writing a letter home. With five hours to go before relief, he had trouble writing a letter to his younger brother, Matthew. To help stay awake, he grabbed his soiled neck towel, wrapped one end of it around the handle of a battered black coffee pot. Heated by a Sterno stove, the pot and cooker was perched precariously on a pile of four broken sandbags in one corner of the bunker. Once their supply of Sterno was used up, they were forced to use some foul smelling oil provided by their Montegnard allies. Luke thought the stench could peel paint, but it did keep the coffee hot and he knew better than to ask what the oil consisted of.

"Nothing like C-rat coffee and a handful of aspirin to work your way into an ulcer," Luke said out loud. The sound of his voice helped break the creepy silence. Then with the towel over his neck once more to fight off the sweat, he returned to his unfinished letter. Between words he took a sip from his coffee stained ceramic mug with some Saigon bar logo and wondered what kind of mischief his little brother might be getting into back home.

Three hundred and ten yards outside the camp's perimeter, a young North Vietnamese Army lieutenant signaled his sergeant to open fire on the compound with their four mortars. At precisely 0158 hours, the first mortar round exploded inside Song Bo River Camp and nearly hit the Communications Bunker, where Luke sat. A shock wave containing jagged pieces of shrapnel peppered the outside walls; the concussion wave sent Luke head over heels backwards against the opposite wall. With hot coffee splattered all over him, Luke's attention draws to the radio. He grabbed up the hand-held microphone, flipped the transmission switch to send and shouted, "Incoming! Incoming!" First in English, then repeated in South Vietnamese and again in the only Montegnard dialect he knew--there were seven of them he knew of.

Not that the warning was needed. The multiple explosions sent the camp's defenders en route to their assigned slit trenches and various bunkers at flank speed to escape the rain of mortar fragments and fiery debris. Though soundly built, Luke knew the Comm Bunker could not withstand a direct hit. The three-foot-thick walls consisted of canvas sandbags and odd-sized sheets of plywood, scrounged lumber, corrugated tin and packed dirt. Luke pushed himself off the floor, grabbed his M-16, ensured he had earlier switched the rifle's selector from safe to semi-auto when he came on shift. A round was chambered when he took over the radio duty. One never knew when an unwelcome guest would sneak through the wire to make a suicide run on the communications bunker. He looked across the room, now filled with dust and saw 1st Lt. Bob Weeks, his A-Team commander, on his knees against the far wall. Lt. Weeks, visibly shaken by the blast, remained conscious with a small trail of blood, trickling from his nose. Luke spotted his lieutenant's smile and understood--*a near miss was still a miss.*

"Get on the radio," Weeks ordered. He winced from a sharp pain in his head. North Vietnamese mortars added to his discomfort when a second series of explosions shook the camp; a clear message to the defenders that this wasn't just routine harassment fire. The S-2 Intelligence Section at Phu Bai Air Force Base had advised Lt. Weeks two days ago that the lead elements of a North Vietnamese regiment had come into his area and he should expect an attack soon.

Major Thieu, Lt. Weeks' South Vietnamese counterpart took the information seriously and left for an *unscheduled* visit to the City of Danang. This left Lt. Weeks in command of the camp, until the Major Thieu's return. For the past week the North Vietnamese Army and Viet Cong had stepped up their attacks on various towns and military installations and the newspaper boys in Saigon called it, "The Spring Offensive". The Song Bo River Camp, a Special Forces stronghold, was located 58-miles west of Phu

Bai, deep within Indian country. Lt. Weeks had the camp on full alert as the sun went down and darkness enclosed the area in a thick blanket of moist blackness.

The US learned the North Vietnamese Army and Viet Cong preferred to attack in the early morning hours before dawn. They expected to find the enemy weary from long hours on high alert through the long night. The Communications Bunker also acted as the A-Team's command post; a major part of the camp's defensive plan because the radio was their lifeline to Phu Bai. Unfortunately, the enemy also knew this and tried destroying the bunker with concentrated mortar fire. If a ground assault were to follow the mortar attack, which Lt. Weeks suspected, the air support from Phu Bai would prove vital to the camp's defense. Lt. Weeks could then direct the fighter's weapons to fire where it was needed most. That being the case, a member of the A-Team manned the radio 24 hours a day. Lt. Weeks didn't trust South Vietnamese soldiers with the duty. He knew among his allies were some VC. As a back up, a second radio with extra batteries was smuggled into camp unseen and buried under the floorboards of the Forward Observation Post. Its existence was known only to the members of the A-Team.

His M-16 ready in his right hand, Luke keyed the radio's microphone with his left thumb to keep Phu Bai apprised of the situation, "Sierra Bravo One under heavy fire by mortars. This is no harassment. I repeat this is no harassment fire. Alpha-One requests air support over our location immediately." Alpha-One was Lt. Weeks and each member of the A-Team was given a designation number in order of rank. Luke, a new member to this team was Alpha-Ten. Luke transmitted his message and a radio operator in Phu Bai could hear the muffled explosions in the background. Within two minutes, Phu Bai advised Luke the air support was being launched.

"Lieutenant, the birds are being sent," Luke advised Lt. Weeks. Getting only a quick nod in response, Luke crawled to the north side of the bunker and dragged the heavy radio along with him. Small openings were built into the walls of sandbags, providing rifle slits for defenders to fire from. From Luke's position he could see sections of barbed wire strung along the northern perimeter. Two hundred Montegnard strikers--mountain tribesmen who hated nearly all Vietnamese--were hired by the US Government as mercenaries, manned the north perimeter. Two hundred eighty South Vietnamese ARVN (Army of the Republic of Vietnam) soldiers and 40 popular force volunteers were spread between the east and west perimeters. The Song Bo River Camp was built on the southeastern side of a large, steep plateau overlooking the Song Bo River. Shaped like a huge triangle, the east and west sides of the camp overlooked the valley below, while the north perimeter faced the remainder of the plateau.

The builders of the camp knew it would be costly for an enemy to attack uphill against an entrenched force, but the north side of the camp presented a problem. A large, thick growth of trees and bushes covered the unoccupied remainder of the plateau, which grew to within 100 yards of the outer perimeter wire. Plans to clear off 500 yards of jungle growth had been put on hold by order of Major Thieu, much to Lt. Weeks' disgust. To prevent a surprise attack on the north side, Weeks placed two well concealed listening posts 50 yards inside the tree line. These positions were 200 yards apart and manned by volunteer Montegnards. A series of trip flares and trip-wire activated claymore mines formed a semi-circle around these posts for added protection. These flares could turn a night's darkness into bright daylight, while the claymore, each containing a piece of C-4 plastic explosive, upon detonation would send out hundreds of tiny steel balls with an effectively aimed killing range of 100 feet.

In addition to the ARVN, volunteers and Montegnards, a 14-man Special Forces A-Team out of 5th Special Forces Group from Fort Bragg also manned the camp. The team consisted of two officers and two-six-man squads; made up of noncommissioned officers.

When the A-Team arrived on the scene patrol activity increased by nearly 80% and the VC lost their control over nearby villages. In retaliation, the North Vietnamese sent an NVA regiment south to destroy the camp during the spring offensive. Lt. Weeks had fortified the camp with six .50 caliber machinegun positions spread out around the perimeter and two 81mm mortar pits positioned in the center of camp. Eight nearly antique .30 caliber machineguns and twelve M-60 light machineguns were placed to provide interlocking fire in support of the heavier weapons. Lt. Weeks also added triple strand, razor sharp concertina wire to enclose the unprotected areas of the camp. Claymore mines were set inside the wire every ten yards with trip flares positioned between them. Added for effect, A-Team members hung used C-ration cans on the wire with rocks inside to make noise when rattled; an old tried and true method from previous wars.

SONG BO RIVER CAMP 0207 HRS, MAY 12TH

The mortar barrage actually caused little damage to the camps few structures, though one round had hit the east corner of the Aid Station, which wounded an ARVN soldier. The man was being treated for a leg infection after he stepped on a VC punji stake. Another round took out one of the large water storage tanks; sending 800 gallons of water into a trench full of terrified ARVN troops. The heavy bunkers and reinforced trenches were doing their job of protecting the troops and by 0207 hours only six men had been wounded. The bad news was how the mortar fire was blowing apart large sections of defensive wire; holes the enemy could use for a ground assault.

"Any casualties, Luke?" Lt. Weeks asked.

"Six WIA so far, sir," Luke repied.

That won't last long, Weeks thought to himself. He glanced out his own rifle slit, then looked back at Luke. He studied his young RTO for a moment. He liked the kid. The two of them had spent many a long night together over the last two months of duty. Often they compared ideologies and religious doctrines. Lt. Weeks found Luke well educated in the areas of religion. He wasn't surprised to learn Luke was the son of a church pastor. Seeing Luke's 6'4", 185-pound frame scrunched up against the far wall of a bunker built for the miniature South Vietnamese made Lt. Weeks smile. He turned away from Luke's idealism to his own beliefs. Lately he felt God had lost touch with his creations. It seemed to him God tended to ignore their many pleas for mercy and compassion. The war had done that to him, caused doubt as he witnessed the brutality of man against his brother. Still, Luke put up a good fight in God's defense when they debated a higher authority; which helped pass the time on those long hot nights. Lt. Weeks turned 26 years old fifteen days ago and the A-team had presented him with a birthday cake made from eight C-ration pound cakes covered in fruit cocktail. He was quite touched.

Running an average of 165 pounds, the Vietnamese sun had turned his skin a dark golden brown and lightened his brown hair to what his school buddies would call *surfer brown*. His graduation photo from college displayed his eyes as a radiant bluish color, but after two months of duty out here in *Indian Country*, they had assumed a weary shade of bloodshot blue. Like Luke and the other members of the A-team, Lt. Weeks wore a heavy flak vest, usually unzipped to expose his sweaty bare chest and stomach. Until the rains came, he often went without a shirt. Unless he knew someone was coming out from Phu Bai to check on the camp, he then pulled on a wrinkled green jungle fatigue shirt. But within moments, his shirt was once again covered in sweat stains and his upper body reeked of a foul odor he compared to jock rot. The heat in Nam had taken its toll; Lt. Weeks dropped ten pounds to Luke's 17.

Outside the bunker the temperature had cooled to a tepid ninety degrees, while inside the bunker it remained well over a hundred degrees. The doorway leading inside the bunker was covered by a green plastic shelter-half at night to ensure none of the lantern's light escaped and in a fruitless attempt to keep the mosquitoes out. With the exception of the four rifle slits, there was no other ventilation and on any given night the occupants inside the Comm Bunker could easily consume over two gallons of water to stave off dehydration. As sweat rolled off them, the mortar barrage continued to rain down upon the camp. Luke, who cringed as each explosion shook the ground, thought he was smack inside a thunderhead and the gods of war were having at it.

Another near miss shook the bunker like a 5.6 earthquake, causing a thick cloud of dust to rise up inside, temporarily blinding both Lt. Weeks and Luke. Another round exploded a mere ten feet from where Luke sat, the sandbags saving his life. It sent a wave of flame against the bunker wall and a shock wave knocked both Lt. Weeks and Luke off their feet. Luke struck the corner of an ammo crate with his chin. He cried out in pain, pushed himself from the floor, inspecting the radio for damage. It was okay. Only then did he take a moment to wipe the blood from a small laceration on his chin. Lt. Weeks lay on the floor, covered with a fine layer of dirt from the ceiling. His helmet, blown off his head, lay on the ground a couple feet from him.

Luke crawled to lieutenant Week's side; relieved to find him conscious, his nose and ears bloodied, but eyes responsive.

"You okay, L-T?" Luke asked.

"Yeah…Ah think so," Lt. Weeks answered hesitantly.

Outside, Luke heard a man shout for a medic, followed by a voice he recognized as MSgt Jones yelling, "Medic!" Luke knew Jones manned the Forward Observation Post on the northern perimeter with 2nd Lt. Jake Overstreet and SSgt. Alan Foster. Suddenly, multiple explosions shook the bunker, followed by more screams coming from the direction of the Forward Observation Post. Leaving Lt. Weeks' side, Luke returned to the radio, attempting to contact the FOP. Nobody answered. Right then a Montegnard Striker burst through the doorway, nearly getting him shot in the process. He bled from a nasty shoulder wound, was out of breath from the run. He ignored the rifle Luke aimed at him shouting, "F-O-P hit! F-O-P hit! Obesteet an' Fosster dead!"

Luke sat the striker down, pulling a battle dressing off his canteen belt, applying it to the man's wound. While doing so, Luke learned how the explosion killed Overstreet and Foster instantly. The sudden news of losing two of his men caught Lt. Weeks off guard. Though dazed by a mild concussion, he lay on the ground unable to speak. He listened as the striker attempted to tell Luke through broken English and hand gestures what had happened. Using Luke for focus, Lt. Weeks pushed the fog from his mind, sitting up.

"Luke, contact Jones an' have him take a squad to rebuild the FOP. Leave Whitehead in charge of the north perimeter for now," Weeks ordered.

With great effort he pulled himself to his feet, bracing one hand on the barrel of his rifle and the other on the bunker's wall.

"Yes, sir," Luke said. It took several calls over the radio before Jones responded. He had to dig his buddies from the rubble in vain hopes of finding one of them alive. Luke watched the scene through a rifle slit, barely able to make out the silhouettes of several men in front of a backdrop of hellish flames that engulfed the FOP. A pile of rubble that once was the twelve-foot tall observation tower, burned like dry kindling. Luke could see the fire, his face darkened by sweat and dust. He thought how a direct hit on this ramshackle bunker would have the same effect. It was not a thought he relished in. He stood the homemade table up, while Lt. Weeks spread out his map, showing the camp's defenses. He shook his head in frustration. An experienced combat soldier, Lt. Weeks knew he faced a well-supplied NVA force.

"They've got to be in the woods to the north, they'd lose too many men coming up the slopes for a frontal attack." Then turning to Luke, Lt. Weeks asked him for the latest casualty count? "We have 44 WIA and 12 KIA, Sir," Luke said.

"All right...notify Phu Bai of our casualties. We'll need medivac birds at first light an' get me an update on those fighters."

"Yes, sir," Luke responded with, his nerves tight; his voice strained. A tense moment passed before Luke turned, advising Lt. Weeks of a flight of Marine F-4 Phantoms that were coming in from Danang, loaded down with 250 pound bombs. "Sir, Phu Bai wants to know if we have a location on those mortars yet."

"Tell 'em to have the fighters hit the woods north of camp with their first run," Weeks ordered. He remembered his two LP positions in the woods north of camp. "Luke, pull those LP's immediately!" He had forgotten the men manning those LP's; which was unforgivable for a camp commander and Lt. Weeks knew it. But Luke had already taken care of it by contacting MSgt. Jones earlier. "Jones pulled them already, Sir."

Luke heard a radio call come in from the lead fighter pilot. He turned away from a relieved Lt. Weeks to hear the transmission. He didn't see the thanks in Weeks' eyes. At that same moment the shelter-half cover for the doorway jerked open. An elderly Montegnard leader entered the room. Luckily, Lt. Weeks recognized him as the leader of the camp's striker force and chief of the local tribe. By the looks in the old one's ancient eyes, Lt. Weeks knew something was seriously wrong. But out of respect for their culture he waited for the old man to speak first.

"Many…many VC all aroun', L-T…They come soon." He made a hand gesture to show the camp was encircled. Before the old man could finish, Luke interrupted, "Lieutenant, fast movers will be on station in five mikes."

The old man nodded his head once and left the bunker without another word. Outside two other Montegnards stood ready to escort their chief back to the perimeter. "That old man is rattled. He's not the type to get scared easily. Advise all posts to implement Operation Plan Alpha-Three. We're gonna get hit hard and I don't want any of those ARVN behind our A-Team positions."

"Affirmative, Lieutenant." Luke knew Alpha-Three meant to destroy all equipment while falling back from their positions and to keep all allied units in front, while they retreated. Since 1963, the soldiers they trained shot several members of the Green Beret in the back. In a country where allies and enemy look alike, it was easy for VC or NVA to infiltrate the ranks of the South Vietnamese Army.

Four minutes and 35 seconds later, the plateau shook and rolled under the impact of six 250 pound bombs, which exploded so close to the north perimeter. Whitehead was knocked to the dirt floor of his bunker. Untouched by shrapnel, Whitehead reported to Luke over the radio he had probably sustained a "…good head knockin', but I'm all right. Keep 'em comin'." Luke could barely understand Whitehead's transmission. The fighters were now directly overhead and on their second run. *They're making it mighty hard to hear anything above the sound of their afterburners.* "They're right on target, sir," Luke yelled across the bunker. He hoped Lt. Weeks could hear him over the sounds outside.

Before Weeks could reply, the radio came to life, "Sierra-Bravo One, this is Sierra-Bravo–Eight, NVA are engaging my position, over," Sgt. Peterson, who commanded the eastern perimeter, reported this before he dropped his microphone. He brought up his rifle to fire on full-auto against a squad of NVA. They charged through holes in the wire and in some cases, using their bodies to bridge the wire for their comrades.

Lt. Weeks realized the NVA had taken advantage of the bombings to launch an assault upon the east slope. He thought it a foolhardy move to say the least; which frightened Lt. Weeks even more. He knew the NVA were good fighters. Their leaders were deadly proficient in jungle warfare. *If they're ready to sacrifice troops this early in the attack…They must have an effective fighting force to back it up. But what the NVA don't know, I got a second flight of Sandy's comin' in an' those beautiful World War II vintage jobs are loaded down with napalm.*

However, before Lt. Weeks could pat himself on the back, SSgt. Medina--who was Alpha-Five--radioed in reporting a large enemy force had moved on his position on the western slope. "Alpha-One, Ah've got ARVN

14

on the run. Those damn cowards are leaving me high an' dry, L-T. You'd better send me some strikers, out!" Medina's abrupt transmission ended and Lt. Weeks knew the man had his hands full.

"Luke, tell Jones he's taking over for Overstreet in the FOP. Have him send two squads of strikers to back up Medina on the western slope immediately and keep two squads ready to support Peterson." Lt. Weeks realized he didn't need to yell anymore. Except for machinegun and small arms fire that came from the slopes, the area seemed to be strangely quiet. No more mortars, no more bombs and only an ominous feeling of what was to come. "I've got to get outside, Luke, to see what's happening," Lt. Weeks said. He turned to face Luke, "You've got to stay on that radio, kid. Do not leave this bunker, understand?" Lt. Weeks reached out laying his left hand on Luke's wide right shoulder, "Make contact with those Sandy's. We're gonna need 'em to hit both the west and east slopes before we get overrun. I'm on my way to Medina's position, but I'll keep in touch by radio. Remember, Luke, Mr. Charlie wants that radio too and some of those ARVN out there aren't who we think they are. You shoot anyone who tries to get in here that you don't recognize as a team member. You got that, sergeant?"

"Affirmative, L-T," Luke said. They shared a brief exchange of comradeship before Lt. Weeks charged from the room with his M-16 in one hand and helmet grasped in the other.

Alone, fighting down fear swelling in his throat, Luke huddled beside his radio pack, keeping rifle aimed at the opening to the bunker. While outside, the night exploded with sounds of RPG and M-79 grenade launchers, which played a weird duet, supported by heavy and light machinegun fire and the occasional hand grenade. Three minutes later the tension inside the bunker was broken when Luke heard the A-1 Sky Raider flight leader's voice came over the radio, "Sierra-Bravo-One, this is Whiskey-Three-Niner, how do yuh read, over?"

"Whiskey-Three-Niner, Sierra-Bravo-One is readin' you five by five and glad to hear you, over," Luke said in relief.

"Readin' yuh five by five and back at yuh, now where duh yuh want thu hot stuff, over?" The pilot had a southern quality to his voice, which gave Luke the impression he was a Mississippi cowboy.

"You can drop your load on those little men climbing up the slopes from the river side of our position, over," Luke advised him.

"Copy…on the slopes above the river…Can do…Stand-by for one hot foot a comin' right up. Tell yuh boys to keep their pretty little heads down now…this stuff will really light up your life…over and out!" The flight leader replied with a joyful finish.

That man seems to like his job, Luke thought. Less than a minute later, the hillsides below the east and west perimeters burst into a raging fire storm, as one Sandy after another released canisters of napalm upon the enemy. Orange, black and yellow flames billowed hundreds of feet into the air as the inferno covered the slopes. Even from inside the bunker, Luke could hear the screams of the NVA soldiers caught in the hellish onslaught. Later, Lt. Weeks told Luke how the scene was like a glimpse into the mouth of Hades, as he watched the enemy embrace the napalm's fiery death dance. For one brief moment, it was as if a volcano had erupted from the sides of the hill, blowing a hot jell like substance that made for instant lava.

Perimeter posts began reporting; the enemy was in full retreat. Dozens of NVA hurled themselves down the slopes to escape the deadly flames. Even friendly forces could feel the effects of the napalm blast when a wave of intense heat moved across the compound, forcing ARVN troops and volunteers to drop to the bottom of their trenches to escape Hell's fury. Air temperatures exploded upward from a sultry 90 degrees, transformed to a searing 300 degrees in mere seconds. Shortly afterward, cooling air currents carried the odor of burning flesh and scorched earth.

Luke was in the middle of thanking the flight leader when he heard Alpha-Eight yelling, "L-T's been hit!" Switching frequencies, Luke learned Lt. Weeks was on his way to the Aid Station with a bullet in his right arm. The news shook Luke up. But the battle wasn't over yet. SSgt. Banks, who manned the mortar pits, sent out 81mm rounds of high explosives to send the fleeing NVA on their way.

A moment later, Luke heard Lt. Weeks' weary voice come over the radio, "Cease fire. I repeat, cease fire." Within a minute the camp fell into an uneasy silence, with only the sound of men in pain and others yelling for a medic heard. Luke glanced at his watch, seeing it was only 0307 hours. The attack lasted only 67 minutes; the longest hour and seven minutes of his life. At 0355 hours, Luke made radio contact with the rebuilt FOP. Sandbags piled up to an eight-foot circular wall--three sandbags thick and a .50 caliber machinegun moved into position--supported by two rifle trenches now created the new position.

Hearing a noise behind him, Luke turned with rifle in hand to see Lt. Weeks stumble into the bunker. He collapsed unconscious to the floor. He refused to stay in the Aid Station escaping SSgt. Oliver's care to resume command. Contacting the Aid Station, Luke advised Oliver of Lt. Weeks location. A disgruntled medic responded, "Turn my back on him for one minute an' he takes off. I'll be there in three mikes, just make sure he doesn't bleed to death."

Luke relaxed a bit while replacing a bloody bandage wrapped around Lt. Weeks arm. He knew Oliver would probably redo it, but at least the medic would know Luke was doing his job too. In little over an hour the camp sustained 88 men killed and 170 men wounded. Of the men killed, four were members of Weeks' A-Team. Song Bo River Camp's defense force had been reduced from 534 effective fighters to 286 stunned, shaken men. With the coming of dawn, the humidity inside the bunker thickened and the heat became miserable. Only when the sun broke the horizon was Luke allowed to open the bunker, by tying off the sticky shelter-half. His body draped in sweat, splattered with Lt. Weeks' dried blood; Luke wondered how God could allow such carnage to occur. With each ounce of doubt, he forced himself to remember his dad's words, "The heart of man is sinful." Luke recalled another conversation with his dad, "God allows man to have free choice. It is within us to make war and kill. We've been doing it for thousands of years, Luke. Yes, God could wipe out the armies of the unjust; destroy his weapons; but where would our free choice be? He cast Satan down to ensure us freedom to decide our own destiny. Even if it means our own death. How God must weep for His children."

The doubt was gone. Luke uttered a short prayer for the dead and their families. Later, he prayed a stronger prayer for faith when his eyes fell upon the pile of body bags lying near the helipad. Using that same soiled green towel, he wore draped around his neck; Luke wiped his face and trudged on toward an undamaged water tank. He hoped to grab a couple hours of sleep, but that faded when he saw MSgt. Jones coming toward him with two shovels in his hands. "No rest for the weary," Luke whispered.

SONG BO RIVER CAMP MAY 13TH, 1968- 0812 HOURS

Luke received word from MSgt. Jones that a second A-Team had been put on alert in Danang in the event Song Bo came under another ground assault. Luke was to assist Jones in an inspection of the camp's defenses, while Lt. Weeks rested in the sun outside the Comm Bunker. Large sections of perimeter wire were gone; replaced by deep craters. Dozens of trenches and a minimum of five bunkers lay in ruin. Some bodies remain buried underneath tons of earth. Acres of scorched earth outside the wire glistened as sunrays struck the hardening napalm jell. It would be hours before anyone could walk across the hot blackened surface. Oliver had his hands full with dozens of wounded who were in need of treatment. Priority cases would be flown to Phu Bai or Danang. Two Vietnamese medics assisted, while volunteer Vietnamese soldiers helped with minor cases. The stench of death drifted across the plateau, mixed with smoke from the fires. The smell forced many men to wear something over their noses to filter the air, but the visual scene was a horror that made even the strongest man wince; while weaker ones ran away sick.

By 0900 hours, the air was filled with arrival and departure of Hueys. First came the dust-offs--medivac birds to remove the wounded. Then supply birds. Finally, the ever-desired mail. Outside the wire, hidden deep in the jungle forest; the NVA forces remained quiet as a fighter cover continually supported the helicopters during evacuation of wounded. Farther out, Huey gunships search for elusive NVA; but the enemy had vanished into the jungle, returning to tunnels, waiting for cover of night to come back.

Lt. Weeks declined leaving camp. He spent the morning relaxing upon a pile of sandbags; while observing the evacuation. His injured arm was worn in a sling. Lt. Weeks gently massaged his sore muscles. Assisted by a jab of morphine, Oliver carefully removed an AK-47 bullet from the LT's arm, which missed the bone and an artery by a quarter inch. The wound cleaned, bandaged, the arm placed in a sling; Oliver handed Lt. Weeks a handful of aspirin, telling him to call him if the pain got too much to handle. "That will be $20 or a good bottle of bourbon." To this, Lt. Weeks replied, "How about three weeks extra guard duty, when we get back to camp?" Oliver smiled, wiped his hands, saying, "All my work is pro bono anyway for you government workers. Do you want a lollipop, lieutenant? I have grape and cherry?" He always carried suckers for the children he worked on. They often followed him around camp in hopes of a free one.

MSgt. Jones told Luke how Lt. Weeks grabbed an M-60 machinegun to repel a large force of NVA. "...after getting himself shot up, he tossed out a couple grenades and saved the day." Luke knew from hearing the story from others that Lt. Weeks' action actually forced a platoon size force of NVA to retreat even before the napalm drop.

"For an officer, that kid's not too bad," MSgt. Jones said. Luke knew that was high praise from an old soldier like Jonesy.

Approaching noon, a CH-46 supply helicopter landed inside camp, its twin rotors blowing clouds of dust over the men. The bird carried needed ammo, rations, another radio for the new FOP, plus a bag of mail from home. Once the supplies were quickly off loaded, half the ARVN bodies were placed on board. The remaining bodies, covered by poncho liners after body bags were used up, would wait for tomorrow's flight. The bodies of the four Americans were flown out earlier by Huey, headed for Danang's morgue and later Hawaii. Once the wounded were gone and supplies stacked up; the defenders began stringing new wire. With the high number of enemy dead, MAC-V hoped the Song Bo River Camp wouldn't be attacked again for some time--but they were wrong.

SONG BO RIVER CAMP MAY 13TH, 1968, 2215 HOURS

When the last Huey departed the camp, the sun dropped behind the horizon. The humidity and blood-sucking mosquitoes returned with a vengeance. MSgt. Jones sent two striker patrols out in the morning. They returned at dusk reporting that the enemy was within three miles of camp. The were prepared to attack the camp.

Lt. Weeks notified Phu Bai thatanother attack was imminent. Confirmation occurred when an enemy mortar barrage began at 2215 hours.

Sgt. Peterson was on radio duty when Lt. Weeks ordered, "Make contact with Phu Bai. Get those sky jockeys back into the air ASAP!"

Barely able to hear over the explosions, Peterson crawled over to Lt. Weeks' side, "Lieutenant, air cover should be on station within ten mikes." Lt. Weeks glared at Peterson. Looking over to MSgt. Jones, who shared the bunker with them, he said, "In ten minutes the NVA will be in here to welcome those fly-boys."

He clutched his M-16 with a tight grasp; thought for a moment of his next move, and addressed Jones, "You get on up to the F-O-P. Keep me appraised of the situation up there. I'll stay here with Peterson for the moment."

"Yes, sir," Jones answered with a shout. He ran outside. "Keep your head down, Jonesy!" Lt. Weeks yelled to an empty doorway.

Luke manned a heavy .50 caliber machinegun on the north perimeter, scrunched behind the bottom of his sandbag wall and holding his hands over both ears to stifle the sound of nearby explosions. He had three young half-dressed Montegnard strikers to assist as his gun crew; while two M-60 machineguns supported his position on each side. NVA mortar crews concentrated their fire on the wire, shredding the new wire. Large bomb craters from F-4 bombardment covered an area the size of two-football fields, leaving blackened stumps, burned trees, and gray ash covering the north side of the plateau.

By 2228 hours, a flight of A1-E Sky Raiders from Phu Bai was overhead dropping napalm on the east slope, below camp. A large force of NVA was sighted with infrared scopes as the wave of liquid flame swept over them. The mortar barrage lifted at 2229 hours, giving Lt. Weeks the impression the NVA might be low on mortar ammo. Though short in duration, the mortar fire had done its job all too well. Several ARVN trenches had taken direct hits, killing or wounding 34 men.

"Send in one of the reserve units," MSgt. Jones advised his Vietnamese NCO counterpart.

A reserve force of 25 ARVN troops--one of two support units--was brought in to replace the dead. The wounded were ordered to stay in place to fight, while bodies were thrown from the trench; used like sandbags to protect the living. Lt. Weeks began feeling better from a mixture of adrenalin and a shot of scotch whiskey from Oliver. He was on the radio to the mortar pits; they would direct 81mm fire against enemy positions to the north.

"Peterson, advise Phu Bai to send in the Mike Force," Weeks ordered. He then turned away the microphone held in Peterson's hand, whispering, "This could be *Custard's last stand* if we don't get help soon." He knew their time had run out unless they got help fast. The Mike Force included the second A-Team and another 90-Montegnard striker force. When the mortars stopped, Luke stood up carefully, peeking over the bunker wall. He spotted movement in the distance, grabbing his radio to request illumination over the north perimeter.

Sgt. Banks responded with, "Two spot lights comin' right up." Once the flare rounds were ordered, Luke advised his small force to prepare to open fire upon his command. Nine seconds later, the pitch-blackness of night exploded with balls of miniature sunlight, when two parachute flares illuminated the area over the north perimeter. The two flares hung 200 feet above the plateau, begginning a slow downward drift towards the horizon.

To avoid glare that came off the parachute flares, Luke shielded his eyes with his left hand, raising his head to see what activity could be seen outside the perimeter wire. He used binoculars. The sight before him caused him to freeze. Only repeated tugs on his arm by a nearby Montegnard brought him back into focus.

"Open fire--Open fire!" Luke shouted. He grabbed his radio microphone, reassuming a low crouch behind the sandbags. He struggled to control his anxiety. Once able to think straight, he contacted the communications bunker, "Alpha-One--this is Alpha-Ten. I've got a large force moving in on my position. I request immediate assistance, over." Luke was surprised how calm his voice sounded, as if he had ordered a hamburger at a McDonald's Drive-up.

"Alpha-Ten, advise estimated enemy strength, over," Peterson asked. His nervous fingers tapped the microphone case, while waiting for Luke's reply. "I've got hundreds of 'em crawlin' through holes in the wire. Hold on, over." Luke popped back up and was forced to shield his left ear from distinct rapid fire sound of the .50 caliber machinegun. "Make that charging through the wire. Estimate battalion strength and ah need help up here like right now!" Luke dropped microphone and binoculars to pick up an M-79 grenade launcher. He popped it open--confirming the single barrel weapon was loaded with a 40 mm white phosphorus grenade--fired it. He reloaded it with a second load of high explosive. After a third round was in the air,

Luke picked up the radio mike, shouting, "Unable to hold, request permission to fall back to secondary position, over." His voice was no longer calm. Lt. Weeks knew Luke wasn't one to exaggerate when it came to enemy strength.

"Order Alpha-Ten to fall back," Lt. Weeks ordered. "Then advise Alpha-Three to send Kendal that reserve unit of strikers. We can't let the north perimeter fall...They'll overrun the camp before the Mike Force can get here," Lt. Weeks said. He was up against the north wall of the bunker. Through dark ringed bloodshot eyes, he starred out the nearest rifle slit to see what was happening up there.

With the heavy rattle of machinegun fire all around him, Luke was unable to hear Peterson's voice over the radio. Not that it mattered anymore. Luke and his heavy weapons squad didn't have time to fall back. The enemy breached the perimeter in strength, sending a platoon-sized force against Luke's bunker. The NVA, strength reduced by half from the previous attack, wore tan kaki uniforms and tan colored pith helmets with a single red star in the middle of the front of the headgear. They were supported by a battalion of Viet Cong in black clothes or whatever they could find to wear. Both units were armed with AK-47's and Russian made bolt-action rifles.

Screaming and hollering, they spilled out of the woods, breaching the wires. Luke seriously needed to shut them up, frightening the ARVN, but his position was about to be overwhelmed by sheer weight in numbers.

Lt. Weeks ordered Sgt Banks to drop high explosive mortar rounds right on the perimeter wire, but the pit crews were in support of the other two perimeters. The area that surrounded the camp, known officially as "No Man's Land", became a killing field, as NVA bodies fell by the dozens under concentrated fire of mortar and machineguns.

"I need more flares!" Luke yelled into his radio. He returned using his M-16 on full automatic against a line of enemy soldiers. Several NVA and VC were already at the base of his bunker wall. One attempted to lob a grenade in, but was cut down by a striker's deadly swing with a machete. The man on the .50 caliber went down, a bullet hole to his forehead. Luke jumped up, resuming control of the huge weapon. He swept the powerful machine gun from right to left, forced by fear to fight down the urge to hold the dual triggers down and run through the belt with abandon. He knew from his training the weapon would be more effective with the use of short bursts and target selection. Luke didn't want the barrel to overheat.

Luke looked down at the young Montegnard boy who assisted him as a loader. *You're about Matt's age...and now you're going to die...oh, God...why?* Unable to speak, his breath control on automatic fast forward and adrenalin his drug for today, Luke knew with sudden realization he was about to die and for a brief second he thought of his parents and the letter they'd receive from the Department of Defense. He visualized their faces as they read the letter, the grief they would feel. He envisioned their tear-filled eyes. This lead to sudden white rage from down deep inside him.

Each one of those enemy soldiers charging him meant another tear on his mother's cheek. With this thought deep in his mind, clarity grew stronger. Luke raised his right hand, now clenched into a tight fist. He shouted, "Give me strength, Lord!" His fear was gone, replaced by a strange sense of excitement he never felt before in battle. He felt a wave of warmth throughout his body and said, "I know you are with me, Lord God, but forgive me for what I must do here today." At that very moment, Luke reached down, lifting the detonation device for the six claymore mines positioned in front of his bunker. He pushed the plungers down, heard the claymores explode outward, sending hundreds of steel pellets outward toward the enemy's ranks. Dozens of NVA and VC fell before the steel wave of death. For a brief moment the enemy's charge stopped. But the respite didn't last long. The NVA and VC began a stomping climb over bodies of their dead to reach Luke's position, seeking their own revenge for their fallen comrades. One belt of ammo gone, the young striker appeared with a new belt of the heavy ammo. Luke returned to the business of the day--to kill the enemy.

SONG BO RIVER CAMP MAY 14, 1968, 0638 HOURS

With a new day's sun in the sky overhead, the morning fog dissipated, Lt. Weeks knelt beside the body of Luke Kendal. Sgt. Banks crouched down opposite of Weeks. He zipped Luke's body bag, while they listened to MSgt. Jones' account of how Luke died. Seriously wounded, MSgt. Jones lay bandaged on a stretcher, waiting for the next dust-off to take him back to camp. Before he left, he wanted Lt. Weeks to know the facts surrounding Sgt. Luke Kendal's last few moments.

"Kid kept firing, L-T, 'til he ran out of ammo. Should of seen him, L-T. Regular John Wayne and Audie my god Murphy, he picked up a rifle an' ordered his strikers to attack. Attack! Can you believe it? No retreat in that boy. He stood there like Paul Bunyun, emptin' his weapon at 'em." Jonesy took a moment to catch his breath and fight down a spasm of pain. A tough old soldier, Jonesy had a story to tell and wasn't going to let a little thing like pain stop him. He refused Oliver's morphine. He had problems with it in the past when he got shot up twice before. But he did except a couple heavy belts of Oliver's 25-year old Scotch whisky he saved for the serious wounded team members.

"Take it easy, Jonesy," Lt. Weeks said. He rested his hand upon Jones' uninjured shoulder.

"You can be proud of that boy, lieutenant. He died like a real Green Beret," Jonesy said before a spasm in the chest forced him silent.

"Put it in your report, Jonesy. You need to rest now," Lt. Weeks ordered.

"Listen, L-T, jus' in case ah don't make it. That kid…Luke, he grabbed up some grenades an' started lobbing 'em. Bombardin' 'em as they poured over his position like an army of ants." Jonesy stopped again. He took a moment to grind his teeth together to fight back the pain. Lt. Weeks held his silence to allow his friend to continue at his own pace. "Even with our reserve force, the perimeter was overrun by sheer numbers. But Luke wouldn't retreat, holdin' his position while they swarmed over him. Saw 'im take two hits, but Luke wasn't through yet…No, not that kid. He went hand-ta-hand with three of 'em, knives and knuckles with two bullets in 'im. Shot to pieces and he still kills three of 'em." Jonesy lowered his voice to a whisper. "I'm proud to of served with him…" Jonesy fell silent. His eyes were moist and he turned away from Lt. Weeks and stared off toward an arriving Huey. Lt. Weeks was unable to see Luke's heroics, but from Jonesy and other A-Team members he eventually learned how Luke went down under the weight of several NVA and though he knew he was about to die, he used his last grenade on himself and the enemy soldiers all around him.

MSgt. Jones, manning the FOP, was the next target for the NVA assault. Shot in the stomach and unable to use his legs, Jones detonated a series of claymores before he lost consciousness. His position overrun, the NVA left Jones for dead as they continued their attack. This was Jones' third Purple Heart. The first one he earned in Korea in 1951 and right now Jones thought a good desk job back in the states might be in order.

Because of Luke's bravery and that of several others, the Song Bo River Camp never fell to the enemy. With no other options, Lt. Weeks called in another bombing strike right on the north side of the camp. He ordered his men to seek cover as the bombardment hit and broke off the NVA's attack. Then enemy survivors fled and retreated back into the forest.

While they searched through the rubble, Sgt. Banks discovered the wounded and unconscious MSgt. Jones under a pile of enemy bodies. Ironically, it was their bodies that protected Jones from bomb fragments.

The attack on the Song Bo River Camp had been costly for both sides. Of the original 534 defenders, only 96 still stood to see the new dawn. Of the 14 A-Team members, six survived and every one had sustained a wound of some kind. The Mike Force arrived in time to see the enemy flee back into the trees, but no one followed them. Now was the time to care for the wounded, identify and bag up the dead, bury the enemy in mass graves and repair the camp's defenses for the next attack. Not only a major military defeat for the enemy, the battle for Song Bo was also a major political defeat for the Viet Cong. In the weeks to follow, several local villages added their support to the camp's efforts to free the valley of VC terrorism.

Although wounded, Lt. Weeks refused to leave until each of his men were placed in body bags and loaded into a helicopter. Following a short briefing of his replacement, Lt. Weeks escorted the remains of his dead comrades to Phu Bai, where they were placed in a temporary morgue. Luke's body was placed in a metal coffin and flown by a US Air Force C-141 transport to Norton Air Force Base in Southern California.

While recuperating from his wounds at the 95th Evac Hospital in Danang, Lt. Weeks began the painful process of writing letters home to the loved ones of those who had died.

Scheduled for transport back to the states, he wanted the letters completed before he left Viet Nam. It surprised him though to find the letter to Luke's parents the hardest one to write.

> *Dear Pastor and Mrs. Walter Kendal:*
>
> *By now you have been notified of Luke's death on May 14th of this year. I am proud to say that I was his commanding officer and that your son fought bravely and with honor befitting that of a Green Beret. At the time of his death, Luke faced a vastly superior enemy force and although wounded twice, he refused to give ground to the enemy. It was due to his courage and that of other such men that our camp was not overrun. I am sincerely sorry for your loss, but please know that Luke's death is also my loss because I considered Luke a friend.*
>
> *I wanted you to know how much his fellow soldiers admired and liked him. He was always there to help when one of the men struggled with a personal problem. I guess you could say he was our resident chaplain.*
>
> *I was proud to have known him and to have served with him. He talked often of his love for both of you and his feelings for his younger brother, Mathew. Sgt. Luke Kendal will be missed.*
>
> *Due to his bravery, I have recommended your son for the Silver Star. I know this can in no way replace your loss, but Luke was a soldier and he deserves this honor.*
>
> *Please accept my condolences and I will try to write again in the near future. I also ask that you pray for our country as this war tasks our very ideals and beliefs.*

Lt. Weeks wrote eight letters and by the time he was finished his cheeks were moist with tears. As with most soldiers who commanded troops in war, with each man killed under his command a piece of him died also. For his own actions at Song Bo, Weeks received a meritorious promotion to captain and was awarded the Silver Star. He also received his second Purple Heart.

UPLAND, CALIFORNIA MAY 31ST, 1968, 1412 HOURS

On Memorial Day, funeral services for Sgt. Luke Kendal were conducted with an American Legion Honor Guard present to provide a military member's salute. The American Flag, folded neatly by the Honor Guard, was presented to Luke's mother. Grief stricken, Jean Kendal silently accepted the flag from a retired Green Beret major. After a few words were whispered in Jean's ear, the major presented a new green beret to Pastor Walter Kendal. "Please accept this beret in remembrance of your son's courageous service with the Army's Special Forces."

As the Legion's bugler blew "Taps", Walter Kendal, a veteran, saluted his son's casket and whispered a final goodbye. Holding tightly to her husband's arm, Jean Kendal continued to weep while their church congregation and Luke's friends from high school shed their own tears. Amongst the mourners, several people could be seen looking around for the missing family member.

"Honey, where's Matthew?" Lorraine Haskel asked her husband.

"I don't know, dear," Bob Haskel answered. He hoped his wife would quit being so concerned about other people's kids and worry about the whereabouts of there 17-year old daughter for a change.

"I just can't understand how he could be so rude to his parents--not attending his brother's funeral. He should be thinking of his mother." Lorraine pulled a white handkerchief from Bob's suit coat and dabbed her eyes, leave heavy black eyeliner spread over his new monogrammed handkerchief.

"Matthew isn't like that, Lorraine. Maybe…maybe this is too tough for him right now." Bob looked at his handkerchief and shoved it into his back pocket.

"He still should consider his mother," Lorraine said in a curt tone.

No one, not even his parents, knew where Matthew was that afternoon. Walter Kendal would discuss the matter later; right now he had a son to bury. He left his wife's side and moved toward the casket to lay a single white carnation upon the casket's lid. It was a fight to control his grief as Walter stood there and watched as the casket was lowered into the grave.

1 – A BROTHERS LOVE

UPLAND, CALIFORNIA JUNE 8TH, 1968, 1018 HOURS

For four days, Matthew left the house with the full intention of going to school. Yet, he never made it. He parked his bike in front of Cornet's Five and Dime Store and spent several hours perched on a hard wood bench across the street from the Armed Forces Recruitment Office. He struggled with a decision: a decision that must, by his own choice, be reconciled today. *Option-A: I attend Bible College, marry Kathy Lee and become the next pastor in the Kendal family. Nice, safe and what everyone wants me to do. But Option-B: I enlist in the Army and volunteer for Viet Nam. Then I can get back at those…those slant-eyed gooks for killing my brother. Do I flip a coin? No, the Bible does say an Eye for an eye.*

Matthew looked into the blue eyes of Uncle Sam and read the words out loud, "I Want You!" He slapped his knees with the palms of his hands, jumped up and exclaimed, "Looks like you got me!"

Matthew walked across the street, straight into the Army Recruitment Office. Here, a tall, smiling black sergeant in a crisp dress summer uniform met him at the door with a firm handshake. "Welcome, young man. Why don't you have a seat and tell me about yourself." Two hours and three cups of coffee later, Matthew left the office with his future laid out before him. First he had to take the entrance exams. Then, it was a quick trip to Los Angeles for the physical, followed by a bus ride to Boot Camp at Fort Ord. Once he made it through those steps, he was promised, in writing, a shot at Airborne. The recruiter, who learned Matthew's brother was a Green Beret killed in Nam, told him he was "…just about guaranteed at getting' your own green beanie if you volunteered and if Viet Nam is where you want to go, I can see no problem in getting you over there. But first you'll have to go through Advanced Infantry Training and then jump school." Matthew, unable to comprehend why the man would lie to him, believed every word. Unfortunately, Luke had never taken the time to warn Matthew about recruiters and their outlandish promises. Luke would learn Army recruiters and used car salesmen had a lot in common--the ability to lie with a straight face.

As he watched Matthew leave his office, SSgt. Allen felt like he could pat himself on the back for such a great catch. "That kid's officer material if he'd only gone to college. But no, he wants to seek justice an' it's an awful shame I couldn't talk him out of it. The Army needs good officers...lots of 'em. I only hope the boy survives Nam." SSgt. Allen looked at his office partner, Sgt. Bartley, and shrugged his shoulders. "Sometimes I really don't like this job, but we just made our quota for the week."

Sgt. Bartley walked over to the coffee pot and poured himself a cup of molten black lava and said, "Least you ain't humpin' the boonies anymore... let the kids do it"

Viet Nam was now in full swing and recruiters were pressured to fill the slots, or they'd soon find themselves with an 80-pound pack on their backs, in leech infested rice paddies. Draft dodgers were on the rise and nearly every night the 6 o'clock news had another newsreel of someone else with a burned up draft card in their hand. Viet Nam was an unpopular war; one where most of the enlistees were either high school dropouts or unemployed youth in search of a hot meal. But as long as they could breathe without wheeze or a heart murmur and follow the yellow line through the Induction Center, the Army grabbed them up.

Somewhere between the recruiter's office and home, Matthew's air of self-confidence began bursting, with realization of his parent's icy glare of disapproval striking him like a lightening bolt. Then, thinking of Kathy Lee, he began hearing thunder roar in his head, "What am I gonna tell her?"

KENDAL RESIDENCE JUNE 10TH, 1812 HOURS

Luke built up his nerve over the next 48 hours and then blurted out the news over dinner. This was a big mistake. Jean Kendal had just passed the mashed potatoes to Walter, who dropped the big serving bowl to the floor upon hearing the announcement, making a mess. But, Jean Kendal wasn't around to clean it up. She glared at Matthew, running from the table in tears, slamming her bedroom door behind her. Walter promptly stood up, grabbing Matthew by the scruff of his neck--not too gently — walking him outside for a little man-to-man talk. Walter fought to keep his anger under control; listening, while Matthew explained his many reasons for choosing the Army over Bible College.

Now it was Walter's turn. Matthew, with a hard look of defiance on his face, remained silent. The exchange reminded Walter of the same talk he had with Luke; a vain attempt to persuade his oldest son not to join the military unless he completed college and went in as an officer. Then and now, he was reminded of his own feelings on the morning of December 7th, 1941. The very next day Walter was in line outside the recruiter's office, waiting for a shot at the Japanese; while his father, a World War I veteran, wanted him to wait to see if the war would last. But Matthew was now his only son, "What does Kathy Lee have to say about these new plans of yours,

28

or haven't you told her yet?" Walter knew the answer by the sheepish expression on Matthew's face.

"I'll take care of that tonight, but I sure hope she takes it better than you and mom did."

Walter frowned at his son and said, "She didn't lose a son."

Matthew knew he'd said the wrong thing, "Sorry, dad, but I can't go on to Bible College feeling the way I do. I'd probably drop out within a month. I have...I must do this my way. Can you please understand that?" Matthew's answer was cold silence and an icy stare before his father turned and walked back inside the house.

KATHY LEE OSBORNE RESIDENCE SAME NIGHT

"You're what!?" Kathy Lee shouted. She tossed Matthew's hand aside, jumping from the couch. She assumed the same icy glare his father had earlier, while she waited for an answer from him.

"Babe, it's something I just got to do and I thought you'd at least understand."

"Babe...Babe!? Don't you dare call me that," Kathy said in a raised voice. Remembering her parents were in the adjoining room--they probably heard all of this--Kathy continued on in a calmer voice, "You want me..." she pointed at herself, "...you want me to understand how you've decided to put off all our plans, our engagement and marriage, while you go ff and play soldier boy? Am I hearing this right, Mister Kendal?" Kathy Lee stood directly in front of Matthew, who decided it was safer to remain sitting because the look on her face could frighten a small child and he felt a cold shiver down his spine. He had never seen her like this before and it shocked him.

"Honey, it's only a two-year enlistment..." Matthew began, but she cut him off.

"No honey either, buster...You'll end up in Viet Nam, right? Probably get yourself killed, right?" Kathy Lee turned away, her long black hair whipping in the air like a circus pony's tail. Without another word she walked out of the living room, climbed the stairs to her bedroom and slammed the door extremely hard. Matthew left the Osborne house straight away, worried he might have a face off with Mr. Osborne for what he had done to his daughter. Worse would be to face her mother, especially after he had witnessed how angry his girlfriend could get.

He walked down the sidewalk, not knowing if he could feel much worse? *My mother's home crying, dad wants to deck me an' Kathy Lee wants to throttle me. Maybe I could hold up a 7-11...or steal a car, make my day a total winner.*

UPLAND HIGH SCHOOL GRADUATION JUNE 15TH, 1968

Over 3,500 people--parents, relatives and students of the 1968 senior class--attended this year's graduation. Kathy Lee, still upset with Matthew, hadn't spoken with him since the night of his big announcement. At the ceremony, she avoided eye contact with him. Matthew avoided eye contact with Mr. Osborne. Sadly, their squabble made them a no show for their graduation party at Disneyland--an event they looked forward to all year.

KENDAL RESIDENCE JUNE 19TH, 1968 0820 HOURS

Matthew stood beside his bed, finished packing his overnight bag; his only baggage for the trip to Los Angeles, and then, on to Boot Camp. He dropped his bag by the front door, walked into the kitchen. There, he was surprised to find his favorite breakfast on the table: strawberry waffles buried under a mountain of whip cream. "Thanks, mom," Matthew said. "Probably be awhile before I get decent chow again." He gave her a big hug.

"Have you heard from Kathy?" Jean asked, as she poured batter into the waffle iron.

"No. I guess I really blew it there, Mom." He fiddled with a forked strawberry, popping it into his mouth.

"You hurt her, Matt," Mrs. Kendal said. "But I know she's very much in love with you. Give it some time and things will work out."

Matthew began to say something, stopping when his dad entered the room and took a seat at the table. They hadn't said much to each other since that night, only polite conversation limited to "please" and "thank you". Matthew didn't want to leave home this way and he hoped his dad would forgive him. *He preaches on forgiveness all the time, you'd think he could spare some for his own son.* When the doorbell rang, the sound startled Jean. Matthew nearly jumped from his chair. "I'll get it," Matthew said. When he opened the main door, Matthew's heart jumped a beat when he saw Kathy Lee standing on the porch. A slight breeze carried the slightest hint of lilac, her favorite perfume, into the living room and Matthew went week-kneed. "You want to come in?" He asked, holding the door open for her.

"Why don't you come out," she answered, then waited as Matthew closed the door behind him, walking out on to the porch. "My dad told me you were going today. So...well, I thought we'd better settle some things before you leave."

Matthew thought it was settled, "Not much time, I catch the Greyhound Bus in about an hour. But ah was hoping you'd write...Or did you come here to break things off?" Matthew asked, afraid of what her answer would be, but desperate for it. Kathy Lee didn't say anything, but simply handed him his class ring minus all the Angora fur she had tied around it to help it fit her finger. He just looked at her, his mouth hanging open, surprised by how heavy the ring felt in the palm of his hand.

"You really hurt me when you made this decision without even talking to me. This affects both of us, but you only thought of yourself and this idiotic quest for revenge. Such a macho…All right, I know you loved…love your brother, but you forgot about me, the woman you wanted to spend the rest of your life with. I was angry, Matt and it took me awhile to get over it. I cried myself to sleep that first night and never wanted to see you again, but I finally talked with my dad."

A small smile broke out on Kathy Lee's face, causing Matthew to respond with a somewhat stupid look on his own face. "You should know my dad had thoughts of skinning you alive for hurting his little girl." Kathy Lee saw that Matthew wanted to say something in his defense, but she cut him off, "No, don't say anything yet, Matt. Let me finish. Dad and I had a good talk about this John Wayne stuff. I was surprised to hear how he actually respected you for your convictions. Well, to keep it short…we decided to keep you."

Matthew was now really confused, "Then why? What's with my ring?"

"I'm wearing another ring now." She held up her left hand. For the first time, Matthew noticed the diamond engagement ring they picked out together, several months earlier. For the total sum of $153.00, the ring held a diamond almost big enough to be seen by the naked eye.

"You're wearin' *the* ring!" Matthew exclaimed. For the first time in several days he felt the warmth of the sun, heard the songs of birds in the trees. Life was going to continue for Matthew Kendal.

"We agreed I wouldn't wear it until after graduation, when we would announce it to our parents. Well, I think it's time you told your parents, because mine already know. Dad took it quite well after mom talked him into putting the rifle back on the rack."

Matthew didn't say another word. He swept Kathy Lee up in is arms, kissing her. A passer-by might have given them a score of eight, maybe nine, but it was probably right up there with some of the more romantic kisses of the 20th century. When Kathy Lee forgave Matthew, Walter's own icy shell collapsed. Both he and Jean gave the kids their blessing. Tears of joy were shed all around as they left to drive Matthew to the bus station. Kathy Lee was still on his arm as he stepped on the bus; the last passenger to board after they separated from a final kiss; causing both to blush as the other passengers broke into applause.

LOS ANGELES ARMED FORCES INDUCTION CENTER JUNE 19, 1968, 1500 HOURS

With only his underwear and a nervous smile to keep him warm, Matthew spent more than two hours on his bare feet in one line after another in cold hallways. Over 3,000 guys, herded like cattle, were driven up one corridor and down another as examiners poked and prodded like meat inspectors. In one room, Matthew sat on a metal stool, answering questions about his sexual preferences from an older woman in a white lab coat. Moved on to another room, he was asked about his religious belief and in the next sentence if he'd ever contacted a social disease. Then off came the underwear and nervous, Matthew looked for the nearest exit.

In line with him are longhaired hippies, Chicanos with greased back black hair and Blacks with huge round Afros that rested on their shoulders. He'd never noticed it before, but hair seemed to type a person's ethnic group. Accept for Surfers, they preferred short wild blonde curls. Bikers, who spent most of their time on their hogs, had hair of every length, texture and degree of cleanliness. The bikers also made it plain to anyone who would listen, how they hated *pigs,* and just about anyone in uniform. Scattered amongst these fine specimens of young manhood are a strange breed of human male, known to examiners as *scammers.* They pretend to be sick; either mentally, physically, or both. One guy is cross-dressed in a tiger-striped dress, wearing high heels two sizes too small, with stiletto heels. Another clown is a flaming homosexual; going so far as to hit on one of the examiners. A guy dressed as a Nazi storm trooper began an argument with a dude quoting communist propaganda from a book in his hands by Karl Marx. The MP's were tempted to let them settle it and take bets. These are the draftees, men summoned by their government to serve in the armed forces to defend the United States of America.

Matthew came to realize the Induction Center was one of the few places in the United States where racism, fascism, communism, homosexuality and other stereotypes seemed to be ignored by authorities and actually applauded by fellow victims of the government's draft service. By 1969, the examiners had seen it all, as one draftee or another struggled to achieve the high government rating of 4F (unsuitable to serve in the military). At 3:22 p.m., Matthew was dressed again. With thirty-one others, escorted into a small room where the American flag was displayed and an Air Force Major stood behind a wood podium to give them the Oath of Enlistment; now official members of the U.S. Armed Services. A quick hand shake from an unknown Army captain, Matthew was directed to follow a smaller group of Army recruits toward a door with a large exit sign above it. This was the first exit sign Matthew had seen since he entered the Induction Center. It made him wonder about fire safety concerns in the event of emergency. *Where were we to run to, I never saw a colored line marked fire exit?*

Outside the door, two husky Army MP's formed them into a single line, while they waited for their government chartered bus. Matthew figured the MP's were around to keep anyone from making a run for it. For one brief moment, he gave it some consideration. The treatment inside the center only reminded him of how he was no longer a senior in high school, but now the property of the U.S. government. Soon, a chartered Greyhound Bus pulled up. The men are ordered by name to the bus. When he heard his name called out, Matthew stepped up to the bus door, noticing the driver had the three stripes of a sergeant on his sleeve. He stopped to greet the rather large bus driver with, "How's it goin, Sergeant?" Luke learned this was a big mistake for a new Private to make.

Sergeant Anderson, an arrogant noncommissioned officer, enjoyed hassling new recruits, answered with profanity enhanced exclamation, "You scumbag maggot!" Matthew, stunned; barely had a chance to recoil before Anderson pulled his bulk from behind the wheel, going nose to nose with him before continue his verbal attack, "You're in the Army now, boy. Open your trap again an' ah'll put mah foot in it. Yes-siree! Now get your skinny-white-self to the back of thu bus an' keep your lily-white mouth shut! Move it, maggot. Move it--Move it!" The tip of Anderson's nose was less than an inch from Matthew's own and all Matthew could do is stare back at the man in disbelief. He'd never been talked to in such a way. *Scumbag... maggot?* Not even his football coach, a man known to twist the English language like taffy, had ever blasted him in such a way.

"Boy, you's jus' had you-self a physical, so ah knows you got good hearin'. Now get that white butt of yours a movin' down dat aisle or ah will personally throw you back there. Now move it. Move it--Move it--Move it!" The sergeant spat out the words, which showered Matthew's face with spit.

Unable to speak, Private Matthew Kendal nodded only once before he ran down the aisle to find a seat in the back row. Once seated, he used the sleeve of his shirt to wipe away the white sergeant's spittle. Five minutes later, the bus pulled away from the curb, heading north on a six hour ride to Fort Ord. His current situation became more bleak, when the bus's diesel fumes began filtering into the back of the bus and the overhead speaker crackled. Sgt. Anderson's calm voice announced, "All right, kiddies, there'll be no rest stops along the way an' listen up--the toilet in the back don't work either. So tighten up and hold'em...Welcome to the US Army." Matthew tilted his head back, closing his eyes, *Six hours of this?*

WILLIAM CASSELMAN

2 - GOING WHERE THE ACTION IS

KENDAL RESIDENCE, UPLAND, CALIFORNIA DECEMBER 19TH, 1968, 1800 HOURS

With six gruesome months of training behind him, Private First Class Matthew Kendal felt a 30-day leave was what he needed to help him forget all those painful 30 mile hikes and 24-hour duty days. Sprawled out on his mother's couch, Matthew's gaze fell upon his brother's photograph, which sat on the mantle. He suddenly recalled a comment his father once made to his congregation that concerned his oldest son.

Luke had just returned home on leave after completing Special Forces Training at the John F. Kennedy Center for Special Warfare. "My son, a new member of the elite Green Beret, has been instructed in the proper use of semi-automatic and fully automatic weapons, endured an extensive survival course and learned various forms of hand-to-hand and knife fighting techniques," At this point, Matthew remembered how Luke sat up in his pew with a look of pride, which radiated from his face and eyes filled with self-assurance and a bit of a gleam that said, "I could disable all of you with only a toothpick" attitude. But Walter wasn't finished yet. "He is now qualified to dismantle machine guns and assemble them in utter darkness, lob a hand grenade and hit a target with it at 50-yards and even read a topographical map. Still, with all this training at taxpayer's expense I might add, you'd think someone would have taught him how to use a ten cent ball point pen." Luke's prideful look transformed to a sheepish grin as several women of the congregation scowled at him for his failure to remember to write home to his parents. The point was made and Luke never forgot to write home at least once a week, up until the notification of his death. In fact, his last letter arrived home three days after his heroic stand at Song Bo River Camp and still remained unopened. The Kendal's had decided to open the letter on the first anniversary of Luke's death. In this way it would help with the grief they all knew they would be feeling that day.

"Well dear brother, fourteen more days an' off to Nam for me. But I have to tell you, Luke, my guts feel like mush inside. Was it like this for you? Can't decide whether it's cowardice or anticipation, maybe a little of both, but sure wish you were here to answer some questions. Then, if you were, I'd probably be in the middle of some boring theology class. Did I do right, Luke?" Matthew looked into his brother's eyes, hoping for an answer from the photograph, but none came. Mounted in a heavy silver frame, Luke's service picture sat in the center of the mantle, over a stone fireplace. On one side, the beret presented to Walter Kendal at Luke's funeral sits and on the other side, two open presentation cases that contain Luke's Silver Star and the Purple Heart. Matthew read and reread the citation that accompanied Luke's Silver Star; how his brother behaved courageously before dying valiantly in the defense of his nation. But since he enlisted in the Army, Matthew viewed the war in Viet Nam somewhat differently than before and since he arrived home he had shared how he felt with his father. "One captain, a platoon commander who served in '68, says the politicians are usin' Nam to prepare us for World War III and raisin' campaign funds from the defense industry."

"You got this from an officer?" Walter asked in disbelief. In his day officers wouldn't speak like this, especially in front of enlisted men.

"Yeah...then he said somethin' that really got my attention...about how we should be sending our best and brightest to win the war quickly. But that's not happening, Dad. Most of the troops goin' over there are draftees--poor schmucks who couldn't get a college deferment or even finish high school. I saw it in my own company; a lot of high school dropouts an' one guy who didn't finish the fifth grade." Matthew took a sip from his hot chocolate, studied the drink as it swirled for a moment and then continued, as his father remained silent. "There's a lot of Chicanos an' Blacks, mostly 18 an' 19-year-old kids who haven't been outside their own neighborhoods before Boot Camp. From what I see, someone in Washington thinks these guys are expendable."

"What about you, Matt?" Walter asked his son. "Where do you fit in?"

"I'm a rarity, Dad, a real life volunteer."

"We'll, I'm not saying your wrong, son. I've watched the news and this war is unlike any in our nation's history. Nearing six years of fighting and we're still no closer to victory than we were in 1963. Yet, it's strange to hear it coming from you, a boy who volunteered for Viet Nam to avenge his brother's death. Take my advice, Matt, don't accept other people's opinions and make them your own. Not when you haven't the facts to back it up. When you're over there, make your own judgment based upon your observations and not second or third hand information."

On the far end of the mantle stood a small gold frame, which held a color photograph of Matthew and two men dressed in starched green fatigues and bloused boots. The three men had new parachute "jump wings" to show off and each man pointed at them above their left shirt pocket. Matthew stood in the middle of the photograph with a big smile on his face, his left arm draped over the shoulder of the young black man to his left, while the Mexican youth to Matthew's right had his left arm draped around the back of Matthew's neck. On the back of the photograph was scrawled, "Won our wings today--Airborne!"

Staring at the photo, Matthew thought of his two buddies, *Man, what a weird trio we made.* Then Matthew suddenly remembered he had a date with Kathy Lee and glanced at his watch, *I'm late!*

KATHY LEE OSBORNE RESIDENCE SAME NIGHT

Kathy Lee waited on her porch, though the night air was cold. Her eyes sparkled when she spotted Matthew drive up in his dad's car. A moment later, they were on their way to a new restaurant in Pomona. Her head on his shoulder, her arm locked in his, Kathy Lee asked Matthew if he'd decided to call either of his new army buddies.

"I decided not to...I'll see 'em in San Francisco, an' knowing those two...they're out partying down an' don't need any interruptions from me."

"You really like those two, don't you?" Kathy Lee asked. The car radio played Christmas music. All the storefronts they drove past were decorated in colorful bright lights for the season. Some of the storefronts had religious scenes from the Bible and Matthew thought there were angels everywhere.

"That's an odd question, babe," Matthew said. "Your tone makes you sound like some racist snob?"

"Watch it, big fella, you know I'm no racist. But you seem closer to them...well, then any of your other friends from high school. With the short time you've known them, it just seems...so unlike you."

"Except for you an' Luke, I don't think I've ever had closer friends than John an' Jose. I told you, because of our colorful backgrounds, our instructors at Jump School referred to us as the Three Caballeros."

"Does that make you Donald Duck?" She said with a laugh.

Before he could answer, Matthew realized they were at their restaurant. He turned into the parking lot. His first attempt to find an empty parking spot was a wasted effort, but Matthew finally found a space on the back row on his third try and pulled in. With lights and ignition turned off, he turned to Kathy Lee, kissing her lightly. "You're right about John an' Jose bein' different from the other guys I used to hang with, but I guess maybe the change is in me. I never took the time to get to know the Chicanos I went to school with an' the only Blacks I knew were from other schools we played in sports. Mom an' dad taught Luke an' I to respect people, no matter what color they were. But I never went out of my way to make one of 'em a friend..." Matthew gazed out over the steering wheel for a moment before he continued, "...and now I've got John an' Jose glued to me like a pair of long lost brothers."

"Lets eat, I'm starved. It's cold out here with the car off and we can talk inside," Kathy Lee said. She shoved Matthew out of the driver's door, following right behind him. They walked hand in hand to the restaurant, stopping to let first one and then another car drive by.

While they waited on the cars to pass, Matthew whispered in her ear "I just hope John makes it to 'Frisco."

"What?" Kathy Lee couldn't hear what Matthew said. "I said I hope John survives his visit back home."

"Why do you say that?" Kathy Lee glued her feet to the ground, she could see by the concern in Matthew's eyes that he needed to talk this out and she didn't want the moment to pass. Over the last two years she had observed her future husband to be one of those people who kept everything locked inside: people prone to develop ulcers. To save him, she would often badger him until he talked about his current concern. With his brother's death, Matthew built a wall even she couldn't break down.

"If you'd met him, you wouldn't ask. His flight to Boot Camp was his first airplane ride an' even that trip was an Army screw up." Matthew saw her confused expression. "Long story, I'll finish it inside, while we wait on our food." The petite hostess with long blonde hair, wearing a black dress seated them at a small table by the window. A couple moments later, a middle-aged bald-headed waiter in a white shirt and black bow tie took their order, leaving them alone.

"Okay, go on," Kathy Lee said. She glanced out the window, taking in the view of colorful city lights and vehicles passing by.

"About what?" Matthew asked. But then he remembered, "Oh...about John. Well, coming from the east coast, he should have gone to Missouri for Boot Camp. But nope, the Army screwed that up, sending him all the way to California. He arrived at Fort Ord with a bad case of jet lag and a real bad case of attitude."

"Too bad he couldn't have come home with you, instead of Washington, D.C. I would've liked to meet him." Kathy Lee looked up as the waiter brought a basket of fresh baked French roles and real butter to the table, along with their dinner salads.

"He needed to take care of a few things before goin' to Nam. I'm only worried because he lives in a pretty rough area of town. They had over 12 murders in his neighborhood alone in the last two years." Matthew buttered half a roll, shoving the whole thing into his mouth. Military chow hall had a dire effect on his table manners. His mother was shocked when he first exhibited them at dinner.

"Murders in Washington, D.C.?" Kathy Lee asked. "I thought our capitol was covered in all sorts of local, state and federal cops."

"Seems our nation's capitol is surrounded by one of the largest ghettoes in the country, and the murder rate is really high. John says there's more poor Blacks livin' there than all of Southern California."

"Wow. You never see that on the news." Kathy Lee paused while she sampled her salad, finding the taste pleasing. "Didn't you say he was raised by his sister?"

Matthew couldn't answer right away because his mouth was again full. "...umm Yeah, an' it must have been a rough upbringing. John got beat up by her boyfriends, until he was too big an' could take care of himself. With all that hate, he grew up to become a militant...a Black activist you could say. Both of his parents died when he was only 11 years old an' his 18-year old sister took over the job with some reservations." Matthew picked up a slice of dill cucumber with his fingers, taking a bite. "Do you know he lived his whole life within a mile of our capitol, yet the only white people he ever saw were either government employees or cops?"

"If he was an activist, why'd he choose the Army?" Kathy Lee asked. She picked up her dinner roll, buttered it and took a small bite.

"He got busted for his second car theft an' a judge gave him a choice of joining the Army or serving two years in prison. Tough choice from his point of view, but in those first days of Boot Camp he wondered if he'd made the right decision." Matthew closed his mouth when the waiter came up to deliver their main course; a rib-eye steak dinner for him with all the trimmings and a swordfish dinner for her. For once, Matthew had some money on him to afford a nice meal and he wanted to treat his fiancé to something special.

While they prepped their meals with sauces and sour cream for their potatoes, Matthew remembered those first days of Boot Camp and how he and John had first met.

US ARMY POST/FORT ORD, CALIFORNIA-BOOT CAMP, JUNE 20TH, 1968, 0510 HOURS

Early morning wake-up came before dawn. It was still pitch black when a new platoon of recruits formed up outside the chow hall for their first G.I. breakfast. Matthew still had sleep in his eyes when he heard a loud obnoxious voice behind him, "Hey, you, white boy! Move's your big honey butt to thu back of duh line an' make room for mah brothers."

Turning around, Matthew saw a Black youth, standing only a few feet away, hands on his hips and hard dark brown eyes. There were two other Blacks standing right behind the noisy one. One of them added his support with, "Don't cry little white boy, we ain't gonna hurt you...yet." They hadn't been to the barbershop yet, so the *platoon* was full of large Afros, neatly styled shiny pompadours and long sun-bleached hair. Due to sports, Matthew's hair was relatively short and it made him stick out as an early target for the mean ones. Unsure of why he was targeted, Matthew was in no mood for their bully-like antics. But with a queasy stomach from the bus ride from Hell and only three hours of sleep, Matthew tried ignoring the guy by turning around. That didn't work.

"C'mon, Honky, don't act like yuh don't hear me. It's yours turn to ride in thu back of thu bus. Thu brothers get up front now, you jus' move to thu back of thu line like a good honky boy an' you don't get hurt."

Matthew refused to respond; not a reaction the Black youth anticipated. Agitated by Matthew's passiveness, the Black stepped forward, planning to grab Matthew by the arm and swing him around for a quick stomach punch. Another white kid saved Matthew, shouting a warning. Matthew spun around, his fists clenched, feet set apart to show his antagonist he was ready to fight. Matthew didn't know this guy or what his problem was, but after a long, smelly bus ride, forced to listen to several irrational drill instructors scream in his face and too little sleep, he felt a bit grumpy.

The two of them faced off as members of the platoon formed a large circle. Before Matthew and his adversary could lock horns, a huge Black drill instructor, SSgt. Riley moved in to separate them. With massive hands, he planted one on each of their chests and shoved hard, which drove them back into the crowd of recruits that surrounded the event. "You mus' wanna fight real bad, boys! But we don't give you time to socialize here. You get just five minutes to eat an' get out. An' now you've used up all that time wantin' to square off and all these other clowns blew it too." Riley ignored the rest of the platoon briefly, looking from the Black youth to Matthew, shaking his head in disgust. "Both of you…down an' give me twenty push-ups…now!" Riley then addressed the rest of the platoon. "I hope you all enjoyed this show. It cost you your breakfast." Riley turned, noticing that only Matthew was on the ground doing push-ups. The Black kid remained on his feet, fists still clenched. He glared at Riley with a bitter look of defiance.

"You want to go one-on-one with me, Boy? Are you really that stupid?" Riley stepped up; went nose-to-nose, while he locking eyes with him. "Make your mind up, I ain't got all day." Reluctantly, the defiant youth backed down, dropping to the ground to begin his twenty push-ups. By this time, Matthew was already on his feet, barely winded.

Standing in starched fatigues, hands on his hips, his G.I. hat slanted forward for effect, SSgt. Riley ordered the platoon back into ranks. Besides his stripes of rank, Riley wore parachutist's jump wings and Combat Infantrymen's Badge over his name tag, which were sewn to his shirt directly above his name tag over his left shirt pocket. The CIB meant Riley had been in combat. His boots, shined to a high gloss, his pants worn

40

bloused. If he had worn his Class-A Uniform with full-sized medals, SSgt. Riley would have a Bronze Star for Valor and Purple Heart, along with Vietnamese Cross of Gallantry with Golden Palm and numerous 'I Was There' ribbons.

New recruits are mostly unfamiliar with military formations, the exception being a few JROTC and ROTC graduates who helped the others. With 16 prior training platoons behind him, SSgt. Riley was used to all types--mommy's boys to big bad dudes--they never seem to change; they came in all colors and sizes. He'd hoped to save his talk for another day, but this morning's episode forced him to use it now.

His breath labored from exercise, the Black young man stood to his feet, giving Riley an icy glare. But the look went unnoticed. Riley simply ordered him to join the last row. "Okay, ladies, stand at ease...no talking. Listen up. You are now members of the United Stated Army, not some high school glee club...or college frat house for you Ivy League dropouts. We don't have honkies; spics; niggers; kikes; nips; breeds; Pollock's or what ever name you used ta call your fellow red blooded Americans. Right now, you're all new meat for me to grind into soldiers. Remember, the guy standin' beside you may be the one who saves your life when you all get to lovely ol' Viet Nam. We're in war an' some of you, probably most of you, will end up over there. Skin colors don't mean a thing when the bullets start flyin'. It's us against them, or you won't survive. So knock this racist crap off. Otherwise, I can make your stay here miserable as all Hell. Now get those lines straight! Now it's time for a trip to the barber, ladies." Riley chuckled when he heard the mournful sighs. It was the same every time and his favorite day of Boot Camp.

For the next three days they drilled, cleaned barracks and learned how to fold their new uniforms properly. Matthew was able to avoid contact with Private John Adams of Washington D.C through most of it. With shaved heads, now decked out in the same baggy uniforms, Matthew began thinking his platoon was beginning to look and march like soldiers. Not an opinion shared by SSgt. Riley, who still referred to them as ladies or girls.

After evening chow on the third night, Matthew heard from John Adams again. The two squads Matthew and John were assigned to were ordered to sweep the barrack's floor to prepare the room for a final inspection before *lights out*. Rounding a set of bunk beds as he swept, Matthew came face to face with three Blacks, blocking his path. John stood in the center, leaning on his broom. Glaring at Matthew with a look of contempt, he said, "You tink that Uncle Tom sergean' is gonna protect you, whitey?"

"Listen, Adams, I don't know what your problem is and I really don't care how you feel about me, but I don't want any trouble. I've got a floor to clean and you're keeping me from it. So, why don't you drop this crap and get back to work." Matthew continued sweeping. hoping John Adams would back off.

"Ah tink whitey here is 'fraid of me," John said to his two companions, standing behind him, exchanging racial jokes at Matthew's expense. Frustrated, Matthew turned his back to John, stepping away. Before he could take two steps, John--egged on by his buddies--jumped on Matthew's back, hitting the side of Matthew's head with his fist.

Though hurt by the initial attack, Matthew used a wrestling move, dropping to the floor on one knee, throwing a startled John over his right shoulder. The fight was on. Not too surprisingly, everyone in the barracks wanted a front row seat. Rolling on his right shoulder on the floor, John leapt to his feet like a cat. An experienced street fighter, John charged in to drive Matthew back against a metal bunk bed. For a brief moment, the two stood their ground, exchanging a series of blows to head and shoulders. When he saw his opening, Matthew stepped in with another wrestling move flinging John over his hip onto the hard floor. He dove down on top of Adams, attempting an arm-lock to keep control. In the heat of battle, Matthew didn't notice how quiet the barracks had become.

With a palm of his hand on Adam's chin, Matthew suddenly felt two strong hands seize him by the shoulders, pulling him up. Tossed to the side, Matthew watched as SSgt. Riley reached down, jerking John Adams to his feet as if he was a toy soldier. "Adams, you've got a severe attitude problem and you, Kendal are goin' to be my cure." Riley turned to face his silent platoon," Finish cleaning this room, inspection in fifteen minutes. It had better shine, ladies!" Riley ordered. He returned his attention to Matthew and John. "My office...both of you, now!" He barked out the order. Matthew took off obediently. Not John. He gave Riley a hard glance before beginning a slow swagger toward Riley's office. John didn't get two steps before Riley kicked him square in the backside, knocking him to the floor with a thud like sound. "I said now, Private Adams. Move it, you..." Riley didn't finish. Fighting to control his own anger, he waited as John pushed himself up off the floor, getting to his feet. "Now are we gonna go at it, or are you going to follow my orders?" Riley asked as he matched John's own icy glare. John didn't answer. He went directly to Riley's office at a fast walk to assume the position of attention in front of Riley's desk.

Riley, an Army veteran of 17 years, saw action in the Korean War and served as an advisor in the early days of Viet Nam. He learned how to handle men from three countries. He walked into his office, closed the door and seated himself behind his desk. At first he ignored the two recruits who stood in front of him, spending the next five minutes with paperwork on his desktop without even a glancing up at these two boots. He knew from experience how uncomfortable they had become.

At last, Riley looked up and studied both young men for a moment with a scowl. He recognized the furled brow and look of arrogance on John's face. He'd seen it often enough. Riley was reminded of his own youth from his teenage years in Harlem. How the hate for the white man burned inside him. But that all changed when he went to Korea, where his best friend ended up being a white kid from Texas; a tall, lanky Texas boy from Amarillo who gave his life in the process of saving Riley from a Chinese ambush.

Riley glanced over at Matthew, sized him up and hoped he was tough enough to handle what Riley had planned for the two of them. *You look tough enough an' maybe smart enough to carry this off...I sure hope so, kid.* He stood up from behind his desk and walked up to each man, inspecting his wounds. Satisfied they'd both survive, he ordered them to be at ease. "Gentlemen, racism is a disease, which can spread like a wildfire through the ranks. Right now, those men out there are picking their sides and the next time you two fight I'll have a small race war on my hands. So, I've got to handle this right now before some officer gets wind of this an' steps in. You wouldn't enjoy that and neither would I. I might lose one of my precious stripes, but you two would spend the next two years locked up in the stockade and then receive a Bad Conduct Discharge or worse. Now you may not know this, not yet anyway, but most good NCO's are a bit more intelligent than those college boys give us credit for. With experience, we've learned how to handle our own problems in our own good way. As a result, the smart officers tend to look the other way unless someone stirs up trouble that we can't deal with in a speedy fashion."

SSgt. Riley returned to his desk. "When this works, the problem is resolved. When it doesn't...we'll you'd better jus' hope it works." Riley reached down, opened a corner top desk drawer and pulled out what appeared to be a jump rope. Except at both ends of the four-foot length of white rope is a single handcuff, exactly like the ones used by the police.

He ordered both recruits to stand at attention and without offering any further explanation he walked behind Matthew and secured one cuff to Matthew's right wrist.

When he tried to cuff John, Riley found Adams a bit more difficult. "You ain't puttin' dat thing on me!" John exclaimed. He jerked his arm away and made a dash for the door, only to find it locked. Adams turned back to face SSgt. Riley and John pointed his right index finger at him and released a loud outburst of strong profanity.

"Shut your mouth, recruit or I will shut it for you. You will not address me in such manner, do you understand me!?" Riley moved in to within an arm's length of John, who has now assumed a fighter's stance.

"Yous can't do dis to me! Ah wanna see a...gen'ral...or somethin'. Ah gots rights!"

"Knock it off, Adams. I've seen your record. You've got two options here; you either submit to my authority right now or spend the next two years in lock-up. Plus, what the Army gives you for insulting a non-commissioned officer. Now make up your mind right now, boot! I'm not playin' games here. We either make this work or I get your butt busted out of the Army an' into the waiting arms of the Washington D.C. Police." Riley moved back away from John and waited for an answer. He hoped the kid would make the right choice. In four years of Boot Camp, he'd seen more success than failure with his hard cases.

With unclenched fists, John lowered his hands and gave-up, "Ah ain't got much choice do I?" His shoulders drooped, the fight out of him, he returned to his position beside Matthew and remained mute, while Riley secured the cuff to his left wrist.

"Sir, Drill Instructor, Sir, permission to speak." Matthew said in a raised voice, wanting his turn to complain about this *absurd* treatment.

"You're at attention, Missy. Get yourself down an' give me twenty!" Riley ordered in a deep bellowing voice.

Matthew quickly dropped to the floor and began his push-ups, while yelling out, "One...Two...Three..."

Seeing his opponent's misfortune, John popped a smile and his timing couldn't be much worse. "You think this is amusing, recruit?" Riley asked.

The smile vanished, but John's cocky attitude got the best of him and he answered with, "Ah guess so."

"You guess so what?" Riley asked in a raised voice. Unsure how to answer, Adams remained silent until he remembered the proper way to talk with a drill instructor, "Sur, ah guess so, sur."

"You got a real poor attitude, boot, but you'll learn to adjust," Riley said in a calmer tone and then glared directly into Adam's eyes. "So, Private Adams, your new buddy is doin' push-ups all by himself...do you think that's right?" Confused by the question at first, John glanced down at Matthew and decided his best choice was to join him. He dropped down to the proper position and began with, "One!"

Well, the kids not stupid. Maybe this will work. I hope so for his sake. Riley listened to the two recruits count off their push-ups and then watched as they returned to the position of attention. John is notably more winded than

Matthew and this doesn't escape SSgt. Riley's attention, "Adams, your in pretty poor shape for a street kid. Your gang must've spent most of their time sittin' aroun' on their duffs, smokin' dope an' ogling sweet young things all day…But we'll change that." Riley switched his gaze to Matthew, "What about you, Kendal? You a jock, maybe some rich boy who swatted little white fuzzy balls aroun' a country club tennis court? Couldn't hack college an' lost your deferment? Rich daddy couldn't get you out of thu draft?"

"Yes, sir…I mean no, sir." Matthew answered.

"Make up your mind, what is it?" Riley asked.

"High school, Sir…played football, wrestled an' threw the shot put in track." Matthew said in rapid fire words.

"Were you a varsity man?" SSgt. Riley asked.

Matthew replied with a quick, "Three years, sir…An' I enlisted, Sir."

"Enlisted?" Riley already knew this from reviewing his records, but he wanted Adams to hear it. "Not too many of your kind around here anymore." Riley gave Matthew a brief nod of approval before he continued, "As of right now, Private Kendal, you're to get Private Adams into better shape, while you two are glued to each other like Siamese Twins. A *real salt and pepper team* as we used to say in Viet Nam." Riley then sat down behind his desk, "Either learn how to get along…or kill each other. That's all for now…so get out of my office!" Riley barked and the two recruits ran for the door, only to collide in the doorway. Following a brief exchange of heated and colorful words, John burst through first and they returned to the bunk area to find them the center of attention.

One of the other Blacks, a kid from San Diego, shouted out, "Hey, they can't do that…It's slavery!"

"Shut up! Yous wanna end up like dis too, tied up ta some honky?" John asked.

When he heard the word honky again, Matthew let out a deep sigh and wondered, *why? Why me?*

FORT ORD, CALIFORNIA, JUNE 22ND THROUGH JULY 12TH, 1968

Over the next three weeks, the minutes and hours seemed to creep by for Matthew and John. With bunks brought together, they begin to lose sleep in this uncomfortable arrangement. Nearly every day the two of them receive extra push-ups for one foul up or another. They are sent back to the barracks for additional duties, while others drilled. Being tied together, it was impossible for them to drill with the platoon. However, Riley made sure they got his personal attention. At chow time they become the focus of attention from all corners and officers turn a blind eye to this treatment because they have seen it work in the past. Only when changing uniforms are they allowed to be uncuffed by their squad leader, giving them a brief chance to rub their wrists, grab a quick shower and stretch.

One day they began working as a team. They passed their inspections and completed their assigned duties without a blow being thrown between them. By the end of the third week, both men begin learning about each other's life and Matthew discovered why John was so bitter toward whites. How an intoxicated white man was responsible for the accident that took the lives of both of his parents when he was only 11 years old. How the man walked away from court with a hand slap because he had a good white attorney with political clout. A friendship began growing and even after the handcuffs were removed the two continued spending their free time together: much to the disgust of John's former comrades who now call him an "Uncle Tom" behind his back. Matthew had his own trouble, some of his white platoon mates now referred to him as a "nigger lover".

Learning how Matthew's father was a church pastor made John feel uneasy, "Listen, Matt, keep tat God stuff to yous'self. Don't preach at me, okay? If tere's a man up dere, he sure ain't done nothin' fur me. Yous an' me cool, jus' lay off thu Jesus rap."

"No problem, John. Me an' the big man upstairs aren't exactly on speaking terms right now. I told you how my brother got killed, how it caused all that grief for my family. Well, I'm not so sure God cares about us anymore. Maybe He's moved on to other things."

"Dat's cool," John said.

THE CHATEAU RESTAURANT, POMONA, CALIFORNIA, DECEMBER 19TH, 1968

With a smile of admiration on his face, Matthew observed Kathy Lee as she returned from the restroom, making her way through the crowded restaurant to reach their table. When she took her seat, she wanted to know what he was grinning about.

"First, of how lucky I am to have such a beautiful fiancé and I was still thinking about John."

"Why thank you, kind sir for the compliment." She reached across the table to grasp his hand. "Matt, I'm sure John is all right." Returning her white cloth napkin to her lap, she picked up her fork, dabbling at her plate.

"I know, but...like I said he's had it pretty rough growing up."

"From what you say, I'm surprised one of you didn't end up dead." She tried imagining him roped to this John fellow for three weeks and couldn't picture her Matthew being able to handle it.

46

"I think SSgt. Riley would've had the live one drag the body around for a couple days as punishment for damaging government property." He smiled when he remembered SSgt. Riley and his leadership. He owed his friendship with John to Riley and wished someday he would have the chance to thank him.

"That reminds me. With you two locked up together...did you read each other's letters?" She now looked at Matthew with a cocked eyebrow and he wasn't sure he wanted to answer this question, but he did.

"John never got any mail, so I let him read a couple of my letters...from my folks." Matthew took a quick bite of steak in an effort to avoid her scrutiny. "No, we gave each other as much privacy as four feet of rope allowed. Still, I did read parts of my letters to him when we became buddies. It helped us grow closer, especially the mail from mom an' dad. Not having his own parents, he seemed to enjoy hearing from mine."

"Did he like growing up in Washington D.C.?" Kathy Lee asked.

"I asked him that once an' all he did was laugh. Turns out he's never seen the monuments or any of the museums, except at a distance. Said it was all white man's history an' then he got real defensive an' asked me why the white man never built a monument to all the slaves who died building our great country? I couldn't answer an' later, it made me wonder why there wasn't a memorial for all the slaves who did build Washington DC?" A polite bus boy arrived to refill their glasses, briefly interrupting their conversation.

Kathy Lee then popped up with a question about Jose Martinez; Matthew's other buddy. "You talk about Jose doing this or that, but you never told me how you two met." She picked up her filled glass of ice water, taking a sip.

"Sorry, thought I did. Well, like I told you before, John and I being friends was a bit tough on some people's way of thinking. We left Boot Camp for A.I.T...that's Advanced Infantry Training. Anyway, John was getting some rough treatment from his pals. You know a lot of that Uncle Tom stuff. Then one night, a few white guys from a rival platoon jumped John an' I behind the barracks. We were outnumbered six to two, but then out of nowhere this little Chicano charged in like a wild man. Growing up in East L.A., Jose knew more about street fighting than anyone I'd seen before. He was no Marcus of Queensberry boxer, believe me, and all of a sudden those jokers are running for cover, dragging one of their wounded off by his shirttails. We were licking our own wounds and headed off to the PX for a coke and this gave us a chance to get to know Jose. Turns out, Jose had been in a foul mood all day and was just looking for a chance to take it out on someone. After that, people seemed to leave us alone. Guess one nigger, one honky an' one spic was just too much to take on."

"Honey, watch your language. People are looking at us," Kathy Lee said, noticing an elderly foursome at the next table looking disapprovingly at Matthew. In his defense, she stuck her tongue out at them. They returned to their meal.

"Now, that's lady like," Matthew said, grinning.

"I don't care," Kathy Lee replied with a pout. But then she perked up asking, "Was Jose drafted?"

Before Matthew could answer he had to wipe his mouth to clean away some of the steak sauce. "Yeah and he nearly went underground to avoid the service."

"Underground?" Kathy Lee asked.

Matthew looked about the room before replying, "Yeah, Jose was a member of the White Fence Gang; a big outfit who ruled the Spanish side of East L.A. But then his mother got sick and before she died, she got Jose to promise he'd leave the gang life to make something of himself. Jose says she was a devout Catholic and that a promise made on her deathbed must be kept or it dishonors her memory. So, he showed up at the induction center as scheduled." Matthew picked up his water glass, "Kathy, you should see that little guy with an M-60; a real animal."

"All right, that's enough about your friends and the Army. Now let's talk about us." Kathy Lee reached across the table again, laying her hand on top of his. She gazed into his eyes and couldn't help but notice how much he had matured over the last six months and wondered what a year in Viet Nam would do to the man she loved.

KENDAL RESIDENCE JANUARY 2ND, 1969

Two weeks raced by as first Christmas, then New Years Day passed by. The day of departure arrived. Matthew stood in front of the family mantel to say a final goodbye to his brother, "We've come a long way, Luke. I only hope I have your strength and courage to survive over there. Keep an eye on me, will you?" He picked up the framed photo in his right hand, glancing from the photo to the ceiling, "Watch over mom and dad, Luke." Then, hearing the sound of someone nearby, Matthew returned the photo to its place on the mantel.

Walter saw his son in the living room, walked up to him, draping his left arm around his shoulders, "Make sure you write often, son, for your mom's sake...and mine. If you need anything, you let us know. If I know your mother, she already has food boxes planned out with enough food for your whole squad." Walter then turned to face his son, his voice taking a serious tone, "Matthew, I know you're not on speaking terms with our Lord right now. But He understands. Just please remember, when you're in combat and fear begins to choke you…Well, He is there for you. Whether you acknowledge it or not, you do know the Lord and there's going to be a lot of young men over there who do not. I know from reading Luke's letters and that letter from his commander, how Luke was instrumental in helping others. I've even come to realize that maybe your journey to Viet Nam is all part of God's plan, to fulfill some purpose." Walter grew silent, studying the look of doubt on his son's face.

"Matt, you're not the only one having trouble with this. But here I stand, honoring my Lord, even in the knowledge that I might be sacrificing a second son to a war very few people understand." Walter finished his lecture with a final word, "I think after you get over there, maybe some of that anger will bleed out. When it does, open your heart to our Lord and always remember, you have my blessing, Matthew." After a brief hug, Walter turned, walking toward the kitchen. Speechless, Matthew watched his father leave the room, noticed Kathy Lee for the first time. She stood by the kitchen door, allowing Walter a private moment with his son before she came in.

"You okay?" She asked, walking up, placing her arms around his neck.

"Sure. Yeah…guess I'd better get my bags." Matthew gave her a quick kiss before pulling away, ambling toward his bedroom.

LOS ANGELES INTERNATIONAL AIRPORT, JANUARY 2ND, 1969

At 7:45 p.m., a man's squeaky voice came over the public address system announcing the final boarding call for United Airlines Flight #802 to San Francisco. Matthew hugged his mother one last time, kissed the tears from her cheeks before moving to his father for a big bear hug and a couple firm slaps on the back. When he broke from Walter's grasp, Matthew felt something being placed in his right hand. Looking down, Matthew saw a small silver cross. "I thought you might want to take it with you." Matthew accepted it out of respect for his father, saying, "Thanks, dad," slipping the cross into his pocket. His anger toward God still burned deep. The parents left the youngsters some privacy. Hand in hand, Walter and Jean walked to the far side of the gate. There they watched as Kathy Lee wrapped herself around Matthew's broad shoulders. The female gate attendant seemed to understand. She didn't hurry them. She saw the young man was in uniform with a destination of San Francisco. She knew; *another unfortunate young man is headed for Vietnam.* The two stood frozen as time ceased to exist in their private little world, afraid to speak; knowing whatever is said could very well be their final words if something was to happen.

The airplane had a schedule to keep and even a romantic gate attendant must do her job, "I'm sorry, soldier, but I must ask you to board now." Matthew could only nod in response. His words were saved for Kathy Lee,

"I love you so much." He kissed her hard, then released her. He gestured to his father to come to her side as he departed.

"I'll be back. I promise you, I'll be back."

"I love you too, darling. Be safe...Oh, please be safe." Kathy Lee continued shouting, "I love you" over and over, until Matthew vanished down the loading ramp into the airplane.

UNITED AIRLINES TERMINAL, SAN FRANCISCO, INTERNATIONAL AIRPORT, JANUARY 2ND, 1969

Impatiently, Matthew checked his wristwatch again, releasing a deep sigh. John and Jose were both late. Their bus for Travis Air Force Base was due to depart in 30 minutes. Suddenly, a dark hand slammed down upon Matthew's left shoulder startling him, followed by a rather loud voice with an east coast accent, "Hey, white boy, t'ought we wasn't gonna make it, didn't yuh?" Matthew quickly turned, seeing his two best friends standing there with big teethe smiles on their faces. Jose's uniform was in a bit of disarray. He'd apparently found a way to sell his government airplane ticket, took a bus up from Los Angeles and saved the difference. John, who'd flown all the way from Washington D.C., had bloodshot eyes and the odor of beer about him.

"I'm gonna have to keep you two away from the MP's 'til I can get you cleaned up," Matthew said, a disapproving look in his eyes.

"So, how was your leave? How's Kathy Lee?" Jose asked.

"We can catch up later, let's head for the bus. We don't need any AWOL charges," Matthew said.

Jose replied in a sarcastic tone, "What they gonna do, man, send us to Nam?" An Air Force Staff Sergeant at the departure counter saw the three of them, ordered Jose to straighten his tie before, directing them to the right bus for the trip to Travis, "Good luck, gentlemen." He didn't get any tougher about their uniforms and appearance because he knew where they were headed.

"Thanks, Sergeant," Matthew replied. The three hefted their olive green duffle bags over their shoulders and marched off to war.

DANANG AIR FORCE BASE, SOUTH VIET NAM, JANUARY 4TH, 1969 0030 HOURS

Following a 21-hour flight, a massive USAF C-141 Star Lifter landed upon the runway; much to the relief of 98 weary soldiers, airmen and Marines, who spent way too many hours in an aircraft made foul by the stench of sweat, cigarettes and vomit.

Twenty-four thousand feet over the Sea of Japan, the aircraft hit heavy turbulence. The crew chief was disheartened to learn he didn't have enough airsick bags on board. Between fear, anticipation of combat and air sickness, he would have to spend several hours today with his aircraft, just in cleanup. He promised to carry an extra supply of air sickness bags in the future, along with an extra mop and a bucket.

Danang, the second largest military base in Vietnam, located 80 miles south of the DMZ, was known unofficially as "Rocket City"; due to the high number of enemy rockets fired at it by the Viet Cong and North Vietnamese Army. A multi-service installation with Air Force, Army, Navy, Marines and even US Coast Guard, Danang's air terminal was a hub of activity for both U.S. and South Vietnamese air traffic. When the massive aircraft approached the terminal, it slowly opened its back doors, allowing a wave of sweltering heat to rush in, blasting the new arrivals.

Jose was the first to complain, "Man, it's hot out there…reminds me of LA in July."

The Marine next to him responded with another wave of nausea. "Get used to it, soldier. This is the Nam," a Marine captain added. He shook his head upon noticing the mess his Marine had made, he helped him to his feet, guiding him past Jose and Matthew.

"Thought those Marines was tough," Jose said.

"Air sickness can get the best of men, Jose…even a Marine," Matthew responded, slowly standing. He felt as if he had walked into a blast furnace.

Walking from the aircraft, they grabbed their duffle bags off a pallet. Jose grabbing Matthew by the arm said, "Hey look! This ain't Vietnam, Matt. We've done landed in Oz." Jose pointed to a large group of South Vietnamese men crouching beneath the aircraft's large wing; tiny, brown skinned people, hired by the military to clean the trash of arriving aircraft. "…an' those gotta be Munchkins."

The South Vietnamese males Jose pointed at all sat crouched down in a particular way--their knees bent, their backsides only inches above the ground. Dressed in a mixture of cast-off uniform items and what appeared to be soiled silken garments. About 30 men, all over 25 years old, several smoking foul smelling Vietnamese cigarettes. They watched with great interest as the new American servicemen filed by. Some smiled broadly, while others looked upon the Americans with blank expressions, having seen so many pass by before.

Entering the terminal, new arrivals are enriched by various smells of Viet Nam: the pungent odor of Vietnamese cooking, a vile stench associated with a mixture of high humidity, filth of open sewage and the odor of death. Off to one side of the terminal lay a row of body bags, tagged and ready for loading on the same C-141 for the long trip home--a somber moment for new guys to experience.

Too tired for casual conversation, the men stand around in small groups; some smoking cigarettes to calm their nerves while waiting. An Army sergeant in green jungle fatigues walked up to greet the new arrivals, "Stow your smokes, grab your gear and head for those buses over there." He pointed to five beat up 29-passenger olive green buses with wire mesh over the windows. "You'll get used to the heat, men, but not the smell," he said. Turning his back to them, he raised his arms as to say *take it all in, boys, this is it.* They walked outside. He yelled, "Welcome to Vietnam!" The sergeant vanished into a crowd of South Vietnamese soldiers awaiting transport to the community of Tam Ky.

"Matt, how come they got wire over thu windows?" Jose asked.

Matthew shook his head, replying, "What'd you do, sleep during all those briefings? The VC love to lob grenades in on inattentive G.I.'s."

"Oh yeah, ah forgot. So, what's inattentive mean?" Jose asked as he boarded the bus, selecting a seat toward the back. Sliding his duffle bag to one side, he removed his soiled dress coat, folding it; dropping into the seat. Jose spotted a bunch of Vietnamese kids waving at him and smiled. He waved back. "Don't these kids go to school? Mus' be close ta 2 a.m., where's deir folks?"

Matthew glanced around and then answered, "Probably war orphans." Stripped off his own blouse, he didn't fold it. The heat was the worst he had ever experienced. His dress shirt was already soaked with sweat and he had only been in country for 45 minutes.

"Ah've ever seen so many people smilin' at me, Matt. Dey look like a bunch of junior car salesmen." John, who was in the seat in front of them with all three duffle bags piled up, turned saying, "They love havin' us big bad American dudes over here ta protect 'em."

The bus driver, an Army corporal, overheard the conversation. Putting down his pocket book, he turned to face the three passengers, "Those gooks out there aren't all friendly and don't let those smiles fool you. The ones who aren't VC are probably cowboys and they're waiting for a chance to rip you off. Cowboys ride around on little Honda fifties, come right up beside a bus and cut off your rings or even a watch. In the process they'll slice off a wrist or a finger and won't mind a bit. They put the mesh up to keep stupid soldiers from losing their appendages. But it also keeps the grenades out too. Now Charlie, he watches the airport to count the new troops coming in; best intelligence outfit in the country."

Matthew, dismayed by the news, asked, "Great. Anything else we should know, corporal?"

The Corporal moved out of the way, allowing another group of men to board. "Watch out for the kids. They'll throw crushed glass at you through the wire and their grandmas sell you a Coke with crushed glass in it. They've even walked up and dropped grenades at some poor slob's feet while he's handing out candy. VC love to use kids. Yeah, Vietnam is a right friendly place. They love us here!"

John looked to his two friends, "Welcome to gloomy Viet Nam that man says. Can we go home now…please?" The airport is lit up for the arriving and departing aircraft, which is unusual during the hours of darkness. Usually, the airport is darkened to prevent the VC or NVA from having good targets to direct their rocket fire toward. But tonight lights are on and dozens of people are hustling about moving baggage and freight as fast as possible, so the lights can be turned off once more. Meanwhile, mosquitoes use the bright light like a homing beacon. The new comers, who cannot close the windows, meet their first enemy. Swarms of mosquitoes seek out naked flesh. The men begin smacking their adversary as the buses fill-up with the flying blood suckers.

"C'mon, Corporal, let's get this bus moving before I lose a pint of blood!" A Marine officer shouts out, while he slapping the back of his neck.

"Yes, Sir," Corporal Hamilton said. He stepped outside the bus, signaling the driver in the second bus and then settled down behind the steering wheel. An 18-minute bus ride left the new arrivals billeted in a fine selection of rust covered eight-man Quonset huts for the night. The compound the Quonset huts were in was surrounded by a triple row of barbed wire fencing and each of the huts was separated by a ten-foot long and four-foot deep slit trench. The trenches were to be used by the soldiers to dive into in the event of a rocket attack.

For some of them, this was only a one-night stay. Tomorrow, they'll board a USAF C-123 cargo plane for a four-minute flight to Phu Bai Air Force Base and from there, a short CH-46 helicopter flight to Camp Eagle; home of the 101st Airborne *Screaming Eagles.*

Between wondering about his future, dealing with the heat and dive-bombing insects, Matthew had a hard time sleeping. Still, after such a long flight, a restless state of slumber eventually came. Twenty minutes later, he was rudely awakened by the sound of several large sirens. The wail and a nearby loudspeaker that blared out, "Rockets…Rockets…Rockets! Danang is under attack. Rockets…Rockets…Rockets! Danang is under attack."

Matthew heard the man's voice over and over, "Welcome to Vietnam!" *In the war zone for less than three hours and the enemy was already trying to kill us.* Matthew jumped out of his metal bunk, making a mad dash outside in nothing but his underwear. Big mistake.

The men leapt blindly into the nearest trench. Whoever made the mistake of diving in first, knew right off they should've waited, as knees and elbows grinded down upon that bottom man. Matthew didn't know who he landed on, but he heard them grunt when he landed in a trench of men who squirmed atop one another in 6-inches of muddy water. But all complaints went unheard, including his when Jose and then John dropped on top of him. Nearly drowned as others dive in on top, Matthew fought to keep his head above water and between gulps of air, he wondered if his enlistment in the US Army was about the dumbest thing he'd ever done? He wondered about ordering a snorkel, if he survived this experience.

CAMP EAGLE/101ST AIRBORNE, SOUTH VIET NAM, JANUARY 5TH, 1969 0400 HOURS

Standing on the helipad, after off-loading from an Army CH-46, the new guys began checking out their new surroundings. Camp Eagle's flight line was abuzz with activity as dozens of UH-1 *Hueys* and CH-46 *Chinook* helicopters arrived and departed in a kind of organized chaos. Within minutes, a single Huey landed close by, letting several soldiers step off. "Man, those dudes look like some serious bad dudes," Jose said.

Matthew didn't comment. He was startled by the condition of the men Jose was talking about. Their fatigues were ripped, shredded, caked in dried mud and stained with dried salt from heavy sweat. But their boots got most of his attention, *they're almost white.* All of them had soiled towels draped around their necks and by their beard growth, Matthew suspected they'd been out in the field for quite awhile. Smiling at one of the soldiers as they walked by, Matthew was spooked when the nearest guy turned, seeming to stare right through him with a glazed overlook. The experience gave Matthew a weird sense of what was to come for him and his two buddies. A young sergeant then showed up, ordering the new guys to fall in. Clipboard in hand, he recorded their names and serial numbers before leading them off toward headquarters for assignments.

As members of the 101st Airborne, Matthew knew they'd be humping a field pack through the boonies of the Thua Thein Province and over the next few months they would learn of the Viet Cong, of poisonous snakes, assorted booby traps, heat stroke, punji sticks, jungle rot and malaria, why to stay clear of angry water buffaloes and why Nam's meat eating mosquitoes prefer American choice. They walked towards headquarters in a loose file, duffle bags and assorted suitcases in various colors in hand, with their attention everywhere. They had come to see the elephant and they all wanted to take in the whole show.

Matthew turned to his friends to say, "Welcome to Vietnam." Only to get, "Oh, shut-up," from Jose and an ugly sneer from John as a response.

Poor John was already sporting three mosquito bites on his face. His scratching only made them worse, and now one was bleeding.

WILLIAM CASSELMAN

3 - THE SCREAMING EAGLES OF THE 101ST

3RD BATTALION AREA, CAMP EAGLE, SOUTH VIET NAM, JANUARY 5TH, 1969 1004 HOURS

"Gentlemen, my name is Sergeant Major Bradley and I would like to welcome you to Camp Eagle. First off, as of right now you are all members of 3rd Battalion; a unit that has served proudly through World War II, the Korean conflict and now here in Viet Nam. We are the Screaming Eagles of the 101st Airborne. Never dishonor this heritage, gentlemen." Bradley paused as the 12 replacements shout out, "Airborne". Bradley replied with the required response of, "All the way!" He grinned and then continued, "Secondly, the closest you'll come over here to jumping out of an aircraft is a quick four to eight-foot drop from a Huey hovering over a hot L-Z." Bradley paused again, giving each new troop a brief once over. *Boys! Always it's the boys who do the fighting…How many of these kids will still be alive a year from now an' which ones are already ghosts?*

He looked into their young faces, recalling his first day in Korea: February 14, 1951. A green kid right out of training, but by the end of his first week he'd killed two men. *Now another war, except this time I'm the one sending these green kids out to kill or be killed. I don't want to know their names, where they're from or who their girl friend is. No, for the next 30 days they're all just new guys from nowhere USA…until I have to write that letter home.*

With a war that has already lasted almost seven years, and troops rotating home after 365-day tours; making friends with new arrivals was too tough on the veterans. So, a new guy is left to himself, until he's shown he has the stuff to hack it and the luck to survive. Only then is he allowed to join their inner circle, to exist as a comrade in arms. This was rough treatment for a kid right out of high school, but easier on the squad members from an emotional tie. Too many new guys were killed within the first month and a lot of them took a veteran along with them.

Bradley continued with his standard *new guy* briefing, "You'll be assigned to your company today. For the next few days you'll spend all your time acclimating yourself to this miserable godforsaken heat. Each man will be issued salt tablets, take them or you'll end up in the dispensary. End up in the dispensary for not taking your salt tabs and I'll personally kick your butt all the way across this compound. Keep your eyes and ears open, and listen to your squad leader. It might save your life. Right now the battalion is trying to rebuild. We've lost some good people over the last month and we're getting' ready for Tet. For those of you who don't know, Tet is the Vietnamese New Year." Bradley saw the look of confusion on several of their faces. "No, this isn't like our New Year's celebrations, not by a long shot. Last year, the North Vietnamese and VC staged an all out offensive throughout Viet Nam, and we sent a lot of body bags home after that little show.

"Okay, next on the agenda is a word about writing home. You will write home every week, even if your writing arm is busted. I really hate..." Bradley's voice grows more intense, "...let me emphasize that, I really, really hate to be called before the battalion commander and informed your mother is upset because her little boy hasn't written home. If that should happen, you'll be very, very sorry!" Bradley punctuated his last word with a cold stare, making sure he'd gotten his point across. "Now each company pulls guard duty on a rotational basis, that and other select duties I won't go into right now. Live with it! This is the U.S. Army, not some National Guard outfit on weekend maneuvers.

"Next, stay away from the local women. The ones who'll talk to you are probably infected with some sort of social disease the VC will use to infect and kill you with. No dope, keep the drinking under control and stay out of trouble, or you'll end up in a sweet little place called Long Binh Jail. Even the rats hate it there." Bradley paused to check his wristwatch and knew he needed to wrap things up. "Finally and most importantly, remember every one of those people out there could be a Victor Charlie... or a plain old run of the mill thief. You leave something lying around and it will be gone quicker than you can blink. Now keep in line, follow orders and you might finish your tour intact." Bradley does a mental check to make sure he hadn't forgotten anything. "My door is always open to you but remember your chain of command," Bradley said and then finished off with a quick nod of his head and a smile before he turned them over to SSgt. Riddles. "They're all yours, Staff Sergeant Riddles," Bradley said in a guff voice and then departed at a quick walk for a meeting at headquarters.

"Okay, you can relax. Smoke 'em if you got 'em," SSgt. Riddles said in a squeaky voice that reminded Matthew somewhat of Mickey Mouse. While several men lit up, Riddles took a moment to look over their names on his clipboard.

"Right, for the rest of the morning you're assigned to me for weapons issue, equipment issue and individual unit assignments. But first, I want to introduce Captain Richards, our Battalion Chaplain."

Standing off to one side, Captain Richards moved in to address the replacements. A tall Black man, Richards was dressed in a set of clean, starched fatigues--a striking difference from the winkled uniform worn by Riddles. "Men, I'm Captain Thomas Richards, a Protestant Chaplain and the only chaplain assigned to 3rd Battalion. So, for you men of Catholic faith and other religions, you're stuck with me for all your spiritual matters. Now I've received instructions on Catholic and Jewish services, but I'm ashamed to say my Hebrew and Latin are a bit weak." Richards hoped to see some smiles from a few of the men, but they either stared back at him with blank looks or ignored him. He was used to it from the new arrivals. It did sadden him to see how many non-believers were coming from the states and wondered if this was an example of what the country had become.

"Once a month, the Brigade Catholic Chaplain makes it in here for a service or two and to hear your confessions. But I haven't seen a Rabbi since I arrived in country. So, do we have any members of the Jewish faith?" Richards asked, but no one raised their hands.

"How many Catholics do we have?" Two men held up their hands and Riddles wrote their names down for Captain Richards, who would then send the names onto Major Reeds at Brigade. "Chaplain Reeds likes to know how many Catholics are in our unit."

"I guess that's it then. My tent is over near Battalion Headquarters and easy to find. I hold Sunday services at 0900 and 1030 hours inside the main chow tent, and a Bible study on Wednesday nights at 1900 hours for anyone who wants to attend. My tent flap is always open if you need to talk, but make sure you advise your squad leader before coming over or I'll have Sergeant Major Bradley paying *me* a visit.

"On a final note, I have a foot locker full of Bibles if you should need one." It again bothered Richards to see the lack of response from the new men, but he decided to go ahead and offer a prayer for their safety before he left. Asking the men to bow their heads and close their eyes, Captain Richards prayed out loud for the Lord's protection over these men. Out of twelve men, only three had their heads bowed and only one remembered to remove his hat out of respect. Matthew kept his eyes open and his head erect while trying to ignore the prayer. He looked out around the camp and was amazed by the size of Camp Eagle.

Surrounding a massive helipad, Camp Eagle was constructed smack in the middle of a grass covered valley. With all the activity, Matthew estimated there had to be a couple thousand men stationed here. New tin roofed Quonset huts were under construction; future barracks and offices. A new post exchange was recently opened and rumor had it the engineers were to install hot showers in the headquarters area.

With Richards gone, SSgt. Riddles waited as the men slung their duffle bags over their shoulders, then marched the men over to a set of metal connex containers. Rolls of barbed wire encircled the drab green boxes, while two soldiers pulled guard duty at a single opening in the fence. Here, each man received a Colt M-16 Automatic Rifle in new or almost new condition. They received two bandoleers of 5.56mm ammo, ten empty magazines in either new or used condition, and a new rifle cleaning kit. "Grenades get issued at platoon level," Riddles advised. When John took hold of his rifle, the first thing he noticed was a blotch of dried blood on the stock of the weapon. He complained to Riddles.

"So what? Little elbow grease will take care of it. Least you're not getting one of the new ones. You'd be busy all night getting the weapon cleaned up," Riddles replied. John also received a 66mm-M72 Light Anti-Tank Weapon, known simply as a LAW. "You won't have to worry about tanks, but it's a perfect weapon for taking out bunkers," Riddles added. He slung it over John's shoulder. Upon request, Jose received a well-used M-60 Light Machine Gun with a dirt stained shoulder strap, 500 rounds of 7.62 mm ammo and a Colt M1911A1 .45 caliber Automatic Pistol in fair condition. Seeing Jose wrestle with the full ammo cans, Matthew and John stepped forward to help him.

Besides a rifle, Matthew was handed a M-79 40mm grenade launcher in good condition and a satchel full of assorted loads for the weapon. New bayonets and knives were issued and once weapons issue was complete, Riddles marched them over to a nearby field kitchen for the noonday meal, giving them a 30-minute break for chow. Today's menu consisted of "mystery" stew and imitation grape drink to wash it down. "Tonight," the cook announced, "There will be burgers and Cokes." Seeing the disgusted looks on the faces of the new troops as he slopped the stew down on their metal plates; the burley cook, with a half-burned cigarette between his lips, pointed to a sign above the cook area that Matthew read out loud, "No complaints and No suggestions."

Another new guy popped off with, "Gotta be better than C-rats," only to receive dirty looks in response from the others.

On post, the Battalion Commander had issued orders to ensure his men received hot meals. Unfortunately, with food supplies low, the cooks were forced to become *inventive* with the stock on hand. In the field, the men lived on C-rations; those little green cans of food--some of them dated back to World War II. Regarded by most as being a lousy meal, the heavy cans also added weight to a weary soldier's pack.

After chow, the men marched in a loose formation to another Quonset hut for additional equipment issue. Here they receive eight pairs of black or green socks, three canteens and a canteen belt, one set of combat suspenders, two new sets of jungle fatigues and an either used or new rucksack. Then, the issuance of first aid packets, ammo pouches and other smaller items they threw into their rucksacks for now. Once complete, SSgt. Riddles had the men line up while he read off their individual assignments.

"Listen up for your name…Lofton an' Whitehall, you go to Alpha Company. Bustamante, Rodriguez, Jones an' Luntz, you're moving in with Bravo Company. Isaacs, you an' Laughferty will go to Charlie Company. And that leaves…Kendal, Martinez, Adams and Waterford for Delta Company. Your company commanders will decide platoon assignments. That's it, so good luck, gentlemen." Riddles began to walk off, but stopped to turn around when Bustamante asked where the companies were located? To which Riddles simply pointed to the north before he walked away at a leisurely pace.

Matthew, John and Jose stow what equipment they can into their packs, slid them over their shoulders and begin dragging their duffle bags behind them toward the direction Riddles pointed. Behind them, Private First Class Jack Waterford, a huge lad from South Carolina, hefted his heavy load over his shoulders and followed. Hearing Waterford shuffle his size 16EEEE feet behind them, Matthew dropped his duffle bag and turned around to meet him. "I'm Matt Kendal, that's John Adams an' over there is Jose Martinez."

"Jack Waterford's mah name, guess we's assigned ta the same company," Jack said in a thick southern drawl. Matthew dropped his duffle bag and offered his hand to shake Jack's and then the big guy grasped Jose's smaller hand with a firm grip. But when John offered his hand, Jack pulled back his and gave John a hateful glance accompanied by spitting on the ground in front of John's boots.

Reacting before John could, Matthew got right in front of Jack and locked eyes, "You got a problem with PFC Adams?"

Jack kept his eyes glued on John and answered, "Don't like niggers!" He took a step back from Matthew.

"Mister, I don't like that word. If I ever hear it coming from your mouth again, you'll be chewing on broken teeth." Fighting down his temper, Matthew backed up a couple inches himself but continued to verbally reprimand Waterford, "This man is my best friend and you'd better remember that." Not knowing what else to say, Matthew picked up his gear and started walking away with Jose in tow. John gave Jack a cold, hard look before he turned away to follow his friends.

Startled by the exchange, Jack remained standing there. In all his life he'd never seen or heard of a white man defending a Black. Born and raised in a small rural section of South Carolina, Jack dropped out of high school at 15 and started running moonshine for his uncle. Standing 6'5" and weighing close to 250 pounds, he made an excellent choice as an enforcer for collecting on his uncle's debts. Brought into the Klu Klux Klan five months before receiving his summons from Uncle Sam, Jack initially thought about hiding in the woods to avoid the draft. But his uncle persuaded him to join up. He didn't want to have the authorities poking around his moonshine business while in pursuit of his draft dodging nephew. Once Jack found out about the pay a soldier made, he began to cotton to the idea of serving his country. His uncle hardly paid him enough to live on and his dream was to own a new 1969 Camaro. He got married only a month before entering the service and Jack's 15-year-old wife, a distant cousin on his mother's side, remained in South Carolina with Jack's uncle.

Finding Delta Company's area, a sweaty foursome dropped their gear in front of a Quonset hut with a sign over the front that read "D Company". Glancing around his new surroundings, Matthew immediately noticed the differences from the quarters at Battalion Headquarters to his new home. Here the men of D Company share a mixture of wood shacks, several run-down Quonset huts and even a few old army canvas tents with wooden floors. Every decaying structure came with its own sandbagged slit trench and the outer perimeter of the area had several large bunkers made from plywood and sandbags. Each battalion area was designed with the capability to defend itself in the event the enemy had penetrated the camp's outer perimeter.

"Home sweet home," Matthew said and he gave Jose a quick wide-eyed expression before he walked through the open doorway to enter D Company's office. Right off, he noticed two Vietnamese men crouched on the wooden floor in front of an old scratched up gray metal desk. When the new guys appeared, the nearest one lifted his head up to present the foursome with a big smile. This exposed a double row of blackened teeth. Matthew, being the closest, flinched back in horror and his reaction brought about an outburst of laughter from both of the Vietnamese.

Behind the desk, SSgt. Rounders, D Company's clerk pulled his nose out from a detective novel and with little interest, he observed Matthew and the others assume the position of attention. Not knowing Jack's date of rank, Matthew took the initiative to report in for all four of them. Yet, even at the position of attention, they can't help but stare down at both of the Vietnamese men and wonder of the local Vietnamese dental plan.

SSgt. Rounders offered an explanation, "Betel Nut juice, the stuff causes their teeth to go black. Has some weirdo narcotic effect too, deadens the pain while their teeth rot out. Stupid people, the juice causes most of the decay, but they won't listen to us. They've been chewin' the stuff for hundreds of years...ignorant savages." Rounders leans to his left to let loose with a spit of tobacco juice into a trashcan beside his desk. "At ease, guys and bring your gear inside. Put it in that corner over there." Rounder pointed to his left, "Didn't Sergeant Major Bradley brief you about theft around here? Vietnamese are the fastest thieves in the world." He stood up, put out his hand and asked for their orders. Because he can type 50 words a minute, Rounders landed this job as Company Clerk. Not that he minded much, not with seven-months in country already and his second Purple Heart. He doesn't mind the next five months in Camp Eagle, while others go play in the boonies. Only when the whole company marched out does he leave the safety of his office to become just another field grunt.

Sitting at another desk directly behind Rounders, Captain Sampson, D Company Commander, gave the replacements a once over as they stacked their gear. Beside the two desks, the hut held four metal folding chairs, a small white refrigerator with its door held shut by a large hasp and lock, a calendar with a sexy blonde' photograph on it that hung behind Sampson's desk, two olive green issued foot lockers, a black electric fan aimed at Sampson and D Company's main radio set up on a wooden table beside Sampson's desk. The only light inside the hut cam from two open windows, an open doorway and one each olive green desk lamp on the two desks.

A graduate of ROTC from Cal Poly, San Luis Obispo, California in 1964, Sampson entered the U.S. Army as a second lieutenant with a young man's dream to make the Army a career. But by halfway through his second tour in Nam, Sampson's hope of making general became entangled with his disillusionment over the way the war was going. A lack of commitment by the upper echelon to win this war has disheartened him and he felt the overall battle plan for Vietnam bore more resemblance to a Monopoly Game played by children than an operational plan of strategy.

"Captain will be with you in a moment, you can smoke if yuh want," Rounders said before he handed the men's orders and files to Sampson. "What platoon, Sir?"

Before he answered, Sampson dropped the stack of folders on top of his desk and stood up for a well-needed stretch. A quick two steps to his refrigerator, he opened it to retrieve a semi-cold eight-ounce bottle of Coca-Cola.

Once he popped the lid off the bottle with a rusting "church key", attached to the refrigerator by a long piece of parachute chord, he downed a gulp before he responded to Rounders, "Give them to Sinclair, his 2nd squad could use these four new guys."

"Yeah," Rounders replied. He shook his head in disgust; remembering that day Sinclair's platoon was mistakenly bombed by a South Vietnamese Air Force pilot out of Danang. Seven men were wounded by bomb fragments and one died later from a wound infection.

63

SSgt. Rounders reached forward to tap the head of the older of the two Vietnamese crouched in front of his desk. The man popped up off his haunches and smiled at Rounders, while he waited for his instructions. "Lt. Sinclair, go find him. Captain Sampson wants him." Rounders kept the instructions brief and simple, the old man's English wasn't very good but he worked for the equivalent of 25 cents a day to run around the compound and perform various errands for D Company. The Vietnamese man left the office, which gave Rounders a chance to return to his detective novel, while the four replacements stood around and sweat.

With a dripping Coke in hand, Captain Sampson offered up a brief smile to the four men and then casually returned to his chair to begin a review of their records and orders. Undermanned by a minimum of 14 men, he was overjoyed to see four new bodies appear. But seeing how uncomfortable the new guys were, he decided not to wait for Sinclair and waved them over to his desk, where to Rounders' surprise he offered them each a Coke from his private stash. "Relax, guys, we're not too formal here... too hot for that rear echelon junk. Remember your chain of command, keep your mouths shut, ears open and you'll make it home. SSgt. Rounders is my buffer, my bookkeeper and mailman. You need to see me for anything, talk to him to arrange an appointment, but only after getting an okay from your platoon leader. You'll find I'm easy going unless you cause problems and I'm sure you've already heard Sergeant Major Bradley speech on writing home. That goes double for me. I get hauled before the C.O. because you failed to write your folks... you'll be on burn barrel detail for a month or two. I like to run things real smooth, no waves and no trips to the Major or the Colonel. We keep it real simple here, in house and friendly like. But in the field, everything is by the book or you'll end up dead. Are there any questions?" There was none. "Okay, relax until Lieutenant Sinclair arrives." Sampson returned to their records while the four new guys finished off their Cokes and made small talk in low whispers.

"What you think, man?" Jose asked both Matthew and John.

"Man seems cool," John answered, as he checked out the sights and watched the lone Vietnamese chew his Beetle nut with enthusiasm.

"I only hope this Lieutenant Sinclair's as easy going," Matthew added.

Jack remained quiet and sipped his Coke. He didn't like officers much: they all reminded him of his uncle in one-way or another, making him feel small and stupid. A few minutes later a short, stocky 2nd lieutenant walked into the room with a tall, olive-skinned sergeant who accompanied him. The Vietnamese runner scurried past them to resume his position in front of Rounders' desk.

Their combat fatigues were faded and nearly threadbare from constant wear. Their boots were a whitish color from too many rocky hillsides in search of their elusive enemy. But both Lt. Sinclair and Sgt. Brodrick knew the proper way to report to a senior officer, when they came to attention in front of Captain Sampson.

Captain Sampson returned their salute and put both men at ease. He then tossed each of them a coke and addressed Lt. Sinclair, "Lieutenant Sinclair, these four new men are all yours. One of them is listed as a proficient M-60 gunner. But use them any way you see fit and try to get them a couple patrols before we get orders to move out again. I really hate losing new guys because they haven't learned how to survive over here. Getting real tired of writing those letters home," Sampson said with a deep sigh.

Captain Sampson gestured first to Matthew and then the other three, "Men, this is Lieutenant Sinclair, your platoon leader and Sergeant Brodrick, one of his squad leaders." Lt. Sinclair stepped forward to shake hands with each of the men. Sergeant Brodrick held back to size each of the men up first.

"Effective immediately, Sergeant Brodrick is your squad leader." Sinclair then addressed Brodrick, "Sergeant, show them their new home and give 'em a run down on our operation here. Select one man to be an assistant gunner for Martinez. I'm going to stay here and talk with Captain Sampson for a few."

"Yes, sir," Brodrick answered and then turned to face his new charges, "Grab your gear an' follow me." As they picked up their equipment, Sampson advised them he would review their records and if time allowed, he would have a talk with each of them individually.

When he saw Waterford pick up his M-16 with his finger inside the trigger guard, Brodrick quickly yanked the rifle out of his hand and released the magazine. He checked to make sure a round wasn't chambered and then returned the rifle to Jack. He advised all of them, "Make sure your weapon's selector is on safe at all times and you've got no round in the chamber, while inside the compound. Now let's go." Brodrick walked out of the hut first, without any offer to help carry their gear.

After they left, Sinclair walked around Sampson's desk and retrieved another Coke from Sampson's refrigerator, without permission. He popped the lid off, pulled a metal chair over and plopped down into it. "Man, it is hot," Sinclair announced before he gulped down nearly half of the bottle.

"I swear, Roger, these kids are all babies, younger an' younger. I half expect some 14-year-old kid to walk in here, his rifle behind him on the ground and his stuffed teddy bear in his arm," Sampson said. He tossed the used Coke bottles the new men drank from into the trash. He knew full well one of the Vietnamese runners would pull them out later. After nearly 400 years of war, the Vietnamese had learned not to waste anything.

Lt. Sinclair was 23-years old, a recent graduate of West Point and often a real pain in Captain Sampson's behind. Sinclair's record showed him to be 5'8" and 201 lean pounds at his last physical and that he had played offensive guard for West Point's football team. *Take those gold bars off him and he'd fit right in with the rest of my company...a bunch of kids playing soldier. But that gold bar on his lapel is like a huge wall separating him from his men. He's a bit uppity, unable to accept the kids in his command who've dropped out of school. Otherwise, he's not a bad platoon leader and gutsy, like the rest of those ring knockers.*

"Roger, are you aware our company is made up of 30% high school dropouts, 10% petty criminals and at least 50% of them are under the age of 20? We've got three kids in 2nd platoon who never even saw the inside of a high school classroom," Sampson said. Then he stopped and noticed for the first time how SSgt. Rounders had vanished again. *That man can disappear so fast, you'd think he had a girl hidden away nearby...naw, he's a Mormon; doesn't drink, much less fool aroun' with the local girls. Now where was I? Oh, yeah--*"When I was over here on my first tour, the majority of my platoon were high school graduates from nice white middle class homes. Even had a couple college grads, guys who opted not to accept a commission. Now I've got these kids, nearly half of 'em are Black or Mex. Before the draft got them, they were probably employed in burger joints, 7-11's or gas stations. It just makes me wonder, Roger, is our country sending us their castoffs? Who'd care if they got zapped? Besides their family I mean. No more upper class college boys who'd rather stay home, smoking dope and making signs for the next anti-war demonstration...or running off for Canada...Bunch of creeps!" Sampson leaned forward and whispered, "Sometimes, when I write one of those letters home, I wonder if the person at the other end can even read them?" He pushed himself off the top of the desk, stood up and walked over to a footlocker. He unlocked it and lifted the lid to reach inside and pull out a small-framed photograph.

"My beloved family," Sampson said. He displayed the photo for Sinclair to see. The guy on my right is my younger brother, real class act. He got himself a deferment to attend some junior college and is probably taking a class on some off the wall drug induced meditation technique...or home economics for the idiots." Disgusted, Sampson dropped the photo back inside his footlocker and slammed the lid down. "He makes me want to puke."

"Brian, you've showed me that picture before and there's nothing you can do about your brother's life. You know as well as I, it's the kids who fight the wars. Rich kids stay home to run the country while the poor and uneducated ones fight to defend it. It's always been that way an' always will. And don't forget, Captain, you an' I are over here too."

Sampson returned to his seat and readjusted his fan so the forced air hit him directly and then gave Sinclair a thoughtful gaze, "Roger, you don't think too highly of your men, do you?"

Lt. Sinclair wait for a quit moment before he replied, "If you mean I don't care about 'em...you're dead wrong, sir." He remembered to add a quick, "Respectfully of course." He smiled and then tossed his Coke bottle into the trashcan. "Look, I admit to having a lack of respect for the ones who dropped out of high school or never bothered to attend. And yes, I have trouble with crooks, pot smokers an' mommy's boys. One of those clowns could cost me a whole squad in a fire fight."

"Roger, we yank an 18-year old out of his neighborhood, train them to kill an' send them across an ocean to fight an enemy they've never heard of before. They don't see the NVA or VC as a threat to the American dream and so they ask 'What are we fighting for?' Can you answer them? I can't anymore. The big picture is clouded over by our lack of commitment to finish what we started and an ally whose government is corrupt. Yet, Uncle Sam sent these boys over here and some of 'em look like they came here fresh out of Boy Scout or YMCA summer camp."

"No disrespect, Captain, but maybe they seem so young because you keep getting older." Lt. Sinclair sat back in his chair, ignored the two runners and propped his feet up on the corner of Captain Sampson's desk top.

"Sure, you're probably right. I'm old enough to remember how the average age for an enlisted man during the Korean War was 26 years old. Now that average age is 19 and they've had no life experience. One day they might be at their high school prom and within a year they end up over here." Sampson recognized the look of apathy on Sinclair's face and stopped.

After a pause of uneasy silence, Sinclair added, "All right, Captain, I can agree with you that these kids got a raw deal. That this isn't our war and most of the Vietnamese can care less who's in charge, but you tell me how to change it?" Sinclair put his hands up in surrender.

Sampson responded with, "I can't. All we can do is keep them alive, get 'em back home to the world."

"Can we change the subject now?" Sinclair asked.

"Sure," Captain Sampson replied. "I gather you want to know about your new men?" Sampson asked in a tired voice.

"It might help me bond with them better," Sinclair said with a smirk.

"Knock it off or I'll cut off your Coke allowance. By the way, I believe the next case of Coke is on you an' we're now down to five bottles." Sampson opened the refrigerator to prove his point.

"Right, sir...I'll get it taken care of, now about the men, sir."

"I'll have to remember to add 'too pushy' to your next proficiency report." He hoped that would get a rise from his favorite lieutenant, but all he received in response was a look of mock disgust. "All right, let's see who we have here," Sampson said. He then opened the first file folder that contained copies of Martinez's last proficiency report, his orders to Nam and miscellaneous correspondence. "Well this Martinez is another high school drop out, but he got his G.E.D. during A.I.T...that's a positive note. Shot expert with the .45 and a note here says 'PFC Martinez is a natural with the M-60'. No father on record an' mother deceased. He's from L.A., so this heat shouldn't bother him too much." Sampson tossed the file to Sinclair and opened the next one.

"Adams had some disciplinary problems in Boot Camp, but worked it out. Another drop out...and he's had trouble with the law. Got a choice of jail or the Army," Sampson said and shook his head, he'd seen too many of these lately.

"Oh, great," Sinclair complained and then asked, "So, how'd he make Airborne?" Sinclair still had Jose's file open. Captain Sampson replied, "Appears he also obtained his G.E.D. during A.I.T. and made the grade for Jump School. Both parents dead, lists a sister as beneficiary for his insurance. Good report on him during Jump School too...Um, that's strange, he turned down a chance at Ranger School so he could come to Nam...He requested his orders be changed." Sampson tossed Sinclair Adam's file. "You'd better keep an eye on him...he sure doesn't fit the norm."

"Now here we have a live one, PFC Waterford is apparently a card carrying member of the KKK. CID did an investigation, but nothing to report. He's married, no education. One ray of sunshine, he sends most of his money home to his wife." Sampson dropped Waterford's file into Sinclair's waiting arms and opened Matthew's file.

"Well, we finally find a glimmer of gold. PFC Kendal has a high school diploma, an actual enlistee and he showed very high scores on his entrance exams. This kid even volunteered for Nam." Sampson glanced through the file further and then added, "Honor grad at A.I.T. and a Letter of Commendation with a meritorious promotion to PFC upon graduation. Wonder why a smart kid like this didn't go to college?" Sampson stopped to read Matthew's Letter of Commendation, while Sinclair completed his review of the other three files. "Kendal apparently assisted Martinez and Adams in obtaining their G.E.D.'s. That is one strange trio for the books."

"Think maybe I should split 'em up?" Sinclair asked.

"No, keep them in the same squad for now. Those three might help with some of the racial tension that's been popping up around here lately. Funny isn't it? Out in the field the men have one color; Army green, but back here they start seein' white, black, red an' brown." Sampson turned

Matthew's file over to Sinclair. "Kendal might make good squad leader material."

"Brodrick will check him out." Sinclair stood up and dropped the files on top of Rounders' desk for future filing. "How about chow ol' wise leader?" the lieutenant asked.

"Give me another ten minutes," Captain Sampson replied. He wanted to finish his daily report for Rounders to type up.

"Roger, take it easy on those boys. Give 'em a day or two to get acclimated before you throw 'em to the wolves. Brodrick's a good NCO, but he can be pretty tough at times. I've also noticed he's been a bit short tempered since that accident."

Lt. Sinclair rubbed a bug bite on the back of his hand, "He lost nearly his whole squad to friendly fire, sir. He's a bit rattled still and you can't blame him. Good man though, best I've got for humping the boonies."

Sampson glanced over at coffee pot and debated whether or not he should have another pot made up, but then decided to do it and tapped the head of the second runner and pointed to the empty coffee pot. The little guy was up and off his bare feet in a flash and with coffee pot in hand headed outside to refill with clean sanitized water from the water trailer. Then Sampson turned back to the lieutenant, "Still, keep an eye on him. If he needs some time off, I'll wrangle him a three-day R & R at China Beach."

"Yes, sir...Thank you, sir. See you in ten minutes, Father Sampson," Sinclair said before he dashed outside. Captain Sampson watched him leave and shook his head in wonder. He then looked down upon his remaining Vietnamese runner, who smiled back at him with blackened teeth. *Yeah, you smile now, but tonight you'll probably be aiming a rocket at me. Wonder which one of you two is VC or maybe both of you are...You both probably speak perfect English and whatever happens here ends up on some VC officer's desk by nightfall...This damn war is so confusing.*

HOME SWEET HOME

Matthew tried hard to look for a brighter side, but he had so little to work with. He stood in front of his new home; a filthy ten-man canvas tent with splintery wood floors and holey mosquito netting draped from the ceiling. Eight wooden cots were positioned inside the tent, each one with an individual mosquito net draped over it by a frail metal frame. No fans, no refrigerator and no pretty ladies to fan them with palm leaves. He selected an empty cot and dropped his gear to the floor. He then tested the strength of the cot by sitting down on it carefully. Only then did he notice a Black man lying on a cot in the rear of the tent. The man was watching Matthew's every move with alert eyes. "Hi," Matthew said. But he received no response from the man who continued to puff long drags on his cigarette and glare at the new arrivals.

John and Jose picked a cot on each side of Matthew. They used their feet to kick their gear under the beds and then laid each of their weapons out on top of their cots. When they spotted the man in the back of the tent and his lack of response to Matthew's greeting; checking their bunk's stability, they slowly stretch out. Waterford wanted to stay clear of John and the other Black guy, so he dropped his equipment down beside a cot near the front of the tent. He wanted to check his valuables so Jack opened his duffle bag, pulling out a stack of car magazines. Laying them down at the head of his cot, he sat down and began removing his size 16EEEE boots.

For the first time since leaving Phu Bai, Matthew, John and Jose actually began to relax and released an audible sigh in unison. Covered in sweat, their muscles cried out and they all hoped for a few minutes of rest. Unfortunately, Sgt. Brodrick had other plans. "Get those boots back on, Waterford. And stand up when I address you," Brodrick ordered. He waited for each man to pull himself up, all except the man in the back of the tent. He continued to smoke and watch the show. "You four are now part of 2nd squad, 1st platoon, D Company. That's PFC Isaac Washington behind you, my assistant squad leader. Isaac, stand up." Brodrick paused as the man came to his feet. Sgt. Brodrick ignored his sour expression. "As you can see, we're still three-men short of a full squad, but at least there's six of us now. First off--get your weapons cleaned. I'll inspect them in one hour. Once you've finished cleaning them, go over them again one more time and check each other's work. Next--load up your magazines with only 18-rounds each. Before evening chow we'll go out to the range an' sight your weapons in. And like I said earlier, while in camp you will keep a loaded mag in your weapon. But do not, I repeat do not chamber a round. Keep the selector on safe at all times, we don't lock an' load until we get out past the outer wire. I find a round in your chamber before then, we'd better be under attack or I make you eat it. Now get squared away. I'll be back in awhile." Brodrick shook his head in wonder as he watched Jack slowly lace up his left boot and pull on his right boot with a grunt. "You move that slow out there, mister and you're gonna be dead." Without another word, Brodrick walked out of the tent.

"What'd I do?" Waterford asked, surprised by Brodrick's statement.

"Slow to move, means slow to think, New Guy. You'll be the first one to buy it. New meat for the slaughter an' the less he knows 'bout you, boy, the better," Isaac said from his cot at the rear of the tent. Enraged, Waterford moved toward Isaac with fists clenched, "Nigger, ah'll..." Waterford froze in place when he suddenly found himself looking down the barrel of an M-16, one held securely in Isaac's hands. He dangled a lit cigarette from his mouth and stood back up to move closer to Jack, while the other three new members of the squad remained perfectly still. "Ah' don't like that word, never did. Call me Black, Afro-American or plain ol' Washington. But you ever use that word again in mah direction or at a friend of mine, an' someone will be putting your lily-white butt in a body bag."

Jack didn't say anything, but he turned and walked out of the tent. Isaac lowered his rifle and dropped his cigarette to the wooden floor, stepped on it to ground it out. He then put his rifle back beside his cot.

Matthew couldn't help but wonder, *was Isaac serious about his threat or had he even chambered a round when Jack made his move? Better not to ask, this place is a whole new world for me.*

When Jack came back in a few minutes later, he saw Matthew, John and Jose busy with their weapons and decided he'd better do the same. He avoided eye contact with Isaac and began to break down his M-16. He used a wire brush on the various parts that he needed to strip down and oiled everything.

Brodrick never showed up before chow and when he did make a show after chow, he offered no explanation. Young for a sergeant, Wayne Brodrick was a serious 22-year old, 6'3" broad at the shoulders and weighed 208-pounds of hardened muscle. He had leather-like olive-toned skin, a product of his long months in Vietnam and a former surf bum from Malibu, California. His time left in Viet Nam matched with his last days in the U.S. Army; he was due for discharge on May 9, 1969. Brodrick dreamed of home and the next year with the waves along the west coast of California. To sweeten the pot, he had ordered a brand new 1969 Chevy Pick-up; a perfect ride for his boards and he had scheduled it to be at his home, when he got discharged in May. So far on this tour, he'd been wounded twice by the enemy and once by *friendly fire* when his squad was bombed. Unfortunately, Brodrick would take home a dark secret; a substantial heroin habit he developed from over usage of morphine from his wounds.

An hour before sunset, Brodrick had his squad out at the rifle range to sight in their weapons. When they later returned to their tent, they had learned various ways to swat mosquitoes and the dire need for their malaria pills, which they washed down with a big gulp of water. The men were now once again on weapons cleanup.

In the background, 3rd Battalion's compound was filled with the various conflicted sounds of modern day music; Jimi Hendrix's heavy guitar rifts battled it out with Merle Haggard's country twang, The Rolling Stone's "Satisfaction" dueled with Peter, Paul and Mary's "Puff the Magic Dragon". The air was filled with country, folk, rock and blues, each man turning his sounds up to outdo his neighbor and it was about to drive Matthew, a Beach Boys and The Association fan, right up the wall.

Washington laid on his cot, where he chain-smoked his cigarettes and through angry dark brown eyes, glared at Jack with utter contempt. And the way Jack felt toward John, Matthew and Jose also created a sad situation for a six-man squad.

"When do yuh think we'll go on patrol, Matt?" Jose asked. He ran a short steel rod with a patch at the end through his .45 automatic several times and gazed upon his pistol with admiration.

Matthew watched Jose for a moment and then answered, "Next couple of days probably. We gotta get used to this heat first an' don't forget, buddy, to take your salt tabs an' drink lots of water."

Jose smiled and he showed a lot of teeth, which always made Matthew laugh, "No problem, white-man. I've lost five pounds since we been here an' on my second canteen since lunch. Now ah see why they give us those extra canteens," Jose said. He then picked up his canteen and took another gulp of water.

"Hey, did you guys see how shaky duh Sarge was?" John asked in a whisper.

"Probably bad nerves from all the combat he's seen," Mathew said.

Before John could reply to Matthew, Isaac sat up and interrupted, "Listen, Brodrick is the man. He'll take care of yuh. Got himself a Bronze Star doin' what he does. Now shut-up so I can sleep." Isaac gave them a hard look and ground out his last cigarette on the floor. He then pulled his mosquito net back over him and stretched out.

Keeping their voices down to a whisper, Matthew, John and Jose talked about what they'd seen since they arrived, while Jack used a flashlight to read his car magazine.

Half an hour later, Brodrick stepped inside the tent and gestured for the new guys to follow him outside for a talk. "I want to talk about your enemy, besides the two-legged variety. You'll be in this blast furnace every day an' there's nothing we can do about it. So we take one of our towels, wet it down an' wear it around our neck. Use it to wipe your face and forehead whenever we take a break. Salt tablets will save your life and regard your water as liquid gold. Don't waste it. Make sure to change your socks often because blisters will cripple you an' the infection can kill you as dead as a bullet. Always look where you plan on stepping, this place is full of trip wires an' punji traps. Keep your eyes moving and never focus on any one thing unless it's Mr. Charlie in your sights. Any questions so far?"

Matthew held his hand up halfway real quick and brought it down. "Sergeant, what can you tell us about the VC?"

"You remember all those John Wayne westerns?" Brodrick watched as Matthew nodded his head up and down. A big John Wayne fan, one of

Matthew's favorites was *Fort Apache*. "Victor Charlie is a lot like those Apache. This is their home and they know how to fight here, because they've been doing it for a very long time. Charlie can live off a single rice ball for days and he lives most of his life in tunnels. A tough little guy, you can never underestimate him because he won't think twice before blowing you away.

He could be a 12-year old boy or girl, a prostitute at the local bar or even one of those runners that Rounders uses. We've got VC and NVA inside the local ARVN units an' I'm still not convinced that wasn't a commie flying that plane that took my boys out.

They called it friendly fire, nice term, but we were in plain sight when he dove on us."

"Are they that good?" Matthew asked. He was a bit curious why he was the only one asking questions.

"A lot of these guys from Hanoi haven't been home in ten years and some of them are veterans from fighting the French. Before that, they fought the Japanese and we trained them to do that. They can make a bomb out of your C-rat can and launch a rocket with your used up flashlight batteries. That's why we try to bury everything in the field and why we burn our trash. But besides him, you face venomous snakes, disease carrying insects, jungle fever an' just plain old fatigue. Anyway, that's all I got for now. Go get some sleep, tomorrow we'll take a little walk in the woods."

CAMP EAGLE, D COMPANY AREA, 0430 HOURS, JAN 6TH, 1969

"Rise an' shine, Mr. Kendal, there's a war on an' ol' Mr. Charlie is waiting out there to drink your blood," Broderick said in a fatherly-like voice. Then he saw a glimmer of consciousness and bent down to within mere inches of Matthew's face.

He switched to a loud bellow and shouted, "Get your butt out of that rack, mister. Time to play soldier an' you got 30-minutes to get ready. Up-Up-Up!" Matthew shot out of his bunk, got wrapped up in his netting and collided with Brodrick, who was now in the process of tipping Jack Waterford's bunk over. "Get up, you big lummox! The war is a waiting and today might be your day to die. Can't keep the grim reaper waiting...So get up!"

With all this yelling, John and Jose are both up and had their pants pulled on. When Jack found himself on the floor, he wiped the sleep out of his eyes and looked up to see Isaac's smiling face looming over him. "Best hurry, white boy. Brodrick is not a man to keep waiting." Isaac was already dressed, his boots were laced and an open can of C-rat fruit cocktail was in his right hand.

"Listen up!" Brodrick growled from the front of the tent. "We're taking a hike to teach you new guys how to handle a combat patrol. None of that A.I.T. crap they taught you. This is reality an' a wrong move can kill you. Carry a full load of ammo, all your canteens will be full an' at least one pair of extra socks, two if you can handle the extra weight. You'll each carry four meals in case we stay out longer than expected. We move out with the rest of the platoon at exactly 0500 hours. So get the lead out, the L-T hates to be kept waiting."

"Washington, hustle over to Rounders and pick-up our chow," Brodrick ordered and then walked out of the tent. He left behind four frightened young men. They stood there with their pants unbuckled, eyes wide and their mouths hung open. At 0522 hours, 1st platoon was formed up and ready to move out. Without further instructions, four squads were loaded onto trucks and hauled out to the northern end of Camp Eagle. From there, the men would walk.

INTO THE BOONIES AT LAST, 0803 HOURS

By the time they stopped for a break, Matthew only felt sheer agony surge and pulse throughout his body. With extra canteens, extra ammo, food and other equipment, the straps of his rucksack cut deep into his shoulder muscles. Once a superb athlete, his heart raced past the 130-mark and his chest sounded like a steam locomotive as it climbed a high grade. His feet hurt, his head pounded and his throat cried out for liquid refreshment. *I must've lost a gallon of sweat.* Matthew was unable to stay on his feet, finally collapsing to the ground. His only movement was digging out his canteen.

John lay beside the trail; his eyes closed against the bright sun; his chest hurting. Jose sat beside Jack. Both men had their heads bowed, while they drenched their heads with water from their individual canteens.

"Matt, howd...dem guys expect me tuh...move wit' all dis... 'quipment?" John asked between labored breaths.

Before Matthew could respond, Isaac interrupted in a tired voice, "Get used to it, bro. You'll carry your load an' sometimes more. When Charlie hits, you'll be happy for every weapon yuh got." Isaac came even closer, "We're in Indian country right now, so keep your mouths shut an' remember the hand signals you was taught."

Indian country? John Wayne an' the Apaches? Matthew gulped down another swig of lukewarm water. Word came down the line to move out. Isaac helped John to his feet; while, Jose and Matthew helped a weary Jack up. With packs in place and weapons ready, they stepped back onto the trail, following the man in front of them. For the next 45 minutes, everything looked the same. The same razor sharp elephant grass hung over the path, broken by the squad on point and the same jungle growth on both sides. *You could hold a whole army of VC out there an' I'd never see one through all this stuff. If I look down to watch for trip wires, how will I be able to keep an eye on the jungle? I watch the jungle an' I'm liable to walk right into some punji trap. I'll never learn this…*

By the time the next break came, Matthew and the others sensed the Angels of Death circled overhead. Their fatigues were drenched in sweat, their shoulders raw from the straps and their vision blurred by heat. The new guys dropped to the ground, cursing the life of their lieutenant. Using towels to wipe their faces off, each man took a moment to wonder if he'd make it the next mile. And all too soon, they're off again down the trail; no one having strength to speak as they broke out of the jungle foliage, entering a strange, giant bamboo forest. Matthew had never seen anything like it; bamboo with trunks a foot in diameter; some standing over 20 feet high. When they cleared the bamboo, Matthew stumbled when entering a field of waist high elephant grass. He remembered his lecture on snakes. Matthew was extra careful with his foot placement, while he secretly hoped Lt. Sinclair would run into a ten-foot long king cobra.

Moving through a wide valley, the platoon covered another three miles before Lt. Sinclair called for a ten-minute break. Exhausted, the four replacements fell to the ground without even bothering to seek cover. Jerked to their feet by an angry squad leader, Brodrick took the next couple of minutes to lecture them on the necessity of interlocking fire and good cover. "Four guys bunched up together, ralphing up their guts makes a pretty good target for a grenade." Brodrick placed them into position and then checked their canteens; he wasn't surprised to see they had gone through more than half their water supply. "Those canteens are supposed to last you four days, not one! Ration your water, make it last. No one's goin' to share their water with you an' don't forget to take your salt tablets. While we're on it, take a couple right now." All four of them dug into their shirt pockets, retrieving their salt tabs. They washed them down with a gulp of water.

"This is an easy patrol to help you get ready for the real thing an' by tonight, you'll think airborne training was a cake walk," Brodrick said. "Check your socks. If your feet are sweaty, change 'em before you develop a blister an' don't forget to use the foot powder either. It works. Now relax, we move out soon." Brodrick left them alone, but stopped to advise Isaac to keep an eye on them, "Keep me advised on their condition, I'll be up front with the L-T."

Isaac looked at his four baby cubs and then replied, "Right."

Lt. Sinclair checked his map and talked to his RTO for a radio check, when Brodrick approached. "Good news, we're not lost," Lt. Sinclair said. He then folded his map and placed it back into a canvas map case he carried.

"How could we be, L-T? We've humped through this valley at least a dozen times I know of." Brodrick reached behind and pulled a battered looking canteen out. Unscrewing the lid, he took three small sips before he replaced the lid and returned the canteen to its pouch.

"How are the new guys doing?" Sinclair asked.

Broderick answered, "Like we expected; ready to die an' puking all over the trail. There's nothing like a walk in the boonies to show a new guy the facts of life."

"I'll give them another five minutes, but you move up an' advise the point I want to switch our heading toward that point." Sinclair pointed to a single round hilltop on the other side of the valley. "Charlie knows we use this valley a lot...I don't want to run into any surprises. We'll spend the night in that old Marine outpost, probably run a couple ambushes an' see what turns up. Maybe we'll get lucky, catch some gook going to Phu Bai for a little R an' R," Lt. Sinclair said.

"Sounds real good, sir," Brodrick agreed. He then turned around and made his way up the formation to where the point element was. He was with Lt. Sinclair on this one; using the same terrain too many times was foolhardy, even if it was in a reportedly secured area of operation.

Three hours later, the platoon reached the base of the small hill Lt. Sinclair had pointed out earlier. With only a ten-minute break along the way, the new guys were on the verge of total collapse. Spread out across the trail and unable to even lift their weapons, the foursome could only stare back with blank expressions, when Brodrick glared at them in frustration. He knew these men were whipped and they wouldn't be able to make the climb up the hill in their current condition. Which meant others would be forced to push, pull and carry them to the top.

Finishing off his second of three canteens, Matthew couldn't remember when he'd been so tired or thirsty. According to Brodrick, they'd only covered ten miles today. *But it feels like fifty. I've never...such...God, I'm bushed.* Matthew laid his head back against a Banyan Tree and stared up at a cloudless sky. His hands were cut by elephant grass and his face was covered with bug bites. All Matthew can do is breathe. *I've spent the las' six hours hikin' through Hell, a bug infested, sweltering Hell!*

Suddenly, Isaac leapt to his feet and began ranting, while he yanked his pants down. All Matthew can understand him say is the word, "leech". Ordering Isaac to shut-up first, Brodrick used a lit match to burn a five-inch leech off the back of Isaac's leg. When it fell to the ground, Isaac ground it into mush with the heel of his boot. "Ah hate those things!"

Following a word with Sinclair, the rest of the platoon moved up the hill with 2nd squad to bring up the rear. With Brodrick and Isaac a dire threat to the new guy's lives, the two experienced soldiers of the squad pushed and shoved the four men until they finally reached the summit an hour after the rest of the platoon. The four new guys crumbled like week old cookies and 2nd squad fell to the ground at the foot of an old bunker. Even Brodrick, who fought the urge down more than once to shoot the four of them, took a knee to catch his breath. By the time they hit the crest of the hill, all six members of the squad were down to climbing on all fours. After a moment of peace, Matthew lifted his head up to ask in a whisper, "What's this place?"

Brodrick stood to his feet and leaned against the ancient fortification, "This used to be a French outpost, then the Marines used it for awhile. But watch out for booby-traps an' snakes. Cobras love to sleep inside bunkers, so stay out of them 'til they've been cleared." With that said, Brodrick left his squad to head over to where Lt. Sinclair stood. Matthew fought down a sudden case of nausea, releasing a deep groan, while pulling himself up with one of the bunker's old sandbags for leverage. He tried keeping his mind off his parched throat, passing on chow of beef loaf. Taking a moment, Matthew stretched out his muscle cramps before everything decided to stiffen up. Isaac was next on his feet, but chow was definitely on his mind. When he saw a small fire, he dug into his pack, pulling out a box of C-rations. "Chow time, boys. Gotta go!"

"Ah'll pass," Jose said in a faint whisper. Closing his weary eyes, within less than a minute, Jose began snoring softly. Beside him, Jack was already asleep with his rifle curled up in his arms like a long lost love. And John, in dire need of a latrine, wandered off in a slow, painful shuffle. He hoped to find the nearest available dark corner before his leg muscles cramped up.

"Watch out for snakes," Matthew warned John.

"Thanks," John replied through clenched teeth. His whole body ached from today's little walk in the woods.

Two hours before sunset, Brodrick brought his squad together for a final briefing on tonight's ambush operation. "L-T wants us to set up our ambush on that new trail we cut across the valley today. First squad is setting up on the other side of the hill, hoping to catch some poor VC slob visiting his girl friend in Phu Bai. Third and fourth squads will remain here on security. Now listen up real good, if it hits the fan tonight and you have ta retreat back up here…the password for tonight is pigskin. Got that? Pigskin. Our counter is touchdown. I repeat, our counter sign is touchdown. Don't forget 'em, or you'll end up dead. You got that Waterford…pigskin and touchdown?" Brodrick said to the big guy, who simply nodded his head in understanding. "Anyone of you get separated from me and can't make it back up the hill, you sit tight and remain silent. Wait for dawn before moving around. Someone will be searching for you at daylight. Okay so far?" Brodrick waited for each man to either reply or ask a question. "Once you're positioned, you will not budge. Make any noise and I'll kill you myself. Got it?" Again Brodrick waited for each man to verify he understood with a nod of the head. "I'll assign your fields of fire and only I will handle the claymores. Our ambush will be L shaped, like you learned in A.I.T."

Brodrick then pointed to Jose, "Martinez, you and Waterford will be at the top right corner with the sixty. Washington, you and Adams hold the center and bottom of the position, while Kendal an' I take the entry point. No one, I mean no one shoots until I set off the claymores. Leave your packs here...take only one canteen...if you've got any water left. No smoking, no eating an' no talking once we leave here. Take off anything that might make any noise and check each other out. If Charlie hears you, he'll sneak up behind you an' slit your throat. Questions?" There was none. "Okay, get ready to move out."

*I'm not ready...Can I really kill someone? I shouldn't be here; this is all a mistake. I should be home with Kathy Lee, not here...*Matthew squeezed his eyes shut. He fought to get control of his fear. But even as he opened his eyes to look upon his friends, he could still feel the doubts that weighed heavily on him.

"You okay, Matt?" Jose asked.

"Sure, no problem." *Right, tonight I'll be lying there motionless, can't swat a bug or shoot a snake...I hate snakes...I'm so smart, 'Vengeance is mine sayeth the Lord', why didn't I leave this to him. Why'd I have to come all the way over here to avenge Luke? I may have to kill someone tonight...or maybe I'll die...*

Matthew exchanged a thoughtful gaze with John and then Jose. He recognized their own uncertainty through their weary eyes. At this moment, each man wrestled with his inner fears and maybe a silent wish to have changed something in his past. "On me and stay quiet," Broderick ordered in a low voice. His voice broke the eerie silence between four frightened young men. With him in the lead and Isaac at the rear, 2nd squad moved out.

4 – INNOCENCE LOST

CHAFFEY JUNIOR COLLEGE, ALTA LOMA, CALIFORNIA, JANUARY 10TH, 1969 1012 HOURS

A loud squelch over the classroom's public address system interrupted the professor's lecture on "Pre-18th Century Classic Literature", followed by the raspy voice of a young man, who announced the time and date for the upcoming anti-war demonstration. Kathy Lee Osborne, who sat in the third row of the classroom, slammed her English notebook shut and shook her head in outrage. *Christmas break is barely over and already they're holding demonstrations to stop the war. Here they sit on their duffs with their college deferments or they're out burning draft cards, while my Matthew's over there defending them. Why can't they hold a rally in support of our soldiers? It gets me so mad I want to...*Kathy Lee's thoughts were interrupted when the announcer ended his spiel with a loud shout of, "C'mon out an' show your support for ending the war in Viet Nam!"

"Right on!" An older boy yelled in agreement. Others in the class echoed similar sentiment and the liberal professor had a smile on his face. Two rows behind her, Kathy Lee overheard two guys bragging to anyone who would listen about how they escaped the draft with altered medical records. A sympathetic medical practitioner helped them. "Got me a big 4F and it was the first time my dad was ever proud of me for getting an F before," the more obnoxious of the two said.

*It just isn't right! Those two big blowhards should be in jail...or at least over there with Matthew. My man stands up for what he believes in and these...jerks...*She felt a presence behind her and Kathy Lee looked up over her shoulder to find Professor Munson at her shoulder. "Are you with us this morning, Miss Osborne?" Munson asked.

"Sorry, Professor," She answered. Then a chorus of snickers sprouted up from a few of her less than kind classmates and her face turned a reddish color.

KENDAL RESIDENCE, UPLAND, CALIFORNIA, JANUARY 10, 1969 1807 HOURS

A cup of hot coffee in one hand, his feet rested on an overstuffed dark brown ottoman, Pastor Walter Kendal relaxed back in his well-used easy chair, watching the evening news on television. In her oak rocker beside him, Jean Kendal alternated between crochet; in an attempt to keep her nervous hands busy, and watching the latest news footage from Viet Nam. A handsome commentator with slicked back black hair and large, perfect bright white teeth, switched to his next story; "The 9th Marines are on the move again and this time their destination is reportedly to be the A Shau Valley. Reports have surfaced on how our South Vietnamese allies continue to come up against stiff resistance in the infamous A Shau Valley and they have suffered heavy casualties."

The station's anchorman broke in with an up-to-date report on the upcoming inauguration activities for President-Elect Richard M. Nixon, which was followed by two minutes of commercials. The network returned for a brief exchange between three political analysts who debated the initial problems the new president would have to face when he took office. First topic of course was the Viet Nam War and whether to stay and fight, or get out before more Americans were killed. With the three of them offering an unusual, unanimous decision to pullout, they switched to the subject of Civil Rights. With the assassinations of Dr. Martin Luther King Jr. and Robert Kennedy, the South was in a state of extreme unrest.

"I think that's enough for tonight," Walter said. He stood up, startled a bit by the loud creak in his right knee and walked over to flip the television set off. He was tired and today was a busy one. He counseled couples with marriage problems and he fought with the red ink to stretch the church's finances, thinking about his son in-between. Walter often turned to his wife for comfort, making his best attempt to admire her handiwork tonight. "Another great looking quilt, dear, who's this one for?"

She smiled up at him, saying, "It's an afghan for the Jackson baby." Jean looked into her husband's bloodshot eyes, recognizing a look coming from too much mental strain. She put her crochet back inside her basket rising to present her husband with a warm embrace. "Let's go for a walk, husband."

"It's a bit chilly, honey," Walter said. But she responded with, "We both can use some night air, c'mon." Jean added, "I'm a little concerned about your knee. You should carefully exercise it more or have it looked at."

He squeezed her about the waist, "Only a bite of arthritis, honey. At my age I'm lucky these old knees work at all." Then in jest she said, "I get you an oil can and start calling you the Tin Man." She led Walter by the hand to the living room closet where they withdrew their coats. Walter remembered to lock the front door and they walked off the porch. After briefly thinking, they ambled off for a tour of their neighborhood. Jean hoped the cool night air might wash away some of their stress.

ON AMBUSH WITH 2ND SQUAD, JANUARY 11TH, 1969 0218 HOURS

A calf muscle cramp in his right leg below the knee made concentration difficult for Matthew. Clenching his teeth to bite off the pain, Matthew inched his hand back to massage the spot. *I've been lying in this spot for hours.* Matthew blew a stream of air, attempting to blow a mosquito out of the way of his nose; while others continued swarming around his face like fighters in a holding pattern. He was concealed in elephant grass three to four feet high. His whole body itched from insect bites, razor cuts from the grass, strained nerves and sweat. Yet only two feet away, Sgt. Brodrick laid motionless, only his eyes darting back and forth between the trail and Matthew and listening behind them for the enemy. Observing Brodrick in turn, Matthew was impressed with his squad leader. *Looks like the guy enjoys this stuff, he almost looks content to be out here with the bugs an' hasn't moved an inch since he lay down. How's he do it?* When he heard another mosquito buzz his right ear, Matthew pulled his damp towel up from around his neck to wipe his face and ears off. But within seconds, the insects are back in play and Matthew was about ready to freak out at any moment.

On ambush duty for over five hours, the squad hadn't heard a sound except for the insect concerto. Overhead, a quarter moon and a few hundred thousand stars provided the only illumination for the men to see by. When he got a nod of approval from Brodrick, Matthew quietly shifted his position and cleared the cramp with some quiet exercises. Although the high grass concealed them, the muddy slime they lay in played host to a number of unwanted pests; to include leeches. Since taking his position, Matthew had the distasteful chore of removing two of the bloodsuckers who worked their way up his leg before he felt their presence. Unable to light a match to burn them off and only after getting permission from Broadrick, Matthew rolled over on his back, and pulled his pants leg up to cut them off with a knife. This was not the recommended way to dislodge the vermin, but it was all he had. He remained as quiet as possible and his minor surgery was complete within three-minutes. Matthew then pulled his pants back down and lay back as a wave of nausea passed. *Leeches, bugs an' snakes, how does anyone live in a place like this?*

He wanted to wash the mess off, but the clinking sound of a canteen could be heard for 20 yards or more, so he settled for a handful of mud. Now he knew why so many of the other guys taped the bottom of their pant legs to their boot tops, a practice he realized to keep the night crawlers out. Simple blousing with a string didn't do the job, but he had learned the hard way. *Ambushes in training were nothin' like this. Fear really separates exercise from reality. No trouble stayin' awake, too scared to blink much less dose off, but I really gotta pee.* Something Matthew would have to wait for until daylight because the smell of urine would carry downwind and warn the enemy off.

Palms sweaty, Matthew worried he might lose grip of his rifle when and if the shooting started. He wiped them on his shirt very quietly, but still got a look of disgust from his squad leader.

Following routine, Matthew glanced down the trail first before looking over his shoulder to make sure no one was sneaking up behind him. But here in the dark, his imagination began to play tricks and he started to visualize a dark shadowy figure in the grass behind him. He could almost make out the large knife clenched between the enemy's blackened teeth and his heart began to race. Matthew tightened up and began to bring his rifle around. But with his adrenaline flowing, his senses suddenly cleared and the vision faded. He now saw only long stalks of grass and a small mound of mud. Relieved, he turned his head around to look at Brodrock. *My heart's beatin' so loud, can't believe he can't hear it. If he did, he'd probably want to cut it out before the VC heard it too. Man's not human the way he can jus' lay there without moving a muscle. Even the mosquitoes stay away.*

He focused on the trail and listened to the night's symphony and after a few minutes he began to pick out the various insect and animal sounds and many of the strange odors. Like most new guys, his first thought was to compare the jungle's aroma to a rotting salad. Now, laying here, only to stare out into the darkness, he started to learn to distinguish the differences in the odors carried by a gentle breeze. Earlier, Brodrick had lectured them on the importance of a good nose, "A man's stench is different than that of an animal, especially with Americans. We carry the odor of bug juice, soap, aftershave, cologne an' American grown tobacco. A cook fire leaves a man with the odor of what he just finished eating; beef, pork an' even beans. With the VC, we might smell the odor of their last rice bowl, or fish. That's why we tell you to leave the bug juice back at camp and why we want you all raunchy for patrols. Old Spice can carry for over a mile and lead the VC right to us."

Matthew watched the trail and lifted his head up an inch or two to sniff in a lung full of air every minute or so in anticipation he could pick up something different. And that's how it began. Matthew's eyes widened when he picked up a new odor only a moment before Brodrick detected it. With a hand signal, Brodrick advised Matthew to keep his eyes locked on the trail below and wait to see what or whom the strange odor came from. A moment later, they both heard a clanking noise of metal on metal. Someone or something was headed right for them and Matthew's heart rate jumped to 120 beats a minute, as another surge of adrenaline worked its way through his body like an Oklahoma oil well gusher. He looked to Brodrick for instructions and acknowledged a hand gesture for *don't move* with a slow nod of his head. Elsewhere, Jose fought to stay awake. That was until he heard the metallic noise on the trail and he was now awake with a tight grasp on his M-60. With bloodshot eyes, he stared down the length of his M-60 and ignored the sweat that dripped from his forehead and ran down his cheeks. He sighted in on the trail and double-checked he had a 100-round belt cleared for action.

Off to Jose's right, Jack Waterford lay curled up like a small child, *Dummy's nodded off again!* Jose gave him a quick kick to the ribs and Jack jerked awake. He glared back at Jose with an expression of annoyance on his face, but the expression quickly faded when Jack became aware of the sounds up the trail. Now both of them are alert--scared out of their wits, but alert. Isaac heard the noise too, but the loudness of it confused him, "Whoever it is, sure don't care how much noise they're makin'." Isaac whispered near John's right ear.

They're splashin' through thu puddles like bunch of kids, not botherin' to sidestep 'em, John thought. He inched forward on his belly for a better view of the trail, but Isaac pulled him back.

Brodrick didn't know what to think at first. *Either it's a large force who care less of making a racket...or...No!* Recognition struck like a bolt of lightening and sent a wave of fear through him. He remembered that foul smell and recalled that night not so long ago. "We got to get the men off the trail, right now," Brodrick muttered out loud. This breech of silence surprised Matthew. But before Brodrick can move, Jose gets overexcited when he spotted someone on the trail and pulled the trigger of his M-60. He released an extended burst of fire on two very large dark shapes that had entered the ambush site.

"No, don't shoot!" Brodrick screamed, but it was too late. One of the massive water buffaloes released a mournful cry of pain and charged up the trail in response. With little recourse and remembering all to well of what a wounded buffalo can do, Brodrick slammed his hand down on the detonating device and two claymores exploded. With terror filled eyes, Matthew saw the world explode in front of him as night changed to bright daylight and grass, mud and steel pellets smashed into a 1500-pound enraged beast. Mixed with the sounds of explosion, Matthew could hear the final roar of the animal before it dropped to the ground with a loud thud, then a splash. The water buffalo settled in a large puddle, its lifeless eyes open and glaring right at Jose.

"Cease fire! cease fire!" Brodrick yelled out. At first Jose hesitated, but then he reluctantly pulled his finger off the M-60's trigger, exchanging a look of, *what'd we do wrong* with Jack? They waited for the smoke to settle. One fifth of a belt; 20 rounds had been expended, most of them missing the huge animal because of Jose's excitement.

Following a brief moment of silence, Brodrick stood, not completely sure if his quick triggered Mexican could be trusted. He stepped onto the trail with rifle ready. Brodrick hoped the claymores had done the job, but his hopes were in vain. A second very mad buffalo was still alive. With a deep roar of rage, the buffalo lowered its head, snorted and prepared to charge. With an animal that weighed well over a 1,000-pounds, this was a fearful sight to behold at night, often sending men in search of the nearest tree. But there was nowhere to run in time. When Matthew saw Brodrick had nowhere to go, he jumped to his feet. His squad leader planted his feet, sighting his rifle at the animal, pulling the trigger on his M-16. Matthew flipped his selector from semi to full automatic with his thumb, bringing his weapon to waist level, blasting the nightmarish creature in front of him with a wave of lead.

Round after round impacted the animal, striking its massive black horns and penetrating its broad chest. The animal bellowed its war cry, charging on its path straight toward Matthew and Brodrick. Kicking up mud and grass, it came closer and closer, with nostrils flared and eyes wide with madness. The massive beast charged, until suddenly, the animal dropped, plowing up the trail for another ten feet before coming to rest only a short distance from where two very terrified men were standing with empty rifles.

Matthew stared at the two dead buffaloes and didn't notice Jose come up beside him saying, "Never shot a cow before."

Brodrick lost it. He tossed his M-16 at Matthew and grabbed Jose by the shirt and shook him violently. "Shut-up! Shut-up! Shut-up! You stupid Spic..." Brodrick stopped abruptly and released his hold on Jose. He glared at him and watched as Jose fell down on his butt and landed hard in a large puddle. He was a mere five-feet from the first buffalo killed. In a strained whisper, Brodrick advised Jose that his cow was in fact one of two water buffaloes and then turned to Isaac, "Go down the trail 20-yards and listen. I'll send for yuh in awhile." He then turned to Matthew, "Give me back my rifle, reload yours an' move to the other end of the trail. Stay out of sight an' keep your ears open."

Matthew nodded his head and then answered, "Right." He handed Brodrick back his weapon and inserted a fresh magazine in his own. He also remembered to chamber a round. With a loaded weapon, Brodrick kicked the nearest animal to make sure it was dead before he approached the other buffalo to do the same. "This happened a couple months ago, too. Only last time the buffalo nearly trampled one of my guys to death. I should've realized it when I heard that noise." Brodrick pointed to large bent up brass cowbell that hung from the larger of the two beasts. "They make 'em themselves, use an old 105 casing. Not like our cowbells back home." Then Brodrick walked back up to Jose, who avoided eye contact. "Who gave you permission to fire, Martinez? That could've been me on the trail or another one of our patrols an' they'd be just as dead as those stupid animals. That's one of the reasons I told you I'd set off the ambush with a claymore, to ensure that I knew it was the enemy we were going to kill." Brodrick stepped in to be even closer and whispered, "You an' I will have another discussion about this when we get back to camp."

He then addressed the rest of the squad, "Get ready to move out, this site is blown for the night." Brodrick then walked off to contact Isaac and returned a few minutes later in silence. Isaac resumed point as the patrol picked up Matthew and headed off in a staggered single line back toward the platoon's position on a new trail Isaac cut through the elephant grass. Before they reached the bottom of the hill, 2nd squad heard two muffled explosions off in the distance, followed by the sound of an M-60 and the distinct reply of an AK-47. Within less than a minute the brief firefight was over and the jungle was once more silent. Brodrick stepped forward and tapped Matthew on the shoulder, "Take rear guard, I'm gonna see what's up." He then passed the other men and moved up to where Isaac had knelt behind a rock outcropping.

Isaac talked in a low whisper and advised Brodrick of what he thought had happened, "First squad must've caught some. Ah think we'd better sit tight, res' of the platoon is gonna be trigger-happy tonight. They might pop a cap before botherin' to ask for the password." Brodrick agreed with him, "We'll set up here and wait for dawn. You stay here an' I'll have Adams join you." He stayed in a low crouch and returned to his squad. "Adams, move up to join with Washington. Martinez, you set up your sixty to cover the trail below us, but keep your fingers off that trigger until I order you to do otherwise. I'll set up one claymore further down and run a trip wire across that last turn. Waterford, you're with trigger happy here an' Kendal, you follow me."

Between a constant barrage of mosquitoes and Brodrick's stone cold glare, Matthew didn't think dawn would ever come. Yet the sun did arrive and 2nd squad began the hard task of climbing back up the hill. Brodrick reported in to Lt. Sinclair, briefing him on the blown ambush. He wasn't happy to hear about the buffaloes. "Now I have to file a report with the CO, who'll have to file a report with the colonel. We're all gonna catch it because some dirt farmer forgot to tie up his buffaloes and ol' Uncle Sam will have to cough up a few hundred bucks to repay him." Lt. Sinclair gave Brodrick a look of disapproval and added a note of sarcasm, "What's this make, sergeant, three dead buffaloes?"

Brodrick hesitated and then answered, "That's correct, Lieutenant." His voice was strained and his fists clenched to hide his tremors. Sixteen-hours passed since his last ride down the road to heroin euphoria and the monkey's claws had dug in deep. He swore to himself, over and over, that he'd never use the junk in the field; but it had gotten harder and harder to keep that promise.

"Well, at least we got three dead Victor Charlie's and no one got hurt." Sinclair looked over to where 2nd squad was stood, "Your men look pretty bad, have 'em eat some chow and rest up. I've got birds coming in for pick-up in one hour. You and I will discuss last night's op when we get back to camp, so go take care of your people now."

Brodrick looked over his right shoulder at his squad, muttering, "Yes, sir." He looked back to watch Sinclair walk over to where 1st squad had milled around.

Frustrated at being saddled with four new men, Brodrick made it quick when he passed on the news, "Fifteen minutes for chow and make sure you bury your cans. Hueys will be here in one hour, so make sure you're ready to go…If you aren't, you can walk back!" He then stomped off to find a quiet place to forget about last night's snafu and fight off the shakes that came with heroin withdrawal.

When the Huey lifted off, Matthew's feet dangled above the Huey's skid. He gazed over the valley floor. The very same valley they had hiked through the night before. *Now I understand why so many guys smoke, helps handle the heebie-jeebies. Wonder if my next 359 days are gonna be as bad?*

D COMPANY AREA/CAMP EAGLE, JANUARY 11TH, 1969 1914 HOURS

Brodrick stormed into the squad's tent with a crazed look on his face and immediately seized Jack's rifle off the big boy's cot and broke it open for inspection. A small flake of dried mud was discovered, which launched Brodrick into a tirade. He threw the disassembled rifle at Jack's face. "You call that clean?" Brodrick asked. He splattered the young troop with spittle, yelling loud enough to be heard all across the company compound, he shouted, "It's time you learned a hard lesson, troop!" Brodrick ordered Jack to pick-up his E-tool (small government-issue foldable shovel), attempting to shove him outside. Jack didn't push easy. He stood his ground. This caused Brodrick to assault him with a blast of profanity.

From the defiant look on Jack's face, Matthew became concerned Jack might swing at Brodrick. He stepped in between the two men. "Jack, don't be stupid. Grab your shovel and do what the sergeant ordered," Matthew said.

"Listen to him," Jose added. "We'll go outside wit' you too."

Brodrick looked at all of them through wild eyes and yelled, "That's right! All of you outside and on the double…and that's a direct order!" Once outside the tent, Brodrick marched over to a cleared spot approximately 20 feet from the tent, turned to face Jack and pointed to the ground, "You'll bury that spec of dirt in an eight-foot long by two-foot wide grave, mister and I want it six-foot deep." He used the heel of his boot to outline the dimensions of the grave. "Now start digging and the rest of you will witness the event," Brodrick ordered.

He's tremblin' all over...What's got into him? Matthew wondered. But not Isaac, John or Jose, they've seen these signs too many times before. They knew Brodrick was in withdrawal and completely irrational at this point. Jose looked over to Isaac and his eyes asked the question, *did you know?* All Isaac would do in response was to slowly shake his head, *no.*

Bordering on near insanity, Brodrick gave each of his men a dirty look before he left to find his heroin connection. He needed a fix bad, but so far he had been unable to find his supply; a deformed elderly Vietnamese beggar, who wandered the camp, doing odd jobs, who secretly sold heroin to his clientel. This old cripple with only one eye was in fact a disabled member of the former Viet Minh; forerunner to the Viet Cong and currently under the employ of a certain North Vietnamese major: An Intelligence Officer for the 29th North Vietnamese Regiment. The major supplied the heroin, which was sold to the Americans at $5.00 a gram; while the old man gathered the intelligence data. Toothless, he lost his right arm to a French grenade and his eye from a Japanese mortar fragment as a kid. Even with these old wounds, the old man proved to be a valuable intelligence resource.

Over the last two weeks, the old beggar learned how the 101st prepared for a major push into the A Shau Valley to support the 9th Marines and several South Vietnamese units of little consequence. This was very good news for the 29th NVA. Since 1965 the *A Shau Valley* was under control of the NVA and every battle fought there has been a victory for Hanoi. The major, dressed in a South Vietnamese Army Captain uniform, was due to return to his unit's new location fairly soon. The 29th NVA moved into its new area of operation—a combined natural and manmade mountain fortress located only three miles from the Laotian border--known as *Don Ap Bia Mountain.*

With his squad's help, Jack performed the burial service with full military honors. When they finished up, word came over that Lt. Sinclair wanted Brodrick. A runner reported he'd missed a squad leader's meeting. Isaac sent the squad out to look for him. When they failed to locate Brodrick, Lt. Sinclair ordered the whole platoon out to search for the absent squad leader. Shortly after midnight, a member of 1st squad came upon Brodrick's body inside a C Company bunker. He was very dead and his body was slumped over with a hypodermic syringe still in his arm. There was a length of parachute chord wrapped loosely above it. The news of Brodrick's death and how he died hit the platoon hard and the next morning, Lt. Sinclair stood before Capt. Sampson's desk.

"Captain, how am I supposed to write a letter home to his parents? How do I tell them he died from a heroin overdose? You know I've written a few of these letters, but those always dealt with a soldier dying in action. Now I'm going to tell his father that his son died with a needle in his arm. Sorry I can't do it," Sinclair said. He dropped his arms and collapsed into a metal folding chair where he gratefully accepted a cold bottle of Coke from Sampson.

"I don't know what to tell you," Sampson said. "None of us suspected Brodrick had a problem and now the Division has CID looking into it. They want to see if he was involved in black marketing or drug trafficking and who his connections might be. My gut feeling tells me Brodrick's will turn out to be another casualty of war, like the guy who gets hit on patrol. He's been a good squad leader, so tell them he was a good NCO and avoid mentioning how he died. They'll have a Bronze Star and two Purple Hearts to show he served his country. Keep it humble and keep it simple."

"They'll find out when the insurance company starts trouble," Lt. Sinclair said.

"Maybe, but let the guys in business suits carry the weight. Times like this I don't mind passing the buck, especially to some civilian sipping martinis safe at home." Captain Sampson stood up and walked over to lean against the doorjamb, "He probably got hooked on the junk when he got hit. You know it's happened before. When I got it, the morphine sure made the world a nicer place to live in." Sampson then turned to face Sinclair, "Let's put him to rest gently, no sense making it tougher for his parents. If the insurance company wants to make waves, we'll let the lawyers work it out. Okay?"

Lt. Sinclair rose to his feet and said, "Yes, sir…Thanks." Sinclair walked over to stand in front of Sampson, "Any ideas for a new squad leader?"

Sampson shook his head and replied, "Nope, but I'm hoping for some more replacements. Battalion knows we're spread pretty thin for NCOs right now. You'll have to let Isaac Washington run the show for now." Captain Sampson returned to his desk and let the electric fan cool him off.

"Thanks, Cap." Sinclair dropped his empty bottle into the trash and headed for 2nd squad's tent. *Whole battalion is hurting for people and now I've got a PFC handling the duties of a squad leader with four new men to boot. Just great!*

With Brodrick's death, the Battalion Commander ordered all companies to begin anti-drug training for their men. While the captains and majors were busy with this task, the higher-ranking officers continued to bend their elbows at the officer's club. It never occurred to them of how hypocritical their actions were as they guzzled down imported wine and rice whiskey from Thailand, and beer from the Philippines.

While they waited for a new squad leader, 2nd squad was handed an assortment of menial duty assignments around the company area. By far the worst job was a chore known as, *burning of the crappers*. Enlisted and officers used separate latrines, both simple wooden outhouses with the bottom half of a 55-gallon barrel used to catch the refuse. Once a day, some poor unfortunate soldier was given the sad duty to pull the drums out, drag them approximately 50 feet away, and set them on fire with the help of diesel fuel. The same soldier was then on standby, hopefully upwind, to insure the fire doesn't spread outside the barrel. Some enlisted people felt this was done, because in the past, some of these fires spread to the officers' outhouses; which burned down only the officer's outhouses. During this task, the soldier needed to breathe, which was nearly an impossible feat. Even with a moist bandana wrapped around his face, the fumes nearly overpowered the soldier. For two days, the men of 2nd squad performed this duty. By the end of the second day they are on the brink of mutiny.

"Ah say we burn down the officer's hole an' show 'um what we think of 'em," Jack said and he received a nod of agreement from Jose.

"You want to spend the rest of you hitch in the brig?" Matthew asked.

"We got to do somethin', Matt," John added.

"Maybe we do," Matthew countered and laid out his plan of action. After hearing the details, Isaac finally agreed to their plan.

A major visiting from Battalion Headquarters made a pit stop at D Company's Officer's latrine. He was reading last month's issue of Field & Stream when he noticed flames below his feet. "Fire...Fire!" He hollered over and over, as he burst through the latrine door and stumbled to the ground with his pants hanging down around his ankles. What was intended to be only a smoke-out got a bit out of hand with too much diesel fuel and ended up as an out of control blaze. The men of 2nd squad fought the flames with shovels of dirt, but the officer's latrine burned to the ground anyway. Suspicious, but lacking the evidence to prove anything, Captain Sampson determined that 2nd squad had most likely failed to ensure the refuse fire was completely out, before they reinserted the barrel beneath the toilet hole. However, they didn't get away with it completely; the next day they were ordered to build a new two-holer latrine facility for the officers. The work completed, the disgruntled men of 2nd squad returned to their tent to find two cases of beer and a note, "The grateful members of D company wish to show their appreciation for actions above and beyond the call of duty."

D COMPANY HEADQUARTERS, JANUARY 15TH, 1969 1315 HOURS

Captain Sampson, sweat on his face and arms, hair moist, glanced up to see the large shadowy image of a man who stood blocking the hut's doorway. Not all that tall, only 5"11 to be exact, the man with sergeant's stripes on his sleeves and a duffle bag at his feet, had a pair of shoulders nearly as wide as the doorway. His muscular neck and massive arms were of such size any pro-football lineman's coach would like to see in his team members. Square jawed and a broad forehead, the man's eyes displayed his prior experience in a hostile environment, but his hand salute was crisp as he reported in.

"Can I help you, sergeant?" Sampson asked. He returned the salute, but he remained sitting.

"Sorry to disturb you, Captain, I was looking for the company clerk." He picked up his duffle bag with his right hand, as if it only weighed ounces instead of pounds and tossed it inside the room and off to one side and then stepped in to the room.

"He's out on errands, what do you need?"

The sergeant marched further into the office and came to stand approximately 18 inches before Sampson's desk. At the proper position of attention, he addressed Captain Sampson, "Sergeant Campbell reporting to the Company Commander as ordered."

"You've been assigned to me?" Sampson asked in surprise. He hadn't expected a new NCO. Campbell stayed at attention and answered, "Yes, Sir."

"Stand at ease, sergeant." Sampson stood up from behind his desk and offered his hand. "No, take a seat…too hot for this. Do you want a Coke?"

Campbell was somewhat surprised by Sampson's laxity in the protocol department and replied, "Sure would, sir. Thanks." Rod Campbell shook hands with Sampson and then plopped himself down in one of Sampson's metal chairs, which put an audible strain on the aged chair. While he waited for the Coke, he noticed the two Vietnamese gentlemen crouched off to one corner and offered them a greeting in Vietnamese. They grinned and replied in kind.

Sampson popped the caps off two Cokes and turned to one of the runners. He issued a quick command and the runner was off to find Lt. Sinclair. Sampson believed 2nd squad was about to have their new squad leader. "I see you speak some Vietnamese, sergeant and by that CIB on your chest I gather this is your second or maybe third tour?" Combat Infantryman's Badge is awarded to men who served in combat in an excess of 30 days.

"Second tour, Captain," Campbell said. He handed his records and orders over to Sampson. A moment later, Sinclair walked into the hut and presented himself to Sampson with a casual salute and then gave Campbell a thoughtful look. Sampson thought they could have been cousins, nearly the same size with Campbell being the broader of the two.

"Lieutenant Sinclair, this here is Sergeant Rod Campbell. Man's on his second tour, so you're getting a veteran." Sampson opened Campbell's records and began reading out loud, "One Purple Heart, an Army Commendation Medal and a Bronze Star for Valor."

Campbell shook hands with Lt. Sinclair and for a brief moment the two men appear to be testing each other's strength as arm muscles bulge. With a nod of approval, Sinclair released Campbell's hand and took a seat on the corner of Sampson's desk.

"You'll be taking over my 2nd squad, made up of only four new men under a seasoned PFC..." Sinclair hesitated briefly and then continued, "You'll hear it soon enough so I might as well tell you now...the man you're replacing overdosed on Heroin. And the new men only have one patrol and scored two water buffalo on a blown ambush." Campbell watched Sampson shake his head and hear him whisper, "Buffalo." Then wipe his face off with a semi-damp towel.

"Yes, sir, those critters can be mighty tough to take down...sort of like taking on a locomotive with a 30-30 rifle," Campbell said. He then asked, "Can you tell me where I can find 'em, sir?" Campbell stood up and prepared to leave.

"You don't have any other questions, Sergeant?" Sampson asked.

"Not yet, sir, but I may have later for the lieutenant." Campbell popped another crisp salute and walked to the doorway where he picked up his duffle and stood, waiting for Lt. Sinclair.

"Guess I'll show him our happy home then, Captain, sir." Sinclair presented another casual salute, resembling more of a hand wave than a military hand salute and led Campbell off to where 1st platoon was billeted.

When he walked into 2nd squad's tent, Campbell tossed his duffle bag down onto the floor to get the men's attention. Campbell couldn't help but smile to see them with their weapons in hand and cleaning tools spread out on the floor, *At least they're not total screw-ups.* "My name is Sergeant Rod Campbell, your new squad leader. I'm glad to see you're busy because you're going to need those rifles tonight. We're goin' out for a walk after dark."

Isaac looked up, "You did say afta' dark?"

Campbell scowled at him, "That's what I said...an' so we understand each other from the get go, this is my second tour. I came over in 67 and

91

went home after eight months with a banged up leg. Hated stateside duty and volunteered to come back, but don't go thinkin' I'm gung ho…'cause I ain't. But this sure beats what I was doin' back home." Campbell looked into the eyes of his men and added, "I've lost my edge an' the L-T thinks I should take you new guys out for some night recon before we get our marchin' orders. We'll have 1st squad along to baby-sit." Campbell opened his duffle bag and pulled out a box of Cracker Jacks, "Do what you're told and we'll get along fine. Now which one of you is Washington?" With their shirts off, Campbell didn't have nametags to go by.

"Right here, Sarge." Isaac held his hand up. "Congratulations, you're now an E-4. So swing by the PX and pick up your new rank. Who's my sixty man?" Campbell opened the box of Cracker Jacks and popped a few candied kernels into his mouth.

Jose answered by picking up his partially assembled weapon from off the floor. "Name's Jose Martinez, Sergeant." Jose presented his best teethe grin.

"Who's your assistant?" Campbell asked. Jack Waterford stood up to which Campbell shook his head in surprise, *little guy carrying the pig and some big dude lugging the ammo…always the army way!*

"I'm Jack Waterford."

Campbell pointed to the both of them, "You two make a real Mutt an' Jeff team. How tall are you, soldier?"

"Six foot-five, Sarge," Jack answered, wondering why his height mattered.

"Well, with you around ol' Mr. Charlie will have an easy target, might leave the rest of us alone." Seeing the look of shock on Jack's face, Campbell added, "Don't worry, I'll teach you to stay low. Now that leaves one of you two to act as my RTO tonight." Campbell looked at Matthew and then John, "Your names and where you're from?"

Matthew spoke first, "Name's Matthew Kendal an' I'm from Southern California." Next was John. "Ah'm John Adams…Washington, D.C." John answered with his thick east coast accent and it made Campbell cringe.

"Tough luck, Kendal, I need someone they'll understand an' that's you. Go over to the company and pick-up a field radio. Have the company RTO check you out on procedures and make sure you get the right codes…and don't forget smoke flares…four of them at least." Campbell held up the four finger of his right hand. "Smoke flares?" Matthew asked.

"Yeah, two green, one red and one blue. In case we need to call for a dust off or we find a tunnel." Matthew nodded his head that he now understood. "On my way," Matthew said. He pulled his shirt on, buttoned it and left the tent.

"Okay, you have two hours to prep for tonight. I got us a ride out by Huey. Later, we'll have some time to get to know each other." Campbell found an empty cot and stretched out for a nap, while the rest of the squad finished putting their weapons back together.

With his eyes closed, Rod Campbell listened to the men as they complained about their sad lot in life. It felt good to be back and for the first time in nearly a year he felt alive again.

Born and raised in Phoenix, Arizona, this was his fourth year in the U.S. Army and he had tentative plans for reenlistment when this tour wrapped up. A high school football star, he got into a scuffle over someone else's girlfriend and lost his college scholarship to Arizona State University. He got off with a sentence of Probation and the Army seemed to be the only outfit who offered him anything to get out of Arizona. Wounded by mortar fire in the Tet Offensive of 68', he was flown stateside for medical leave and found his wife in the proverbial arms of another man; a fellow NCO. A month of divorce proceedings and several nights of drunkenness and brawling led him to the conclusion he was happier in Nam. In need of good NCO's, the 101st Airborne was gracious to grant his request within short notice. He only needed to heal up from his leg wound and settle any further legal problems he had with breaking the man's jaw: the one who was playing house with his wife. In this instance the Army sided with Campbell, they felt harshly about men who lived with other men's wives when that other man was off to war. That other man went off to an Alaska radar site to learn his lesson.

Though not enjoying the prospect of carrying a field radio out on patrol, Matthew listened to the company RTO's instruction on proper radio procedure. The hardest part was to remember all the call signs: Black-Jack One (Battalion Commander), Bravo-One (Company Commander), Charlie-Three (artillery), Echo-Six, Red-One and all too many others. During a firefight the RTO (Radio Telephone Operator) may have to call in artillery support, make contact with a flight of fast movers or possibly call for a dust-off for the wounded. Matthew released a sigh of relief when the RTO handed him a spiral notebook which contained all the call signs.

"Listen, Matt, when the bullets start flyin', I've forgotten all this junk from time to time, so keep the notebook handy and don't lose it. You'll do just fine."

Matthew thanked him for the notebook and then asked, "How do you keep the snipers from seeing the antenna?" This question got a wide eyed expression from the RTO, who glanced about the room and then replied, "Stay close to an officer. Snipers would rather zap an officer than waist a bullet on an RTO. But after that you dig a hole so the only thing they'll see is your antenna."

Matthew laughed and said, "Thanks, but will you now show me how to put the batteries in?"

The RTO agreed, "Sure," and then showed Matthew how. But afterward, he watched as Matthew inserted the batteries three times before he was satisfied that Matthew knew how to do it. "Rule # 1, think of this radio as a toy you got for Christmas…the kind that always said 'batteries not included'. You never want to assume the radio has batteries in it when you take it out to the field. You want fresh batteries in it when you leave the company area and take two extra sets with you. It's hard to find a Western Auto out there in the boonies. Okay?"

Matthew nodded his understanding and replied, "Gotcha." He gathered up the radio, notebook and extra batteries. But it didn't make him feel any better to notice the bullet hole in one corner of the radio's casing. He then remembered the smoke grenades Campbell wanted and before he could ask, the RTO handed him four of them. At the top of each grenade is a thin strip of colored tape showing what color the smoke was.

D COMPANY AREA, JANUARY 15TH, 1969 1840 HOURS

Squad inspection showed each man carried on either his belt and combat suspenders, or in his field pack the following items; four full canteens of water (Campbell located an extra canteen for each man), three boxes of C-rations, 12 magazines of M-16 ammo, one OD wet green towel, three pairs of OD green or black socks, one container of foot powder, one first aid pouch and large battle field dressing, one poncho liner, one sheath knife of their preference and a bayonet, one flashlight with extra set of batteries, fragmentation hand grenades and their M-16 rifle. Jose and Jack each carry two belts of 100 rounds of M-60 ammo, while Isaac carried one belt of M-60 ammo. John had a LAW tied to the top of his pack and Jack carried a pouch of 40mm grenades for his recently assigned M-79 grenade launcher. Matthew lugged the weight of a field radio and also carried a pouch of 40mm grenades for his newly assigned M-203 grenade launcher attached to six his M-16. By the time Campbell finished his inspection the men of 2nd squad were soaked in sweat and moaned their complaints. Satisfied, Campbell ignored their mournful cries and led them out to where they joined up with 1st squad for a short hike to the helipad. In quick pursuit came a swarm of mosquitoes, which grouped in a flight formation above their human targets. Those pests were not about to lose this wipe herd of beef.

Matthew walked behind Campbell and he noticed the weapon his new squad leader carried and decided to comment on it, "Hey, Sarge, what's with the shotgun?"

Campbell held a Remington 12-gauge shotgun with a modified choke on a sling over his shoulder; the model was equipped with a pistol grip instead of a normal stock. "I carried one last time I was here and it's a very effective weapon in the boonies. VC have this religious thing about shotguns, something against all the holes it makes in a body." Campbell also carried a second LAW and a medic bag attached to his rucksack. There would be no medic coming along on this little jaunt and he wanted to make sure they had some medical supplies in the event one of his guys stubbed a toe or stepped into a punji trap. He was a cautious man and took it upon himself to receive 120 hours of emergency medical training while state-side. On Campbell's last tour in Viet Nam he had learned to be ready for anything.

Two loaded Hueys lifted off from Camp Eagle, while darkness closed in from the east. Campbell wanted to catch the local VC by surprise and 18 minutes later and 14 miles northwest of Phu Bai, the Hueys descended quickly over a field of elephant grass. The birds swooped in fast and hovered several feet above the ground, which allowed the men of 1st and 2nd squad access to a cold LZ. Still, they quickly formed a defensive perimeter while the helicopters departed the area. A reportedly secured zone and cleared by the 9th Marines a month earlier, the birds were scheduled to return at 1400 hours the next day.

Before taking off on patrol, Sgt. Ulston of 1st squad briefed the men, "According to Battalion S-2 (Intelligence), this area is supposedly safe and secure. But one thing you can be sure of over here, there is no such thing as a secured area. From the time we hit the LZ consider yourselves in enemy territory." With only 13 days and a wake-up before heading home, Sgt. Ulston believed in being extremely careful. "We have a saying over here, 'the night belongs to Charlie'". That got the new guys on 1st squad's attention.

With two men from 1st squad on point, the men moved slowly and silent through waist high elephant grass, a grove of Banyan trees and a forest of giant bamboo. Overhead, patchy clouds played a game of hide and seek with the moon and this made it tough for the men to see more than ten feet in front of them. Campbell had his men listen to Sgt. Ulston and added to it, "That man knows his stuff. He's a survivor and I want every one of you to survive this tour, too. Keep your eyes open and mouth shut. Listen for every sound and if you question it, get my attention."

He watched each man and occasionally stopped them along the way with a whispered word of critique or encouragement. "Jose, you got to keep pace with the man in front of you, but still maintain your distance. That pig has to be ready, but you can't be too ready and zap the three guys in front of you because you got too excited."

"Jack, hold your weapon level and maintain a 90-degree visual range, but keep your finger off the trigger. I don't want you killing Jose because you think you saw something," Campbell advised him in an encouraging voice and slapped him on the shoulder in a way of support. "The men saw right off Campbell was of different sort than Brodrick, more instructive and less shout. "Keep your eyes moving, Matt and don't stare at the ground. If there was a trip wire in front, John would have already killed you with the way he's ambling along looking for babes."

"John, quit checking out the streets for ladies. You don't need to impress anyone but me with your style. That's the enemy out there and he wants to kill you dead. Got it?"

John grinned, but it was too dark for anyone to see it. "Yeah, I got it, Sarge."

Finally, Campbell called a break after the men had covered nearly three miles of rough terrain. Two men: John and a man from 1st squad were sent out to set up an LP 50 yards up ahead. The remaining men formed an NDP (night defensive perimeter) and once both NCOs were satisfied with their position, Campbell and Ulston gave the okay to chow down. "Open those cans quietly and after you eat, make sure you bury 'em!" Ulston ordered. Campbell walked up the line to make sure every man got the order. He added a good word here and there. He knew tonight was not the night for harsh criticism, unless it was something dangerous a man was doing.

They continued to keep a vigil while they consumed a cold meal. Each man knew at any moment the VC could rain mortar fire down upon them, a thought capable of disquieting a man's digestion system. Matthew sipped fruit cocktail juice from the can and then reached into his shirt pocket to pull out a snapshot of Kathy Lee. Though he was unable to see it in the darkness, holding it in his hand brought him a sense of calm. Three times he had tried to write her, but each time he struggled with what to say to her. The same matter wasn't resolved with his parents, *what do I say? Weather's great, wish you were here? Killed a water buffalo last night, my last squad leader overdosed?* Still, he knew he'd better get a letter off soon or he'd be standing in front of the Sergeant Major.

Leaving the squads, Campbell made his way out to check on his LP, only to be greeted by a pair of M-16's in the hands of two very nervous young soldiers. "It's Campbell," he said in a faint whisper.

"C'mon in," John said, when he recognized his squad leader's voice.

"Is everything okay?" Campbell asked. He crouched down beside John. Such a big man knew his silhouette made a good target.

"Not sure, Sarge," the other man said. "I keep hearing a clinking-like sound. It's aways off, but I'd swear it's manmade." PFC Connors kept his voice low, a veteran of five months in country he knew the value of silence on an LP.

John started to speak and Campbell stopped him with a soft, "Quiet." For the next few minutes the three of them listened to the sounds of the jungle: a concert of insect life and small animals being pursued by larger ones. Then, Campbell heard the noise too and suddenly his plans for night recon abruptly ended. He didn't expect to find any VC activity in the area, but that single metallic sound had changed everything. "You two stay here, while I bring up the rest." Campbell then added in a low whisper, "Stay real quiet and don't get curious or I'll kick your butts with my size 13's." He checked his shotgun first and then began to crawl off. That old feeling gushed through him, *Different this time, I'm the one responsible for keeping these kids alive and it looks like we've walked right into it.*

Campbell knelt down beside Ulston, "LP's picked up something, could be some mamma-san washing out her cooking pot or a buffalo dragging his chain."

Ulston nodded his head, he understood, "And it might be some Charlie cleaning his rifle."

Campbell, looked over his shoulder at his squad and then replied, "Right, there's no sense taking any chances. I'll have the RTO notify command and let 'em know we're checking on suspicious activity. Accordin' to our map, there shouldn't be any villages in this area." Campbell looked to the moon and then back at Ulston, "I'll take my squad up first, pick up the LP an' you bring up the rear to watch our backs. Sound okay with you?"

Ulston rubbed the beard stubble on his chin, "I'm getting way to short for this...but let's do it." He then went over to talk with his assistant squad leader and brief his people. C-rat cans were quickly buried while Matthew made contact with Battalion Command.

When Matthew made contact on his third attempt, Campbell yanked the handset away, "Able-Niner, we're checking on possible, I repeat possible enemy activity at the following coordinates..." Campbell, who used a flashlight cuffed over his map, read off a series of numbers. "We'll keep you advised of situation, out." Campbell handed the radio handset back to Matthew, "Saddle up, buckaroo."

John breathed out a sigh of relief when Campbell returned with the rest of the squad. They were in the middle of a field, a small knoll in front of them and with only one other guy. This didn't make John a happy camper. Besides, he'd already cut one leech off his leg with his bayonet because he couldn't risk lighting a match and he was sickened by leeches. The thought of one on his leg nauseated him. He sliced the slimy pest up into several pieces and tossed the remains out into the grass. Only then did he wipe his leg off and pull his pants leg back down.

Directly in front of the LP, some 40 to 50 yards away, stood a long line of Banyan trees. With Isaac on point, the squad cautiously moved forward until they reached the first grove of trees. The wooded area reminded Matthew of a dark closet, he couldn't see anything in front of him but black. Moments earlier they had some moonlight, but the thick growth of trees didn't allow the moon's shine to filter through. Several times Matthew reached out to touch Campbell's pack. *How'm I supposed to see the VC? I can't even see my hand, much less a booby trap...Hope I don't goof up and get someone killed.*

The squad moved forward like blind men, with each step paced between ten and 12 heartbeats as they bounced off the trees. Matthew then heard the metallic sound several times, but then it stopped completely and his heart quit beating. The stench of soiled uniforms and his own sweat made him teary eyed, but he didn't want to risk a towel wipe of his eyes; afraid any movement would alert the enemy. For what seemed like an hour, but actually only a few minutes, the patrol moved through the forest until suddenly, Matthew felt Campbell's sweaty palm on his face. Surprised at first, he followed suit by reaching back to stop Jose and so forth down the line. Then, as if someone had pulled back a thick black curtain, Matthew spotted the glow of a small fire through a thick row of trees. Matthew knelt down on one knee and began to see other fires in the same area and soon counted a total of four small fires. When Isaac spotted the first fire he brought the squad to a halt. He used his hand to touch the man behind him and waited for Campbell to join him up front.

Crouched behind a tree, Isaac briefed Campbell on his observations, "Four...maybe five huts. They got some cookin' fires out front an' some women sittin' aroun'...No men, but one water buffalo to the rear that ain't picked up our stink yet." Isaac pointed with his right index finger, but his elbow was bent to limit his arm extension.

"Good eyes," Campbell said. He then pulled out from under his shirt a small set of binoculars and observed the scene. Though they were not infrared equipped, the binoculars still allowed the wearer to have better visibility at night.

"Yeah, I can see five women, two babies and one child poking the fire with a stick. They must've moved in recently, but this is a mighty strange spot for a village. Too far from water an' too small...Charlie'd eat 'em up in a minute...unless they are Charlie. You stay put." Campbell made his way back to where Ulston had positioned his squad in a defensive position off the trail.

Campbell briefed the other squad leader and then asked, "So, what do you think?"

Ulston remained silent for a moment and then he answered, "I Don't wanna move in while it's dark, better to wait for dawn."

Campbell agreed with him, "Okay, you set up 1st squad for an ambush back where we entered the tree line. My squad will set up here inside the tree line to keep an eye on the place," Campbell said in a feint whisper.

"So much for a simple training op. Down to thirteen and a wake-up, and you got me out here playin' John Wayne. You're gonna owe me big time...What do you wanna use for a password?"

"Uhhh...challenge will be Bonanza an' counter will be...Little Joe," Campbell answered.

"Bonanza fan, right?" Ulston asked.

"Nope, you reminded me of it with that John Wayne stuff."

Ulston gestured to his squad, "I'll bring my guys up at 0600 hours, Little Joe." Ulston then crawled off to relocate his men. *Thirteen and a wake-up...Thirteen and a wake-up...I'm gonna die out here!*

Campbell returned to Matthew's side, grabbed him by his combat harness and gave him a yank to follow him. Some distance back, Campbell contacted command and briefed them on the situation. They confirmed no report of a village in this area, which only heightened Campbell's suspicions.

Their two Hueys would now return to this new location at 0700 hours, escorted by two AH-1 Cobra Gun ships in the event air support was needed. But for now, the next nine hours would pass by very slow for the men of 1st and 2nd squads. Mosquito dive bombers would wage an air assault, while slithering night crawlers staged a ground attack.

Jose, who fought down a case of combat jitters, kept his M-60 trained on the village and waited for any sign of VC activity. Then sometime around midnight the fires dimmed and the women broke up their coffee corner and returned to their huts. Without even the glow of fires to focus on, the night now became a test of nerves.

Matthew jerked when John crawled up beside him and whispered into his ear, "Dis place is worse than duh Red Cross. Ever'ting wants our blood, but at least duh Red Cross gives yuh a doughnut and sum orange juice." Hearing John's voice be carried through the trees, Isaac snaked back to John's side and clamped a dried mud-caked hand over his mouth. Message received and Isaac took the hand away.

At approximately 0200 hours, the men heard a series of muffled explosions way off in the distance. *Sounds like Phu Bai might be getting hit or somewhere near there.* Campbell thought.

He pulled on Matthew's shoulder and led him back to a spot where he could contact command. He learned a small hamlet near Phu Bai was hit by mortar fire, but there were no casualties reported yet. When he signed off, he pushed Matthew ahead of him and they returned to their former positions.

At 0550 hours, Campbell was alerted to the sound of movement in the village. The black of night was slowly beginning to brighten with the coming dawn. He used his binoculars, which nearly tripled his night vision and spotted six men. The Vietnamese men were entering the village from the west and they carried weapons, *Good evening, Mr. Charlie.* Two of the men were lugging a mortar tube, which hung from a bamboo pole carried on their shoulders. A third man carried the heavy metal tripod, while a fourth labored to haul the steel base plate. The remaining two men were armed with long rifles, *No AK-47's?*

While four of the men remained standing, two men knelt down to shove aside an unused fire pit.

Through binoculars, Campbell watched them open a wooden trap door from under the fire pit. *Tunnel...storage?* Campbell ignored the insects that buzzed his head and kept the Vietnamese men in view as they lowered the mortar tube, tripod and base plate into the hole. They then placed the rifles inside before they sealed the tunnel up and moved the fire pit back into position. For added camouflage, they placed a cooking frame over the pit and an empty pot hung from it. *Not bad...who'd suspect it?* In his last tour, Campbell had learned how well the VC could conceal things; from tunnels, weapons and food storage areas and large underground hospitals.

Finished with their task, the Vietnamese separated into their various huts and never suspected a squad of American soldiers had observed them. Campbell crawled to each man, whispering the same thing, "We don't move until dawn, stay loose and remain silent."

At 0600 hours, Sgt. Ulston abandoned the ambush site, pulling his men in and leading them back to where they joined with Campbell's squad. Ulston wasn't exactly overjoyed to hear the good news and he made it plain with his suggestion, "Maybe we could fall back and forget all this...what'll you think?"

To which Campbell replied, "I know, thirteen days and a wake-up." He put his hand on Ulston's shoulder, "You're senior man here, Sgt. Ulston. Do you really want to forget all this?" Campbell asked. "You can run this show if you want, I won't say anything to Lt. Sinclair…but I did radio in what we found and it might be a bit sticky."

"Naw, L-T said you were in charge of this op," Ulston said with a sigh and added, "So where do you want us?"

Campbell smiled and whispered, "Ah the warrior lives on." He laid his hand on Ulston's shoulder.

This got Ulston to reply, "You're laying it on a bit too thick, Campbell…now tell me where you want us and if you get me killed, I promise to come back and haunt you." He pushed Campbell's hand off and glared at him, "…and don't get my squad shot up. I'd like to turn them over all in one piece when I sign off as their squad leader and take that glorious *freedom bird* home to the *World*."

Campbell's voice took on a serious tone, "Enter ten or so yards down that way," he pointed to a natural pathway between two large trees. "Stay parallel with the huts. I'd like to have your sixty-crew take up a position to the far right and hold a flanking position to cut off anyone fleeing that way. But make sure they understand we want prisoners, not corpses." Campbell then used his hands to show how he wanted Ulston's squad to move forward in a line formation, "But stay to the right side of that pathway you went in on. Focus on that hut straight ahead," Campbell pointed to the hut he meant. "Watch out for booby-traps, they're bound to have this area wired." Campbell pointed to his men, "Then I'll move my squad in a line formation to the left with my gunner to the far end of the line to catch anyone running that way. Both gunners to fire only straight ahead or to their unprotected side. I don't want to get shot by an over excited new guy. This way we can cover nearly three sides of the village an' there's little chance of us shooting each other." Campbell looked at his watch, he could just barely make out the hands on the dial, "Give me five minutes to put my squad together and my first man will move out. When you see him, cut your men loose to move in. Once we're inside the village, we separate into two-man search teams and round-up those Victor Charlie's. Okay with you?"

Ulston answered, "Sounds good, but let's hold off on waking 'em up until we're all in there and ready to bag 'em as they wake up. Once we get the place surrounded, we'll fire off a few rounds in the air and grab 'em as they come out."

Nodding his head, Campbell agreed and added, "Well make some veterans out of these rookies." He then mentioned, "Just think, Ulston, tomorrow its only 12 days and a wake-up." This time it was Ulston's turn to shake his head in dismay, "Funny guy…How many days you got left?" Campbell had a strange smile on his face, which bothered Ulston, "Me, I'm here forever…I love this place. I'm only out here to check on real estate values, might buy a farm and raise chickens."

Ulston backed away from Campbell and whispered, "I should've known…you're nuts. Guys like you are bound to get me killed…a real certified apple pie hero."

Campbell left a weary eyed Isaac on watch. He wanted to make sure no one came up behind them, when they entered the encampment. He then used the next few minutes to brief his new guys one by one. Then it was time. With a stealth that even surprised Campbell, the men of 1st and 2nd squad surrounded the small village and closed in. They didn't wake up the villagers of the hamlet, nor the water buffalo, that seemed disinterested with the Americans. But then it happened all too quickly—a Vietnamese woman with a baby in her arms came out of one of the huts and spotted the enormous Jack Waterford. She let out a terrified shriek, almost dropped the baby and nearly got herself shot. It was probably only the baby in her arms that prevented that from happening.

"Get in those huts fast! Wake 'em up an' get 'em out in the open!" Campbell yelled. His order was followed by a similar command issued by Ulston, who kept his rifle trained on the woman with the baby. Once before, he'd seen a hand grenade pulled out from a baby's blanket and he wasn't about to take any chances this short to him going home.

Twelve men quickly closed on the huts with bayonet tipped rifles leveled at the waist. Matthew burst through the door of one hut, with John right behind. Both men were wide eyed to find a half-naked man and a woman in their bed on the floor. A small baby was suckling the mother and the man had his arms up in surrender. With his adrenaline on overtime, Matthew aimed his rifle at the man's face and though he could sense his fear, he can't understand a word the man said. "Outside!" Matthew ordered. "Hands up…get outside. Make a move an' I'll drill you!" Matthew shouted.

John, who stood beside Matthew, was an echo to Matthew's commands, "Outside-Outside-Outside!"

Without having to fire a shot, six Vietnamese men, seven women and six children are moved to the center of village. With the exception of the babies, who continued to feed, the four children were frightened. Matthew stood beside one man and was surprised by how harmless he appeared. *This is my enemy?*

"Kendal, you and Adams start a search those huts for a tunnel entrance or any underground storage," Campbell ordered. He then turned to Jack, "Waterford, you keep these people together while Washington and I check out this fire pit." Campbell smiled at the Vietnamese men when he moved toward the pit and saw the look of surprise on the faces of the Vietnamese.

"I gotta tunnel here!" One of Ulston's men yelled out from inside one of the huts.

"Pop a smoke grenade down it, see where it comes up," Ulston ordered. Within less than a minute a plume of green smoke began to rise from a tree line approximately 45 to 50 feet off. Another one of Ulston's men dashed over to keep a rifle leveled on the spot.

"Drop a frag down each end," Ulston ordered. A grenade would collapse the tunnel and often kill anyone inside of it, which was always the enemy. Very few soldiers, with the exception of the *tunnel rats* ever wanted to journey down into one of these tunnels. They were almost always booby trapped with everything from poisonous snakes nailed to a wooden beam to punji traps in the floor.

Listening to the explosions and feeling the ground shake, Matthew and John entered the hut where they found the family of three. Using his bayonet to pull away a pile of grass mats, Matthew made a discovery. "I got somethin' here!" he shouted. His whole body was juiced with excitement and he even had the nervous jitters to complicate things.

"What is it?" Isaac asked from outside the hut. Matthew knelt down to push aside several bamboo poles to reveal a long wooden box with Russian writing on it. "Bamboo poles, looks like an open box of rifles. Old ones… must be Russian made if I remember their hammer an' cycle logo right." Coming out of the hut with an arm full of old bolt-action rifles, Matthew heard someone shout, "Grenade!" He thought it was one of their guys giving a warning before he dropped another grenade down a tunnel shaft. It wasn't.

A Chinese made pineapple grenade flew through the air in a high arc and landed at the feet of a stunned PFC Jack Waterford. He froze up, too frightened to move to save his own life. While everyone else dove for cover, including the Vietnamese, Isaac charged in and hit Jack at the waist to drive him backwards and only a microsecond before the grenade exploded. Two men from 1st squad caught shrapnel in the legs and went down with screams, while they grabbed their wounded legs. One Vietnamese woman was blown sideways by the shock wave, her back ripped open by the blast. Another Vietnamese fell to the earth like a downed bowling pin when the blast wave hit him and he is rendered unconscious. But surprisingly, the lethal wave of shrapnel missed all but the one woman.

Matthew rose to his feet, rattled by the blast and clutched his rifle for security. Then he saw a blur of movement to his right, quickly turned and spotted an older Vietnamese male alone in the tree line. The man was holding another Chinese grenade in his right hand and was about to pull his arm back for the throw, when Matthew brought his rifle up, took aim and fired off a short burst. Riddled by automatic fire, the lifeless body of the man collapsed to the ground and the live grenade rolled out of his hand and exploded. The blast hurled the body into the air and the shattered remains fell within clear sight of where Matthew stood. Stunned by what had occurred in a matter of seconds, his rifle aimed at the bloody pile of rags before him, Matthew fell to his knees and upchucked on the ground.

Everyone yelled at everyone else and frightened soldiers with rifles pointed, herded the Vietnamese prisoners together into a tight clump in the center of the small village. Campbell ordered Jose to keep that tree line under a close eye in the event there might be other VC in the area. Men from 1st squad were providing first aide for their two wounded soldiers, while Campbell checked on Isaac and a terrified Jack. From behind him, Matthew heard his name called out but his mind was having trouble, he could not register anything but the mangled remains of the man he had killed. "Oh, God..." Matthew muttered and then he began to tremble. The horror at his feet took focus. Unable to stand, he dropped down to all fours where the fresh stench of death assaulted his senses and he continued to vomit.

Jack lay on his back. He patted his body down to make sure he was still in one piece. Isaac was beside him on all fours, he shook his head back and forth in an attempt to clear his ears. The concussion of the grenade had left him temporarily deaf. But though the grenade had knocked them to the ground the shrapnel had miraculously passed over them. Jack sat up and looked over at Isaac with a shocked expression on his face, while realization dawned on him. A black man had actually saved his life. Isaac was too busy with his deafness to notice Jack and he panicked when the big southern boy picked him off the ground in a big affectionate bear hug and shouted, "Thank yuh! Thank yuh! Thank yuh! Thank yuh!" To this, Isaac yelled back, "Let go of me!" Jack refused to release him.

Campbell moved in and separated the two men. He also checked each of them out to ensure they weren't wounded.

"You did a good job, Washington. That took a lot of guts."

Isaac shook his head, pointed to his right ear and shouted, "Sarge, I can't hear a thing. I got this ringing in mah ears." Nodding his head that he understood, Campbell checked Isaac's ears and gestured at him to go sit down by where the other two men were being given first aid.

Then Campbell spotted Matthew and walked over to him. He knelt beside him, put his hand on Matthew back and said, "Puke your guts out, Matt. I threw up all over the place my first time too." When John walked up, Campbell stood up and said to him, "Stay with him. Get some water down him and a couple salt tabs before he gets dehydrated. I'll be back in a few."

Campbell reached down and gently removed the radio pack from Matthew's shoulders and carried it over to where Ulston was standing. "Birds should be here in about ten mikes, suggest you take three men and set up a DP. I'll leave four men here to watch the prisoners and bring the whole bunch down when the Huey's arrive. If we hear any shooting before then, we'll come a running...Okay?" Campbell asked and Ulston responded with a simple nod of agreement. An hour later the first Huey lifted off with the two wounded soldiers and three of the five male prisoners. The remaining members of 1st squad squeezed on board the second Huey with the rest of the prisoners and left for Camp Eagle. Campbell watched the two birds disappear over the hill and then sighted two more Hueys coming in with Lt. Sinclair, Captain Sampson and the men of 3rd squad. While the Huey's rotors still rotated down, Sampson and his party followed Campbell to the village. Overhead, two Cobra gunships continued to provide aerial surveillance in the event there was more VC in the area. As they made their way through the thick woods, Campbell briefed the two officers on what took place and finished up when they entered the small village to see a stack of captured weapons and two dead bodies; the Vietnamese woman killed by the first grenade and the man Matthew killed.

"They hid the mortar under this fake fire pit, pretty good job of concealment too. We found the rifles buried under one of the huts and must've blown up their mortar rounds when we fragged a tunnel. Part of the tunnel collapsed over there and we had a pretty good sized secondary blast," Campbell said.

Sampson picked up one of the rifles and examined it, "Russian Simonov SKS, 7.62 mm. Soviets supply them to the NVA mostly, but some of them must have made their way down to our local VC cadres." He finished his inspection of the weapons and then ordered them destroyed along with the rest of the village. Captain Sampson then walked up to Matthew, who now stood uneasily between John and Jose. Sampson congratulated him for a job well done, "From what your squad leader says you saved a few lives out here today with your actions. Not something we expect from a new guy." When he recognized the look of pain in Matthew's eyes, he suggested, "If you need to go see the chaplain, you got my okay and Lieutenant Sinclair's too."

Sampson reached up and laid his right hand on Matthew's shoulder for a brief moment, "Son, I hope you never get used to it. Taking a man's life should never come easy." Sampson then left Matthew's side to go have a talk with Isaac.

"Look, man, I told you it was nuthin'. So, jus' cool it okay?" Isaac pleaded with Jack to give him some room, but Jack stayed by his side like an over protective watch dog.

"You saved mah life. All this time, they tol' me you people was so bad and hateful, but you saved mah life." Jack looked so serious and ridiculous at the same time, he made Jose laugh.

"Man, I've tried to tell you...Lord, ah wish ah was still deaf, mah head hurts too bad to talk anymore. Jus' go away, please," Isaac begged. Nothing worked. However, Jack remained on watch to safeguard his new buddy. Then Jack saw Sampson and Sinclair close-by, so he popped to attention and saluted. He forgot all about a policy of enlisted men not to salute officers in the field to safeguard against officers killed by snipers. Isaac shook his head in disgust and told Jack to drop the salute.

"Washington, your quick action today and at the risk of your own life saved PFC Waterford from certain death. I've asked Sergeant Campbell to write you up a recommendation for a Bronze Star and I'll endorse it." Sampson offered his hand and Isaac brought up his own in return.

"Thank yuh, sir. But ah was jus' the one close enough."

Sinclair added his two cents, "Maybe so, but it sounds like everyone else had their own skins on their minds. Glad to see your promotion to E- 4 came through, maybe before this tour is up you'll make sergeant."

Isaac nodded his head a couple times and said, "If you'll excuse me, sir, ah need to gather up my gear."

Sampson released him with, "You go ahead and take Waterford with you, Washington. He seems to be a bit rattled still." Isaac got his gear together and piled it with the other's stuff for the hike to the LZ, but when it was time to leave, his pack hung off Jack's shoulder.

"Don't yuh think you got enough ta carry already?" Isaac asked. Jack wouldn't concede and Isaac decided his head hurt too much to push it at the moment and he only carried his rifle to the LZ.

CAMP EAGLE/D COMPANY AREA

Second Squad returned to Camp Eagle and drifted back to their tent and the first duty was to strip down their weapons and clean them. Once that chore was completed, they turned their attention to ammo check and third, to washing out their uniforms, underwear and socks. The stench of soiled uniforms was nearly powerful enough to drive the mosquitoes off, but not completely.

When Matthew finished up with his rifle, he leaned back against his cot, lowered his head and closed his eyes. The scene of that mutated dead man on the ground replayed in his mind, again and again. Tears trickled down his cheeks as all his previous plans for revenge and his role of avenging angel faded away. Bitterness, once a blazing fire, was replaced by a sickening feeling of repulsion. His insides were queasy, *who was he? Did he have a wife, some kids? I shot 'im down, killed 'im. Who am I? Was he defending his home as I would?* He ignored the concern his friends showed and leapt up to dash out of the tent.

"What's wrong wit' him?" Jack asked. His face and arms were covered in bug bites and his bloodshot eyes a look of bewilderment.

Jose shot him an icy glare. "Let's see, Big Man...Matt's only 19 years old, his big brother got killed here las' year an' he probably misses his folks an' his special lady friend. Plus, he's livin' a long ways from home wit' people who wants ta kill him. Oh yeah, he kill't a man today...his first. Maybe that's what's wrong wit' Matt."

"Sorree," Jack said. "Guess Ah talked 'fore ah think."

Jose continued to nod his head and said, "Maybe that concussion did yuh some good, big guy." His wide eyes and raised eyebrow routine got Jack to smile, but inside, Jose remained deeply concerned for his friend Matthew.

The squad continued with their chores while they listened to the singing talents of Elvis Presley over the Armed Force Radio. Outside the tent, a Black soldier from 3rd squad shouted out, "Turn that white boy off, I can't stand no whitey tryin' to sound like a Black man singing the blues." Jack started to reply, but a hard look from Jose shut him up, when John shouted out, "Elvis may be white, bro, but he sure know how to sing the blues a whole lots better than you ever did."

After a long walk to Battalion Headquarters, Matthew finally located the chaplain's tent. The flap was up, so Matthew ambled up and knocked on a wooden tent pole. Chaplain Richards lay stretched out on his cot, with a pocket book in his hands. When he saw Matthew, he swung his legs around and sat up, "What can I do for you, soldier?"

Matthew hesitated briefly and then said, "Excuse me, sir. My name is PFC Matthew Kendal...from D Company. I was wondering if I could have a moment of your time."

"You bet, young man. Come on in and have a seat." Richards pointed to a couple of wooden chairs. He put a leather bookmark in to hold his place and laid the pocket book down on top of an OD green footlocker. He then turned to face Matthew. "What's up, Matthew?"

Eyes began to water, again and Matthew lowered his head to whisper, "I uh...umm, I killed a man today."

WILLIAM CASSELMAN

5 – THE DEAR JOHN LETTER

KENEDAL RESIDENCE, UPLAND, CALIFORNIA, JANUARY 23RD, 1969 1518 HOURS

Jean Kendal was flustered. She sat at her kitchen table with a tough decision to make as to whether or not she should open the letter that lay before her on the kitchen table. The mail arrived and among the usual utility bills and pester some giveaway adds was a plain white envelope, delivered without a stamp, that carried the return APO address of South Viet Nam. The problem lay in that the envelope was addressed, in large black printed letters, to "Pastor Walter Kendal" and not "Pastor and Mrs. Walter Kendal". By using only her husband's title and name meant only one thing in her mind: *For dad's eyes only, mom, sorry. Probably man talk and my son thinks it will cause me some degree of concern. Well, the next letter had better be for me or he can forget about receiving any more cookies from this mother.*

She pushed herself from the table to avoid further temptation, especially since this is his first letter they had received from Viet Nam. Jean then picked up the letter, stood up and carried it into her husband's den. She placed the envelope on his desk. Out of sight and out of mind wasn't working though. Three times that day she nearly caved in with a desire to rip it open and read the contents. But each time she stopped herself with the realization her son had his reasons for addressing the envelope to only his father.

Walter arrived home from another long day of counseling sessions and dealing with other church matters, to receive a warm embrace from his wife and then the news of Matthew's letter. He could read her mood, so he went into the den and retrieved the letter in order that he might eat his dinner tonight without his wife glaring at him.

Walter relaxed into his favorite chair and used a penknife to open the envelope. Jean gave him some space and took her own chair, but she was unable to do much of anything as she waited to hear how their son was.

With reading glasses perched on the bridge of his nose, he begins to read:

Dear Dad, I wanted some man-to-man talk without getting mom upset. I just left the chaplain's tent where I've been for the last hour. Had an interesting talk with him and he suggested I write you. I think you'd like him, although he is a Baptist and I remember that argument you got into a couple years ago with that Baptist pastor concerning rapture.

Anyway, this is kind of hard, Dad, doing this by letter but we're stuck with it. Something happened this morning in a small village near here. We were out on a night recon, supposed to be a secure area, but that's the Marines for you, because they must've missed this bunch and we stumbled upon some Viet Cong they bypassed. They call them Charlie over here, sometimes Mr. Charlie, Victor Charlie or just plain gook. We entered the small village after dawn, woke up all the people and their kids. I was so scared, pointing my rifle at them and shouting. I can't speak Vietnamese and they didn't understand me either. Everyone was scared and the kids are screaming. Except this baby, she or he, I don't know, just kept feeding off his or her mother. Everything happened so fast, a grenade landed and we all dove for cover. A woman got killed and two of our guys were wounded. When I stood up, I saw this guy behind one of the huts and he was getting ready to toss another grenade. I shot him, Dad, killed him too. Next thing I remember I'm getting sick all over the place and Jose was trying to make me feel better. It didn't work. I just kept looking at this man's body, all mangled from the grenade he dropped when I shot him.

Dad, I used to listen to all those stories you guys would tell about World War II, but you never told me about what you felt when you killed someone. To stare into his lifeless eyes, see his torn up body. Why didn't you tell me about that, Dad? I came over here for revenge, but there is no revenge left in me. It died with the man I killed. I'm now just another soldier over here that has a job to do and counting the days until I can come home. I'm no John Wayne, no hero like Luke was. Will I have nightmares, Dad? Is that why you and your friends never talked about death? Maybe when I come home you and I can talk about it then. Don't worry, I'm okay now. I love you. Love, Matthew

Walter carefully folded the two pages, inserted them back into the envelope and placed the letter inside his Bible cover. He clutched his Bible to his chest and closed his eyes as a single tear began to trickle down his cheek. He thought back to that night in France so long ago when he too had killed his first man and how sorrowful he felt. He remembered it was a dark night in a cold land. So long ago, yet it was never far from his mind. A night when he took the life of a German soldier no older than himself and it wasn't the last man he would have to kill before the war was over.

"Yes, son, you'll have nightmares and there's nothing you or I can do to stop them from haunting your sleep, except to pray. Only the Lord Jesus

Christ can heal our wounds, but the memories still continue," Walter whispered.

Can you read me the letter, Dear?" Jean asked. She saw the tears and knew the letter contained something very important.

"No, my love," Walter said. "I know you're extremely curious and when Matthew comes home I will share it with you, but this one was son to his father letter. I am sure the letter to follow will be for you too. I do hope you understand."

"No, but I trust you and I love you both. *I knew I should've steamed that letter open when it came…but no, that would've been wrong. But dang it!*

D COMPANY AREA, JANUARY 25TH, 1969 1420 HOURS

As with every war, mail had a strong effect on a soldier's morale. Letters from home were an emotional tie to one's loved ones, news of family and words of affection to bring a smile to a lonely young man so far away from home. Company clerks announced mail call and then quickly tossed out various sized letters, rolled up magazines and hometown newspapers, and packages to waiting hands. A letter could tell a soldier how much his wife or girlfriend missed him, of future plans and maybe for the family man how the kids had grown. For a lucky one, a recent snapshot of that special lady or the new baby who had recently learned how to walk. For a few of the men, a package contained several dozen homemade cookies to be shared with the members of his squad and that always helped boost the morale for everyone--unless the sender was a poor cook and the cookies went to the dogs who roved the camp.

Yet sometimes, and far too often to many a broken heart, a soldier received bad news in the mail. Such mail not only affected him, but also possibly his whole squad as well. Stuck in a war, far from home, the unfortunate soldier can't help if a friend or relative was in trouble; someone was sick or had died and his depression could affect everyone like a disease. But by far, the worst piece of mail to receive was the infamous "*Dear John*" letter. Unkind words like, "Sorry, honey, but I've met someone else who can satisfy my needs better. Can we still be friends?" Even worse was, "I want a divorce, I've moved in with your best friend." Such letters seemed to always finish with, "I never planned for this to happen…"

Next down on the list was the informative letter from a friend or relative, "I just thought you should know I saw your wife with another man last night." A tough one for a man who doesn't know who or what to believe and a suspicious mind could cause an extreme amount of mental anguish. A man would say, "I trust her. Really, I trust her." Then doubt came into play and the day-after-day of mental tug-of-war lingered on. This worsened when he went a long time without any mail from home.

PFC Jack Waterford, happy to get some mail finally, received such a letter from his cousin back home. It even came with a photograph of Jack's wife dancing rather intimately with another man. "He's living with her, Jack, in your house and they look pretty darn happy. Even saw your uncle over there a time or two, stayed all night and he tends to brag some about their nocturnal activity." Teary eyed and angry, Jack tore both the letter and photo up into small pieces. His anger burned and turned into a rage and he began to throw around whatever he can lay his big hands on. First Jose, then John and also Matthew grabbed Jack and wrestled the big guy to the ground in an attempt to keep him from injury to himself or anyone else. It was a struggle, but they got him to stop. Then his eyes began to leak tears and in a mumble, Jack told his friends of the letter.

When Campbell walked in, he found his squad on the floor with a mournful Jack.

Matthew saw Campbell and stood to his feet and informed him of the letter. Campbell's first expression was one of sympathy for Jack, but he became angry as he recalled his own past experience with an unfaithful wife. He took a seat on the floor with his men and shared a few ideas with Jack for a righteous plan of attack. "Write her right away and confront her with these accusations," Campbell said. He then added, "When was the last letter you got from her?"

Jack looked into Campbell's face and said, "Not since I got here."

Campbell hesitated for a moment and then said, "Okay, then it sounds like you have a problem, Jack." Campbell paused for a moment and before he continued, Jose asked, "Yeah, Sarge, so what's he gonna do 'bout it?" Campbell ignored Jose and spoke to Jack, "Now your wife is still entitled to her quarter's allowance by law, but you can stop sending home the rest of your money. Have it sent to a new bank account, maybe use a whole different bank, but anywhere she can't get her hands on it."

Jose spoke up, "Change your insurance too." Later that day, Jack wrote a letter home to his wife and asked her about the accusations made by his cousin. He also sent a letter to his bank, requesting a statement on his savings. His wife never wrote back, but the bank statement arrived and it showed his account to be in the amount of $5.00. Exactly the amount needed to keep the account open. Not only was his wife involved in adultery, but his dreams of a new car were shattered. He threw his wife's photograph into a half-barrel of burning outhouse refuse and then added in his pile of car magazines. Jack then wandered the company area like a lost soul for the next few days. With Matthew's counsel and assistance, Jack wrote another letter home to his wife. He asked her to leave the other man and honor her marriage vows. That letter returned eight-days later with *Addressee Unknown*. Jack's depression continued to linger on.

In late January 1969, word was received at Battalion Headquarters of how the 9th Marines had initiated Operation Dewey Canyon in the eastern part of Quang Tri Province. Their objective was to drive south into an area known to the American military as Enemy Base 611; located in the northern tip of the A Shau Valley and also right smack on the Laotian border. The operation would last through the end of March with 130 Americans killed and 920 wounded during the month long fight. U.S. Intelligence believed over 1700 NVA soldiers were killed during the offensive.

Though driven out of Enemy Base 611 by the Marines, the enemy promptly returned from their camps in Laos when the American forces left. They quickly set up death traps to the eastern edge of Enemy Base 611 for any American or South Vietnamese unit who was foolish enough to enter.

The Tet Offensive of 1969 erupted all over South Viet Nam, which hit 115 villages, cities and military installations with rocket and mortar fire. Following Tet, a second communist offensive, named by the U.S. media as the Post Tet Offensive, was launched. This attack ran from February 5 through February 22, 1969. One hundred twenty-eight Americans lost their lives during those 18 days of intense fighting.

CAMP EAGLE'S SOUTH PERIMETER, FEBRUARY 17TH, 1969 0305 HOURS

D Company was on perimeter guard duty and 2nd squad was groggy, but their half-closed eyes turned to wide open alert when the first rockets sailed overhead and exploded inside the camp. Their latest intelligence briefing reported there was no major enemy force in the area to stage a ground assault and the 1st lieutenant who conducted the briefing had stated, "Any rocket or mortar fire should be considered harassment in nature."

"You feelin' harassed, Matt?" John asked when he peeked over the rim of their new trench.

Matthew answered, "My Dad told me how the people in London went through this stuff for over four years during World War Two." John shook his head in response.

Jose said, "Yeah, I remember how our D.I.s talked 'bout how the 101st and 82nd kicked German butt big time." John and Jose ducked down when another rocket passed by with the explosion coming only a few seconds later. Matthew saw a fiery plume erupt from where he knew a helipad was. Three rows of concertina wire separated the men from a *free fire zone*; an area referred to as *no man's land* in other wars. Soldiers who manned the trenches and bunkers on the perimeter were the Camp's first line of defense. They were supported by Huey and Cobra Gun ships, 105 mm artillery and 81mm mortars. Two such mortar pits were assigned to the south perimeter, to provide flares for illumination and high explosive (HE) rounds in the event of a ground assault. Campbell sat inside one of the larger bunkers with the other three-squad leaders and conferred with Lt. Sinclair. They listened to the radio traffic from inside the camp. With them was SSgt. Joe Franklin, the new platoon sergeant.

"Sounds like they hit one of the storage buildings, but no casualties," Sinclair said loud enough for everyone to hear.

"I need to get back to my men, L-T. You have anything else I need to know?" Campbell asked.

"No, just have 'em keep their heads down. Alpha Company of the 1st Battalion will relieve us at 0800 hours," Sinclair said. He then turned to the radio when a transmission reported another hit on the north side of the camp.

"What about coffee, sir?" Campbell asked. He knew his men could use a little pick-me-up once the attack was over and their adrenalin faded.

"We'll try to get some out before dawn, but no promises, sergeant."

Campbell popped him a salute and said, "Yes, sir." With his shotgun slung over his shoulder, he left the bunker and ran to where his 2nd squad was positioned some 25 yards away. He really hated to sit around and get pounded. He knew all too well how rockets and mortars never cared where they landed, and how the VC weren't known for their accuracy. VC would sit a rocket between a roped together bipod of bamboo, aim it at a large base and hope for the best. However, the NVA used actual metal rocket tubes on tripods with sighting capabilities and were known to hit their targets quite effectively.

Campbell found Isaac lighting a cigarette for a very nervous new guy by the name of PFC Edward Andrews. He and a SPC 4 Amos Riley had arrived two days earlier. When Campbell jumped into their trench, he popped up suddenly beside Andrews and asked, "How do you like the war so far?"

Startled by his sergeant's sudden arrival, he caught his breath and then answered, "Rather be home feeding my chickens, sergeant. Least they don't want to kill me. Peck me some for stealing their eggs, but that's all."

Campbell loved country boys. They were hard workers and great shots. "Washington will take good care of you." Campbell tossed Isaac a nod and a pair of raised eyebrows, as if to say, *Chicken farmer?* He then worked his way to a small bunker where Jose and Jack had their M-60 positioned for inter-locking fire with the machine gun bunkers on each side.

"Stay awake, Jose. I catch you noddin' off again and I'll make Jack the gunner." Campbell said in a stern voice.

"Not me, Sarge, must've been some other Mexican you saw," Jose replied.

Campbell shook his head in frustration. Try as he may, he couldn't stay mad at Jose. Especially when he did his Bandito impression with two belts of M-60 ammo strapped around his chest and that big teethe grin of his. "One Mexican's enough for this squad, Cisco. So stay awake or I'll kick your butt."

Next to the bunker, Matthew and John took a moment to man the shovels and dig their trench a bit deeper before the next rocket flew over. "Saw you got another letter from Kathy, is she okay?" John asked between loads of brown dirt and tossed one load a bit further to hit Jose with some of the dirt.

"She misses me. Newsboys are saying a bunch of stuff about us not trying to win this war. She gets confused by what she sees on TV and hears on the campus. Jokers are telling her how we're all out smoking dope and getting the clap. When I get home I'm gonna have me a little talk with some of her classmates."

"Hey, take me 'long. We'll show 'em all thu fine things we learned over here." John rested on his shovel for a moment to wipe his eyes, "I can't believe we still have ten more months of this."

Matthew leaned his backside up against the side of the trench and looked off into the distance to see a good-sized building burning. "Don't mention time," Matthew said.

John then asked, "You got anything new from your folks?"

Matthew shot him a confused look in response. "Hey, buddy, you're always there when I get the mail. You know who I get letters from as well as I do."

John put his shovel on the rim of the trench and replied, "I know, but sometimes I forget and hey, man, you gots anythin' else ta rap about?"

Matthew laughed and answered, "Right, Bro…Anyway, some jerk wanted to stage a moratorium at the church in support of the anti-war demonstrations. My ol' man blew a fuse."

John hefted another sandbag up to line the trench and gave Matthew a thoughtful glance, "Been noticing you readin' that Bible thu chaplain give you. Is it helpin' you much?"

Matthew collected his thoughts before he answered, "I thought I had walked away from God when I came over here, but seems He never walked away from me. After what happened in that village, I needed Him again an'

He was there for me. Still don't understand a lot, especially 'bout this war, but I know I got to keep my head in the right frame to survive this place."

John went to the bottom of the trench and Matthew couldn't see him clearly, but he could hear his voice, "Maybe you read me some from thu Bible when we get back to thu tent?" Matthew was surprised by John's sudden interest in God, but he laid his hand on John's shoulder and started to tell him how happy he'd be to share with him from the Word of God, when an explosion suddenly interrupted their conversation. The shock wave drove both men to the bottom of their trench and debris began to fall on them. Matthew struggled to dig himself out while John clawed his way up the sides of the trench to get to his feet. They were both spitting dirt out of their mouths and wiping their eyes when they heard the hated call of, "Medic!"

Matthew immediately recognized Jose's voice; "Medic-Medic!" Jose shouted. "Oh God, someone help me." Jose's shout turned to a scream of desperation. An enemy 122 mm rocket is six feet long, and filled with a rolled up sheet of serrated pieces of metal ½ inch square. Upon impact, the canister holding this shrapnel blows apart and the shrapnel-pieces fire out like 400 bullets in all directions. This rocket exploded only 25 feet from Jose's bunker, where it collapsed one wall of sandbags inward to bury Jack and Sgt. Campbell. Jose, who stood to the rear of the bunker, was blown outside through the doorway. Shaken, but still conscious, Jose jumped up and ran back inside, only to find a ton of dirt had buried the two men. Jose dug frantically and reached Campbell first. He began to pull him out by his ankles, when help arrived.

"Jack, get Jack out!" Jose shouted at Isaac, who was first on the scene. But all Isaac could see was one of Jack's huge boots and it was mostly buried under a several hundred pounds of ripped open sandbags and mangled wooden beams. Once Jose got Campbell clear, his breath starting between violent coughs, Jose ran back inside to help Matthew, Isaac and John. There wasn't enough room for anyone else to enter the damaged bunker and now Jose was in the way.

Matthew shoved his friend back, "Go outside and get some air. We're doing all that can be done." But Jose pushed past his friends and the hysterical Mexican reached out to pull Jack free, while the others slung 25 pound sandbags, some of them burst open, to the next man and out through the narrowed opening. Outside, others formed a line to clear the bags and other debris. Others, shaken by the blast and some lightly wounded could only standby and watch.

Lt. Sinclair, who was focused on the rescue, suddenly remembered they still had a job to do. He ordered most of his men back into position and used men from other squads to fill into 2nd squad's position. A long moment passed before they were able to pull Jack free, but he wasn't breathing. Matthew, John and Isaac lifted him outside, where Jose carefully lay him down on the ground. There a company medic began CPR. While they watched in stunned silence, the medic thumped Jack's chest hard, rubbed his arms and shoulders and tried everything he could think of to get Jack back from a dark abyss. But to no avail, Jack was dead. With resignation, the weary medic looked up and shook his head, "Sorry, he's gone."

With tears on his filthy face, Jose dropped to the ground, cradling Jack's head tenderly in his lap. The rest of the dirt covered men of 2nd squad stood over their fallen comrade, while Jose used his hand to gently wipe the dirt away from Jack's face and in a whisper of a voice, "Adios me amigo...viya con dios."

Jose looked up at Matthew and asked, "Why, Matt? Why Jack?"

Matthew didn't know what to say and said, "I don't know, Jose." He was at a loss, unable to answer his friend's question. Second squad stayed with Jack until the field ambulance arrived. They watched the medic fill out the body tag and looped it around a button on Jack's shirt. The tag showed the time and date of death and a brief synopsis of how it happened.

Matthew felt like he should say something and knelt down beside Jack, where he now lay on a stretcher. He placed his right hand on the big man's broad left shoulder, saying "Lord," he stopped, not knowing what to pray. *My friend's dead, yet he lay here so peaceful. Not a mark on his body, no blood or wound to show how he died. Why Jack? I don't know. I just don't know?* "I just don't know!" Matthew shouted to the heavens. He struggled with his attempt to understand God's will.

When he saw the stress in Matthew's face and the look of panic in his eyes, Jose reached over Jack's body and touched Matthew's hand. In a soft whisper, he said, "It's okay, amigo. Jack knows now."

John helped Matthew to his feet and led him back to their trench. Where John returned to the chore of digging out their hole and Matthew remained silent. He stared off in the distance and a moment later, Matthew said quietly, "I never even asked Jack about his beliefs, where he stood with God. He could be standing at the Gates of Hell because I never took the time."

John came within a couple inches of his friend's face, "Knock it off, Matt." He threw a shovel full of dirt over his shoulder and glanced back at Matthew.

"But it's my fault if he..." Matthew didn't get to finish.

John was suddenly inches from his face again, "Look, jus' shut-up, okay? Jack's dead, that's it. Now drop it, before Jose does a rat-a-tap-tap with his sixty on your head."

Campbell remained at the aid station for the rest of the night. He suffered from a major headache and a bloody nose from a mild concussion. When he was informed of Jack's death by Lt. Sinclair and how Jose had saved his life, Campbell's first order of business was to thank Jose. When he returned to 2nd Squad's area, Campbell found him stretched out on his cot. "Thank you, compadre. I owe you big time an' I'm sorry about Jack."

Jose nodded his head once and said, "No sweat, Sarge." He then went back to staring at the ceiling.

Later in the day, Campbell came back into the tent to pack up Jack's stuff for shipment back to the states. His ammo was divvied up among the squad and the rest of his equipment was returned to SSgt. Rounders. Before he left the tent, Campbell walked up to PFC Andrews and assigned him to be Jose's new assistant gunner. Before darkness, 2nd squad returned to their security positions and although the machine gun bunker had been rebuilt, Jose didn't go inside. He wouldn't even talk to Andrews, but the new guy understood and didn't push it. The enemy's rocket barrage began in the early morning hours and seven rockets hit the interior of the base. One Huey was blown up and eight men were injured when a terrified 2nd lieutenant drove a three-quarter ton truck into their quonset hut. The clerk wasn't sure if this would be categorized as friendly fire or not?

After two more nights of perimeter guard duty, D Company received a well needed one-day R & R at Eagle Beach; a white sandy beach used by the 101st for the men's relaxation. Similar to China Beach further south, Eagle Beach resembled the famous beaches of Hawaii or California and allowed a weary soldier a chance to forget all about the war. The illusion was only spoiled when one noticed the concertina wire and machine gun bunkers that protected the area and the steady flow of Army helicopters flying overhead.

Matthew spent the day trying his skill at body surfing with Campbell, while Isaac, who didn't know how to swim, spent the day drinking beer with John, Jose, Andrews and Riley. Later in the afternoon, 2nd squad entered into a game of touch football with the other members of D Company, which resulted in several contusions and a couple of missing front teeth. Several of the men had eaten a fare share of sand and were now on the sidelines washing out their mouths and there were a few near drownings when the man with the ball was tackled in the surf. Touch had turned to tackle after the second play was called and a lot of pent up anxiety was released in explosive gang-piles. Sometimes there wasn't even a ball involved.

That evening, the men of 2nd squad sat around an open fire with two cases of beer and talked of home. Jose, who had consumed several bottles of beer, stared at Matthew for a moment and suddenly burst into laughter.

"What's so funny?" Matthew asked.

"Ah just thought 'bout Jack's loving widow. Ain't she gonna be mad when she finds out he changed his insurance over to his mom." Jose continued to laugh and was soon rolling across the sand. Inspired by the beer, the whole squad joined in. The time of mourning Jack's death had drawn to a close. Six semi-intoxicated young men hoisted their beers in a final salute to former KKK member PFC Jack Waterford.

WASHINGTON D.C. /HOPSITAL EMERGENCY ROOM, FEBRUARY 23RD, 1969 1955 HOURS

Abby Adams, John's older sister, lay face-up on a hospital gurney. Her face was covered with blood stained bandages and her misshapen right arm was in an air splint. Paramedics put the splint on when they found her lying unconscious on the floor of her apartment living room. Her boyfriend; a drunk and belligerent bully, was dragged off by two members of the Washington D.C. Police Department and incarcerated. Witnesses told police how he came home from work and started to beat on her right from the time he entered the apartment. The landlady informed the admitting nurse over the phone how her only relative was some soldier over in Viet Nam. With the E.R. swamped with the victims of a drive-by shooting, Abbey was left in an overcrowded hallway, while they waited for the next vacant treatment room. Five hours later, someone noticed the woman on the gurney was dead and the autopsy would show her heart had simply given out. Doctors, who wanted to protect the hospital, would say her condition and death was due to extended drug usage. Without insurance, her body was shipped to a city-financed funeral home and Abbey was laid to rest in a very inexpensive grave. A week later, the Red Cross sent a notification onto John and the next day, John was advised of his sister's death.

D COMPANY AREA, MARCH 2ND, 1969 1115 HOURS

"John, maybe you should go home? Captain Sampson said. He could arrange an emergency leave for his young troop. Campbell had also recommended the leave, while he escorted John from company headquarters.

But John remained quiet until they reached the squad's tent, "Ah don't think so, sarge. Nothin' back there now. Sis was all I had, but thanks for coming with me." John didn't walk inside. He needed to be by himself and drifted off.

When Campbell walked inside without John, Matthew asked, "Where's John?"

Campbell shook his head and pointed his right thumb over his shoulder. "His sister's dead, but he doesn't want to go home on emergency leave."

Matthew understood. "We're his family now, Sarge...There's nothing back at home for him now." Matthew walked outside to search for his friend.

D COMPANY AREA, APRIL 3RD, 1969 0814 HOURS

Orders were given from Division down through 3rd Battalion to Company level; a major operation was coming up. Captain Sampson stood before his platoon commanders and issued commands, "Have your squad leader's check their men's equipment. Whatever they need get it issued ASAP and make sure they've got their wills made out."

On the morning of April 13, 1969, Campbell's 2nd squad and other elements of the 3rd Battalion were flown out to the northeastern corner of the A Shau Valley. The objective: knock the NVA off a little known hill known as Dong Agai Mountain. The task was a lot tougher than anyone suspected it would be. For thirteen days the Battalion played a game of King of the Mountain with the NVA, with each force fighting to hold ownership over this worthless mound of dirt. Before the last assault, fighter-bombers were brought in to rain thunder and lightening down upon the top of the mountain and kill as many of the NVA as possible. By the end of the day, the 3rd Battalion had won the contest at such a costly price: five men dead, 54 wounded and one of them a member of 2nd squad.

DONG AGAI MOUNTAIN, APRIL 25TH, 1969 1311 HOURS

Bone weary, Matthew sat on a cool spot of a blackened log and waited for his squad's turn to be airlifted out. He couldn't remember when his body had suffered such abuse, every muscle and every joint cried out in pain and even his skin was in rebellion. He also noticed he carried a foul stench of decay about him; which came from having worn the same uniform for the last 13 days. Even the mosquitoes left him alone because his body was covered in dried mud and nearly two weeks of stale sweat. The odor of burned flesh, combined with the scent of scorched earth was everywhere. Bombs and artillery left the summit and sides of the hill resembling a lunar landscape made of ash.

During the sixth day of battle, Matthew destroyed one enemy bunker with a LAW and afterward, stood there, his eyes frozen on the bodies they found inside. Mangled remains, blackened from their fiery death. It was a sickening sight, but Matthew didn't get sick this time. He only pushed it out of his mind and continued to climb on.

At the end of the battle for Don Agai Mountain, Matthew was accredited with eleven confirmed kills. This statistic brought words of praise from Lt. Sinclair, but only a deepening depression for young Matthew.

Still, the squad fought well together and Campbell felt a sense of pride for the job they'd done. Only one snafu, Andrews caught a chunk of mortar fragment in his right shoulder--a minor wound.

"Matt, next time I complain 'bout pulling security, remind me of tis place," Jose said. He rested his head upon Matthew's leg and closed his eyes for a moment of peace. The squad was a tired looking sight. They all lay around on top of each other, too tired to budge another inch and too emotionally drained to care anymore.

"Don't wanna climb another mountain," Matthew added as he closed his eyes and licked his dry chapped lips. They were out of water and had been for the last 18 hours and all he could taste was smoke.

"All right, get up," Campbell ordered. "We've gotta walk a few more yards, so grab your gear an' lets move out." Campbell had a dry raspy voice. "Jose, got any 60 ammo left?"

Jose could only shake his head, but seeing it was Campbell he replied, "Nope. Ah was gettin' ready to use it like a baseball bat if we had to go on." Using the butt plate of his weapon for support, Jose boosted himself up and pulled Matthew up behind him.

"Isaac, when we get back to base camp make sure they all get a full supply of ammo and refill their canteens. I'll check on Andrews and join you all for chow." Campbell then led off with his wobbly-legged squad slowly following behind.

The 3rd Battalion would be presented with a unit award for valor for their actions on Dong Agai Mountain, but all the men of 3rd Battalion wanted was 24 hours of sleep, something to drink and some decent hot chow.

When they lifted off, Matthew gazed down upon all the bodies of the dead NVA that lay scattered about the hillside; *I never want to go through anything like this again, never never again,* Matthew thought, closing his eyes to the grizzly scene below.

But the men of 2nd squad still had another mountain to climb; another tough objective to take deep inside the A Shau Valley, where a mountain known as Dong Ap Bia awaited them.

Officially designated as Hill 937, Dong Ap Bia was also known as The Mountain of the Crouching Beast by local Montegnard tribesmen, and for the members of 2nd squad the beast was about to show its ugly fangs

6 – NEW FRIENDS AND ENEMY'S

29TH NORTH VIETNAMESE HOSPITAL, INSIDE AP BIA MOUNTAIN, A SHAU VALLEY, SOUTH VIET NAM, MAY 8TH, 1969 1640 HOURS

Private Medic Lin He Que, a 19-year old, was assigned to the 29th North Vietnamese Army Regimental Hospital. A North Vietnamese youth, he once enjoyed a carefree bicycle ride through the narrow streets of downtown Hanoi and now lived in a world of tunnels, dim lights and stale air. He routinely struggled with bouts of claustrophobia, while wandering and occasionally stumbling through the dark caverns inside the mountain. Foul smelling oil lamps and bright burning torches provided the only light to see by and the air circulating down through the mountain had already turned bitter before it reached the lower levels where the hospital lay. Born into communism, Que was proud to be assigned to a unit recognized by Ho Chi Minh himself for its various acts of gallantry. For years he had learned of the capitalist Americans, and their barbaric ways. He looked forward to his regiment's upcoming action against these honorless bandits from the United States.

For the last few days the medical personnel had heard the muffled explosions that carried down through the mountain. Que's supervisor, an NVA Medical Captain of Surgery, informed his staff the explosions announced the American's arrival.

"These foolish Americans, their bombs inform us of their coming and our Intelligence officers know how many soldiers they bring to die a cowardly death before the rifles of our brave comrades. We shall prepare for wounded, but our men will fight and win a strategic victory over this barbaric enemy." The captain walked off, while Que stood there wide eyed with excitement.

For three years, VC laborers and NVA engineers worked to hollow out this mountain, molding it into one massive stronghold. The hospital, large enough to treat 50 patients, was connected by tunnel to Regimental Headquarters and the main kitchen. Unlike American hospitals, an NVA bed consisted of a rice mat, a wood washbowl and a pile of folded cloth to be used as bandages. At full strength, the hospital staff consisted of one surgeon, 12 female nurses and seven male field medics. Tweve hundred men of the 29th NVA are housed at either the encampment located outside the foot of the mountain or inside the natural fortress itself. The NVA fortified the mountain with two encircling rows of hidden bunkers, connected by rifle trenches. Snipers were positioned in dozens of spider holes to surprise the enemy; and as a last defense, the mountain's summit is carved with one series after another of reinforced rifle trenches and additional bunkers.

Que's tour of the mountain's defenses left him with a feeling of security. *No one can defeat us. Not here and certainly, not the Americans.* Going about his duties, Que unintentionally overheard two field officers have a conversation in the tunnel as they stopped for a smoke, "Are we sure…can we be sure which area the Americans will come? They have so many bombs and they destroy our beautiful jungle forests with little or no care."

The second officer replied, "Truly, they bomb many locations in an attempt to confuse us, so we will be vigilant and wait. Our spies will inform us when the American devils leave their camp and we will be ready, comrade. They will come like the overconfident fly into our spider's web. We are the patient ones and the A Shau has always belonged to us."

On April 25th, a C-130 Hercules began dropping 15,000 pound bombs, known as Daisy Cutters, on the valley floor below Hill 937 and throughout the A Shau. These bombs delivered a devastating explosion, capable of leveling the jungle growth to knee high kindling in an area big enough to easily land five UH-1 Hueys. The 101st Division Commander, hoping to confuse the enemy, ordered 30 of these landing zones to be made before the operation commenced. So, from April 25th through May 9th, these massive bombs rained down upon the A Shau and the ever watchful eyes of the NVA.

When the two officers walked off, their conversation faded in the distance. Que was encouraged by what he'd heard. He resumed his chore to fill water containers. Fresh water would become hard to come by once the battle began. Que carried two full water buckets over to the far side of the cavern, pouring them into one of a dozen large clay pots. In doing so, he passed by a darkened room, separated from the main room by a brown threadbare blanket. This was the cold dark den reserved for the dead. Here the bodies would be stacked up like cordwood and await cremation for when the battle ended and the bodies could be taken outside.

D COMPANY AREA, CAMP EAGLE, MAY 8TH, 1969, 1220 HOURS

Long awaited promotions had come down from Division, which brought E-4 status to Spec 4's Matthew, John and Jose. But before they can celebrate, 3rd Battalion was placed on alert status. The Three Caballeros had barely enough time to get their new rank sewn on their uniforms before they boarded a Huey for a windy flight to Camp Evans. There, the men of D

Company were packed into hastily put up ten-man canvas tents and their gear stowed before briefings began for the upcoming *Operation Apache Snow*.

When SSgt. Franklin heard the objective was in the A Shau Valley, an icy jolt traveled down his spine. In 1965, a young PFC Franklin fought and nearly died in the A Shau, while helping rescue of a badly chewed up Green Beret A-Team. For over four years he lived with nightmares from that operation, where he lost his squad leader and two best friends in a heated withdrawal to escape a large enemy force.

Lt. Sinclair knew of Franklin's prior experience in the A Shau and called upon him, "Sergeant Franklin, could you enlighten us on what we might expect in the A Shau Valley?"

With a deep sigh, Franklin stepped up and said, "Yes, Sir." He made his way forward to brief 1st platoon and while he made his way forward, Lt. Sinclair addressed the men, "Sergeant Franklin was involved in a smaller operation in the A Shau in 1965. I thought maybe something he remembered might help one of you stay alive. Go ahead, Sergeant Franklin." Lt. Sinclair moved off to one side and Franklin took center stage.

"Yes, Sir," Franklin said nervously. He could feel his hands tremble and took a few deep breaths to get control before someone else noticed. The men formed a half-circle, everyone sat on the ground, their eyes on him. They watched when he cleared his throat several times and then begin, "This deep into the A Shau Valley is the closest you'll ever come to Hell on earth." That certainly got their attention. "The NVA own it, all of it, and they know every creek, crevice and gully in it. You'll deal with unbearable heat, long hours of pitch black darkness and they've got some real nasty bugs in there that make a tarantula look like a common house spider. You've got towering trees that shoot up for over 100 feet and form an impenetrable canopy that keeps the heat in and the light out. Temperatures rise above 100 degrees by noon and the humidity can nearly drown you. Keep your eyes open for traps, trip wires, spider holes and hidden bunkers. Remember the lesson you learned on Dong Ngai, we're not gonna run up some mountain and post a flag like some dumb Marine. The NVA have been here for years. They've got bunkers in there older than most of you. So take it slow; listen to the lieutenant, Captain Sampson an' your squad leaders."

Franklin took a breath. "Take plenty of water an' all the ammo you can possibly carry. Getting re-supplied may take a bit of an effort and time you no long have, and if the Division people think we can take this place out in a couple of days...they're very sadly mistaken. They thought Dong Agai was gonna be an easy hump too," Franklin said. He paused for a moment, spotting Jose, he knew what he wanted to say, "I recommend you sixty gunners carry an extra 200 rounds with you. You'll use it up quick enough. And LAWS: best thing for hitting those bunkers. Don't forget your salt tablets and don't try no John Wayne tactics up there. Ole Duke never went up against anything like this." Franklin nodded to Sinclair and walked back to where he sat back down and gulped down the bottom half of his lukewarm Coke.

"Okay, no one said this was going to be easy. Squad leaders, I concur with Sergeant Franklin's suggestions. All the ammo you can carry and lots of water. We'll be flown out to Firebase Blaze tomorrow afternoon, so everyone is to be ready at 1030 hours." Sinclair was about to dismiss the men when he remembered another item, "Get a letter written home and get it to Sergeant Rounders. That's it for now, you're dismissed." Lt. Sinclair gazed out over his platoon as the men broke up, *I'm getting' a bad feeling about this one.*

WITH 2ND SQUAD

"What yuh think, Matt?" John asked. The squad was busy inspecting their equipment, loading magazines and in Matthew's case; darning his socks.

"I think Mrs. Kendal's little boy better get a couple letters written. You can write my folks if you want." Matthew slipped the needle through the toe of his sock and released a loud, "Ouch!", when he drove the needle into his thumb.

"So, you think this is gonna be a bad one?" Jose asked. He thumbed .45 rounds into his spare magazines, slipping them into the outside pockets on his rucksack.

"Sgt. Franklin sure thinks so and he's been there before," Matthew said. He pulled the thread through again and tied it off to close the hole in on the toe of his sock. Now he only had four more socks to do. "This place is sure rough on socks."

"Maybe, yuh know, we could tell 'em we all have stomach aches or somethin'. Or you could shoot my little toe off an' ah'll shoot yours." Jose was beginning to feel uneasy about this operation. It reminded him of the time he participated in a drive-by shooting when he was only 12 years old and he spent the night before throwing up in a deserted alley. When the drive-by went down the intended victims were better armed and prepared for the attack. Jose and his best friend barely escaped with their lives when the driver, his 16-year old cousin and the other guy in the front seat; a 17-year old, were both killed in a hail of automatic weapons fire.

"You go right ahead and blow your own toe off, they'll send you to the hospital first and then to lock-up for five-years for damaging government property and probably toss in a little charge of cowardice to make your court-martial more interesting. Besides, Kathy Lee prefers me with all my toes." Matthew gave his friend a *We'll be okay* look and returned to his socks. After a full afternoon of preparation, Matthew and Jose were tasked with carrying the platoon's outgoing mail to Company Headquarters.

SSgt. Rounders wasn't happy to receive another bulky load of mail. His desk was already covered with several bundles of letters from the other platoons. "Everyone wrote home, some of them two or three letters," SSgt. Rounders complained. He had to box them up and deliver them to Battalion Headquarters and it was a task he couldn't pawn off on a lower ranking enlisted man. Mail was a priority, not to be trusted to just anyone.

On the way back to their tent, Jose asked Matthew if he'd remember to mention him in his prayers, "I ain't feelin' too good 'bout this one, Amigo."

Matthew patted Jose on the back, "You said the same thing before we climbed up Dong Agai and you ended up fine. So do me a favor, forget those stupid feelings. As long as we're together, nothing is gonna happen."

Jose was all teeth, "Okay, okay, but you say a prayer for me anyway."

Matthew had to grin, "You've been a Catholic all your life, why don't you pray anymore?"

Jose crossed himself in the Catholic fashion with his right hand, "I still believe…a little, but I never saw God in my neighborhood or next to my mom's bed when she died. Mah gang took care of me, covered me when I needed it. I think maybe God's jus' too big. He don't care 'bout someone like me." Jose remembered his mother's last moments of life and stopped walking. He reached out, grabbing Matthew by the arm to stop him, "You 'member how angry you was over your brother's death? I feel like dat 'bout my mom. She's thu only one who cared 'bout whether I live or die. Now, 'cept you, John an' maybe the squad…I'm alone."

Matthew nodded his head, smiled, saying, "Okay Amigo, I understand."

Jose wasn't finished though. He asked, "You still wanna be a preacher, Matt?"

Matthew chewed on the inside of his cheek briefly, answering, "I think so, but I still have a lot of unanswered questions; especially after what I've seen here. But deep down I feel that nudge. Dad called it my call into the ministry."

Jose pointed to the heavens and added, "You could become Catholic, you'd make a good priest."

Matthew grinned and replied, "No thanks. The thought of all that celibacy and wearing black all the time is not my style, Amigo."

They walked a few more steps and then Jose asked Matthew, "Maybe I'll come to your church someday. You'd let Catholics in, right?"

Matthew gave him the quizzical eyes and answered, "What a question. The House of God is open to everyone."

Jose shook his head, "Not so sure, Matt. Last time I was in church the priest chased us out."

Matthew stopped and asked, "Why?" He had trouble believing that one, until he heard the reason.

"We was tryin' to steal the offerin' box," Jose said. He then chuckled as he recalled that day so long ago, "Fat old priest nearly had a heart attack, but he chased us down the street. He recognized me an' told my mom, she nearly beat me to death and made me pray for forgiveness. Only time she ever used a belt on me and she was cryin' all the time...Me too and I was the one with the welts."

Matthew laughed, "You're a class act, Jose."

Later, the two of them entered the squad's tent and found Isaac gliding around the room with the latest dance step. With a burning cigarette hanging from his lips, Isaac stepped out to a Jimi Hendrix song, which blared out of Amos Riley's boom box. Nearby, poor PFC Andrews was in utter misery. A Country music fan, Hendrix reminded Andrews of a cross between a dentist drill and a cat with its tail caught in the door. Matthew stretched out on his cot, looking up to notice a soldier who stood in front of the tent, *he looks lost*. The man carried an old rucksack over his left shoulder, a new, unscratched M-16 in his right hand and a bandoleer of ammo hanging from around his neck.

"Isaac, looks like we got company," Matthew said, pointing to the new guy.

"Turn the sounds down, man," Isaac told Riley, who replied with, "Aw, man." Andrews was extremely grateful for the reprieve, hoping it might last. He wished he had gone ahead and bought his own boom box. He'd show these guys what real music was, *I'd show 'em some of my Charlie Pride, maybe some Johnny Cash.*

"You lookin' for a home, boy?" Isaac asked the new man in a loud voice. "Is this 2nd squad?" He asked with a note of hesitation.

"Looks like you're home." Isaac pointed to an empty cot," Stow your gear over there, load all your magazines, fill your canteens an' clean that rifle. I'll check on your work when you get finished. We're movin' out in the mornin', so ain't you the lucky one," Isaac said. Then with a smirk on his face, Isaac pointed at Riley, "Give me some tunes, man, ah need to feel the flow an' my feet a movin'." With the volume near max, Andrews was forced to clamp his hands over his ears in protest and escape outside. The new guy, who tried to ignore the loud music, dropped his gear onto the empty cot and reached out his hand toward Matthew. "I'm Bob Baxley from Seattle, Washington," he yelled in hopes of being heard over the music.

Matthew shook his hand, "I'm Matthew Kendal and that bandito looking fellow is Jose Martinez. Over there is the Jimi Hendrix fan club... that's Riley on the box, Isaac Washington's the one with the moves and John Adams is the one cleaning his rifle. The guy who fled the scene is Edward Andrews and he's our resident chicken farmer...Welcome to the 2nd squad." Baxley began to relax. Matthew was the first one to offer him any sign of friendship since his arrival in Vietnam and until his arrival here with the squad, he was beginning to feel like he was carrying some form of plague.

Isaac tossed Riley a quick smirk and shook his head. If Matthew wanted to cater to the new guy it was okay with him. Right now all he wanted to do was fade out and imagine he was back on the gym floor, dancing with Sally Ann Reed. *Oh she could dance that girl.* The camp rocked that afternoon with heavy jazz, swinging country and down and gritty rock & roll. From the Beatles, the Beach Boys, Janis Joplin to the Supremes, the air was filled with the music of a new generation. Added in, but at a lower volume were the new folk tunes of Bob Dylan, John Denver and even a couple die-hard Peter, Paul & Mary fans. It was driving some of the older officers' crazy, but the word had come down from Battalion, "Give the men some time to unwind, in a few hours they'll be jumping off and no one would be listening to any music for several days to come."

CAMP, MAY 9TH 0900 HOURS

Second squad shouldered their packs, following the rest of 1st platoon over to the nearest helipad. For the next hour they stood, waiting, while one CH-46 Chinook Helicopter after another, airlifted men to Firebase Blaze. Finally, it was their turn. The squad entered the belly of the huge double rotor helicopter for a quick 20-minute ride. Matthew looked out a small window on the side of the helicopter. He was amazed to see hundreds of men milling around a large helipad lined with dozens of Hueys. "Looks like we're holding some kind of convention down there," Matthew said. But no one could hear him over the roar of the Chinook's heavy rotor sounds. Located on a flat hilltop, Firebase Blaze was a massive helipad surrounded by 105 mm and 155 mm artillery positions.

Campbell addressed the squad, "Kendall, you and Adams team up... Riley goes with Baxley...Martinez and Andrews, and Washington will be with me. Let's get moving before all the good real estate is grabbed up.

Afternoon chow consisted of C-rations, lukewarm coffee and for the smokers, all the cigarettes they can light up. Once they hit the field tomorrow, the smoking lamp was out. It was a deadly habit to begin with and a burning cigarette or match made a sure target for an enemy sniper.

For the 14th time, the men once more go over their equipment and checked their socks, foot powder and supply of salt tablets. Campbell then handed out additional supplies; each man received six hand grenades and additional belts of M-60 ammo was spread around, along with two extra LAWS. Campbell made sure each man had 20 loaded M-16 magazines in their possession, with the exception of Jose--who carried four extra magazines of .45-caliber pistol ammo. "Every man carries two canteens on his belt and two in his pack, no exceptions 'cause I'm not sharing my water with anyone."

Ready to pass out from the heat, PFC Baxley can barely stand and he can't believe they expect him to carry this much weight into battle. *I'll die!*

FIREBASE BLAZE, MAY 9TH, 1969 2215 HOURS

An eerie stillness settled over the camp and nearly everyman's thoughts are tuned to the upcoming battle. Thick smoke from various cook fires hung over the area, which brought with it the pungent odor of G.I. coffee, cast aside C-ration entrees, good old American sweat and burning tobacco. There were also the various smells associated with machinery; assorted fuel oils and hot engines. For some of these men, who sat alone on a sandbag or lay stretched out in their tent, they began to hear a whisperer of a voice deep inside their heads, "This one's a one-way trip, buddy. You're not coming back from this one." Others, not wanting to be alone, share a story with a friend or gather together in small groups for a bull session or maybe some corporate prayer. For the veterans, the ones who had fought in the A Shau before, they could be heard referring to it as the Valley of Death and this had the desired effect on the younger soldiers. "Not to worry, lad. You'll make it back and you'll have a story to tell your grandkids...and then again, you might get your butt shot off."

For the last couple of weeks, Matthew would spend a moment each night with John and read out loud from his Bible. John would listen as the various Bible scriptures were quoted. At first, he'd question Matthew on nearly every verse. Occasionally, even arguing a point with Matthew, who would more than often respond with, "This is what my Dad told me when I asked." Tonight they lay in their tent, using a flashlight to read by. Matthew noticed there was something different about John. He was hungry to hear the Word of God. Matthew read from the Book of Hebrew. He could sense the longing in his friend's heart; a thirst burning deep inside. "For the Word of God is living and active. Sharper than any double-edged sword, it penetrates even to dividing soul and spirit, joint a marrow; it judges the thought and attitudes of the heart. Nothing in all creation is hidden from God's sight. Everything is uncovered..."

Matthew stopped when John touched his arm and asked, "Matt, can we talk?"

Matthew looked to his friend and replied, "Sure."

John then asked in a whisper of a voice, "Why does this Jesus dude mean so much to yuh?"

"Well," Matthew closed his Bible and turned off his flashlight. "I'd better start with how I came to know him." Though darkness covered the land and feelings of uncertainty and fear fill the minds of men, a strange sense of tranquility surrounded the tent shared by two friends. For during this long, sleepless night, John Adams made the decision to offer his life to the Lord Jesus Christ and the heavens above rejoiced with the voices of a thousand angels.

7 – INTO THE VALLEY OF DEATH RODE THE 600

FIREBASE BLAZE, SOUTH VIET NAM, MAY 10TH, 1969 0545 HOURS
DAY 1

Only the scattered remains of a morning fog hovered over the hilltop and it was a rare moment when even the insect world seemed to be asleep. The chill in the air signaled the arrival of a new dawn and the commencement of Operation Apache Snow. Since 0400 hours, Army cooks prepared a hot breakfast for the men of 3rd Battalion and it would possibly be the last hot meal these men would see until this operation was completed. Cooks, supply sergeants, helicopter crews and field commanders had all been awake since 0300 hours or even earlier, as preparations were made for this morning's massive airlift into the A Shau Valley.

Silence was shattered by the thunderous voice of the Regimental Sergeant Major, "Get 'em up!" He shouted. "Wake your men up and get them fed. Let's get this bunch ready to move out!"

Campbell wiped sleep from his eyes and stumbled from tent to tent as he awakened his squad, "Rise an' shine, you lunkheads! Get up, Farmer Boy...the war's waiting for you." When he reached Jose's tent, Campbell grabbed Jose's foot and began to shake it, "C'mon Jose, no breakfast in bed today."

Jose moaned and pleaded, "Aw Sarge, jus' five more minutes," His eyes were still closed and he was trying to keep the dream from ending, *so beautiful, so white...who are you?* "Hey, get your foot out of my face!" Jose growled at Andrews. "Man, you jus' made my special lady vanish."

Andrews put his hands up in defense and said, "Wasn't me, Jose. It was the Sarge."

Campbell gave Jose's foot another hard tug, "You got two seconds, Amigo!" He then dropped it and added, "Either I see those bloodshot eyes of yours outside or I'm coming in after you an' it won't be pretty." By the tone of his voice, Jose knew he was serious.

"I'm comin', I'm comin'," Jose snarled back and tried to get his *pig* out from underneath his left shoulder.

"Hey, Jose," Campbell said.

"What, Sarge?" Jose had one eye propped open and waited to hear what Campbell had to say before he opened the other one.

"Sorry I ruined your dream, but the Army calls." Since Jose had saved his life, Campbell had taken a friendlier touch with his M-60 gunner.

"No sweat, Sarge…she was mucho too pretty for this Chicano," Jose replied and his other eye popped open, giving Andrews a dirty look. Campbell grinned and then he saw Isaac, who stood outside his tent, stretching his arms out wide, when a big yawn escaped his mouth.

Campbell walked up to him, "Get 'em fed, we don't have much time." Isaac nodded his head, dropped his arms and replied, "Sure, Sarge," He then released another wide mouth yawn.

Campbell walked away shaking his head. "You'd think you guys never got any sleep."

Breakfast was a half-hearted attempt at best for the men of 2nd squad. Pre-operation anxiety was a sure fire way to curb one's appetite. "If I eat, I'll puke," Jose said and Campbell completely understood. His own nervous stomach complained with each bite he forced down, knowing he needed the energy and just the scent of greasy fried Spam patties on his plate was enough to make him feel queasy.

By 0630 hours the fog had lifted and the morning sun began to crest the eastern horizon. They moved by platoons to the helipad and the men of 2nd squad had nothing to do but stand around and wait for their turn. Rumors quickly traveled through the ranks; suspected enemy strength was in the thousands, hot LZs were waiting for them and then bets on who might get zapped first. New guys nervously talked amongst themselves and chain-smoked cigarettes, while veterans relished these last moments of peace.

Tired, some of the men take a knee or plopped down on top of their rucksacks. Squad leaders surround their platoon leaders for last minute instructions and company commanders remain inside the temporary headquarters' tent to ensure the paper pushers have all the necessary equipment lined up to support their men. Wise enough to escape this chaotic confusion, the Battalion Commander; radio call sign "Blackjack-One", was already airborne. He flew 800 feet above Firebase Blaze and would remain in the air during the initial stages of Operation Apache Snow.

Matthew hoped to relieve his own anxiety with a few words from his Pocket Bible. He pulled it out and when he found the appropriate scripture, he began to read out loud, "Though I walk through the Valley of Death, I shall fear no one for Thou art with me…" John, who was with Isaac, heard the Word of God spoken and walked over to listen. Jose and Andrews soon joined them and before long, more than ten men listened to Matthew read from the Bible. His calm voice and God's Word brought a feeling of peacefulness to the men. Rationally, soldiers fear the uncertainty of what lay ahead and like all soldiers who fought in battles before them, they realize there is a chance some of them won't be coming back. A painful thought, but it was a reality and now was a good time to get things right with the Big Man upstairs.

Jose ran an oily cloth over his M-60 *pig*, something to do to keep his hands busy and his mind off that voice inside his head. He knew Matthew was right, he'd heard the voice before, *an' I'm still alive.*

Sitting beside Jose, John began to smack his chewing gum as his thoughts focused on several possibilities, *could be a hot LZ, then we fight it out. But a cold LZ means we haf'ta dig 'em out like ants an' they'll be waitin' for us, either way it is bad news.*

Isaac pulled Baxley off to the side and briefed him on what to expect, "You hit the ground fast, make a quick visual 'fore you move again, an' watch Campbell. Keep your finger off that trigger, unless you mean to shoot. You be pumpin' a lot of Gs, trigger finger will feel like a chicken drumstick. Stay on semi, no rock& roll. You get the order to move…you move an' don't stop 'til you get told to. Got it?"

Baxley looked back at Isaac and replied, "Yeah, I think so." His face covered in sweat, he refrained from touching his canteens and this made Isaac happy. Nearby, Riley and a Black soldier from 1st squad were working their way through a lengthy version of the "dap", while other Blacks watched. Isaac, finished with Baxley, moved in and joined in the ritual handshake. Can you teach me that?" Andrews asked John.

"You kiddin' me? White boys ain't got no rhythm to be taught that." Andrews was confused by John's answer and he looked over at Matthew with a *what!?Is he kidding me?* expression on his face.

"He's right, we white boys just ain't got no rhythm. That's why they put Black guys out on point. VC just love to watch 'em dance down the trail," Matthew said with a look of innocence on his face.

"Say what!?" John burst out with, but he was interrupted when Lt. Sinclair stepped up to shout, "First Platoon, line up for inspection!"

At precisely 0650 hours, sixty howitzers from five hill-top batteries opened up on the A Shau Valley. For the next forty minutes they relentlessly pounded the five LZs selected today for the men of 3rd Battalion. "Now that's what I call fire power," Andrews said. His ears ringed from the near deafening booms of the nearby cannons.

"Every round landing on some gook might keep you alive a bit longer." Campbell advised his men.

While he flew overhead, Blackjack-One studied his Timex wristwatch and counted the last few seconds down until it was exactly 0700 hours. By radio, he issued the order for the men to load up and 600 combat soldiers slowly converged on their assigned Hueys. Once loaded, the pilots were signaled to start their engines. Much like a desert sandstorm, brown dirt was blown up from the turning rotor blades as 66 helicopters prepared to fly. From other nearby Hueys, harsh wind drove dust pellets at the men crammed aboard these troop carriers.

Waiting to lift off, door gunners received word to feed ammo belts into their M-60 machine guns mounted on their Huey's skids. Crew chiefs were busy getting the men seated and strapped in for the short ride ahead of them. For the men assigned to Firebase Blaze, it was an amazing sight to witness when this immense flight of helicopters began to lift off. First two, then three Hueys and before long, the entire flight was airborne. What first resembled a massive state of chaos transformed into five organized flight formations of thirteen Hueys; each bird assigned to one of five LZs. Out of the thirty landing zones blown by using Daisy Cutters, five would actually be used for launching the battalion's cleverly arranged attack.

Matthew watched the firebase grow smaller and smaller in the distance and he began to wish he'd become a door gunner or a crew chief. The feeling of flight was exhilarating, like the rush he got from playing sports. From up here the jungle appeared so harmless. *Can't see the deadly, foul smellin', leech infested compost pile for what it really is.*

From up here the jungle's thick growth is hidden below a massive forest that covers an endless series of rolling hills. No cities, no skyscrapers or rush hour traffic entangled upon some super highway…Nope, only a plush green land which hasn't changed much in the last 5,000 years or since Noah's boat trip.

With his head bowed, Matthew relished in the coolness of the air and took a moment to whisper a prayer, "Lord, I don't wanna end up in a body bag. Mom an' Dad have suffered enough with Luke's death. I know, why didn't I think of that before volunteering. So stupid! But Lord, keep me an' my buddies safe and help me to be brave. I'm a bit frightened right now… Amen." Matthew looked over at John, his friend's eyes were clenched shut and he wondered what John might be thinking? Jose was all tensed up, his scarred up hands locked around his M-60, as if he was clenching his childhood security blanket and Andrews, he seemed to be enjoying the flight, taking in the scenery with a look of awe to his face. Not Baxley though, Matthew recognized that unhealthy shade of green on his face and knew the new guy was airsick.

Matthew tapped Campbell on the shoulder and pointed to Baxley. All Campbell could do was nod his head in sympathy. Riley and Isaac were sitting on the other side of the Huey, both of them swaying back and forth with the wind, they handled their pre-battle jitters by pretending this was just another joy ride.

The crew chief, who wore a flight helmet decorated with the bright yellow patch of the 1st Air Cavalry, received the word from the pilot through the Huey's intercom and he signaled Campbell their 35-minute flight was about to end. "We're going in!" Campbell shouted out to his men." He struggled to be heard over the sound of the rotor blades and made several hand gestures so all his men got the word. Below them lay a sea of green, a giant canopy of towering trees where the landscape is unbroken but for the manmade clearings to be used as landing zones for the approaching helicopters. Nearing the ground, the men can make out the deep craters brought about by this morning's artillery barrage.

"Lock an' load!" Campbell ordered and each man chambered a round. They then thumbed the selector from safe over to semi-auto. Second squad's Huey was the fourth one down and Matthew was the first man to leap clear. He took two deep breaths and ran three steps forward before he took a dive face down to the ground. He aimed his rifle toward the tree line and waited for orders. Only after the helicopter was lifted off did he realize the LZ was cold and not a single shot had been fired.

"So, where's Charlie?" Baxley asked to no one in particular.

"Close enough to hear you, stupid," Isaac warned him.

Campbell ordered the squad into the tree line, "Move out, but stay low." Holding their rifles at the ready, 2nd squad rose to their feet and cautiously moved toward the nearest section of forest growth left undamaged by the bombardment. The LZ had to keep clear to allow for additional troops to land.

Second Squad took up an initial defense position that bordered the LZ and the men glance back and forth between areas to watch the Hueys come in with more men and also keep an eye on the dark forest ahead. Surged adrenaline pumped through them and worked on overtime and as an added duty, this morning the various squad leaders had to keep a close eye on the new guys to prevent an accidental shooting. A nervous trigger finger on a new guy was as dangerous as an enemy sniper.

Andrews had his feet on the ground less than a minute before he dropped on all fours and vomited up his breakfast of scrambled eggs and Spam patties. "Least you didn't do it in the Huey," Campbell told him as he knelt beside Andrews to get him moving again. Jose had crawled on ahead to set up his M-60 to cover the landings, but he needed his assistant and the ammo Andrews carried.

The landing zone provided excellent cover for the men; deadfalls and shattered tree stumps blown apart by artillery and a single Daisy Cutter bomb. Some of the enormous trees were cut in half with shrapnel. Second Squad jumped over logs, crawled around dirt mounds and dashed between points of cover like crazy men. The squad finally stopped to set up a temporary perimeter 20 feet inside the first row of live trees. Campbell found a spot behind a large deadfall and waited for Lt. Sinclair to bring up the rest of the platoon.

"Keep your eyes open an' watch for snipers," Campbell ordered. Then for the next hour the men stared into the forest and watched for any sign of the enemy.

By 0801 hours, the last Huey had dropped its load of men and began to ascend. At that same moment, Andrews was the first one to spot a grass hut less than 40 yards from their position. "Get your head down, idiot!" Campbell ordered. But then he popped up himself for a better look. After making sure first that his men were in good position, Campbell left Isaac in charge and went off in a low crouch to locate Lt. Sinclair. He found him in a few moments, "L-T, we've got a large hut and maybe two or three more of 'em over to our right. Request permission to recon the area?" Campbell asked. "After seeing where Campbell had pointed, Sinclair gave him the okay.

"Move your squad straight in. First squad will move on your left with 3rd squad on your right. I'll keep 4th squad in reserve."

Campbell nodded his head once and said a quick, "Yes, sir." He moved back to his men to brief them on the plan, "Take it slow. Watch for traps, spider holes and tunnels. Call out if you see anything and make sure it's Charlie you're shooting at. All right, any questions?" There was none. "Then let's do it."

Observing the huts, 2nd Squad watched where they stepped and kept an eye on the trees above for snipers, making for a slow and cautious approach. But before long, 2nd Squad found themselves smack in the middle of a recently abandoned NVA encampment. "I count fourteen huts!" Matthew yelled over to Campbell. Each hut came with its own vegetable garden and several still warm cook fires.

When there was no sign of resistance reported, Lt. Sinclair moved up with 4th squad in tow, "What have you got, Campbell?"

Campbell was not happy, "Sir, looks like we've done landed right on top of a major NVA base camp. Our artillery must've ruined their breakfast and they vamoosed. From the size of these huts, I'd estimate regimental strength and the fires are still warm. They're not that far away, L-T."

Sinclair didn't say anything for a moment while he studied the surrounding area. He turned to Campbell, ordering him to place his squad on the far side of the huts, "Set up security while the rest of the platoon inspects the huts further. Tell your boys not to follow any trails. We're on hold for right now." Then he surprised Campbell by breaking out in a big smile, "Boy, our Intel people are going to go crazy with this. We've caught them with their pants down, took over their whole camp without firing a shot."

Campbell's eye's grew wide, "Yes, sir," Campbell said. "But you might notice their camp is empty. That means we could have a whole regiment of really upset gooks out there waiting for a chance to take a shot at us."

Sinclair looked doubtful and said, "An enemy that runs has already lost the war, Sergeant." He then turned to address his RTO. *Guess I've been dismissed. Officers, they all think the same. We've got 11--maybe 1200 NVA out there, we number around 400 and he thinks we've won the war.* Campbell let out a deep ominous sigh and walked off to join his men.

While 1st platoon searched the huts, D Company's 2nd platoon located a wide and well-used trail that led through the forest and up onto a lower ridgeline of Hill 937. With orders from Captain Sampson, 2nd platoon moved to the foot of the ridgeline and set up perimeter security across the trail and within shouting distance of Lt. Olson's 3rd platoon, who was given the responsibility to set up security between the LZ and the encampment.

Matthew, though surprised by the number and condition of the gardens, was more concerned by the actual size of the huts, "They're big enough to hold a whole platoon in each one, maybe more," he told Jose. "Multiply the number of huts by the possible number of men an' we got us a whole lot of NVA out there."

Hundreds of sleeping mats were discovered inside the huts, plus various articles of military equipment and all the evidence that the former occupants left in one big hurry. Amazingly, the artillery barrage and even the Daisy Cutter missed the camp. Not a single round of artillery landed within 100 feet of any of the huts.

John studied the trees and was astonished by the sheer size of them and how they formed a triple canopy that not only blocked out most of the sunlight, but would also interfere with the moonlight. "Gonna be mighty dark in here when dat sun go down," John said.

"A regular sauna too, no wonder crawly things grow so large in the A Shau," Matthew added. By early afternoon the heat throughout the valley floor was 99 degrees and the humidity was the highest level any of the first timers had experienced before. But Franklin remembered and he had brought two extra neck towels along, wrapped in foil wrap he obtained from the kitchen. He planned to have a clean towel every three days and hoped to be out of this godforsaken place by the 10th day.

PFC Baxley looked as if he was about to pass out. Matthew draped a moist towel on the back of his neck and forced another salt tablet down him.

When Matthew wasn't looking, Baxley grabbed one of his canteens and began pouring it over his head.

"Gimme that!" Matthew ordered. He yanked the canteen out of Baxley's hand.

"That's my water, give it back," Baxley pleaded.

"Shut-up," Matthew said. "I know your miserable, but this stuff is life's blood an' it has to last."

Campbell stepped in between them, "What's going on?" He had just returned from another meeting with Sinclair and felt irritable. He couldn't believe the L-T was so blind to what was about to happen here.

"Baxley's okay, he's having trouble with the heat," Matthew answered.

"He ain't the only one," Campbell said. He then went over to readjust Jose's position.

Later that afternoon, D Company was tasked with clearing an area to be used for Battalion Headquarters and a new base camp. The only equipment they had to use is their individual E-tools and several dozen machetes Captain Sampson had brought in by Huey on the next supply run. After only 15 minutes of hacking at the terrain, Baxley collapsed. When two soldiers helped him to his feet, he angrily pushed them away, "Leave me alone! I can do my share," he growled. A moment later, Baxley was right back down again and this time he was unconscious. With the platoon medic already busy with the new aid station, Lt. Sinclair ordered the same two men to carry Baxley over there and drop him off.

Shortly after 1600 hrs, orders come down from Battalion placing D Company on security for the new base camp. Meanwhile, the remaining three companies began to move toward the base of Hill 937 and set up a night defense perimeter.

ON PERIMETER SECURITY

"Martinez, you an' Andrews set up your gun over there in that shallow depression. Carry some logs over for cover an' dig deep. Adams, you an' Riley set up over on Martinez's right. Isaac, you and Kendal dig in on their far right. That puts 1st squad off to Jose's left an' 3rd squad on Washington's right." Campbell paused briefly to take a sip from his canteen. "Don't know when Baxley will get back, but when he does he'll replace you, Isaac." Campbell looked out into the jungle, he could feel the enemy's eye boring into the back of his head and he hated this feeling. He knew if a large force did attack, this battalion could be overrun before air cover could be provided.

"Now keep your eyes open. Remember, we're in the enemy's living room tonight. Going to be real dark in another twenty minutes or so and I want everyone dug in before then. We'll set up the LP when I get back from talking with the L-T. I just thought of another question for him." Campbell walked off, leaving behind six fidgety young men who now wonder who will get stuck with LP duty?

"Dig 'em deep he says…sounds like we may have company commin'," Isaac said. He pulled out his E-tool and began to dig into the soft, but root filled dirt, while Matthew kept watch. They'd switch after Isaac got tired, which took about four minutes in this heat and heavy humidity.

An hour before sunset, the valley resounded with the sounds of a violent exchange of gunfire and explosions. M-16s on full automatic battle it out with AK-47s. B Company's M-79's and NVA rocket propelled grenades (RPG) let Battalion know they'd met up with the home team at the foot of Hill 937. Within minutes, the first casualties began arriving by stretcher.

"Man-oh-man, someone really stepped into it. Must be a whole lot of firepower up there and that heavy gun has got to be a Russian 51," Andrews said. He continued to dig, glancing up toward the mountain with every shovel full of dirt flung over his left shoulder. With the darkness came the sightings of tracers; bluish tint for the Americans and a more greenish tint for the NVA. At the moment it appeared the NVA had a whole lot more guns.

"You jus' keep diggin'. I want a basement apartment and a pool," Jose said. He sighted his M-60 at the base of the mountain and waited for the enemy's advance.

Campbell returned to the squad with news, "Bravo Company walked smack into a line of bunkers. Lost one man and three more wounded. Like we figured, we're facing a sizeable force…maybe a battalion…maybe more. B Company was forced to retreat, but the old man wants that ridgeline taken tomorrow. No patrols tonight. So dig deep and stay sharp. We can also expect mortars tonight…maybe even a sapper or two." Campbell looked into Jose's hole and then continued, "We'll be on 50-50 watch 'til midnight, after that…everyone's gonna be awake." Campbell started to turn away, but then remembered something, "Kendal, you an' Adams on LP. Go out 25 yards, but wait 'til I get a field phone from the L-T. You two both grab some shut eye now, you've got an hour." Campbell walked off and quickly vanished in the darkness.

"Thanks," Matthew said in disgust. "Wish we could've gone out when we still had daylight," Adams didn't say anything. He stretched out on the ground and closed his eyes. With only an hour to go, he wanted as much shut-eye as he could get.

By 1650 hours the humidity was unbearable and the stench of their own sweat drove the mosquitoes into a feeding frenzy. Matthew tried to snooze, but the mosquitoes made it difficult. He slipped his helmet over his face in self-defense and nearly suffocated.

The valley floor was dark, but above the tree canopy the late afternoon sky had turned a deep golden in color. Yet here under the trees, twilight had come and gone quickly. Campbell returned from Company Headquarters with a field phone and PFC Baxley. His hands still trembled and his face was pale, but the medic said he was fit for duty. Campbell noticed the walk from the aid station had left Baxley exhausted; which concerned him.

How long are you gonna last out here and who's gonna have ta carry you when you collapse again? Campbell wondered. "You stay here with Washington," Campbell told Baxley and then addressed Isaac, "Get some more water down him if you can. They had an IV in him when I dragged him off, but he's still dehydrated."

Isaac looked at the new guy, shook his head, sighed and said, "No problem, Sarge."

Campbell knelt down beside Kendal and Adams, "Here's your Ma Bell with a spool of comm line. Run it out about twenty-five yards directly in front of us. Find yourselves a nice place to call home an' dig deep." He then added, "...as quietly as you can."

Campbell checked his wristwatch, "I've got 1722 hours, adjust yours to mine. Check in with me every thirty minutes beginning with 1800 hours. We'll make it simple...say 'lima-poppa' an' I'll respond with a quick 'roger'. Now if you hear anything, pick up the phone an' click it twice. I'll be listening throughout the night, me or Washington."

Campbell moved in closer to make sure they both understood what he was about to say, "Remember this, if you fall asleep out there...you'll both be dead. The NVA are out there, they've been watching us since we arrived. So, thank you for volunteering your services...any questions?"

John grinned widely and asked, "Can ah quit an' go ta jail now? Ah'll tell thu judge ah made a real ba-a-ad decision."

Campbell couldn't help but smile, but then he replied, "No. Are there anymore bright questions?"

Matthew looked at the phone and then asked, "Yeah, what do we do if we come under fire?"

John, whose eyes grew wide, nodded his head in wanting to know that answer too.

"Just stay down an' return fire. I'll bring the squad up if possible. But don't, I repeat don't try to come back here. One of these trigger-happy jerks

142

will shoot you for sure. Leave your gear here. Take only one canteen between you and your shovels. Make the water last. But stay awake and remember your reports every half-hour."

Matthew released an exaggerated sigh and said, "This sounds like a whole lot of fun," Matthew released a second audible sigh for Campbell's benefit. He grabbed up the spool of comm line and the Ma Bell field phone. "Ready, Mr. Adams?"

John looked to Campbell and asked, "An' ah gotta spend all night out dere wit' dis honky? Why can't we have women, the NVA have women soldiers?"

Matthew jabbed John with an elbow and muttered, "What are you complaining about? At least you got natural camouflage." Then they both received a *get moving* gesture from Campbell's thumb.

"We's a leavin', Mr. Boss man," John said. He then moved out in a low crouch, with his rifle at the ready and Matthew following behind with the communications equipment.

After only ten yards of moving forward, both men were down to their stomachs and it took them approximately 15 minutes to cover the remainder of the 25 yards. John wasn't in a hurry to walk into an ambush or some booby trap. But in this darkness, caution didn't prevent John from tripping over several tree roots early on and having to bypass one large boulder. When they reached the end of the wire, they're forced to feel around till they find an outcropping of dead trees roots to use for cover. They also wanted to use a shallow hole of soft dirt from the dead tree as a good place to start digging. John kept watch first, while Matthew dug out a hole. The position was done by 1820 hours and by 1830 they'd made their second check-in. Both men were sitting back-to-back at the bottom of a four-foot deep foxhole. This way they could survey 360 degrees of total darkness and with silence being the key to their survival. They don't talk, sleep, eat and they even breathe quietly. The only things they can do normally is sweat, observe the darkness and hopefully keep their imaginations in check.

Matthew could hear all the noise the Americans were making back at the base camp and even a few loud mouths from either 3rd squad or the men from the other platoon. Even the sounds of the mosquitoes begin to grow louder with each passing minute. The forest was alive and Matthew wondered if it was natural or noises produced by the NVA? *So quiet, I can hear my own heart beating an'...I can feel John's through his back. That's weird.*

Jose has his M-60 loaded with a belt of 100 rounds and two additional belts ready if needed. Behind him, Andrews finished off a can of peaches, nearly dropping the can when Campbell dropped into their hole, startling him. "You boys look pretty snug. Just make sure you keep an eye behind you. The next guy in here could be Mr. Charlie." Campbell put his hand on Jose's M-60, "You got an LP out there, but if anything moves in front of you, you blast it. Don't worry about the guys in the LP, they were warned to keep low and not to come back here without my okay." Campbell then knocked his knuckles of his right hand on top of Jose's helmet and asked, "You need anything, Amigo?"

Jose stared straight ahead, worried about his two buddies. "Naw, Sarge, we've got enough ammo an' water." Jose then added, "Keep your head down, Sarge. I'd hate ta have some sneaky sniper bag you for a trophy. You'd be tough to stuff."

Campbell grinned and replied, "Nice to know you care so much."

Jose smiled, but in the darkness Campbell couldn't see it. "You'se my favorite Sergeant…Gonna name my first kid afta' you."

Campbell put his hand on Jose's shoulder, "You're going to stick your tiny Hispanic boy baby with a name like Rodney?"

Jose shook his head and answered, "Nope, gonna name him Sarge…Sarge."

This got a laugh from both Andrews and Campbell, who patted Jose's shoulder and said, "Makes me feel all warm and cuddly inside the way you look after me, Jose. I hope you have all daughters. Now stay awake or I'll show you how unfriendly your favorite sergeant can be." Campbell gave Jose a friendly slap on the shoulder and began to crawl off, but then he remembered Andrews. "You keep the ammo ready for him, kid and make sure he's alive come morning…both of you."

Andrews knew of the strange bond between Campbell and Jose, and he replied, "I'll take care of him, Sergeant."

Campbell climbed out of the hole, then turned to Andrews and added, "You do that."

His body was tense from a constant state of alert and soon Matthew's body began to jerk, which alarmed John into thinking, *we got visitors?* "What?" John turned his head to the right and asked in a low whisper directed into Matthew's left ear.

"Sorry…nothing'," Matthew whispered back. He then prayed his voice wasn't loud enough to carry through the darkness and bring the enemy down on top of them.

The only way they can keep track of time is with the luminous dial on Matthew's watch, which now lay at his feet to keep it from being seen. *We got nine hours to go, 18 security checks and I'll be a nervous wreck by morning… If I'm alive by morning. How'd Luke ever handle all this? He never wrote about this stuff, maybe he should've and I'd be at Bible College and marching in anti-war parades...not!*

At 2231 hours, NVA mortars exploded between 1st platoon's NDP and 3rd Battalion's Headquarters. Two Cobra Gun ships, already in the area, were ordered in to find the mortar sites by flying at tree top level in hopes they could see the flash when the mortars were fired.

At 2244 hours, one of the pilots spotted a flash of bright light below him and thinking it's an enemy mortar, radioed the other bird, "Eagles Niner-One, this is Niner-Two, I've got a target below. Follow my lead, I'm going in hot."

The other pilot replied, "Right behind yuh, Niner-One." Using the running lights of the first bird to guide him, the two Cobra's dive toward the tree canopy like birds of prey and cut loose with their quad M-60's and 40 mm cannon. Sadly, it wasn't an enemy mortar site they were firing upon, but instead the light that emanated from 2nd Battalion's Command Post (CP). A deadly blunder that sent terrified men scrambling for their lives. Soldiers dove into slit trenches and hid behind trees as the world exploded around them. A few men took cover inside tents, foolishly thinking thin canvas could shield them from the Cobra's teeth. It doesn't. Shrapnel, exploded outward from point of impact, slammed into trees, sliced tents and shredded bodies. Frantic orders were issued and the gun ships ceased-fire.

Stunned by what had taken place and sickened by the realization they had opened fire on their own men, the Cobra crews left the area for a long silent flight back to Firebase Blaze. An intensive investigation into how such a thing could have occurred would follow, but for now, survivors would initiate a search of the area for the wounded and dead.

As an eerie silence returned to the perimeter, as Matthew kept his eyes open. He began saying a silent prayer of healing for the men wounded in camp. He had trouble believing what he had just witnessed as their own gunships tore into the American's lines. In dismay, he continued in prayer and also asked for the Lord's peace for the families of the ones killed. From their position, Matthew and John listened in horror when the two-helicopter gunships launched their attack on their camp. Within such close proximity, for the first time Matthew learned to understand what it was like to experience the tremendous and awesome might of an U.S. air attack upon ground troops. Immediately following the cease-fire, they heard the dreadful cry of "medic!", followed by angry shouts of soldiers cursing the pilots for their costly mistake.

Wiping his brow of sweat, Matthew froze in mid-movement when he heard the sound of movement off to his left. He may not be able to see anything, but his sense of hearing was only heightened by fear. *Someone or somethin' scraping against a tree; maybe brushing some branches...could be a foot stepping on a pile of dried brush.* These were sounds he probably wouldn't normally take notice of, but are now loud enough to cover the sound of his own racing heartbeat. *Someone's movin' through the trees, but who or what?* Matthew pressed against John's sweaty backside and reached back to tap him on the elbow. John picked up the same sounds. When Matthew touched him, it startled him. Moving cautiously in slow motion, praying he doesn't make any detectable sound, Matthew picked up the handset and tapped the handset twice to send a signal to Campbell. *Sure hope Campbell's listening.* Matthew's imagination transformed every tree into an enemy soldier, every rock into the helmet of some NVA and he began to feel like the proverbial fish in a barrel. Unable to prevent himself, he poked his head up for a better look. Right at that very moment, someone on the perimeter yelled out "Incoming" and within seconds, the CP comes under mortar fire. Staff members had only enough time to hurl themselves to the ground when the main CP tent found itself on ground zero. Yet oddly enough, only three mortar rounds exploded inside the camp. Silence followed, as men begin crawling out of their trenches and picking themselves off the ground to observe the damage caused by the attack and caring for the wounded.

However, the mortar attack was a planned diversion to allow a small NVA suicide force to approach the perimeter without being detected and it worked to some degree.

Suddenly, five NVA soldiers stood up from concealment and charged the perimeter with their AK-47s blazing on full automatic fire. Screaming and shrieking like wild men, they race right past the LP before Matthew and John are able to fire upon them. Once they passed by, they fear hitting someone on their own perimeter and all they can do is duck down and pray they don't get killed in the firefight.

"Fire-Fire-Fire!" Campbell shouted out when the NVA rush their position. Warned by Matthew's signal, 2nd squad was ready and they sent out their own wall of death with M-16 and M-60 fire. Riley screamed curses as NVA charged. He emptied one whole magazine in a wide spread and then he slapped in a second one. Beside him, Campbell pumped round after round of double aught buck shot into the attacking force. Surprisingly, Jose kept his cool this time, firing quick four and five round bursts from his M-60, while Andrews continued keeping the belt of ammo flowing freely and his M-16 ready if needed. Isaac and Baxley, hidden behind a pile of logs, each emptied a magazine at the enemy, even as AK-47 rounds impacted all around them. In a matter of seconds, the six-man squad filled the air with hundreds of rounds of ammo and yet in all the excitement, less than 10% actually impacted the enemy.

The NVA are soon cut down, killed by return fire from the men of 2nd squad and some from 1st squad. During the brief firefight, Matthew and

John scrambled to reach a new subterranean level in their home; while overhead, bullets ricocheted off the trees. Both men, doing their best impression of playing a mole, seeing how much of their body they can hide under their helmet-turtle style, listen to the rounds zinging above their heads.

A stray M-60 round hit their field phone. Several metallic pieces bounced in the hole off the top of Matthew's helmet. Thinking a grenade had just been lobbed into their hole, Matthew freaked out, frantically tossing the remainder of the phone out of the hole. "Grenade!" He yelled before he dove on top of John, forcing him to the bottom of the hole, a terrified 200-pound man on top of him. Both men waited for the explosion, but it never came. They slowly they begin unwinding from each other.

While the Battalion CP made contact with D Company for a status report, Lt. Sinclair responded to Campbell's position with 4th squad at his heels. By the time he arrived, the shooting was all over with.

At 2347 hours, Campbell attempted to make contact with his LP, but was unable to raise them on the radio because the line was dead. Campbell was forced to recon the area himself with Riley right behind him. Using the comm line to lead him out, he estimated 25 yards and began whispering, "It's me, Campbell."

He's not only worried the two men might be a bit trigger-happy after what just went down, but there might be more NVA in the area. After his third call, Matthew responded in a low growl with, "C'mon in, Sarge. Coffee's on."

Leaving Riley in place, Campbell crawled into their hole, "You two okay?"

Matthew responded by handing Campbell his helmet, "Too close."

Campbell felt the bullet crease along the top of Matthew's helmet and asked, "Any other damage?"

Matthew replied, "Phone got nailed, thought it was a grenade when it fell in on top of me. Don't remember leaving it outside, but we got real busy digging when all that shooting started." Matthew handed Campbell one of the larger pieces from the phone.

"How you doin', Adams?"

John didn't reply to Campbell right away, but then after a quiet moment he said, "Got duh shakes, Sarge, but ah'm okay. You get 'em all?"

Campbell answered, "Yeah, I checked 'em as I came up. Five dead NVA regulars. They must've been a Kamikaze hit to check our security. So, stay sharp, there's probably more of them out here."

Matthew asked in a low whisper, "What are we gonna use for a phone?"

Campbell thought about it for a moment, "A new phone will have to wait. Just pull on the phone line once every half-hour like we did before. I'll pull the slack out of it as I go back an' give you a single yank in response. Doubt we'll see any more NVA tonight, but you hear anything pull on the line hard three times. Questions?"

Matthew had one, "Yeah, you got any Aspirin?"

Campbell wished he had brought some, but said, "Nope...See you in the morning." Campbell gave each man a reassuring pat on the shoulder; then crawled back into the darkness to collect Riley. Matthew and John grabbed a quick drink of water, returning to their back-to-back position of fighting mosquitoes and waiting nervously for the sun to show.

With daylight came the reports: Third Battalion suffered two KIA and 35 WIA as a combined result of friendly fire from the gun ships and enemy mortars. The five dead NVA were removed from the front of 2nd squad's position and shortly afterward the Battalion's Duty Officer of the Day sent a "Good Job" to Captain Sampson. With small welts covering their faces, Matthew and John finally gave up on swatting mosquitoes and with resignation they allowed the flying things to have access to their blood supply in a sacrifice to some A Shau Valley bug god. Matthew had one bad bite on his lower lip, but chewing on it helped him stay awake during the last two hours of darkness and he had the satisfaction of chomping down on the mosquito. He had heard the rumor that if you ate a mosquito you'd never get attacked again. He had learned this rumor was bogus.

Shortly after dawn, when the first light filtered down through the trees, Campbell crawled out to bring his two weary men back in. While doing this, he sent Isaac to obtain an ample supply of hot coffee from the Battalion CP. Along with the coffee, the men of 2nd squad were informed how D Company would be moving forward to assault the ridgeline. "Time to go to war," Campbell added.

"What was las' night?" Jose asked.

"Only a sample of things to come, compadre," Campbell said before he walked off to find a soft mound of dirt to lay his own weary head down upon. The squad resumed 50-50 watch after morning chow was divided up. For the men of 2nd squad, Day two began with a cold breakfast of C-rations and a flip of the coin to see who got to sleep first. In Matthew and John's case though, Jose and Edwards stayed awake to let both of them conk out for five hours.

8 – LIONS, TIGERS AND BEARS – OH MY!

2ND SQUAD, D COMPANY, A SHAU VALLEY, HILL # 937, SOUTH VIETNAM, MAY 11TH, 1969 0800 HOURS--*DAY 2*

"Chow time!" Isaac hollered, dropping a half-full case of C-rations to the ground. "Yuh got cold turkey patties, beef stew, piggy slices, cow patties, scrambled eggs an' the beans an' weenies are yours truly…so hands off." The boxed meal contained several assorted tins: Certified by the government to be edible, with each entrée accompanied by either a tin of fruit cocktail, pear slices or peach halves. Depending on the entrée, each meal came with a desert packet of either two chocolate bars of an unusual not quite chocolate taste, or a hard coconut patty coated in a thick substance resembling chocolate; again, not quite that Hershey taste the manufacturer promised. Plus, crackers, suitable to be used as training tools for Olympic discus throwers. A tin of a jelly-like compound, or cheese paste capable of locking the strongest jaws together. To complete each meal, a sealed foil packet, containing a miniature book of four cigarettes (various brands), a book of matches, an individual size package of toilet paper, a plastic spoon and a pouch of powered juice mix or hot chocolate. Some of these boxes dated back to World War II. The medic advised in the case of the older boxes to leave the powered juice and hot chocolate alone, or risk a terrible case of Montezuma's Revenge.

"How can something that costs the government so much taste so bad?" Andrews asked. He picked through the meals, selecting ham slices. "I mean those little green cans of scrambled eggs are guaranteed to give you a case of galloping trots. Only can you throw to the Vietnamese they throw back…smart people."

Jose was the last one to make a selection and unfortunately, this meant he got stuck with the eggs. After opening the box and removing the tin of powered eggs, he turned to Matthew, "Maybe we can give dis stuff to the NVA. You know, a peace offerin'."

Matthew shook his head, "Can't do it, Jose. It's against the Geneva Convention. Too cruel and falls under inhumane weapons."

Jose stared at the unopened can in his right hand. "But it's okay for me to eat this crud, but too inhumane…what's inhumane mean anyway?" Jose asked. He tossed the unopened can of eggs into a trash hole. Not getting any response from Matthew, Jose attempted to beg bites off the others, but they all do their best to ignore him.

"Kendal, you an' Adams rack out an' catch some Zs. I'll try to give you five hours, but no promises." Campbell then handed Jose a half-finished tin of beef stew to keep him from pestering the others. Matthew and John moved back from the perimeter taking up residence in one of the large huts. Although cleared by the engineers, they took a moment to conduct a quick security check of their own for any booby traps or tunnels. Once John was satisfied, he stretched out on one of the grass mats and quickly dropped off into a heavy slumber. Matthew was still too wired from earlier action. He stared at the ceiling for a bit before finally falling asleep. But his was a restless slumber. Nightmares haunted his sleep and he awoke several times to escape his dreams.

"C'mon, let's get this place policed up," Campbell ordered. He then advised Isaac he'd be over with the L-T, "I'll be back in a few." Twelve minutes later, the mountain came alive with the sounds of war, as B Company moved against the NVA.

"Looks like another tough day at the office, Mr. Martinez," Andrews said with false bravado.

Inside, his guts churned with the thought that he'd be going up there too. "You stick with me, Farm Boy...you be okay," Jose reassured him.

When morning turned to afternoon, temperatures in the valley rise upward of 100 degrees and D Company continued remaining on perimeter security. Above them, A and B Companies engaged in heated battle with an enemy who refused to give ground. C Company, having already lost a lot of men, tried blasting through a line of well concealed bunkers. As the action continued, weary soldiers, burdened by stretchers, cautiously watched for snipers, while they carrying wounded down the mountain.

INSIDE AP BIA MOUNTAIN, MAY 11TH, 1969 0835 HOURS

Outside the mountain U.S. Army medics fought to save the lives of their wounded and dying. Medic Que worked feverishly to save his own comrades in this man-made catacomb of a hospital. The foul stench of death and the moaning of the wounded caused him to curse the Americans for the carnage they caused to his brave comrades. Blood spurted from a young NVA soldier who lay on the hard ground in front of Que. There was little he could do for the wounded man. New wounded arrived by the minute, only to be left outside in the tunnel. There was no room left inside the hospital. The smaller side room, reserved for the dead already held 31 bodies in it. Que, looking into the eyes of his young patient, watchedd as his life faded away, knowing his young patient will be added to the pile of bodies soon enough.

"Am I dying?" The wounded soldier asked in a weakened voice.

"I am sorry, comrade, for I can do nothing to save you. Rest now and let Lord Buddha hold you in his mighty arms," Que answered.

"No, not Buddha…" life seeped out and the man released a whisper of a moan and died. He shook his head in frustration and fought back the tears. Que rose, gesturing to two men to remove the body. With space to treat another patient, Que walked into the tunnel to locate his next case. The sounds of battle caused several patients to cry out in panic. Their fear was contagious. Even Que could feel it, for the battle was not going well and already there were too many wounded for the medical supplies on hand.

2ND SQUAD, A SHAU VALLEY, MAY 11TH 1243 HOURS

The expressionless faces of the men he killed on Dong Ngai faded away, replaced by the blur that came before being awakened from sleep. Matthew hearing his name called out, sat up and stretching out an arm. He rolled on his side, spotting Campbell, who stood in the doorway of the hut.

"It's time," Campbell said and then left. Matthew checked his wristwatch; he'd been sleeping only four hours and 12 minutes. He took in a deep breath and slowly exhaled. "Nice hotel, but can't say much for the mattress…how about you?" Matthew asked John, who sat up, facing him, with heavily bloodshot eyes.

"Call room service, Matt. Mah mouth's dried out, mah head hurts, mah back aches an' mah left eye won't stop twitchin'." John rose and stretching, while Matthew stood, rotating his head around to release some of the tension felt in his neck. They left the hut together, their rifles slung over their shoulders. They casually ambled up to the squad's position. "What's up?" Matthew asked. It didn't look to him like the platoon was ready to move out.

"Orders got changed. We stay here on reserve, while the other companies hike the hill. Captain thinks the Battalion Commander wants to give us a break for all the action we saw on Dong Agai," Campbell said.

"How bad was it?" Matthew asked.

"Lots of wounded comin' down," Andrews answered. Matthew was about to ask another question when the squad looked up toward the distinct whine-like sound of a mortar round as it sailed over their heads.

"Incoming" was shouted out first by Campbell, but quickly echoed down the line by more than a dozen men.

Campbell dove down beside Matthew, who had already dropped into a shallow hollow behind a huge grayish deadfall. And like last time, the mortar attack stopped abruptly after only three rounds impacted inside the camp. Several men who stood around the CP went down with shrapnel wounds and the call for medics rang out. "Everyone okay?" Campbell asked when he stood to his feet.

"Looks like they're done," Riley said in a tone of fear and hesitancy. The squad crawled out of their holes cautiously and Matthew looked back toward the CP. He winced in horror when he saw a decapitated body stuck 15 feet up a tree. Two men from Headquarters staff were ordered to bring the body down and Matthew knew it was gong to be a grisly task. "Keep your eyes to the front," Campbell ordered. At that very moment a bullet zinged right by John's head and he reacted quickly by a five-foot leap into the hole shared by Matthew and Campbell.

"Move over!" John yelled. He then fell against the front lip of the hole and brought his rifle up to return fire in short bursts.

NVA snipers opened up on 1st and 2nd squad's positions and pinned the men down with a heavy volume of fire. Bullets impacted trees, deadfalls, boulders and one soldier from 1st squad screamed out when he got zapped in the leg by an AK-47 round. Matthew slowly lifted his head up and hoped to see one of the snipers, but Campbell clamped his sweaty hand on Matthew's helmet and forced him back down, "Stay down, you idiot."

Then contrary to what he had ordered Matthew to do and in hopes to get a better view of the front, Campbell did a fast crawl over to Jose's hole. He slid in beside Jose and suddenly sighted an enemy soldier on a low run between trees. Campbell sighted in and was about to pull the trigger, when Andrews shouted a warning, "Look out, Sarge! They're right behind you!"

Campbell dropped and rolled on his stomach. He twisted around in time to see four NVA soldiers charging straight at him with bayonets. "Hose 'em down, Jose!" Campbell yelled. He then brought his shotgun into play and cut loose with two rapid-fire rounds of double aught. Jose swung his M-60 to the right, pulled the trigger and fired off an extended burst. The enemy, behaving like wild beasts, fired their rifles toward 2nd Squad's position in an attempt to knock out Jose's machine gun. But the little bandito refused to back-off and dropped two of them in mid-stride.

"On your right, Riley!" Campbell yelled. Riley moved his rifle to the right and zeroed in on an NVA preparing to lob a grenade toward Jose and Andrews. But Riley was able to drop him with a three-round burst and the followed it up with quick *thanks* wave to Campbell.

The two remaining NVA attackers had taken cover behind a deadfall to change their magazines and heard the pause in the M-60 firing. They leapt up, charging forward. Jose and Andrews wrestled with a jammed machine gun. An AK-47 bullet struck a log only an inch from Andrews' head and he reached for his rifle to return fire. Campbell was faster. He popped up over the top of one log and caught the nearest one with a shotgun blast that slammed the man backwards against a tree. Baxley, shaking with adrenaline, downed the last man with a single shot from his M-16. As quickly as it had begun, the firefight ended and the men looked about in silence to see if there was anyone else in the near vicinity to be worried about. Not having hit anything but a few trees and possibly a large boulder, Matthew visually checked the path the enemy had used and found it clear. He took a moment to calm himself and then walked around the tree that had offered him protection during the firefight. On the opposite side of the tree he counted five bullet holes at chest height.

John, whose rifle had jammed after the second round, set behind a deadfall and was quite upset. He cursed the weapon until he had broken it down and had every part separated. Only then did he find a thick sliver of wood in his magazine that prevented the next round from being chambered. *How'd that happen?*

Captain Sampson, Lt. Sinclair and all of 4th Squad were on scene within a few minutes. They were both relieved to see everyone up and walking. "How many NVA?" Sampson asked.

"At least five and all KIA," Campbell answered.

"Battalion thinks these suicide squads are bringing up their own mortars, firing off three rounds and then attacking the perimeter with a suicidal rush to probe our defenses for a possible major ground assault later. So, they want that ridgeline secured ASAP to give us some advantage if that were to occur," Sampson said. He wanted the men of 2nd Squad to hear what Battalion wanted and why.

"Well, those men aren't going to be telling us anything," Lt. Sinclair said. He was referring to the dead NVA.

"No, but maybe something on them will. Have your 4th squad bring up some stretchers and carry them back to the CP for examination," Sampson ordered.

"Yes, sir," Sinclair answered. He then gestured to the squad leader to carry the order out. Campbell would later learn that from these bodies and the ones turned in earlier, they were facing the 29th NVA Regiment and a suspected force of 1200 men.

For the men of 2nd Squad, they're beginning to wonder why their position is the only one on the perimeter singled out by the enemy and if they might be able to change places with another unit for the night. "Hey, Sarge, how come we're so popular?" Matthew asked.

"Because that ridgeline trail is right above us, Kendal, which means we're sitting right on their supply-trail." Campbell pointed to the ridgeline, "They don't want us up there. Once we get a foothold on that mountain they know the battle's ours."

Andrews, who was still excited from the brief firefight added, "Wow! Aren't we the lucky ones to pick such a fine place…Back home my Uncle Zack would say, 'With luck like that you can expect a drought an' a twister, too.'"

With A, B and C Companies taking the blunt of the action, D Company found them assigned to other duties as directed. While 1st and 2nd platoon handled perimeter security, 3rd and 4th platoons were tasked with moving the wounded to evacuation points and digging additional trenches as desired by the Sergeant Major. Hueys lifted off with the wounded, while additional litter cases were carried down the hill and by late afternoon, word came down that the second assault on the hill had also failed.

A1-E Sky Raiders (Sandy) were ordered in to pound the mountaintop with 250-pound bombs, rockets and 20 mm machine gun fire. The World War II vintage aircraft were perfect for these missions; capable at flying at reduced air speeds over a target. But even with air support, the NVA refused to relinquish their hold on the high ground.

"Matt, you need any ammo?" Isaac asked.

"A bandoleer would be nice," Matthew replied. "We'll probably be loading magazines all night from the sound of things up above."

Baxley asked, "Wonder who's gonna gets stuck with LP duty tonight?" His voice nearly crackled from nervous reaction to killing his first NVA. He didn't get sick though, he didn't shed a tear, but he stared off into the distance for a sometime and the others left him alone.

"Yeah, that's great duty. You wait all night for some gook to snake his way through the brush, drop down into your hole an' slice your throat," Matthew said. "I really wanna know what's on top of this mountain that makes it so damn important? You'd think Uncle Ho had a vacation house up there the way the Air Force has been hitting it." Matthew stood up and stretched his legs and then walked off to locate Campbell. He found him lying on the ground behind a large deadfall, with an open letter on his chest and he appeared to be lost in thought.

"Sorry to bother you, Sarge, but you got anything else for us?"

Campbell was startled, "What?" He had a perturbed look on his face for being disturbed, but he relaxed when he saw it was Kendal. "No, just hang loose and keep your eyes open."

To which Matthew replied, "Okay."

He began to turn away when Campbell called to him, "Kendall, you an' Adams go back on LP duty again tonight."

"Again…why us, Sarge?" Matthew whined. "That's two nights in a row."

Campbell growled back at him, "I can count, Kendal." He didn't plan to offer an explanation, but seeing the anger and fear in Matthew's eyes he changed his mind. "Matt, its simple…you two got some sleep today and you'll stay awake out there. Now any other questions or can I get back to my deep thoughts of becoming a wealthy man after this war is over and buying my chicken ranch here in sunny South Viet Nam? I thought I'd call it Campbell's A Shau Eggs…small and tiny…Grade C. You wanna know what the C is for, Kendal?"

Matthew answered, "Nope." But Campbell looked at him, grinned and said, "I'm going to tell you anyway…the C stands for *cemetery*. This whole valley is just one big cemetery. Over 400 years of warfare. I heard one whole army vanished in this accursed valley once, never to be heard of again…a whole army. Now get your butt back to the line and try to get some rest. You can tell Adams, too."

In a sarcastic tongue, Matthew replied, "Thanks. Thanks a whole lot, Sgt. Campbell." He then turned and headed back to break the news to John. Hopefully he could still get another hour of snooze time before they went back out

Campbell watched him walk away and could only sympathize. He wasn't concerned with the kid's attitude. No sane individual would want to pull two nights of LP duty back-to-back. But what he didn't explain to Matthew was that out of this squad he trusted Matthew and John with the responsibility. He knew they would stay awake. *Jose and Andrews need to stay on the gun, Baxley's too new, Isaac needs to be ready to take over for me if the need arises and frankly, I don't trust Riley one bit.* Riley had transferred over to D Company from another battalion after threatening to kill two other men over a mamma-san problem. There wasn't enough evidence to bring him up on charges, but Division decided it best to move him to keep things from escalating. He hadn't caused Campbell any problems yet, but the field wasn't a place to test someone when other lives were at stake.

When he heard the news, John snarled and tossed his hands in the air. He was about to blast out with a phrase of profanity, but saw the unhappy expression on Matthew's face and stooped himself. Instead he stomped off to find a hole by himself to calm down and took a quiet moment to talk with God. Meanwhile, overhead the sound of war continued on.

"Lord, ah's knew to dis stuff…an ah hope ah don't get you all mad at me for duh way I was a thinkin'. Ah is real sorree for that, but it jus' makes me mad. LP does scare me, but ah'll do mah job. So you jus' watch over duh squad an' maybe tonight you could keep an eye on Matt an' me? Uhhh… amen." *This prayin' stuff is okay, cool havin' someone ta talk wit'. Makes me feel kinda warm knowin' he's up dere watchin' over me. Don't understan' much, but dat's cool too.*

At 1630 hours, Lt. Sinclair showed up at 2nd Squad's position for a routine check of his men. Everyone was awake, except for John, who was snoring away in a shallow depression near Jose's foxhole. Matthew, who couldn't get into a sound sleep, woke John in time to hear the L-T's briefing. "Word from Battalion is we're facing a sizeable force, probably regimental strength or better. They've withstood the combined strength of three of our companies and a joint Army, Air Force and Marine bombardment. Headquarters think they probably have the whole mountain honeycombed with tunnels." Lt. Sinclair stopped to take a sip from his canteen.

"Now the bad news…our people want this hill taken and 3rd Battalion has got the job. So, D Company stays on security tonight, but we move out in the morning to replace C Company. They're pretty well chewed up and moving back to replace us, while they rest up and get re-supplied. We'll move up the ridgeline to fight a line action with A and B Companies. Our goal is to reach the summit by late afternoon and I plan to be on time," Lt Sinclair said. He then turned to Campbell, "Make sure they have plenty of ammo, grenades and water for tomorrow's assault." Lt. Sinclair then faced the squad and asked if there were any questions?

"Sir, how come they don't just clobber this place with a B-52 strike?" Baxley asked.

"That very question was brought up in Officer's call," Sinclair said. He seemed surprised that a new enlisted man would ask such a question. "Division feels that if the NVA see us falling back, they'll know to expect the heavy stuff and will escape into Laos through their tunnels. Then all we'd do is blow up an abandoned tunnel complex." Sinclair ignored the looks of *Yeah, so what's wrong with that* from most of the men. "No, the brass wants the NVA knocked down a peg and taking out the 29th NVA will give Ho Chi Minh's communist party something to explain to his Chinese and Russian allies." There were no more questions, "All right then. If you need me I'll be down at the CP, but I'll be back around midnight or earlier if something happens." Sinclair's pep talk was punctuated with the sounds of gunfire from up the hill and the men of 2nd Squad knew it was going to be another long night for those men stuck up there.

LISTENING POST (LP) DUTY

At 1647 hours, Matthew and John cautiously and silently made there way out to another LP site. They knew better than to use the same hole twice, for that was a good way to get killed. With a new field phone and the same spool of comm wire unraveling as they crawled forward, Matthew led out this time.

Satisfied with a spot, they took turns and dug out a deep hole, while the other guy kept watch. Even so, the man who dug stopped after each shovel full to listen for any sound of the enemy. Once the hole was finished, they snuggled down back-to-back for a long night of bug swatting, leech tossing, sweating profusely and listening to every single sound.

Matthew checked his wristwatch and at the right moment he made his prearranged check on the half-hour. But every time he did he imagined a grenade landing at their feet. Campbell hoped to go with just the comm wire, tugging it back and forth for signals, but Lt. Sinclair insisted on the field phone being used.

When the last noticeable degree of light vanished, Matthew and John were left in complete blackness. They were now forced to rely on their senses of smell and hearing. They weren't having trouble with the nose part; the whole valley floor had a stench of rot and decay from all the moisture and heat. From the mountain they could still hear the sporadic sounds of gunfire and the faint sound of voices coming from the CP area. Besides man-made noises, the jungle was alive with the sound of crawling and flying insects, and other predators that hunted the jungle floor in search of prey. The ones not frightened off by gunfire.

Weary of fighting off the mosquitoes, Matthew mixed some water with soft dirt, mixed with jungle growth, to make a mud paste to coat his face with. He tried draping his soiled towel around his ears, but it interfered with his hearing. So, he smeared mud paste on his ears, cheeks and the back of his neck.

John did the same thing, but he had to fight down a sudden urge to laugh, *Ain't no white man or black man out here tonight, jus' couple ol' boys playin' in duh mud.*

When Matthew rubbed the paste too close to his nose he became nauseated and struggled with the desire to vomit. He knew the vomit would stink and give their position away and after some difficulty, he was able to keep his last meal down. Minutes slowly turned into hours for the wearisome, but time was suddenly forgotten when John suddenly tensed up and pressed his back against Matthew. Not hearing anything yet, Matthew didn't reach for the phone. But within seconds, he not only heard the enemy, but he saw movement of what had alarmed his friend. A lone shadowy figure was moving through the darkness only a couple feet from their hole, his movements separated from them by a chuck of deadfall. If the man had taken a couple steps to his left, he would fall face first into their hole.

A moment later, a second figure and then a third, fourth and fifth figure followed the first. Two of them pass by John's view and move with a silence that would envy any American Indian. Coming beside Matthew, they are within twenty-yards of the camp's perimeter when the five figures stop abruptly. Surprisingly, Matthew can just barely make out the hand gestures they used between themselves and he estimated their distance to now be about ten to 12-feet to his extreme left and on the camp's side of the LP.

Matthew squint his eyes to make out their movements and he nervously watched as one man took something large off his shoulder and placed it on the ground, without making a sound. Another man lowered his load; a large squared off plate and suddenly, Matthew knew these men were in the process of setting up a mortar tube.

I need to warn Campbell, but the NVA...they're too close. They're gonna hear me for sure. Then Matthew understood what he must do. He slowly pulled a grenade off his harness and reached around to put it right in front of John's face. This way he'd know what the plan of action was. He then placed the grenade into his throwing hand and reached behind him with his other hand to grab John's side. After a slight squeeze, he began to press his fingers against him one-by-one in a silent countdown of five. Then he removed his hand to pull the pin on his grenade and with an overhand swing he lobbed the grenade at the NVA. John, who was ready with his own grenade, did the same thing. With both grenades in the air, they dove back down only a micro-second before the earth rocked and night instantly turned into day. A double explosion created a fiery death dance for five unsuspecting NVA and struck the LP with all forms of debris. Both men jumped to their feet and sprayed the scene with automatic fire to ensure the enemy was really dead. But their actions caused most of the perimeter to open up, forcing them to duck back down or risk getting shot by their own side.

Mathew grabbed the field phone up, after clearing dirt off it and after a few seconds of trying, he finally heard Campbell's excited voice, "What happened?"

"Tell them it's all over. Cease-fire before someone gets lucky and kills one of us!" Matthew yelled into the phone's handset.

"Cease-fire! Cease-fire!" Campbell shouted and it's echoed down the perimeter line. Within seconds the gunfire began to taper off.

"They ain't sendin' me out here 'gain, Matt. I done wit' this spooky stuff," John said. He clutched his rifle and braced himself against the side of the foxhole in fear one of his own guys might be the one to send him home in a body bag. "Day may call it friendly fire, Matt, but nothin' friendly 'bout it I know of."

"It's over, John," Matthew said quietly. Nearly deaf from the grenades and all the gunfire, Matthew lowered his rifle and ejected the empty magazine. After inserting a fresh one, a sudden wave of fatigue passed over him and he fell against John.

"It's okay, man...We is still alive," John said to his buddy and patted him on the shoulder.

"Lima-poppa, Lima-poppa, do you copy? Over," Campbell said in a loud voice. He was concerned he couldn't be heard over the phone.

Matthew slowly picked up the phone and replied in a soft, "Go ahead." He was still concerned there was other NVA out there.

"What's your status? Over," Campbell said as he breathed a sigh of relief.

"Five NVA are KIA...mortar tube destroyed...Over," Matthew said.

"You both okay? Over," Campbell asked.

"Affirmative...Over," Matthew said and then he thought, *what's okay mean?*

"Stay where you are, I'll be out at first daylight...understand...Over." Campbell listened to make sure Matthew got his last message. He didn't want his two men to risk coming in and getting shot by their side.

"Copy message...Staying put...lima-poppa is out." Matthew returned the handset and picked the canteen up for a long gulp before he handed it to John. "We'll, back to work my friend," Matthew whispered and then assumed his position of sitting back to back with John.

John remembered he needed to insert a fresh magazine and he did so as quietly as possible, which made Matthew smile. Both Matthew and John spent the rest of the night off and on in silent prayer, praying some avenging NVA grunt didn't pay his respects.

For Matthew, between prayers, he spent the time staring at the five mutilated bodies. What the darkness covered, his imagination provided a clear picture. *Death...it comes so easily, so violently. Death an' destruction, such carnage that man is capable of. Last year I was wrestling for some high school medal an' now I'm killing' people over a mound of dirt. What's that make me, what have I become to carry out such an' act with so little thought?* Matthew hoped for an answer, but none came.

Shortly after morning light broke through the canopy, Campbell led Riley and Baxley out to inspect the dead NVA. He noticed how quiet Matthew was, but passed it off to weariness and adrenaline burn out. The five bodies revealed little of value, except for captured weaponry. The mortar tube, which was damaged by the grenades, was tossed into the LP hole and the bodies carried back to the perimeter with the help from members of 1st squad. "You okay, Kendal?" Campbell asked.

"I'm fine, Sarge...just fine." Matthew answered in an all too calm voice. He looked down at the men he had helped kill and a weird sensation poured through him. Emotionally he began to distance himself from the dead men.

For most of the night he could do nothing else but think of their lives, their families and their dreams. Yet now, he can't seem to care about what he'd done and that thought alone seemed to bother him more than any feelings he had over what he'd done to them. If he'd had to describe it, he'd have said it was as if he was numb to the idea of killing.

Rejoining 2nd Squad, they find Lt. Sinclair waiting for them. "What happened?"

John gave Matthew the *You go ahead* look, so Matthew stepped up and gave the L-T a matter-of-fact style briefing, which caused Campbell some level of concern. "Five NVA were in the process of setting up a mortar tube. I knew that if I tried to contact Sergeant Campbell, the enemy, who were less than 15 feet from us, would detect us. So, we used grenades to take them out and followed that up with rifle fire. At the time we were prevented from examining the bodies because the perimeter opened up, forcing us to remain in our hole. After the cease-fire, Sergeant Campbell made contact with us and ordered us to remain in the hole until daylight. At sun up we found one mortar tube, three mortar rounds and five Ak-47s, Sir."

"Good report an' a job well done. I'll let the captain know what you two did out there, probably saved a lot of lives by taking them out before they could hit us again. Unfortunately, you two won't be getting any sleep...the company moves out in 30 minutes. Get some chow and wash your faces, you both look like you've been wallowing in the mud," Lt. Sinclair said in an uppity way.

"Yes, sir," both men answered in unison. They then walked over to where Jose was cleaning his weapons. In this high humidity, a soldier either kept a constant vigil on the conditions of his weapons or rust would set in and prevent them from working correctly — or not at all.

"Hey Amigo, how's it goin'?" John asked. He plopped down beside Jose and borrowed a piece of cloth to wipe his own rifle down.

"Bad for dem, not for us," Jose replied. "You guys did good." He watched as Matthew opened a box of C-rations and removed a tin of pound cake; a favorite item for most soldiers. "Pretty tough, huh?" Jose asked. He grew concerned as he watched his friend eat in silence.

John answered, "We zapped five of 'em, real hairy stuff." John then opened a box of C-rations and removed a tin of beans and weenies. Not bothering to use a spoon, he opened the can with his P-38 (individual can opener) and gulped down a large mouthful of greasy but flavorful brown and reddish fluid mixed with very tiny bits of highly processed meat. Once breakfast was over, John decided to ask Matthew a few questions about God, "Matt, what you think God thinks 'bout all dis stuff?"

Looking off in the distance, Matthew remained silent for a moment and John waited. Then with a deep sigh and a drop of his shoulders, he turned to his friend, "Do you mean the whole war or this one small sad episode?" Matthew took another scoop of cake and popped it into his mouth.

"Thu war. Will he forgive us fur all thu killin' we do?" John's question spiked Jose's interest too.

In a weary voice, Matthew responded, "The Word of God says if you ask God to forgive you for any sin, He will forgive you and forget you ever accomplished that sin. But as to whether or not the killing in war is a sin? I don't have the answer for that. Lately, I've been wondering why the Lord even allows this to continue…why he doesn't just stop it."

John dropped his can into a nearby trash hole and said, "Yeah, how come he don't? He could jus' wave His arm an' all the fightin' all over dis world would jus' stop." John covered the can over with dirt.

Matthew continued to look off toward a stand of trees, "I remember my Dad telling me it's all connected with us having a free will. He could have forced His will on us, made us slaves to spend our lives worshipping Him… but He already did that with His creation of the angels. No, He wants us to live our own lives an' gave us the gift of free choice. But man is always trying to take that free choice away from his neighbor and wars result." Matthew stopped to pull out the empty magazine he had used on the NVA mortar team and begin reloading it with bullets from his bandoleer.

"Matt, you is one smart dude," John said in admiration. "Maybe you got some Black in you."

Jose objected, "Naw, he's got more Mex in him than Black." This got Jose a half-grin from Matthew and a definite sneer from John.

The men of 2nd Squad went about preparing their personal equipment for moving out while the jungle forest remained quiet on the valley floor. Still, the occasional shot could be heard from up above and it continued to spook the men of D company. With the rise in humidity, a pungent odor of burnt sulfur drifted down the hillside, a bitter reminder of the action that had taken place during the night.

On Hill 937, the summit shook from under an artillery barrage as A, B and D Companies prepared to launch the Battalion's third assault. Day three of Operation Apache Snow began--a day many a soldier on both sides would never live to see the coming of nightfall.

9 – PROMOTIONS COME FAST IN WAR

CHAFFEY JUNIOR COLLEGE, ALTA LOMA, CALIFORNIA, MAY 12TH, 1969 1325 HOURS

A chant of "Hell no...We won't go!" was led by a longhaired, bearded young man. He held a large white bullhorn to his mouth and his chant was echoed by over seventy students that stood in the foreground. A tall lanky Black kid with a huge Afro shared the stage and he waved an upside down American flag in front of five White teenage girls, who held their right arms out in a Nazi salute to the flag. Behind them, several other teenagers, who looked young enough to be skipping high school, flashed big smiles and had both their arms extended over their heads and they displayed the two-finger peace symbol for all to see. Having no security force on campus to deal with the growing anti-war demonstration, the Dean of Students had asked several of the professors and instructors to stand around in an attempt to keep things from getting out of hand. But when the crowd began to behave unruly, the Dean had no recourse but to make a call to the San Bernardino County Sheriff's Office and request their assistance.

The demonstration had begun with a few quiet political speeches during the lunch hour period and then took on a change of venue when the bearded youth took over and dozens of students refused to return to class. In a matter of minutes, the political rally had grown into a large mob and was fired up by the kid with the bullhorn, who challenged the students to make a stand against the war. "Bring our boys home! It's not our war, bring our boys home, now!" He repeated over and over again.

Kathy Lee had remained in her classroom, confused by the commotion outside and the statements made by Mr. Bullhorn. She stood at the window when a sudden spasm of pain burned through her lower stomach and caused her to double over. She was forced to return to her chair with the help of another female student. "Thank you." *That's all I need right now-cramps!* But the pain faded away, though it left her with a tinge of nausea.

A moment later, an announcement came over the classroom's P.A. system, "Attention! Attention! Be advised, Chaffey Junior College Campus is now closed until further notice. All students and visitors are to leave the campus immediately. The rally currently being held outside the Student Activity Center is an unlawful assembly and law enforcement agencies are responding. I repeat, this campus is now closed by order of the Dean of Students."

Kathy Lee's instructor, Mrs. Alkerson addressed the class, "Please gather up your belongings and depart the classroom in an orderly fashion. I suggest you call the Administrations Office later today concerning tomorrow's class schedule."

By the time Kathy Lee reached the parking lot, the rally had grown to more than 500 students. Rather than leave as they were instructed, several hundred students stayed behind. Some remained from curiosity and others stayed in a desire to make their own political statement. Before she reached her car, Kathy Lee spotted several Sheriff's cars that had pulled into the main parking lot. She could see even more county units driving up the hillside road; their red and blue flashing lights rotating. Besides the Sheriff's cars from San Bernardino County, there were several black and white California Highway Patrol units on scene.

That evening the local news station was awarded with three minutes of coverage on the LA evening news: "Today, Chaffey Junior College in Alta Loma joined a long list of learning institutions that have fallen victim to violent anti-war demonstrations." A handsome news anchorman looked intensely at the camera in an attempt to show how concerned he was over this story, but in fact he was more concerned about his upcoming date with the new weather girl after work. "A scheduled rally got out of hand when students refused to return to their classes, reportedly causing a student walkout that brought hundreds of youth out of their classes to join in on their protest against war in Vietnam. Eyewitnesses report the burning of an American flag took place in front of a mob that grew to an estimated 1500 students, who all stood by and watched this disrespectful gesture. To deal with the unrest, the Dean of Students ordered the college closed for the day so school officials could end the rally in a peaceful manner." The face of the newsman was replaced by taped footage of the demonstration, which was narrated by an on scene reporter.

The newsman returned to finish the story, "Following a brief scuffle with police, the man believed to have incited the riot was arrested and charged with several counts of Disorderly Conduct and Resisting Arrest. Several additional arrests were made before the campus was cleared and this station has recently learned the man arrested for leading the rally was in fact not a student at Chaffey, but reportedly a member of the Students for a Democratic Society--normally referred to as the SDS." In the footage to follow, viewers were shown a wounded Marine being placed aboard a Huey, two Navy Phantom F-4 Fighters strafing a hillside and several large pieces of artillery firing off a salvo against an unknown target. With the help of television, the Viet Nam War was brought right into the American homes, giving the American public a first hand account of modern warfare.

Kathy Lee still felt a bit queasy when she returned to school the next day. She had thought of staying home, but all the excitement of the previous day made her want to attend and there was a test she couldn't afford to miss. Surprisingly, she found the campus quite sedate, not a single police car to be seen and faculty were acting as if nothing had happened. The only evidence of the demonstration was some flyers stuck to various bushes in front of the activity center. She picked one up and became horrified by what she read. The handout was actually a copy of the front page of a SDS Newsletter and with a few minutes to wait before class began, she found a vacant bench to sit on. She reviewed one of the editorials printed in red ink. *Guess it's supposed to symbolize blood.* The first article was entitled, "Nixon's Gestapo Strike Again!" It accused American soldiers of murdering hundreds of Vietnamese children. A grainy black and white photograph displayed a scene of naked dead children lying in the dirt. The photo sickened her, bringing on a sudden wave of intense nausea. She threw the flyer to the ground, but when she attempted to stand she was struck by a spell of dizziness. Stumbling to the nearest restroom, she threw herself toward the closest stall and tore her dress in the process, before she vomited into the toilet. A victim to the latest strain of Asian flu, Kathy Lee's feverish mind began imagining a scene where Matthew was killing a small child with a bayonet. Another flash showed him raping a Vietnamese woman, only moments before she lapsed into an unconscious state.

Discovered by another student, an ambulance transported Kathy Lee to Mount San Antonio Hospital where an E.R. doctor advised her mother of how Kathy Lee suffered from a very high fever and dehydration, "We've had a dozen of these flu cases come in within the last eight hours."

Her mother, a worried expression on her face, asked, "What should we do?" Mrs. Osborne then asked without waiting for an answer to her first question, "Does she need to be admitted?"

The doctor calmed her down with a gentle voice and his reply of, "No. After we're finished getting some fluids into her you can take her home and put her to bed for a few days. A lot of liquids--preferably water and ice chips for the first day and two Aspirin tablets every six to eight hours. But, if her fever goes above 103 degrees you bring her right back."

OSBORNE RESIDENCE

Home in bed, Kathy Lee decided it was time to write her dear fiancé a strong worded letter. Still under the effects of the fever, the words she chose to use were not rational and ones she would dread at a later time. She spoke out loud as she put the words to paper, "You don't bother to tell me what you're doing over there and I've heard so many terrible things." *I would've sent you that flyer, but it got lost.* But she does tell him about the demonstration and asked him pointed questions, "Did you kill anyone? What does that feel like, Matthew? Did you enjoy it? Have you slept with any prostitutes? You have to be honest with me...I do have a right to know! I just can't live with a murderer or a whoremonger." Folding the letter, she sealed it in an envelope, addressed it and left it by her lamp before she dropped off into a restless and feverish sleep.

D COMPANY/ 2ND SQUAD, A SHAU VALLEY, MAY 12TH, 1969 1000 HOURS: DAY-3

Matthew loaded twenty M-16 magazines, eight of them stored in pouches and the rest tucked away for quick access in his rucksack. Two of his four canteens hung loosely from his web belt, the other two were placed in the bottom of his pack along with five pairs of clean OD green socks and one pair of black socks. He also had four hand grenades, a banged up flashlight; damaged from crawling around on his stomach, and a sharp survival knife that hung upside down from his combat harness. He kept his washed out and stained OD green towel, even though it carried its own vile stench and pulled it around the back his neck. He got rid of his M-148; under the M-16, barrel grenade launcher and was back to lugging around an M-79, which he kept strapped to his pack, with a pouch of 40 mm rounds. His well-scratched up E-tool was also strapped to his pack. He placed his meal of beans & weenies into the top of his rucksack for his first meal. Once finished, he nodded once and then strapped it closed. Matthew then looked to John and asked him, "Are you ready, Bro'?"

John gave him a hard look and asked, "Do my toe offer still sound so stupid?"

Matthew chuckled and replied, "Not with your aim, I'd lose a whole foot and we'd both be stomping around the prison yard on crutches."

Humidity was on the rise and it kept a steady pace with the temperature. Jose wiped his forehead and slung his M-60 strap over his shoulder. He then watched Campbell approach the squad, his shotgun, hung at his side.

"You keep that pig ready, Compadre. We'll be in a real shooting war soon enough." Campbell then turned to address the whole squad, "This is their playground, their home field an' they know everything there is to know about this choice neighborhood. So, keep a sharp eye out for spider holes, snipers an' all forms of booby traps designed to maim and kill you. Keep your intervals when we start climbing. We will go slowly, to watch for traps, but I'd hate to lose two or three of you because you got bunched up. Watch for my hand signals and those coming down the line. If there's an explosion, no one moves until I tell you. If I'm dead, Isaac takes over. Then it goes to Matthew here." Campbell then pointed to Isaac, "You're up front." He then pointed to Baxley, "And you're on tail, but just remember 3rd squad will be right behind you."

Campbell checked his wristwatch and quickly wrapped things up, "No talking. Limit your water consumption. Above all, stay alive. This is a rotten place to get yourself killed for." Campbell gave each man a once over, adjusted Andrews' pack with a jerk and then went over to join up with Lt. Sinclair for a final briefing. "Five-yard intervals at all times and always remembers the enemy can slip in between you if you're not vigilant."

A couple minutes later, Captain Sampson sent the order of movement down the line, "D Company, move out." Lt. Sinclair added his bit too, "We've got ten hours to take this hill, let's make it in nine!"

Isaac frowned, "What's that man been smokin'?" But he was only loud enough for Campbell and Matthew to hear him.

"The L-T has big expectations. I only hope he doesn't pave the way with our blood to meet his timetable," Campbell replied. For his remark, he received a look of surprise from both Matthew and John. It was the first time either of them had heard Campbell say anything against the lieutenant.

I think Campbell's scared, at least now I know he's human 'cause this place terrifies me. Not sure why--just another hill like Dong Agai...but something...there's a strange darkness...I don't understand it. But I sure wish I was somewhere else. Matthew couldn't escape the feeling something bad was going to happen and it reminded him of how Jose felt a couple days ago. *Gotta shake this gloom and doom off.*

Prior to the next ground assault, Hill 937 shook under the combined bombardment of air attacks and artillery. Not a tree was left standing upon the summit or for 50 yards down the hillsides. Craters blasted into the earth covered most of the ground and it caused a once thriving mountaintop to look diseased, pot marked and very dead.

INSIDE AP BIA MOUNTAIN, MAY 12TH, 1969 1005 HOURS

The mountain top rumbled from relentless attacks and Medic Que fought to save the life of his cousin, Corporal Tse Le-Tung Que. The two of them were related through his mother's sister. The wounded soldier had sustained a severe injury--a gaping hole in his shoulder caused by a 20 mm round. Que attempted to clean the wound and he looked up when the doctor approached for a cursory exam. "Have him placed with the dead."

Que objected, "But sir, my cousin still lives," Que pleaded with the doctor, while he attempted to hide the defiance in his eyes.

An NVA sergeant who was lightly wounded from bomb fragments to his left arm, walked up and requested the doctor go on about his business, "I know this man, sir, please let me handle this." The weary doctor, who had been on his feet for more than 30-hours, glanced between the sergeant and Que. Then the officer nodded his head and walked off. He badly needed a cigarette and a breath of fresh air.

The sergeant addressed two volunteer orderlies, "You two, assist me by carrying our comrade to the other room. Be careful, he has suffered great pain."

Que remained mute while his cousin was lifted and moved to the room for the dead. He ignored the orderly's expressions when they recoiled from the stench of death and lowered Corporal Que to the floor. Only a shallow whimper escaped the wounded man as they removed the bamboo stretcher from beneath him--it was needed elsewhere. The sergeant shielded his nose and mouth with a rag, and then entered the room. Before Que could interfere, the sergeant pulled out his pistol and pointed it at Corporal Que's head and pulled the trigger.

"No!" Que screamed in horror and the two orderlies quickly stepped in to grasp him by the arms and hold him back before he could attack the sergeant. His pistol holstered, the sergeant faced Que and ordered the two men to let him go. But Que didn't attack him. He only stood there and stared down at the body of his dead cousin.

Though he was in pain, the old sergeant looked into Que's eyes and said, "I have fought with this man through many battles and found him to be a man of great courage. He would have wanted it this way…as I would have also. So do your jobs well, medic, for this will be a hard fight and many of us will die before it is over." With that, the sergeant wrapped a bloody rag around his arm wound and walked away to disappear into the tunnel.

Does this mean I should begin shooting all my wounded? What do they expect of me? I joined to save lives, not watch them be murdered by my countrymen. Que returned to his other patients and listened with sympathy to the deep moans and soft whimpers of the wounded. He cursed this war and the Americans for the pain they caused and the feeling of heartache deep within his chest.

D COMPANY/ 2ND SQUAD, A SHAU VALLEY, MAY 12TH, 1969 1010 HOURS

"Medic…Medic!" The call was relayed down the line from man to man. A soldier from 1st squad, 1st platoon, had fallen, a victim to a sniper when D Company began its climb to the ridgeline. The platoon medic came at the run and reached the wounded man, while three others crouched over him.

"Give me room!" The medic ordered. He had to push two of the concerned men away so he could begin his work. "It's Gus!" One of the men said. He was shoved back by the medic, but he had already looked down upon his buddy and tears came to his eyes. He saw the front of Gus's shirt stained a dark red in color and noticed his chest no longer rose to breathe in the foul air of the valley floor. The medic checked for a pulse and when he found none, he quickly checked the man's eyes and found them already fixed and dilated.

"Sorry, guys, Gus is gone." The man who stood above them shouted, "No, you gotta work on him. That's Gus. He's my bud. We we're goin' home next month for R & R and I was gonna meet his little sister...That's Gus, man!" The man dropped down beside his friend's body and began to weep.

Meanwhile, the medic began the sad duty of filling out a body tag and afterward, he removed one of the dog tags for the lieutenant to have. "Steady there, partner. You got to go on. Your buddy here would want you too. I'll take care of him, don't worry," the medic said. He looked to the squad leader and gestured to him with a wave of the hand. "You want to give me a hand here, Sarge and get these guys moving before I've got half-a-dozen here beside ol' Gus."

Other men stopped to look at the body of their friend and it prompted the sergeant from 3rd Squad into action, "You jerks wanna stand aroun' in a circle to mourn your buddy? I'm sure the NVA will do their best to put you right down beside him in the same condition! Now move out!" Then with a quick, but casual salute to this fallen soldier, the squad leader pushed and shoved his men forward to keep the line from getting jammed up. The rest of D Company filed on by, each man looking down upon the body of Spec 4 Augustus Langtry, a 20-year old from Montgomery, Alabama. Tomorrow or the next day, his parents would receive notification of their son's untimely death. The pain didn't stop with Gus's last breath. It would continue on for years to come.

When Matthew gazed down upon Gus, he couldn't help but wonder, *what you were thinking about in those last moments of life. One second you're climbin' up some dirt trail in Viet Nam an' then bam! You're dead.*

Up ahead, the point had an eye out for Gus's killer. But the NVA were a tricky lot, experts in the art of camouflage and patience. When another shot rang out, this one wounded a man toward the front and he went down with a scream. When his squad leader rushed up, the man's right leg was bleeding and clearly broken. The sergeant pulled out a large battle dressing and pressed it hard down upon the wound to stop the bleeding. Again the call went out, "Medic! Medic!"

This time the sniper had made a deadly mistake- two men from the point element had spotted him. "Spider hole!" They raced up the rocky hillside and shoved aside a grass mat that revealed a trapped NVA. The two soldiers stared into the frightened eyes of their enemy, while he shrieked in panic with his hands up in surrender or simply a reaction to being caught unaware. They felt no compassion for the man and pointed their rifles at him. While others watched, the two men wore an expression of cold indifference as they both emptied half a magazine into the man who had wounded their comrade and had probably killed their friend. Revenge or retribution, or was it only a sad aspect of war that was covered under an eye for an eye?

Andrews stood off the trail and waited as the wounded man was carried by. Sweat dripped off Farm Boy, while he swatted at persistent mosquitoes that follow his every move. Soon, D Company was brought to a halt when 1st platoon's point man raised his hand to signal a stop. The rest of the men took a breather and kept an eye on the surrounding trees. Lt. Sinclair, staying in a low crouch, moved up to see why forward movement had ceased.

"Sir, ah didn't want ta keep movin' forward 'til yuh could see this," the corporal on point said. He then slowly moved up, turned a bend in the trail and abruptly stopped with Lt. Sinclair right behind him. In front of them lay a huge ravine with a narrowing river at the bottom of it. "Gap looks to be about 100…maybe 125-yards wide and I'd say the climb down is close to two hundred feet or more. Not too far to go and the river looks shallow, but this embankment has me worried," the young corporal said.

"You were right to stop," Lt. Sinclair said. *Embankment? Looks like a cliff to me.* "I need to give the CO a chance to see this before we go any further. By the sound of things, it looks as if B Company is hitting strong resistance up ahead." Lt. Sinclair scanned the area around with binoculars and listened to all the shooting up the mountain, "Hang tough for a few minutes while I send for the CO. I'll have a couple men come up to keep you company, but don't go any further." Lt. Sinclair ordered and then disappeared back down the trail.

Enjoying the rest, Campbell looked down the line to check on Baxley. *Tough climb for a new guy, better keep a closer eye on him.* Campbell stopped wondering about Baxley when Captain Sampson passed him by without even a *How you doin'?* Campbell looked down at his shotgun and took his towel from off around his neck to wipe the weapon down.

A moment later, D Company began to move again and always upward. Campbell reached the bend in the trail and saw how they were now forced to circumvent a rocky outcropping and the sight the ravine and the 25 to 30 degree slopes worried him. Plus, they would then have to cross that river, all while completely exposed to any enemy forces in the area. Studying the ravine, Campbell can't help but wonder if the NVA were waiting on the other side, "Perfect spot for an ambush, L-T."

Lt. Sinclair shot him a dirty look and said, "Can it, Campbell. You know the orders," He then fell silent when Sampson began to speak to 1st and 2nd Squads, as they began to bunch up a top the knoll.

A moment later, Sampson addressed the 3rd Squad leader and his men, "Pass it down the line, everyone take five, keep your intervals and stay sharp." Captain Sampson then continued talking after taking a single sip from his canteen, "All right, I know this looks hard, but we have no choice but to go on. To assist B Company, we must move forward and that means crossing that ravine; which for some reason isn't even on my map. We'll cross one squad at a time, leaving one squad up here for fire support. We'll keep a 60-team here at all times to keep that hillside under fire if problems result. Once across, 1st Squad will set up on top that knoll and stay in position until the entire company is across."

Overhead, a flight of gray Marine F-4 fighter-bombers zoomed by and made a bomb run upon the summit. The men watch the aircraft release their bombs. Though the trees above prevent them from seeing the explosions, they feel the earth vibrate when hundreds of pounds of TNT detonate.

"Campbell, your squad will pull security while 1st squad climbs down," Captain Sampson ordered. "Then each squad will cover the one before. The rest of you move back, keep the line single file. I don't want this whole company all grouped together like a set of bowling pins." Sampson then stepped back to watch 1st squad begin their climb down into the ravine. "Jose, you set up your gun over there," Campbell pointed to a large rock outcropping. This gave Jose a good line of fire against the opposing slope. "Kendal, Adams and Baxley, you three set up on my left. Washington, you and Riley on my right. Now keep your eyes open for any movement or reflection, there could be a whole company of NVA over there and we wouldn't know it." Unhappy about it, Campbell quickly directed them into position.

While they maintained a vigilant eye for the enemy, 1st squad descended with one careful step after another. Before long, they slide down on their butts, struggling to maintain their balance and keep control of their weapons. When the sides of the ravine become even steeper, the men had to stop, while the man in front was forced to climb down the last 20 feet with his backside glued to the embankment. No one thought to bring a rope, mainly because somehow the ravine wasn't identified on any of the U.S. Army topographical maps.

Then it was 2nd Squad's turn to climb down, while 3rd Squad moved in to replace them on the knoll. Isaac went first, followed by John, Baxley, Jose, Andrews, Riley, Matthew and then Campbell. When he hit the steeper parts,

Matthew was forced to grab for clumps of grass, rocks, a small bush here and there, and any tree roots he could clutch on to. Twice he tore his pants on sharp rocks and his hands and arms bled from dozens of small scratches and scrapes. When they dropped the last five feet to the floor of the ravine, they quickly took up fire positions near the riverbed and ducked behind several rock formations and large piles of driftwood logs brought down the ravine during heavy rains.

Still on their side of the river, 1st and 2nd squads remained spread out while they waited for the rest of the platoon. Once the remainder of 1st platoon had joined up, offering a good protective field of fire in the event the enemy showed up, Captain Sampson ordered the next platoon down and finally the rest of the company reached the bottom. Sampson had the men spread out along the riverbed for a ten-minute rest. The climb down was stressful and they still had the climb up ahead of them. Sampson ordered Sinclair to set up a defense position up riverbed and down river both. "We'll cross the river once the men have rested."

Lt. Sinclair looked both ways before he agreed, "Yes, sir." Sinclair then pointed to his squad leaders and issued orders, "First Squad, down river twenty-five yards...Second Squad, up river twenty-five yards. Let's move it!"

While the security positions were set up, a company of NVA silently moved in to position themselves on the opposing ridgeline. They had attempted to flank the Americans with plans to eventually attack the enemy's CP at nightfall. But when their advance scouts came across D Company down in the ravine, the NVA company commander couldn't believe his good fortune. The ridgeline, which set 60 to 70 feet above the river bed and was heavily covered over in foliage to hide the enemy. This provided more than adequate cover for the enemy to move in unnoticed by the Americans. The NVA Company Commander had planned to use the river bed for easy access through the ridges, instead, when he found an American unit at the bottom and his men now holding the higher ground, he couldn't turn away from this opportunity. Still, the American's air power concerned him, but with hand signals, he silently directed his men into position along the ridge.

Captain Sampson couldn't escape his feelings of uneasiness or the simple fact he had placed his men in a very poor situation at best. *I'd better get some men up that slope, we're sittin' ducks down here.* "Lieutenant Sinclair, move your two remaining squads across the river an' up that hill. I want fire support up there while we bring the rest of the company up."

Lt. Sinclair nodded his head and replied, "Yes, Sir, I'll get 'em movin' right now." He ordered 3rd and 4th squad into the water.

Less than three feet deep; its current flowing gently over the rock bed, it doesn't take the two squads long to cross the narrow span and begin their climb up the steep embankment. Up above, concealed by thick shrubbery, the NVA await their commander's order, 'Open fire." When he saw the Americans advance, he waved his hand. Captain Sampson's worst fear became a nightmarish reality. An RPG was fired from above; shooting through the air; exploding in the middle of the river. The blast, only a few feet from where Lt. Roundtree and two of his squad leaders stood let the Americans know they had been ambushed. The firefight was on.

"Take cover!" Sampson ordered, while he pointed to out enemy positions along the ridgeline, shouting, "Return fire...Return fire!"

Killed instantly, Lt. Roundtree's lifeless body was thrown back against a large boulder by the concussion wave. He sank beneath the water. Sgt. Engles was nearly cut in half by shrapnel. The other squad leader, Sgt. Madia had severe upper body wounds. Madia crawled behind a driftwood log. Using his one good arm and a strained voice, he shouted, "Medic-Medic!"

Men dropped everywhere. Some wounded by the hail of fire and exploding shrapnel from RPGs. Others dive for ground cover to escape a wave of enemy bullets from above. Captain Sampson, visualizing his command being wiped out, grabbed his RTO by his radio pack's strap, physically dragging him behind the cover of a large deadfall. Seizing the radio handset, he took his map out to locate his exact coordinates. After a brief moment, with bullets zinging about; striking rock and wood debris around him, he frantically called for air support. His frightened RTO continued shooting wildly at an enemy he couldn't see.

"I need fire support on the following grid coordinates and hurry, man! We're taking heavy fire!" Sampson read off the numbers, while fighting to remain in control of his company. He watched his world explode around him. Second squad opened up from their position up river and under Campbell's direction. They began wading across the river waters. "Washington, get across an' lay down some fire. Jose, you an' Farm Boy next...an' get that pig workin'!" Campbell gave Jose a hard look; making a mad dash for a pile of rocks on the other side of the river. But he didn't make it. A bullet struck the heel of his left boot, sending him tumbling face first through two feet of water. His helmet flew during the fall; his head bounced off a submerged log. For a brief moment he resembled a huge walrus rolling through the water. The impact rendered him unconscious. He lay face down in the river--drowning.

When Isaac saw Campbell go down, he yelled for cover fire; running back into the water to help him. An NVA rifleman, waiting for such an opportunity, sighted him in and Isaac fell backward when three bullets slammed him in the chest and shoulders.

Without a cry, Spec 4 Isaac Washington fell into the water and lay still. The Bronze Star he was to be awarded for saving Jack Waterford's life so many weeks ago would be awarded posthumously.

Stunned by Isaac's death, Matthew then went into action, springing from behind cover; sprinting forward. This was his best-ever broken field running. He side-stepped rocks, dashed across narrow sections of sandy beach, and leapt over washed out trees before entering the water near Campbell. With arms in the air to keep his weapon from getting wet, he didn't bother to take the time to return fire. He miraculously reached Campbell without being shot. Winded from his run, Matthew slid his hands under the big man's arms, flipping Campbell on to his back to get his face out of the water. He yelled to Jose, "Give me covering fire!"

Jose hollered back, "What you think ah'm doin' here!?"

Matthew grabbed Campbell by his combat harness. With some exertion, he dragged Campbell to cover behind a large boulder; all the while bullets impacted the water around him. "Give me some help here?" Matthew yelled. His eyes clinched shut as he struggled to move the big sergeant.

Seeing how much trouble his friends were in, Jose grabbed Andrews by the shoulder, telling him to take over the M-60. He reached for a LAW. "Keep shootin' Farm Boy," Jose said, while he assembled the LAW for firing.

Andrews raked the ridgeline back and forth with long bursts; hoping to force the enemy's heads down to give Matthew a chance. Jose got the LAW ready, placing it on his right shoulder; aiming for a point of impact several feet below the center of the opposing ridgeline. When ready-- making sure Andrews wasn't behind him to get burned by the round's blast — he aimed and fired. The large explosive rocket burst from the weapon in a fiery explosion; roaring across the river; stiking the embankment. The blast sent a massive wave of dirt and debris, providing a cloud; enabling Matthew a few seconds to get Campbell behind the rocks.

Andrews, crawling on his stomach, moved the M-60 to a log. Jose took over. He was in the midst of burning off a 100 round belt of ammo when Andrews shouted, "Go, Matt!" Jose shouted, "Get your head down!"

Jose pulled Andrews back behind the log. Farm Boy Andrews was nearly hit when an AK-47 bullet struck the spot where he had been only seconds before. Jose saved him and he knew it. He was too busy to even say thank you. Andrews picked up his M-16, supporting Matthew with one-handed rifle fire, while he using his other hand to keep the M-60 belt flowing freely.

An NVA soldier fell off the ridge top, rolling down the steep slope, landing near the water edge. Jose shouted, "Gotcha!"

The walls of the ravine prevented Sampson from getting a clear signal to the CP. "Say again, Delta-One," the Command Post (CP) RTO said. He couldn't understand the message due to static. Disgusted, Sampson turned to Lt. Sinclair and Lt. Olson, "Get your men moving down river before we lose the entire company." Lt. Olson was confused by the order. "Lieutenant, I can't get air cover while were in this valley and we can't climb out. Our only choice is to follow the river down the hill until we can find a good position to make a stand. I'll stay here with two squads from Sinclair's platoon, while you get the rest of the men out."

"Brian, it's my job to stay," Sinclair said. He had already lost three men he knew were dead and didn't want to abandon the wounded. Captain Sampson admired Sinclair's courage, but he didn't have time for it.

"Obey my order, Lieutenant. I got us into this mess and Lt. Roundtree's dead...along with others. Now you get his platoon moving!"

In response, Lt. Sinclair growled a, "Yes, sir." He moved up the beach line in a low crouch, taking cover when possible, issuing orders for 1st and 2nd squad to stay with Captain Sampson, while taking 3rd and 4th squads and the remnants of 2nd platoon with him.

Captain Sampson, his RTO beside him, watched the men move down river, jumping from one point of cover to the next and all the while, returning fire. Sampson then yelled out to Campbell's 2nd Squad, "Campbell, can you hear me?"

Matthew shouted back, "He's banged up, Sir," He hoped the captain could hear him over the weapon's fire. *Its like we're in a big shooting gallery and we're the clay pigeons.*

Captain Sampson shook his head in frustration, heavy sweat dripping from his brow; his hands clammy. He tightened his grasp on his rifle, making a single hand gesture toward the upper ridgeline; he shouted to Kendal, "Keep your heads down an' keep firing at the enemy's flanks."

Sampson gave his RTO a reassuring wink, before he shouting to 1st squad, ordering them to take up positions behind a long pile of logs and a dam of river rocks. "We're holding here while the rest of the company moves down river," Sampson told them.

Heavy machine gun fire continued raining down upon them, assisted by RPG and AK-47's. Bullets ricocheted off rocks. The stony beach became a death trap. The dead and wounded lay where they fell. It was far too risky to recover the bodies. Two men from Roundtree's platoon were wounded when they attempted rescuing a fallen medic. Now, all three lay in the water, their blood turning the water crimson red, as they called out, "Medic-

-Medic!" But no one came. The last available platoon medic was down with a chest wound. His wounded buddies struggled to keep his face above the surging waters.

Yet, they can't leave the wounded. So, five brave soldiers jumped up from behind cover, racing into the river to retrieve the wounded medic and the others from the river bed. Seeing the movement, 1st and 2nd squads opened fire on the hillside using full automatic fire. The five men high stepped through the water; two falling from miss-steps on hidden rocks. They picked themselves up and all five made it to the wounded. They roughly grabbed the three men between them by their battle harnesses, pulling them back to safety in a heroic effort.

Lt. Olson sent one squad back for those wounded men on the beach. With all their wounded in tow, the rest of D Company followed their captain's orders, moving down river. They stopped frequently to return fire along the way.

"I need ammo!" Jose shouted. He was on his last belt. The only other ammo was a single belt wrapped around Isaac's body. Three more NVA bodies lay spread out on the slope on the other side of the river, victims to Jose's accuracy with an M-60. Over 50 yards away, Sampson continued his attempts to make contact with Battalion or anyone else.

"It's no good, sir," The RTO advised. "Keep tryin', maybe a FAC bird will pick up the signal or Lt. Sinclair will get through downriver." With a sickened feeling in his gut, Sampson gazed upon the bodies in the river. "My fault...should've sent a patrol across right away to take the high ground. These men are dead because I didn't do my job!" Trembling from a mixture of fear, guilt, adrenaline rush and rage, Sampson struck the boulder in front of him with a closed fist. The pain felt good.

"Sir, a squad would've been wiped out...That's at least a full company up there," the RTO told Sampson. He wanted to reassure Sampson; though his words were ignored.

"Keep trying, son," Sampson told his RTO.

"I will, sir." *Not like I got anything else to do. And to think I could've gone into the Navy with my cousin?*

Campbell was now conscious. He grimaced, releasing a painful sigh as Matthew dropped him on the ground. The water Campbell swallowed gushed out. He pushed himself to his hands and knees, allowing the last drops to empty from him. The worst over, Campbell turned to a sitting position. He immediately spotted Isaac's body lying in the water only a few yards away. "What happened?" Matthew briefed him while changing magazines and reloading Campbell's shotgun. Because he had the sling looped over his neck, Campbell hadn't lost the weapon when he went down.

Campbell's face remained unchanged. Matthew saw the man's true feelings through his watery red eyes. "He was coming for you, Sarge...bravest thing I ever saw." Campbell remained mute; staring at Isaac's body. Matthew continued reloading his shotgun.

"Five dead men, five," Sampson said. He fell back against the boulder; staring at the sky. "Sir, the Company is moving out of range," The RTO said. He hoped to get Sampson's mind back in the game. *C'mon, Cap...Don't flip out on us now.*

While providing cover fire for the retreat, Riley got shot in the left arm by an AK-47. He bounced off a rock wall; falling to the ground on his side. Baxley moved to Riley's side; quickly wrapping a field dressing around the arm, while Riley bit his towel to stifle his cry. With only two squads to shoot down at, the NVA began to pick and choose targets; while intensifing their firing.

Knowing the squad needed M-60 ammo to survive Andrews slowly crawled from behind a log, snaking his way into the water, reaching for Isaac's body. He hoped the NVA would take him for another casualty if he moved slowly enough through the surging waters. His hopes are shattered when a bullet impacted only inches from his face. He jerked back. Knowing he had no other choice, he leapt to his feet, making a mad dash to reach Isaac. Stumbling over river rocks, he fell once. Then he was close enough to dive forward into the shallow water only a couple feet from where Isaac lay. He scrambled to Isaac's body; while bullets hit all around him--one impacting Isaac's upper body--he wrestled to free the ammo belt. He was forced to use Isaac's lifeless body for cover. *I'll be back for you, I promise.* Soaked through and through, Andrews exhaled deeply; springing from the water, running a zigzag pattern, making him a more difficult target to hit. With only a few steps to go, he leapt into the air to clear a large boulder, somersaulting across the hard ground, he collided with a bewildered Jose.

"You is one stupid farm boy," Jose said. He then added, "Mucho brave, but so very stupid." Jose gratefully accepted the belt and fed it into his machine gun. Andrews leaned against a boulder, catching his breath. With an expressional leer of vengeance on his face, the little bandito began to raking the upper slope with carefully aimed three and four-round bursts.

The rest of the company vanished from view. Campbell moved to where Sampson and his RTO were positioned. Upon reaching Captain Sampson, he heard Lt. Sinclair's voice from down river, yelling for cover fire. Both Captain Sampson and Campbell were surprised by Lt. Sinclair charging back up river like an All-Pro fullback. "Cover him!" Captain Sampson ordered the two besieged rifle squads. Twice Sinclair went down, each time he pulling himself back up, continuing to trudge forward, finally collapsing, out of breath, between Sampson and Campbell. Winded, exhausted, but apparently unhurt, he stared into the angry eyes of his commander. "Don't you know how to obey an order, Lieutenant?"

Lt. Sinclair's reply was mumbled, "I...I wanted to be with my men, Sir. The...company's safe...set up a good DP down there, Sir...and called for air support." Lt. Sinclair returned Sampson's glare with a strange faraway gaze that escaped Captain Sampson's notice for the moment.

Captain Sampson nodded his head twice, raising his rifle, firing off a quick burst over the boulder he was using for cover. In return, NVA fire splintered a large log near them. A five-inch piece of wood imbedded itself in the RTO's thigh. The young lad screamed, thrashing about, exposing himself to fire. Captain Sampson and Campbell, both grabbing the man, wrestled him back behind cover. The RTO bit his lip to fight off the pain, drawing blood. Sampson held the man's leg in place, while Campbell cut the splinter free, placing a battle dressing around the wound.

"First purple heart?" Campbell asked the grimacing RTO. The man only nodded his head, in response. His eyes filled with tears. Captain Sampson glanced around checking the men's positions. Grudgingly, he knew they couldn't move without air support. Putting his hands together around his mouth, forming a chamber, he shouted, "Stay under cover, only shoot when you have a target."

Realizing Lt. Sinclair had been unusually quiet, Sampson looked him over. Sampson decided the run through the enemy's gauntlet frightened Lt. Sinclair more than he showed. *Can't believe you came back, more gumption and loyalty to your men than I gave you credit for.* Lt. Olson raised the Battalion CP on his fifth try of changing positions. Fifteen minutes later, a flight of A1-Es made a run on the NVA position. With the Americans so close to the enemy, the aircraft couldn't use bombs or rockets. They strafed the upper slope with .50 caliber machine gun fire. Hundreds of rounds pounded the earth, sending terrified NVA fleeing in all directions. Seeing the enemy too occupied to shoot at his men, Captain Sampson ordered his men down river to hold; while the rest of the company moved down river to join them. NVA survivors headed up the mountain. They wouldn't bother D Company for awhile. John and Baxley carried Riley, while Matthew provided cover fire. This left Campbell an opportunity to attempt reaching Isaac's body. Captain Sampson, seeing what Campbell was thinking, shouted loudly, "Campbell, leave that man! We've got to get these men out while we have air cover. We'll come back for our dead later."

Freezing in his tracks, river water splashing around his knees; Campbell forgot the NVA. He turned, facing Sampson with a defiant look. "Sergeant, I promise you, we'll be back for all of them," Sampson said more quietly. Campbell turned, looking at Isaac's body; then faced Captain

Sampson, reluctantly nodded his head in understanding, he rushed back to the water's edge.

From log pile to boulder, the men moved from the ambush site. Captain Sampson half-carryied his wounded RTO. Jose--out of ammo again--slung his now useless M-60 over his shoulder, reached down to pick up Lt. Roundtree's M-16. "C'mon, Farm Boy, time to leave dis place," Jose said. He led. Andrews, visibly shaken from Isaac's death, followed. The two squads left this place of death. The enemy scattered. Only an occasional shot rang out as the two squads proceeded down river.

Twenty minutes later, Sampson was relieved, seeing Lt. Olson and his company intact. Six wounded men lay on the ground, attended to by their buddies. "Lieutenant Olson, take two squads down river and cut out an LZ. We need to get these men on a medivac. If they can't make it down through the trees, maybe they can lower a basket. Just see what you can find down there." Sampson said. He knelt on one knee, catching his breath. He looked into weary eyes and exhausted faces of his men, who had stood their ground. He was proud of them.

"Thanks, men. You guys really earned your pay today. And I meant what I said...we will go back for our dead." Not waiting or expecting a reply, Captain Sampson stood up, walking over to check on his wounded RTO. Captain Sampson received minor wounds to both arms from flying debris and for the moment he ignored them. With each step he took, he felt the weight of guilt for those dead men he had left along the river. *I made a major mistake back there and my men suffered for it, I won't do that again...But what do I say to myself about those boys I lost? They'll haunt me for the rest of my life and I deserve it. They entrusted me with their lives and I blew it!*

Lt. Olson set up the DP on a curve in the river bed. The river water lay to their northwest. It wasn't long before the first sniper opened up on them, wounding a man from 2nd Platoon. The company returned fire. A sixty-gunner from 2nd Platoon expended a long burst. Once again, an eerie stillness fell over the mountainside. It doesn't last long. Thirty-five minutes later Captain Sampson was in radio contact with the helicopter pilot flying overhead. With the thick trees, the pilot reported he couldn't see the river or D Company. With such thick foliage, the pilot couldn't land, finding their position when Lt. Olson popped a blue smoke grenade, after hearing the distinct *whump-whump-whump* sound of the Huey overhead. A bush cutter was lowered first--a saw used to cut a path through the heavy canopy. A moment later, an empty basket pushed its way through. A man yelled out when he saw it coming down. Gently, the first man was carried over and loaded into the basket. Word was then given over the radio, "Secure, take him up." Captain Sampson said and then handed the handset back to his wounded RTO.

When the basket lifted off the ground, Captain Sampson called SSgt. Franklin over, "You're taking over Lt. Roundtree's platoon...You have any problem with that?"

Franklin looked at his filthy boots, then back into the dark face of his captain, saying, "Only got one, sir." Franklin said, "I don't have to become no officer, do I?"

Captain Sampson grinned on the right side of his face--the left side was bruised. He replied, "No sergeant, I wouldn't wish that fate on you."

Franklin agreed, adding, "Sorry 'bout Lieutenant Roundtree, Captain. He was a good man...I'll do my best."

Captain Sampson patted him on the arm, saying, "I know you will."

WITH THE NVA ON THE RIDGELINE

The NVA Commander limped from a ghastly leg wound, moving the remnants of his company across the ridgeline trying to stay parallel with the river. Keeping his point element out front to keep the enemy within sight, he waited for the last stragglers to drift in. Several were wounded by the air attack; others were still missing and presumed dead. What he saw in front of him brought a feeling of deep satisfaction. From his vantage point on the upper ridge, he observed an American helicopter hovering over the tree canopy, lowering a rescue basket through the trees. With less than 30 men left in his company, a dozen walking-wounded; he knew he couldn't stage an effective ground attack that his mission called for. But taking out a helicopter wouldn't be much trouble at all. When he thought about all the men he had lost--more than 40 soldiers--the red-cross painted on the sides of the Huey meant little to him. A jolt of extreme pain shot through him. The NVA commander looked down at his bloody bandage. He knew he was going to lose the leg. Knowing he'd most likely never see his home in North Viet Nam ever again, he grew angry. He reached down rubbing the foul smelling bandage on his leg. He glared at the American helicopter with contempt. No, he had no mercy for this medical helicopter and gave the order for one of his best RPG men to come forward. He positioned the sergeant with the RPG beside him. "Kneel down; take aim, but do not fire until I give the order."

When the NVA commander saw the basket vanish in the treetops, he tapped the anxious sergeant on the shoulder saying, "No, not yet, sergeant. Wait for my order." He wanted to make the Americans suffer, to avenge the death of his men. "We'll wait for the basket to come back up." He watched through icy cold deep brown eyes, observing the helicopter's crew chief hang outside the Huey, one foot on the skid; a gloved hand guiding the cable holding the basket. When the basket broke through the upper tree tops, the commander tapped his sergeant on the shoulder a second time and ordered, "Fire!"

ON BOARD THE HUEY

The 24-year old co-pilot, a young warrant officer from Salcha, Alaska, kept an eye on the basket as it cleared the canopy, the 25-year old pilot, a 1st Lieutenant from Seattle, Washington, scanned the surrounding area. He turned to his left when the ignition flash of the RPG alerted him. He spotted three NVA troops on the upper ridge. He was about to shout a warning when his blue eyes locked on the missile coming straight at them, "Oh, my god!" Before the co-pilot could turn to see what the problem was, the Huey exploded in a fiery ball of flame. The rocket propelled grenade impacted on the helicopter's nose, killing both pilot and co-pilot instantly. The blast's concussion wave threw the 20-year old crew chief off the skid; his flaming body coming to a sharp jerk, when he reached the end of his burning safety-belt. He hung in the mid-air below a dying bird, his screams of terror and pain startling the jungle critters below.

D COMPANY

Eyes wide in disbelief and their ears filled with the sound of the explosion, the men of D Company watched dazed as the burning helicopter plummeted through the trees. First, the basket carrying the wounded man dropped through the tree tops. The men below heard shrieks of the terrified man in the basket. The burning crew chief came next--engulfed in orange and yellow flames, flapping his arms in a wild frenzy in an effort to put them out. When the helicopter hit the tree tops, its fall was halted briefly by the upper branches. The cable and safety belts snap off the basket assembly, freeing both the crew chief and wounded man to fall to their deaths. They bounced off the lower branches like silver balls shot through a pinball game; then, fall to the ground with a sickening thud-like sound.

Stunned by what they have witnessed; the soldiers look up as they hear the helicopter break its way down through the trees. Amidst a bellow of black smoke, the flames of the dying bird set the treetops on fire. "Get out of the way, it's comin' down!" Lt. Olson yelled.

Terrified men try escaping the huge fireball; the air filled with the sounds of the Huey ripping and tearing the branches away from towering trees. Then the dead Huey struck the ground with tremendous force, bouncing twice, breaking the Huey's spine, propelling the blackened bodies of the dead pilots through the broken windshields. The Army pilots of the 1st Cavalry landed in a broken heap, 30-feet from the burning hull of their once proud bird.

The on-board medic, killed in the initial blast, was thrown from the bird while it descended. His body hung in the branches over 50 feet in the air. Shrapnel from the exploding Huey blasted in a 360-degree radius, snapping several trees at various heights like a wild logger with a chainsaw, sending them to the ground like guided missiles. Boulders the size of beach balls and smaller were tossed about and the large rotor blades--which were bent at several points from the fall--bounce off the ground rotating one final time. The blade action kills two of Olson's men, instantly in grisly fashion. Two others are struck by debris; one man hit by a large rock that sending him tumbling head over heel, the other caught in the back by a chunk of deadfall.

Captain Sampson pulled himself from the ground. The scene before him left him speechless...Dozens of trees on fire...Debris covered nearly an acre of ground...Bodies of dead and wounded scattered...The call for medic echoes over and over.

SSgt. Franklin picked himself up. A small log flying through the air caught him in the gut, knocking the air out of him. He rubbed his stomach. In a quiet pain-filled voice, he ordered, "Check...Check the wounded. Move stretcher cases over...over there." Franklin pointed to an open area to his left, well away from burning trees and smoldering helicopter frame.

"Where's my RTO?" Sampson asked when his voice returned.

"Right here, sir," His RTO said, limping over. Contacting Battalion, Sampson advised them of what happened. He requested air support to hit the ridgeline above their position. Once the wounded are all collected, the men go about the painful task of gathering up the bodies. For nearly fifteen minutes the area is quiet, except for the moans of the wounded. Leaning against a tree, Matthew was suddenly thrown backwards. A sniper's bullet smacked the tree only a couple inches from his head.

"Sniper!" Jose yelled out, as he dove for cover behind a pile of rocks. The hillside across the river came alive with automatic fire as NVA riflemen open up. "Take cover and return fire!" Sampson ordered; an order repeated by both Olson and Franklin. Not Sinclair, he remained silent. He sat on a log watching the men move around him. His peculiar actions concerned Sgt. Campbell.

With bullets ricocheting from rocks and trees, a man from Sinclair's 3rd squad cried out after getting zapped in the shoulder. M-79s come into play. The distance is too great for the 40 mm grenades to be effective. Jose lay behind a boulder, cursing up a storm for being out of M-60 ammo and after a short burst, Lt. Roundtree's M-16 was now empty too. With nothing else to shoot with, he pulled his .45 from its holster, chambered a round, with a defiant look, he popped up, emptied a seven-round magazine at the upper hillside. In response, two AK-47 bullets struck the rock face in front of him.

Seeing Jose's foolish stunt, Andrews grabbed Jose by his web belt, yanking him down. "Who do you think you are, Pancho Via?" Jose was too angry to speak. He sat on the ground in a frump. Andrews retrieved a loaded M-16 magazine from his pack, tossing it into Jose's lap. "Here, jus' remember you owe me one fully loaded clip." Not bothering to say thanks, Jose slapped the magazine into Lt. Roundtree's rifle, chambered a round, takes his pent up rage out on the enemy's position.

For ten long minutes the firefight rages with D Company holding its own. Lt. Sinclair, stands, waving his pistol around, decided it was time for offensive action. "First Platoon, fix bayonets!" Sinclair ordered, giving Campbell instructions, "We're gonna take that hill, sergeant. Have your squad lead off…cross that river an' charge that hill."

Hearing the order Sinclair shouted out, Captain Sampson dashed to the lieutenant's side, "Are you insane?" Captain Sampson looked to the men, "Stay down an' shoot only when you have a target. Don't waste your ammo." Ignoring Sampson and observing that Campbell still remained standing behind a tree and not complying with his order, Sinclair walked boldly through a hail of fire, reaching Campbell's side, accosting him.

Grabbing Campbell by the shoulder, Sinclair jerked him around, enraged, screaming in his face, "What do you think you're doing, sergeant? I ordered a bayonet charge!"

Momentarily interrupting their face-off; two Cobra Gun ships zoomed in from the south; their quad-60s blazing. The Cobras extensive fire forced the enemy to retreat in a mad run up the mountain. Some, in foolish haste, ran down the hillside and right into D Company's lap. On the upper hillside, the Cobra's 40 mm rounds exploded as crews seek their own vengeance for the death of the medivac crew.

A brief fire fight occurred with the fleeing NVA, but then Captain Sampson ordered, "Cease fire!" He then instructed the men to check for wounded and dead. Once that was done, SSgt. Franklin was ordered to check the bodies of the dead NVA, but not to approach the ridgeline. Sampson didn't want his men walking into another ambush.

Campbell had to fight down the urge to knock Lt. Sinclair on his butt and spoke his reply through clenched teeth, "Sir, the captain has issued a cease fire order."

Lt. Sinclair glared back at him with insanity in his eyes, "They're still up there, Campbell. Prepare the men for attack an' that's a direct order!"

Campbell forced himself to use a calm voice, "Sir, I remind you the captain has ordered a cease fire. We have to take care of our wounded now." Campbell realized the man had apparently flipped out.

"Sergeant Campbell, you are relieved." Sinclair looked around for a moment, his hand still gripped tightly around his .45. "Kendal, you're my new squad leader. Get the men ready, fix bayonets!"

Matthew was confused, "What? Uhm…Sergeant Campbell?" Matthew was unsure of what he was supposed to do. He's also concerned with the way Sinclair is waving that pistol around, using it as a pointer and his finger firmly planted on the trigger. But before Sinclair could berate Kendal, Captain Sampson was on the scene.

"What in the blue blazes are you two arguing about, we got wounded men here?"

Lt. Sinclair swung his pistol around, "Sir, this man," He now pointed his pistol right at Campbell, "…refuses to obey a direct order. I want him placed under arrest immediately and marched off to the stockade." Campbell wasn't going to take any chances. He'd rather be court-martialed for assaulting an officer than shot by one. He side-stepped the weapon, moved in and quickly disarmed Sinclair by wrestling the pistol out of his hand. In the process of doing so, Sinclair's helmet was knocked off and both Campbell and Sampson recoil when they see the massive head wound on the right side of Sinclair's head.

"Oh my god, I can see his brain," Sampson said. He moved in to help restrain Sinclair, who has now gone completely crazy and it took both Captain Sampson and Campbell to wrestle the wounded lieutenant to the ground.

"Battle dressing!" Sampson ordered. Matthew ran up and while the two men held Lt. Sinclair, he began to wrap it around Sinclair's head. The seriousness of the head wound horrified Matthew, but he got the bandage on and secured it. "Must've happened when he came running back up the riverbed. I saw him go down twice, but thought he was just trying to avoid being hit." Campbell fought to keep Sinclair's head still while Matthew tied the bandage off.

"Campbell, you're my new platoon leader. You've got the experience; so don't even bother arguing with me. Assign two men to restrain the lieutenant until we can get some morphine down him." Sampson looked at their position and poor shape of his men.

"We're moving out," Captain Sampson ordered and then addressed Lt. Olson, "Assign a squad to pull drag, but keep them tight. Alpha Company is on its way over to join with us down river. I want two men on each stretcher and one man ready to relieve them in rotation. Any questions?" There were no questions. "Then do it. I don't wanna lose any more men," Sampson said. He gave Sinclair a look of sympathy and went off to find a medic to get a count on the wounded.

Campbell quickly glanced around his new platoon and then ordered, "Sgt. O'Brian, assign two men to help with Lt. Sinclair. Tie his wrists with bandages and have them wrap their web belts around him, arms to his sides, to keep him from hurting himself or them."

This wasn't what he wanted to do. The responsibility of a squad was one thing, but a whole platoon? He wasn't happy, but he accepted the responsibility as ordered. "Martinez, you take over the L-T's weapons an' ammo."

Jose quickly slid the L-T's .45 underneath his web belt and stashed the L-T's bayonet and knife into his rucksack. Now he looked even more like a modern day bandito with two automatics on his hips and two M-16's slung over his shoulder and an M-60 carried in his hand. *I get any more guns they gonna think me a drug dealer for sure!*

"Kendal, the L-T picked you, so you're my new squad leader."

"What? But, Sarge..." Matthew tried to get out of it, but Campbell interrupted him, "Like the captain said, don't argue."

Matthew kicked a rock and replied, "Right," in a surely way and got a nasty look from Campbell.

"Take it like a man, Matt." Campbell slapped him on the helmet, "Your squad pulls tail-end Charlie for the platoon and you'd better keep my men alive...you got that?"

Matthew locked eyes with him and answered, "I got it."

It was 48 minutes later when Lt. Olson's point made contact with Alpha Company and D Company let out a deep sigh of relief. After briefing A Company's CO on today's tragic events, Sampson moved D Company further down river to set up camp for the night. With A Company now between them and the enemy, the men hoped for some rest as the afternoon sun gave way to a thick blanket of darkness and a new wave of bugs.

With listening posts in position, the wounded cared for and a 50-50 watch in place, Sampson took a moment to critique today's screw-up. According to his map, D Company traveled a total of 800 yards up Hill 937 and in the process they sustained 31 casualties. *And tomorrow we'll be ordered to make another assault. But first, we'll recover our dead.* Sampson's thoughts then turned to the letters he'll be writing home. *Dear, God...what can I tell them?*

One hundred yards up river, Alpha Company came under heavy sniper fire. The battle for Hill 937 is far from over and the men of D Company can barely keep their eyes open.

10 – WHO'S COUNTING?

"Matt!" John whispered sharply, but got little if no response. "Hey, Matt…c'mon, its mah turn ta catch some Zs an' the sarge wants ta see yuh." Matthew slowly opened one eye and than allowed the next one to slowly open in stages. His dream faded in a gray mist and he was struck with cold realization that he was still here on good old Hill 937. Nearly four hours had passed since midnight and even in these early morning hours sweat still continued to drip off Matthew's brow and cheeks. He touched his right cheek to count the mosquito bites, *score four more for the Mosquito night patrol.* "Sorry, Amigo, but Campbell wants yuh an' mah eyeballs got ten-poun' weights draggin' 'em down. Hurry up an' get back or this boy's gonna be passed out," John said.

Through heavily bloodshot eyes set deep in blackened sockets, he watched Matthew vanish into the darkness. It was a sobering thought to realize how easy an enemy soldier could sneak up in this blanket of blackness and he felt a cold shiver run down his spine, which provided enough adrenaline to wake him up again.

When he heard a buzzing by his ear, John brought his hand up and smashed another pesky bug against his skin before it could dine on his blood. *One down an' anudder million ta go!*

Cautiously and silently, Matthew made his way back to where the wounded lay behind a barricade of logs. He then tripped over one sleeping soldier and startled another when he landed on the guy's chest. The passwords for tonight were Juniper and the counter was Redwood, and Matthew ended up using both a half-a-dozen times by the time he reached Campbell.

Exhausted and edgy, Campbell was clearly not in one of his more pleasant moods when his new squad leader showed up, "Hope you enjoyed your nap, Kendal because I got a job for 2nd squad."

Matthew took a shot at being amusing, "Well, we could use some R&R…"

But Campbell cut him off. "Alpha Company reported a lot of fires up on the mountain an' Captain Sampson wants it checked out. Get 2nd squad up and ready to move in ten minutes an' make sure nobody's carryin' anything that might jingle and that includes canteens." Matthew began to turn, but then faced Campbell and asked, "You leading it?"

Campbell replied a curt, "That's right."

Matthew was glad and he said, "Okay, Sarge, ten minutes…we'll be ready." He turned around and used two of those minutes working his way back to 2nd squad's position and another minute waking everyone up. He had to do it quietly, so he didn't alert the enemy to their exact position.

"Who cares 'bout some fires?" Jose asked Matthew, and then he turned to Andrews, "I don't care. Do you care, Farm Boy?" Andrews only shook his head in response. His head was still filled with cobwebs from too short of sleep and he was still trying to wake up.

Five minutes later, Campbell showed up to lead the squad out through the company's perimeter. In their absence, two men from 1st squad and two men from 3rd squad moved in to their position. "Jus' remember to challenge us before you start shootin'," Baxley warned the replacements before departing.

After crawling over logs, dirt mounds and large boulders, they entered the water and waded across the river in a staggered line with each man within touching distance of the man in front. It was a case of the blind leading the blind as they left the river and felt their way up the ridgeline. *I feel like singing a round of 'Three Blind Mice'. This has got to be the stupidest thing I've ever done…I can't see a thing. Could be following a gook patrol an' I wouldn't know it. There could be a hundred traps out here and we wouldn't know it until we walked right into one. How can Campbell know which way to go or does the big man even know?* Matthew spit to the side and cautiously placed one foot down in front of the other, while he remembered each time to quietly pat John's shoulder to keep his interval. With Campbell up front, Matthew took up position in front of Jose. They were not using a point man due to the darkness and this made the men real uncomfortable.

After a harrowing hour they finally reached a height on the ridge that allowed a splinter of moonlight to make its way through the thick tree growth. They are now able to see their hands in front of their faces and they begin to increase their pace. Twenty-two minutes later, Campbell brought the patrol to a halt and stepped back to where Matthew stood. He advised him to have the squad hold here, while he moved up on his own for a quick look-see. Campbell removed his binoculars and wiped the lenses with a semi-clean OD green handkerchief he always kept in his right shirt pocket for this purpose. "I'd better go with you to watch your back," Matthew suggested.

"Okay," Campbell agreed without an argument and then grabbed Adams by the shoulder, "You're in charge while we're gone. Don't go anywhere and no noise." He patted John on the shoulder, who responded,

"No, Sarge." *Ah wouldn't know where ta go 'cause ah sure don't know where ah am!*

The two of them moved up the ridge for another 25 yards or so. They used a narrow pathway made by the constant travel of NVA troops between their old encampment and their mountain fortress. Campbell stretched out on top a large rock outcropping and used his binoculars to scan the upper hillsides. While he was doing that, Matthew kept watch and took advantage of the moment to admire the nearly three-quarter moon. *Wonder if Kathy Lee is lookin' up at the moon right now…Can't remember the time difference…is it dark there too right now?* Matthew quit thinking about home when his eyes fell on the outline of Hill 937 and he came to realize how far they still had to go to reach the summit. He knew from the designation that Hill 937 was 937 feet above sea level and it looked to him like they had 900 feet to go to reach the summit. He also knew that whole climb was under the guns of a highly trained NVA regiment. Troops that held the high ground and were also dug in well enough to withstand the constant aerial bombardment and artillery barrage. Matthew didn't like the odds for a successful operation in only a few days.

Campbell spotted the fires burning off in the distance and tapped Matthew on the shoulder, "Take a look." Matthew used the binoculars and thought, *Man, that's a lot of campfires…wonder if they got marsh-mellows?* He tried to compute the number of men who might need that many cook fires and he didn't like the numbers he came up with. *Hundreds…maybe thousands of little men with automatic weapons and they're not hanging out the welcome sign.*

His survey of the hilltop completed, Campbell led Matthew back to where they left the squad, "I'll take point," Campbell whispered, "…you bring up the rear, Kendal." It took them over an hour to reach the perimeter and Matthew breathed a sigh of relief when he heard a man's voice challenge Campbell. Captain Sampson was at their squad's position and told Campbell he'd only a moment earlier finished injecting Lt. Sinclair with another jab of morphine to keep him quiet. His last loud outburst of profanity and accusations brought them all under sniper fire.

"What'd you find, sergeant?" Sampson asked. His weariness was clearly evident by his feint voice. By now, both Lt. Olson and SSgt. Franklin had joined them inside the perimeter.

"Alpha Company was right about the fires, Captain. I counted over a hundred of 'em up there and there's a lot of people moving around. If you ask me, sir, it looks like the NVA are boiling their rice." Sampson looked from Campbell to Olson, then to Franklin and back to Campbell.

"You mean those people are up there having a barbecue up there? I can't believe it. We've blasted this hill with everything short of an atom bomb and they come out to cook their TV dinners and..."

Campbell interrupted him to calm him down, "Sir, those soldiers live on rice. They have to come out an' cook it...otherwise the smoke will foul their tunnels. Probably the first chance they've had since our attack began." Franklin looked up toward the top of Hill 937 and said, "Sir, I'd say we should ignore the fires for now." Captain Sampson thought about that for a moment and then said, "All right, forget about the fires. But I'm calling artillery in on that lower ridgeline. We've got to knock those snipers out so we can move our wounded down river." Sampson walked over to where his RTO was sleeping. He didn't want to wake the boy up because he knew it took the lad quite awhile to get to sleep because of his painful wounds. So he pulled out the handset and made contact with Battalion. Within moments, a nearby firebase was handed the job and the sweaty and shirtless men who manned the big popguns were more than happy to oblige. The first 175 mm round whistled overhead and shook up the men up when it exploded less than 300 yards away. More than a dozen men promptly yelled out "Incoming", but they were abruptly shouted down by Captain Sampson, "That's our stuff, but keep your heads down...one of those could land right in our lap."

Campbell hustled over to brief his men, "Captain's issued an eviction order to the NVA."

Matthew had no reply. He simply reached down and loaded a white phosphorous, also known as a Wiley Peter or WP round, into his M-79, while the earth beneath him vibrated from under the Army's barrage across the river. Several trees wet set afire and this illuminated the area where the snipers had concealed themselves. Whenever an enemy was sighted up in a tree, the men of D Company dropped him from a half-dozen rifles.

"At what Uncle Sam pays for one of those bad boys, this eviction notice is costin' the tax payers back home a pretty penny," Baxley said to no one in particular.

"Better to pay for them than have one of those gook snipers send Mrs. Baxley's little boy home in a large baggie," Matthew replied. Baxley, at first surprised by Matthew having used the word *gook,* simply nodded his head in agreement. With everyone in the squad knowing Matthew was a Christian, this was the first time any of them had heard him use that defamatory term to describe the enemy.

When the barrage ended, a thick and ominous silence returned to cover D Company like a thick layer of fear. The men begin to feel somewhat better when they began to notice the first hint of a gray dawn as it appeared above the trees. With the barrage, holes had opened up in the tree canopy and within an hour sunlight could actually be seen covering parts of the jungle floor.

Sampson, Olson, Franklin and Campbell were crouched in a semi-circle around the RTO, who was awakened by the artillery. Captain Sampson talked with Battalion and once he was finished, he traded the handset with the RTO for an open can of peach halves and said, "Thanks." Captain Sampson pulled a well-chewed upon plastic spoon out of his shirt pocket and gulped down a quick bite before he spoke. "This is how it's going to go down." He pointed to Lt. Olson with his spoon, "You an' Sergeant Rounder will use your 3rd platoon to take the wounded down to the CP. Alpha Company's own 2nd platoon will follow with their wounded. You should make the CP by 0900 hours if you keep moving. Then once the wounded are handed over to the aid station, re-supply for the entire company and head back to rendezvous with us at this end of the ravine. I'm going back for our dead an' Battalion doesn't know anything about that, nor do they need to know. Does everyone understand that?" Sampson looked from Lt. Olson to Sgt. Campbell. He was keeping his promise and Sgt. Campbell responded with a grateful nod. "Ammo, food an' water for the company…I got it, sir." Lt. Olson answered. "Sergeant Rounder, you're to stay with the wounded. Make sure they get well cared for."

Rounders looked please to be going back to the CP and replied, "Sure, Captain, I'll make sure they take real good care of our boys."

Although no one said it, they all knew the captain was sending Rounder back because he had only 9 days left in Viet Nam and less than 18 months before retirement. This trip in to the A Shau Valley had made him a nervous wreck and he suffered from a severe case of short-timer's syndrome. Sampson also knew Rounder would be able to find a job around the CP to keep him busy until he was able to score a flight back to Camp Eagle.

"All right then…Good luck and get the heck out of this valley," Sampson said as he shook hands with Rounder and then ordered Lt. Olson to send one squad out on point to clear the way. "No sense taking any chances, Lieutenant, but make sure your men know to expect A Company's people." Lt. Olson agreed and did as he was ordered. He sent out his 2nd Squad to assume the point and then shook hands with Captain Sampson. "See you soon, Captain and good luck." Captain Sampson suddenly grasped Lt. Olson by the arm, smiled and then walked away to be with Sgt. Campbell and SSgt. Franklin. "Let the men know we're going back for our dead. It's going to be rough, but we can't leave them out there in this heat. Prepare to move out in ten minutes." Sampson then added, "Campbell, I want your 1st squad on point." Campbell replied with a quick, "Yes, sir." He was bone tired, but the thought of retrieving their fallen comrades had restored some of his strength.

Captain Sampson checked his canteens and soon discovered he had only a half of one left and he wasn't about to fill up with river water. Not with the bodies of his men lying in the water to the north. "It looks like it's going to be a long dry day ahead." Sampson told his expressionless RTO. "Captain, sir, if you need a drink... I've got another full one in my pack? I'm going back with the wounded and can refill then. We'll just switch them."

Sampson smiled at the boy and said, "Thanks, lad, I appreciate it." Sampson also needed to find someone else to handle his RTO duties and after some thought he selected a man from SSgt. Franklin's 1st squad who had some experience.

Campbell found Matthew and John crouched behind a large tree, both reloading M-16 magazines with the last loose rounds off one bandoleer. "Adams, run over an' find Eiger, Reynolds and' Waters. I'm holding a squad leaders meeting right here an' right now."

John said, "Sure, Sarge." He pushed himself up off the side the tree and stood up, slid a rifle magazine into his pouch and headed down the line of positions to locate those men.

With 1st platoon down to 80% of its original strength, D Company was currently at 70% strength when they entered the fourth day of Operation Apache Snow and it was going to get a whole lot worse.

Once the squad leaders showed up, Campbell began his briefing, "We're going back for the men we left behind." Campbell gave Eiger a glance, "Eiger, 1st squad is on point and I want you eagle-eyed for trouble. They'll be expecting us...they know we always return for our dead and they may have already booby-trapped them. So tell your men not to touch the bodies, any bodies, until a senior man gets up there."

Eiger looked over Campbell's shoulders and asked, "What's with those guys movin' out to the south?"

Campbell glanced back and then turned his attention back to his squad leaders, "Third platoon is taking our wounded back and getting the company re-supplied." Campbell then looked to Matthew. "I'll be with 2nd squad an' you..." he pointed at Reynolds, "...will follow ten yards back with 3rd squad. Waters, you bring up the rear with 4th squad. Franklin's platoon will be ten yards back from you. Maintain your intervals at all times an' be ready for anything." Campbell then remembered, "Oh yeah, Alpha's got a platoon on its way back here, so watch out for 'em. You got any questions... any of you?"

Matthew raised a hand and Campbell pointed to him. "What?" Matthew pointed over to where Jose was sitting and said, "Jose's out of 60-

ammo, can he get a belt from one of the other gunners?" Campbell could see the reluctance in the other squad leaders. No one wanted to give up machine gun ammo. "Check your gunners and pass some ammo over to Jose. Anything else?" There were no more questions.

For Jose it was like Christmas morning when Campbell showed up with two belts of ammo for his pig. "Try shorter bursts, Amigo. When this is gone, it's really gone...until 3rd platoon gets back. Make every shot count, Compadre or you'll be using your pig like a baseball bat." Jose smiled that teethe grin of his and said, "Thanks, Sarge," He handed one of the precious belts to Farm Boy. "One for you an' one for me...This is an equal opportunity Army."

Farm Boy complained, "I asked for flowers and you give me bullets." Andrews spoke in a squeaky voice, in a stupid attempt to sound like a girl.

Seeing how pale Baxley looked, Matthew walked up to him and asked, "You okay?"

Baxley didn't look up at him from where he was sitting, but he replied, "Yeah, I'm fine...just fine." Matthew knew the look and he asked, "How much water you got left?"

Baxley hesitated at first, but then answered, "None. Not since last night, but I didn't wanna say anything...an' I don't wanna drink out of that river. I've heard the guys talkin', they say it looks red." Matthew frowned, "I doubt that, but I wouldn't drink from it either." He pulled his own canteen out and handed it to Baxley and said, "Here, take a long drink and pop these in your mouth." Baxley accepted the canteen and two salt tabs and was grateful. After a long gulp he began to hand the canteen back. "Thanks, Matt."

"No, you keep it. I've got another one in my pack," he lied. He was beginning to understand what being a squad leader meant. He was responsible for these men, his men.

"I won't let it happen again," Baxley said.

"I know," Matthew then checked every man in his squad for water and wasn't happy with what he found. No one wanted to get water out of the river, at least not until they got above the ambush site.

D Company split up as 3rd platoon headed south and the others pushed up river to reach the ravine before mid-afternoon. When the sun rose above the A Shau, the heat caused a thick layer of mist to rise above the jungle floor. Above D Company's position, most of Alpha Company had become engaged with the enemy's first line of bunkers.

To the west, B Company's 1st platoon came under heavy fire from NVA .51 mm heavy machine guns and lethal RPGs. Taking one bunker at a time with LAWs, guts and hand grenades, the men paid a high price for every blood-soaked inch of ground.

INSIDE AP BIA MOUNTAIN, A SHAU VALLEY, MAY 13TH, 1969 0920 HOURS

Having not slept for more than two hours in a row during the last three days, Que began to fall ill from fatigue and nausea. He was sick of death, weary of the cries and moans of the dying and wounded, and disgusted with having to breathe the foul stench emanating from the hospital. Studying the room full of broken and bleeding bodies, Que stifled the urge to upchuck. Once again the room for the dead was stacked high and only yesterday it was cleared to make room. Volunteers, with scarves wrapped around their noses and mouths, their eyes filled with tears, carted the bodies off through the tunnels for cremation outside.

Unable to take it any longer, Que approached the doctor in charge and pled for a few hours of rest. "What will these brave soldiers do while you crawl off to rest, Private Que? Will they wait patiently in pain while you sleep and dream?" The doctor looked around the room for a moment, while Que stood there trembling from fatigue. The doctor then turned to address his young medic and in a tone of compassion, said, "But yes, I do know you have worked hard these last few days. Go refresh yourself in one of the upper tunnels and breathe in some fresh air…you have two hours." Que replied with a courteous, "Thank you, Sir," He immediately left, afraid the doctor may change his mind and slowly found his way through a maze of passageways until he found a bunker complex near the summit. For the first time in 12 days, he saw daylight streaming through the opening and breathed in a lungful of fresh air.

Que ambled about and looked for a spot out of the path. A small hollow in the tunnel looked agreeable and he lay down to grab a few moments of sleep. Yet it was not a restful nap, the nightmares from the days before haunt his mind. Dead soldiers returned to torture him with their taunts and accusations. He was finally brought awake by the sudden appearance of the bloody face of his dead cousin. Que rolled over and jumped to his feet and shook his head to clear the rest of his nightmare away. He took in one last lungful of clean air, sighed and wandered back down inside the mountain to return to his duties.

In the last four days, Que had seen too much suffering and had watched while many of his comrades had died on the cold stone floor. Yet his hatred for the Americans had diminished somewhat, instead he began to focus some of his bitterness toward the war itself. He had held these dying men in his weary arms and his uniform soiled in so much blood, he looked into their tortured faces when a last breath escaped through their lips. As he closed their eyes a final time, he wondered about their lives and their memories. He couldn't help but think of the loved ones they left behind and he prayed for them. Now, after all these long hours of treating these brave men, more than ever he wanted to see the killing cease and the war brought to an end.

Two orderlies carried a bamboo stretcher in and placed it on the ground before Que. On it a young soldier lay. This was a boy of 18 who remained in a semi-conscious state. He was missing a right arm from the elbow down and his right leg above the knee. The boy, who had shed too many tears and could hardly talk from all his screaming, opened one eye partway and looked to Que for some sign of reassurance, "Be…all right?" Que lied, "Yes, you'll be all right." His two-hour break was now only a memory, and he began to wash the young man's face and adjust the tourniquets. A moment later, the boy's chest failed to rise again and Que summoned the orderlies over. "Be gentle," he requested and the orderlies simply nodded. They too were tired of the carnage and remained mute as they lifted and carried of the boy's body to the side room.

2ND SQUAD/ D COMPANY, MAY 13TH 1969 1014 HOURS- *DAY 4*

Matthew glanced from right to left and back again and he repeated the procedure over and over again, while he watched for any sign of the enemy. At any moment a sniper could fire down from a tree or open up from a concealed spider-hole and with each step, he looked for a trip wire or a hidden punji trap. The stress over the last five months of life had aged him by nearly ten years. He had become an experienced jungle-fighter and was ready to react at any given moment and to any given situation. And like the armies before them, the men of D Company had come to loathe the A Shau Valley.

In only a few short days the battalion has lost nearly 25 % of its strength and they still hadn't cleared the first line of bunkers. The big brass hadn't anticipated how hard the NVA would fight to hold this putrid mound of dirt and it had cost both sides dearly.

While D Company approached the ravine to reclaim their dead, the NVA lay in wait. They knew the Americans would return, especially the men who wore the eagles head patch on their shoulder. When they came upon the helicopter's crash site, Captain Sampson had all the bodies placed under poncho liners. They would leave them here for the time being and pick them up on the return trip. No one remembered the medic, who still hung from the trees above, not that they could do anything if they did. There was no way to reach him- not hanging 50 feet in the air. Several trees would have to be cut down and for that they would need an axe or a chain saw, and D Company had neither.

B Company had launched their assault, but within an hour they were bogged down under heavy machine gun fire. Their casualties mounted quickly and they were forced to withdraw. The company commander advised the CP of their situation, "I've lost forty percent of my command and my men are beat up. I've got to have more men if we're to take this hill." He wasn't aware of it at the time, but A Company had reported much the same thing and they both asked the Battalion CO, "Where's D Company?"

Campbell's 1st squad's point man spotted the first body in the river, he was lying face down in the running water. With his deplorable condition and that of the others, the men were glad they didn't refill their canteens earlier. Twelve to fifteen hours in this heat did a lot of damage to a dead body. Campbell ordered him to leave the body and move on to the next one to ensure they are indeed dead. The point cautiously moved up and the lead man was surprised to see an M-16 beside the second man. *NVA wouldn't have left that rifle if they were still around.*

Giving the immediate area a quick once over, he decided the ravine was clear and summoned the rest of his squad up with a hand signal. One by one, the men moved up and having seen all the dead, they forgot all about proper security measures and formed a circle around one of the bodies- a friend they now mourned. "Man, he don't look human no..." Eiger didn't get a chance to finish. Several AK-47's opened up from the hilltop above them and Eiger went down with a scream in his mouth. A round had caught him in the hip and spun him around like a child's top, until he landed face down in the water. Then a second bullet smashed into his left ankle, breaking the bone.

While others took cover, a courageous man charged over and lifted the wounded Eiger up over his shoulder. With some exertion, he hefted him into place in a fireman's carry and made a dash through the water to seek cover behind a pile of driftwood logs. But before he could reach safety, he dropped Eiger to the hard rocky beach when a bullet zapped him in the shoulder. He landed hard and now lay unconscious on top of a very wide-awake Eiger. The point man went down when a bullet shredded his left arm, which sent his rifle flying out of his now useless hand to land in two-feet of river water. He then painstakingly picked himself up with his good arm and hobbled over to a pile of rocks and collapsed. Only a couple survivors of 1st squad were able to return fire, while they waited for 2nd squad to move up and assault the enemy.

Captain Sampson heard the firefight break out and ordered the men of 2nd platoon to hold fast south of the ravine. He attempted to call for air support, but the ravine walls caused the radio to act up again and he couldn't reach Battalion CP. Luckily, a FAC pilot overhead picked up the call, but he doesn't have good news. He advised Sampson that it could be several minutes before he could have anyone in the area.

"Be advised, Red-One has expended all their ordinance and they are returning to base for rearming. I should have a flight of Marine F-4s in the area in ten-mikes, over." Sampson replied, "Roger, we'll be here waiting, out!" Sampson slammed the handset down and ordered SSgt. Franklin to position his men in a defensive perimeter to support 1st platoon's retreat.

Campbell couldn't believe this was happening all over again. It was like getting struck by lightening twice the same day and standing below the same tree. They expected some sniper fire, but not another firefight. He watched his men move into position and was thankful to see that three of his squads were safe for the moment, "You all keep your heads down, we don't move until we get air cover!"

Using his thumb, Matthew moved the selector on his rifle from semi-auto to full automatic. He popped up from behind a large boulder and fired off a long burst at the ridgeline and within seconds he had quickly finished off a 30-round "banana-clip" magazine in four bursts. John knelt beside him and he too had emptied his rifle and dropped back to change magazines. Jose, seeing the trouble 1st squad was in, positioned his M-60 between two-large driftwood logs and raked the hillside with shorts bursts until his first belt was used up. Baxley hid behind an uprooted stump and spotted a man down some thirty-feet away. Without even thinking about what he was doing, he sprang up rushed over to rescue him.

"Cover me, Jose!" Baxley shouted when he leapt over the stump and dashed toward the fallen man. Bullets raked the sand behind him as he ran, but he made it into the river and dove into the shallow waters beside the man. Several rounds ricochet off the rocks only inches from his head and impact the body Baxley had intended to save. "Oh, God!" Baxley yelled in terror. The body was from the previous fight and when he turned the man over the horror he found caused him to recoil in fright. Suddenly, he forgot all about being in the middle of a firefight and jumped back to escape the grisly scene before him. An Ak-47 round slammed him in the middle of his back and the bullet drove him forward, to where he landed unconscious a top the decomposed body of Lt. Roundtree.

"Baxley!" Matthew shouted. He had ordered Baxley to stop, but the young man never heard him and now he stared speechless when Baxley was shot down. "Cover us, Jose!" Matthew yelled out. Then he and John left cover to reach young Baxley. Matthew returned fire as they ran into the water with John. They both grabbed a hold of Baxley's harness and jerked him off Lt. Roundtree's body and with great effort, dragged him behind a large boulder. Temporarily, he was out of the shooting gallery.

John checked him for a pulse, while Matthew knelt behind a deadfall and continued to return fire. John shouted out, "He's still alive, Matt!" John took a battle dressing out and began to apply it to the bloody wound. "You idiot, who do yuh t'ink you is, Audie--by god--Murphy?" As before, Campbell's M-79 and shotgun are useless at this range and while looking for a rifle, he noticed his young RTO was nowhere to be seen. Back tracking, he found the young PFC lying behind a log with a leg wound a couple inches above the knee.

"Lie still," Campbell said and then applied a bandage and tied it off. "How's it feel?" He surprised Campbell by smiling, "If you get me out'ta here, I got myself a ticket home. Course my dancin' days are..." He stopped talking when a severe jolt of pain passed through his leg and left him gasping.

"This will help," Campbell said. He pulled an ampoule of morphine out of his medic bag and jabbed it into his RTO's upper thigh. *If this keeps up, I'm going need a lot more battle dressing and morphine!* Because of his emergency combat medicine training, Captain Sampson had authorized the Field Hospital back at the CP to issue Campbell 6 ampoules of morphine. With the growing shortage of medics, Campbell was being needed more and more to assist with the wounded. Within a quick moment, the RTO's eyes began to become glassy and he said, "Oh, yeah...Good stuff."

Right then, the hillside blew up from a thunderous explosion when a Phantom F-4 pulled out of its dive and passed over the ravine. A second F-4 attacked, strafing the hilltop with 20mm machine gun fire, which again scattered the enemy. In their panic, two NVA forgot which direction to run and leapt down the hillside in front of 1st and 2nd squad's guns. In a few strides and sliding down on their behinds, they ran right toward where Campbell was with his wounded RTO. "Look out...Sarge!" The semi-stoned RTO yelled in warning. His voice was slurred slightly by the calming effects of the morphine.

Rolling on his right side, Campbell came up on one knee, brought his shotgun up and pumped three rounds of buckshot into the two NVA. The enemy tumbled to the ground and their lifeless bodies came to rest only a couple feet from where a smiling, but shaken RTO lay. "Wow...that was real cool."

The deafening roar of the F-4 faded as the aircraft vanished over the hill and left a strange silence over the ravine. The firefight had ended abruptly and surviving NVA troops escaped up hill to lick their wounds and regroup for later action.

By late afternoon, D Company had collected all the bodies. They placed the dead and wounded upon stretchers constructed of shelter halves or poncho liners. Ten more men were wounded in the second ambush and three of them now lay on those stretchers.

"We'll have to wait for 3rd platoon to return before heading back. There's just too many wounded to carry and still maintain some resemblance of security. Set up our NDP 100 yards south of here," Sampson ordered. Both Franklin and Campbell answered with a tired, "Yes, sir."

With what's left of six squads to set up a position, Sampson sent two squads up river to fill the company's empty canteens. He couldn't believe it when the water detail came under sniper fire, "We clobbered them and now they're back for more. This mountain must have a maze of tunnels and they probably have a subway running from here to Hanoi!" Sampson then looked to his feet, "I'm half expecting some gook to pop up in front of me like some gopher."

Back at the CP, Lt. Olson nearly got himself relieved of duty following a heated exchange with a supply captain. The argument was over how supplies were to be signed for and that the company commander was needed to sign for amount of supplies Lt. Olson was in need of. "Captain, look I've got two platoons waiting for me up there... they need my men and all this equipment and we need it now, not tomorrow!" Lt. Olson got right in the captain face, his eyes cold and his teeth clenched tight as he backed the frightened supply officer up against a large wooden crate.

The Battalion Commander, who was en route to the helipad, overheard the ruckus and decided to investigate. He arrived in the nick of time to prevent the captain from finding himself flat on his back and a 200-pound gorilla with gold bars jumping up and down on his chest. After hearing both sides, he calmly turned to the supply officer and ordered him to provide the lieutenant with everything he needed in a quick and timely fashion. He then instructed Lt. Olson to follow him behind the CP Tent for a brief chat.

The CO checked to make sure they were out of sight and hearing, and then the Colonel lit in on Olson, "Lieutenant, I do understand what's going on up there and how tough it has been on you and your men. But, if you ever raise your voice in my CP or threaten another superior officer in my command, I will personally have you court-martialed! Do you understand me, Lieutenant!?" Lt. Olson replied with a curt, "Yes, sir." But he failed to show any sign of fear or anger. He was simply too worn out and now that he had a chance to calm down, he couldn't believe what he'd done either. *Not the sort of thing they taught me at Officer's Training School.*

"Now get your men fed and bedded down for the night, Lieutenant. It's getting dark. You won't be able to rejoin your company until tomorrow morning. I'll contact Captain Sampson myself and advise him of the situation and my decision to hold you here." The Colonel started to walk off, but then turned around, "Come see me around 2030 hours and you can fill me in on what happened yesterday."

Lt. Olson looked at the Colonel for a moment with a blank expression on his face and then answered with a courteous, "Yes, sir…Thank you, sir." Olson then returned to his men and briefed them. Like them, he looked forward to a night's rest. That was unless the enemy decided to mortar the base camp again or his platoon got stuck with perimeter security.

When he received the news from Battalion, Captain Sampson briefed Campbell and Franklin, "So, that's the way it is. We're stuck here with hardly any food, little ammo and ten wounded men to care for." Sampson then looked to Campbell, "Have some of your men drag those bodies down the ravine, no sense putting up with that smell all night long. I know they were our comrades, but for now that's what we have to do. Post two men on them, relief every four hours…I don't want the NVA sneaking up during the night to deface those soldiers." Captain Sampson then addressed Franklin, "Place the wounded in the middle of our perimeter and have the men build a log wall around them to protect them from sniper fire. We stay on a fifty-fifty watch until twenty-two hundred hours--then we go on full alert. I want a listening post up and down river and use those old-field phones we brought with us. I'll handle the radio until zero-two hundred hours and Franklin you relieve me then. Are there any questions?" There were none.

As squad leader, Matthew now had the job to select two-men for LP duty. With Washington dead, Riley gone and Baxley wounded, it left only John, Jose and Andrews to pull the detail. His squad has dwindled down to four men, including him. "John, you an' Farm Boy got LP tonight. Report to Campbell an' he'll brief you. I'll stay with Jose. And before you start complaining, all the squads are shorthanded." But they didn't say a word. Their gear was gathered up and both men wandered off to find Campbell.

With enough time for each man to get an hour of sleep, Matthew flipped an empty shell casing into the air while Jose watched. When it landed, the open end was closer to Jose and the Little Bandito didn't even bother to say good night. Before darkness covered the valley, Jose was already snoring with a soiled poncho liner over his face and Matthew kept busy by swatting mosquitoes. But with the darkness of night came the snipers, but shortly after 2100 hours the first drops of rain began to fall. In mere seconds a light sprinkle turned into a downpour. Men took off their helmets and stripped off their shirts to let the rain rinse off their filthy bodies.

Matthew let his helmet fill with water and washed his towel first and then started on his socks. He may not be able to dry them, but at least they'd be cleaner. When he finished with his washing chores and a quick sponge bath, Matthew continued to monitor the jungle for any sign of the enemy. From his own experience, he's learned how the NVA preferred fighting in this kind of weather. It was hard to get air support when visibility was reduced to near zero and Matthew knew it was going to be a very long and wet night.

WILLIAM CASSELMAN

11 – CANNON FODDER

PFC Erwin A. Walstein, a skinny, freckled face boy of 18 from New York City, stood with a small group of replacements and waited for a hop into the infamous A Shau Valley. 160-pounds of lean muscle and 71-inches in height, Walstein was dressed in a new set of military-green jungle fatigues and wearing a slightly dented steel helmet perched on top of his head. Slung over his shoulder was a brand new unloaded M-16 rifle and at his feet lay a full field pack- the contents of which were only issued to him a couple hours earlier when he arrived here from Camp Eagle. The first of many to come, PFC Walstein had arrived from Travis Air Force Base only 28 hours earlier with the promise of an all-expense paid trip to glorious South Viet Nam. When he showed up for sick call at 0500 hours at Camp Eagle, his stomach knotted up and sweat on every inch of body surface, the medic on duty recognized the symptoms right off and said, "Simple case of 'scared out of your wits an' you're in Nam'. So, get used to it, troop…Airborne! Next." With two Aspirins and some foul tasting white milky substance dissolving in his gut, Walstein arrived at Firebase Blaze aboard a Ch-46 Helicopter and was ordered by a sergeant from Battalion Headquarters to standby for another short hop to a place called the A Shau Valley. "Got another Huey going that way in a few, you new guys wait here 'til I come back and get you. An' don't load those weapons!"

Not a smoker himself, Walstein stood off to one side while the other replacements lit up and made nervous small talk. A loner by nature, he sat down on his bag and watched the air traffic overhead. More than a dozen Hueys circled overhead and waited for their call to come in for refueling when a space opened up. A flight of six Cobra gun- ships zoomed overhead, circled once and then landed at a revetment area. There several shirtless men waited to rearm them.

From the other side of camp Walstein heard the sounds of artillery and saw the plumes of gray smoke rising from a battery of howitzers, *Big guns! Wonder what they're shooting at?* Walstein glanced around and wondered-- *why is everyone acting so strange? We're not boots anymore, but they're all treating us like we got the plague. Don't do this and don't do that…don't load that rifle. You're not sick, you're just terrified and what this A Shau Valley they're talking about?* Walstein's attention was drawn away from the action when he heard his name called out. *Now what?* "Walstein...PFC Walstein! Which one of you is Walstein?" An aged Chief Warrant Officer shouted in a loud booming voice. He felt like a kid being summoned to the principal's office. But he stood up and replied, "That's me, Sir. I'm Walstein."

"Good, thought I might've missed you." The man held up a small package, "I got a package here that needs deliverin' to a Captain Sampson of D Company. The clerk told me you were being assigned to his outfit." Walstein nodded his head, "Yes, Sir, I'm on my way out to D Company now." The Chief Warrant Officer put a small box in his hand, "Can you deliver this for me, son and make sure it reaches him today?" Again Walstein nodded and replied, "I can do, Sir." The Chief Warrant Officer gave Walstein a friendly smile and added, "Hang loose, kid. You'll be going out there soon enough...an' keep your head down. I hear that's a real shootin' war out there." Walstein looked at the small package that fit into the palm of his hand. It was covered in brown paper and thick straps of wrapping tape. Walstein also saw by the return address that Mrs. Brian Sampson had mailed it from *The World*. "Great! Not only am I flying into a raging battle, but I get to play mailman for my new CO...and all because I took some stupid bet!" Walstein whispered under his breath. Grudgingly, Walstein knelt down, opened his pack and tossed the package on top of his newly issued OD green socks.

The youngest son of Abel Walstein, Erwin had grown up in the old Jewish neighborhood on the north side of New York City. He rode the subway with some friends, all of them working as apprentices in family owned businesses, into town for some fun one day and by late afternoon they found themselves standing outside the Armed Forces Recruiting Station. The young men began daring each other to see who would go in to talk with the enormous Afro-American army sergeant who sat behind the gray metal desk. Erwin, not wanting to be outdone, took up the challenge and two weeks later he found himself boarding a train for Boot Camp. Now he stood here on a dirt helipad a top Firebase Blaze and thought of his friends back in the old neighborhood. *I'm a schmuck...a real schmuck!*

3RD BATTALION CP, A SHAU VALLEY, MAY 14TH, 1969 0955 HOURS
DAY 5

A lone Huey hovered 3-feet over a grassy plain and five men took a leap of faith. They collected their gear and walked toward a man waving them over. They had arrived at base camp and one of the first things PFC Walstein and the other four men see are the hundreds of black flies swarming over 14-body bags. Walstein was already air sick from the rough ride in and he and two others had lost their breakfast within moments after landing--much to the disgust of SPC 5 Hudson, battalion clerk, who was now leading them away from the helipad.

"Get used to it," SPC 5 Hudson said in a sarcastic tone. "This one's a real meat grinder and that's our second load of stiffs in five-days."

Walstein didn't like SPC 5 Hudson one bit. Not only was he a staff clerk, but he showed absolutely no reverence for the men who had died for their country. He wiped his mouth with his sleeve to clean the vomit away, and then took a swig from his canteen to wash his mouth out. Walstein then waited outside Battalion headquarters, while Hudson sent the other four men off to Alpha Company.

"You..." Hudson pointed his pen at Walstein, "...go to D Company. You'll find a Lieutenant Olson over at supply and he's from your unit." Hudson accepted Walstein's orders and walked off without another word. *Nice guy! He must've been my welcoming committee...this is going to be a long year.* It didn't take Walstein long to find Lt. Olson, but he was surely surprised by the way the lieutenant looked. Unshaven, Olson was dressed in a soiled uniform, a filthy OD green towel held in his left hand, rifle slung over his right shoulder and a dirty helmet hanging from a canteen on his belt.

"Sir, PFC Walstein reporting to the lieutenant," Walstein said. He stood at attention and presented a crisp boot camp salute. "Didn't anyone ever tell you not to salute in the field? Snipers love to shoot down the officers." Walstein wasn't sure what to say, "Sorry, sir...Uh, no one told me, but I've only been here...in Viet Nam for two days." Walstein relaxed his position some, but it made him uncomfortable to stand at ease before an officer. A graduate of Airborne school, he still thought officers stood on the right hand of God.

Olson gave Walstein a good once over, admired his clean uniform and new rifle and then remembered what the kid had said, "Did you say only two days in Nam?"

Walstein nodded his head, again confused by the expression on the lieutenant's face, "Yes, Sir, I've been here in Viet Nam for two days...including today, sir." Olson shook his head in dismay, "I can't believe this. They've sent you out here with only two days in country. What are those people thinking? Never mind. So you've been assigned to D Company?" Walstein replied, "Yes, Sir," He wondered what the lieutenant was upset about. "What's your name again?" Olson asked. "Walstein, Sir... PFC Erwin Walstein."

Lt. Olson gave him a once over and asked, "Walstein...Is that a Jewish name?" He'd grown used to that question since joining up. "Yes, Sir, I am

Jewish." Half the people asked if he was Polish and the other half Jewish. *No one ever asked if I was sixth generation American from New York City.*

"Okay, I'm in command of 3rd platoon and we are about to leave here for a short hike up the hill for a rendezvous with the rest of D Company. The CO, Captain Sampson, will decide what platoon you'll be assigned to. We're all short at the moment. So make sure your canteens are full, you've got salt tabs with you and twenty magazines loaded." Lt. Olson mentally thought over the list of things Walstein needed and then remembered another item and asked, "Has your rifle been sighted in yet?" Walstein answered. "We did it right after breakfast this morning, Sir." Olson pointed toward the direction his men were stashed for the moment, "Good, follow me." A bewildered young troop, Walstein grabbed up his gear and fell in behind Lt. Olson to follow him through the base camp. A new arrival to Viet Nam, Walstein was startled by the unruly appearance of the camp, the generally poor condition of the men and the lax attitude toward military bearing.

Behind a large NVA hut, he came face to face with 3rd platoon and their filthy uniforms and general overall disarrayed appearance startled him. Some of them were playing cards, others were sleeping and no one bothered to stand up when the lieutenant approached them. Lt. Olson stopped in front of one group, pointed to Walstein and said in a tired voice, "This is PFC Walstein. He's a new replacement with only two days in country. Take good care of him, he may be assigned to us after the CO takes a gander at him."

Walstein looked at the men and was not impressed. Their uniforms were torn and tattered, layered with dried mud and sweat stained, and the looks on their faces were hard. By their harsh expressions, Walstein began to feel like an unwanted houseguest. *Their eyes, so icy cold and it's like they're looking right through me.*

Third platoon moved out a short time later and climbed the ridgeline at a cautious pace to join up with Captain Sampson. Not knowing where to line up, Walstein attempted to fall in behind the last man, only to get himself reprimanded for his decision. "Ain't no new guy going to pull tail while ah'm aroun'. Now get your skinny butt up dere an' keep that rifle pointed down," The man said, "Ah Survived nine months an' fourteen days in dis hole an' sure ain't gonna get mahself shot by some trigger-happy punk wit' a nervous twitch."

WITH D COMPANY AND 2ND SQUAD

Matthew moaned out in pain, which woke him up with a brain-blaster of a headache. Beside him, Jose maintained a silent vigil on the tree line in front of their position and ignored his friend. The rain had finally stopped, which had left Matthew and the others soaked clean through from several hours of downpour and their shallow foxholes several inches deep in a mixture of soupy mud and murky water. "Geez, I got a headache and a half. You got any APCs or plain old Aspirin on you?" Matthew asked his friend. APC were what the Army issued to their medics, but most troops thought they only carried half the power Aspirin did.

"Do I look like a medic?" Jose replied with a snarl. "Hey, don't cut my head off. I only wondered if you had some…that's all." Matthew lumbered out of their hole and while he stayed in a low crouch, he went behind a Banyan tree and used it for cover as he stretched his arms out in an attempt to get the blood flowing again and relieved his bladder. Satisfied for the moment, he crawled back to his hole and grabbed up his rifle. Jose, in his weariness, shot daggers at him through blood shot eyes, but Matthew only left the hole again and wandered off to find Campbell. He hoped Campbell had some Aspirin in that magical medic bag of his. With his fatigues soaked he began to feel the first signs of a rash between his legs, *Jus' somethin' else to complain about an' no one's listening. Hey, God, are you listening? I sure hope so, don't want to think I'm doing all this complaining and no one was hearing me.* Five minutes later, Matthew was back beside Jose with two APCs in his stomach and he said, "Good morning, Amigo."

Jose apologized for his earlier silence, "Sorree, Matt, Ah'm a leetle out of it. All night I watch these trees an' soon they start to move. So, I shake my head an' they back where they started. But then, they start to move again. So, I shake my…" Jose got abruptly cut off with a wave of Matthew's hand, "I got it- I got it." Jose's explanation had only added fire to his headache.

"Ah need a good sleep…maybe eight or ten hours in a nice dry bed," Jose said in a low voice. "Next week, Amigo," Matthew said. But he wasn't looking at Jose. He had popped his head up and looked around when he suddenly heard a rustling noise behind them. It was Sgt. Campbell. He dropped down beside the two nervous men and tossed a can of pear halves to Jose he owed him and then spoke to Matthew, "Adams and Andrews are coming in, so be ready for them. I don't want any accidental shootings and everyone out here is worn out."

"Who's makin' the assault this morning?" Matthew asked. Up ahead they could all hear the sound of heavy machine gun fire. "A and B Companies are making a move on that first row of bunkers again," Campbell answered. He then quickly swiped a pear from Jose's spoon and gulped it down. "Hey!" Jose complained and Campbell ignored him.

"When your boys get in, make sure they drink a lot of water and get some chow down 'em."

A moment later, John and Farm Boy appeared on their bellies in front of 2nd squad's position. Both men have heavy bloodshot eyes and mud caked all over their faces and the backs of their necks and hands to protect them from the bugs. Together they down a full canteen and popped salt tabs, but they refuse the chow and quickly fell into a restless sleep in a hollow behind Jose and Matthew's foxhole.

Nearly three hours later, Lt. Olson's platoon arrived with the needed supplies for D Company. Jose broke into a big grin when he received 500-rounds of M-60 ammo and promptly wrapped two belts around his torso. He gave two belts to Farm Boy and asked John to carry the extra belt. "No problem," John replied. Groggy from too little sleep, he hung the belt over his shoulder. Each man received two C-ration meals, a bandoleer of M-16 ammo, four more grenades and ammo for the M-79s as needed. There were no dry socks and as happy as Captain Sampson was to see Lt. Olson, he was clearly upset when he learned Battalion had failed to send up additional officers. "They know I've lost two officers, what are those people back there waiting for...the next graduating class from West Point to show up?" His mood only worsened when Olson presented PFC Walstein to him.

"One man...they sent me only one man?" He then noticed how his ranting had shaken the new guy up some and lowered his voice, "No offense, soldier; I'm glad you're here. But I was expecting more men." Olson can't help but add, "Ask him how long he's been in country, Captain." Captain Sampson glanced at Lt. Olson, shrugged his shoulders and asked Walstein, "I'm not so sure I want to hear this, but...all right, how long have you been in this Asian paradise?" Walstein looked between the two officers and then answered, "This...this is my second day, Sir. We arrived night before last...so, maybe it's my third day...Sir." Walstein breath was labored, the heat and the hike up hill had really drained him and with all his panting, he resembled a man who just ran a mile at record speed.

"They sent you out here with only two days in country?" Sampson fought to control his temper, seeing how his foul mood was frightening the new kid. "It's not your fault, Walstein...Walstein, is that Jewish?" Sampson asked. "Yes, Sir," Walstein answered. *Aren't there any Jewish soldiers fighting over here?* "Sergeant Campbell, step over here for a moment," Sampson ordered. Campbell was loading his 40mm pouch with ammo, but stopped when he heard his name called out. He walked over to where Captain Sampson, SSgt. Franklin and Lt. Olson stood around a new troop. Campbell knew he had to be new, his uniform was nearly spotless and the young man looked as if he was going to pass out at any moment. *Heat always gets to them first, heat and the high humidity. He needs more water and salt tabs or he's going to fall down.*

"Campbell, this is PFC Walstein and he's yours. Sadly enough, this is his third day in Viet Nam, so please try to be gentle with him for the next 72-hours...if you can."

Campbell gave Sampson a wide-eyed look and asked, "Third day?" Sampson nodded his head in response and said, "You heard me." Campbell shook his head and then grabbed Walstein by the arm. "Come on, kid," Campbell said and led him over to where 2nd squad held their position. "Wait a second, sergeant...I forgot something." Walstein dropped his pack, opened the flap and retrieved the package addressed to Captain Sampson. "Sorry, Sir," Walstein said. "I forgot this." He handed the package to Captain Sampson. "A helicopter pilot gave that to me and asked that I deliver it to you."

Captain Sampson recognized the return address and said, "From my wife. One of the guys must've made sure it got to me today. It's our wedding anniversary...or at least I think it's today. Thanks, Walstein." Sampson turned away from the men and walked over to a large log. He sat down, leaned his rifle against the log, but within a quick reach, and pulled out his K-Bar knife to cut the package tape. *She always wraps these things up like they're going to the moon.* A moment later, Sampson returned and Olsen asked, "Well, what did she send you?" Sampson held up a bright silver bracelet, "It's engraved with her name on it. She says we'll switch them when I come home." He took the bracelet and dropped it into his shirt pocket. Combat was no place to wear a flashy jewelry, but he'd keep it in his pocket to remind him of her.

Campbell approached Matthew, who was busy trying to find a pair of reasonably dry socks inside his field pack- preferably ones that wouldn't stand up on their own. "Matt, this here is PFC Walstein. He's now assigned to your squad. Take good care of him, he's still on West Coast time." Matt was confused by Campbell remark and said, "What?"

Campbell pointed at Walstein, "This is apparently his third day in country an' you have about twenty minutes to teach him how to survive here." To which, Matthew replied with a sarcastic, "Thanks." He then looked Walstein over and after introducing him to Jose, he pointed at the others, "The men walking around over there in a daze are John Adams and Farm Boy Andrews, and that's the whole squad." Matthew knelt down beside his bag and then remembered to add, "Oh yeah, welcome to Viet Nam." He then continued in his search for wearable socks.

"Five of us...there's only the five of us?" Walstein asked. "I thought a squad had nine men in it?" Jose shook his head in frustration and glared at Walstein. "Okay, new guy, you listen up real good," Jose said in a gruff voice. "One of mah friends is wrapped in a poncho over dere, another is lyin' on a stretcher over dere." Jose pointed to where the wounded were put for the night, "...an' another is back at the CP aid station. So, don't think! You jus' watch an' learn. Maybe you might live anudder day. Right now you is a new guy an' new guys keep dere mouths shut! Got it?" Walstein was startled by the rough treatment, "Hey, I didn't mean anything." Matthew then told Walstein to shut up, pop some salt tabs and drink a lot of water. "The way you're sweating; you'd better change your socks too. You don't need blisters out here. Your feet get infected and you could lose a foot from some god awful jungle rot." Walstein glanced down at his boots, nodded his head in response and followed Matthew's orders. He drank nearly half a canteen of water down and popped two salt tablets into his mouth. He also took his Malaria tablets, which were huge and tasted just awful.

By midday, D Company was on its way back to Battalion and the center of their line was made up of their wounded and dead. Captain Sampson stood off to one side and remained mute while the stretchers passed him by. Walstein couldn't believe it and had to voice his complaint, "I hiked all the way up here, nearly dyin' from heatstroke and now we're goin' back down to base camp? Why couldn't I have just stayed there and waited?"

Jose pointed his right index finger at him and in a stern tone, said, "Clam up, new guy…The walk did yuh good." Walstein snarled, but held his tongue. *When I get back home I'm going to kill that smilin' recruiter and then go after my so-called buddies who got me into this mess.*

By late afternoon, D Company passed through C Company's outer perimeter and began to relax. But not before a new replacement on security fired off a shot at the point man and thankfully the bullet missed him. PFC Bridges immediately realized how close he had come to killing one of his own, when an enraged soldier rushed up and laid a right cross on the new guy's chin. Lt. Olson broke up the scuffle and ordered the new guy to report his actions to his platoon leader. He then dragged his man off by his shirt collar, "C'mon, you idiot. You're still alive."

Overworked and bone tired, the medics began to treat the new wounded men as soon as they came in. Baxley was still unconscious and was tagged to go out on the first medivac. Riley was still waiting since his wound wasn't considered life threatening and he was glad to see Matthew and the others. After a short meeting of comrades, Matthew and John wandered over to where Baxley lay with an IV line running into his arm and another into his hip. A large blood stained bandage was taped on his back and Matthew watched while a man from 1st platoon, a guy who had sustained a minor leg wound, swatted flies away from Baxley. They were all waiting for the next helicopter.

Matthew knelt beside his friend and laid his right hand tenderly on the back of Baxley's head. He then began to pray, "Lord, give me strength… help me find the words to say," he muttered. After a moment of silence, he then continued, "Dear, God, I pray healing for my brother…" While Matthew prayed, John crouched down and added a couple words of his own in agreement. This praying stuff was still new to him, but he felt a sense of calm when he prayed over Baxley. Matthew finished with a quiet, "Amen", and looked at John, surprised to see his friend's eyes were tear filled with compassion. "Thanks," Matthew said quietly.

"You t'ink he'll make it?" John asked.

"Yeah, I think so. We asked God, now it's up to Him. I've given up trying to understand God's ways and why so many men die so young." Matthew looked back down at Baxley, while both he and John stood to their feet. He looked back down at Baxley, "Praying for him reminded me of my hate I carried towards God for allowing my brother to die. But we all make choices and Luke chose to be over here in a war zone. Now I have to wonder if Luke's death was a part of God's plan for me to end up over here. Screwy huh?" Matthew looked into John's confused expression, "Yeah, I know... too complex for simple grunts. C'mon, let's go grab some chow." Matthew said. He tossed Baxley, who remained unconscious, a casual wave and walked off. John glanced at Baxley, smiled and then followed close behind.

"You've got one hour for chow an' cleaning those filthy weapons. Platoon meeting at 1630 hours and everyone will be there. Got it?" Campbell gave every man a hard look to make sure they understood, but he broke out in a smile when Jose blessed him with a big teethe grin.

Second squad decided on a Mulligan stew and before Walstein knew what was happening his helmet was yanked off his head and hung upside down over a cook fire. Without so much as a "Thanks", Jose tossed him back the helmet liner and Walstein watched dumbfounded as the men dumped their C-ration entrées into the helmet. In went the round pork slices, chunky beef stew, crumbling beef steaks, a foul looking corned beef hash and a can of turkey loaf and all were stirred together with a canteen's worth of lukewarm water. When the water came to a boil, the overflow dribbled over the edges of the helmet and fell into the fire, which caused the flames to cackle.

Jose miraculously came up with a half-full bottle of Ketchup, refusing to say where he got it and mixed it in with the ingredients. Afterward, the bottle of Ketchup was quickly buried to hide the evidence. A good thing too, for within the hour an angry officer from headquarters came snooping around for his missing Ketchup.

After twenty minutes of cooking, the men of 2nd Squad feasted on their first hot meal in five days. Walstein, being the newest member, was the last one to get a serving and he was not too surprised to find only a spoonful of Mulligan left in the bottom of his blackened helmet. Taking mercy on him, Matthew tossed him a can of peach slices before he reminded him to get his helmet cleaned up. "You need to have it handy, never know when we'll get another mortar attack."

211

John, Jose and Farm Boy nearly choke on their food when they started laughing at Walstein's expense. The new guy stood there by the fire and stared wide-eyed at his burned helmet and sighed like a 12-year old boy who found a flat tire on his new bicycle.

At precisely 1630 hours, Campbell began his platoon meeting. Normally there would be 36 soldiers in attendance, but today only 24 men remained and they sat in a semi-circle in front of him. They all looked like a pretty tired bunch of boys, but Campbell knew better than to coddle them. "You bums keep your mouths shut and I'll get this over with. Any of you nod off and you'll get the toe of my boot up a very comfortable spot." *These guys look like they're gonna pass out in front of me. Makes me wonder how bad I look?*

"Captain Sampson says no guard duty tonight, but you better remember we're still in Uncle Ho's backyard. We can expect a mortar barrage or even a ground assault at any time. That means you keep your weapons with you, but make sure they're on safe." Campbell emphasized this by looking straight at Walstein and asked for his rifle. Still busy trying to clean his helmet with handfuls of dirt and rock, he was startled by Campbell's request. "My rifle?" Walstein asked. "Yeah, that thing you shoot with. Hand me your rifle, private," Campbell ordered. "Yes, Sergeant," Walstein answered. He lifted the rifle up and handed it stock first to Campbell. Sgt. Campbell confirmed the rifle's selector was still set on *safe* and that a round was chambered. He then handed the rifle back, nodded his head to let Walstein know he had done right and then continued on.

"At dawn tomorrow, D Company moves to B Company's LZ one click west of here. Then, if everything goes according to plan, which we know it never does, we'll attack the ridgeline from there and move upward. Command, in their infinite wisdom and expectation, hopes to secure the summit by nightfall. We'll of course be supported by artillery an' air support, but if we reach the summit tomorrow I'll buy each and everyone of you a case of beer." Campbell saw the look on their faces and he too shared in their lack of faith for taking this hill by tomorrow night. *Probably not until next week if we can do it at all.*

"Now the downside, we can expect heavy resistance and some of you guys are gonna get hit--especially if you make stupid mistakes...Never, I repeat, never assume an area is safe. This is a blood an' guts war zone and if you forget that fact...you'll end up dead. Thinking smart and staying alive is the name of the game. Any questions so far?" Campbell looked around, but no one popped up with a question or raised his hand.

"Captain Sampson promised replacements, but the whole battalion is short of men. But if we get anymore, make sure you take them aside and teach them about what's happening over here." Campbell turned to stand in front Walstein, who was all eyes, ears and a stomach full of butterflies at this point. "PFC Walstein, our latest lamb for the slaughter, was sent out here with only two days in country. I'm surprised he's not at the aide station with a case of heatstroke. Okay that's it. Squad leaders stay behind, the rest of you go get some rest. But remember we're still on a fifty-fifty watch, I don't want to catch the whole platoon off sawin' logs."

As the rest of the men filed off, the four-squad leaders closed in around Campbell. With Eiger out of action, SPEC 4 Jackson was assigned to lead 1st squad. A young Black man from Detroit, Jackson was working on an assembly line for Ford when he received his invitation from Uncle Sam.

"It's goin' to be pretty rough tomorrow, I want every man to have in his possession twenty loaded magazines, four grenades, four canteens and two boxes of C-rats. Each squad will carry two LAWs and two M-79s, with plenty of 40mm ammo. We're goin' up against bunkers, so we'll need heavy stuff to clean 'em out. Now before your guys pass out, have your men wash out their socks an' underwear. In this heat they'll dry quickly enough. That's about it, any questions?" No one had any. "The next meeting will be at 0500 hours... unless we get hit tonight."

Matthew found his squad staked out in a small crater, the result of an NVA mortar blast, with the addition of several logs pulled over and a few large rocks added to provide protection. Waking Walstein from a light sleep, Matthew tugged on his arm and ordered, "C'mon, follow me." He led Walstein over to the company's munitions supply area. After checking in with a supply sergeant, Matthew loaded Walstein down with several bandoleers of ammo and a box of hand grenades. He then piled on two cases of C-rations and directed Walstein back to the squad area, where Matthew found Farm Boy nodding off. "No shut eye yet, Farm Boy. Everyone load their extra magazines up, get your grenades and rations, and then wash out your personals." He ignored their complaints, especially those of Jose's, who had hoped to catch some Zs.

Matthew filled his helmet with water and began to wash out his socks. He used soap shavings from a bar of well-used soap he had obtained in a trade for some gum. With this little bit of soap, he was able to wash out five pairs of socks and four pairs of underwear. He used the rest of his soapy water to wash out his towel and it was a struggle to get it reasonably clean.

Moments after the valley was cloaked in a blanket of darkness, NVA snipers began harassment fire. At 2208 hours, six-mortar rounds impacted in the area of C Company's perimeter, but no one was injured. During the mortar attack, Matthew lay behind a large log and clutched his eyes shut as he mumbled a prayer of desperation, "God, I feel like I'm losin' it. I wanna run, to hide and I don't know if I can handle this anymore. Lord, you gotta help me...Please hear me, Almighty God...I gotta have some help before they find me up some tree."

John lay in front of Matthew and between explosions he looked up to see his friend's scrunched up face and his lips moving. He sensed Matthew's fear and crawled up closer to put his arm over Matthew's shoulder.

"It's okay, Matt. Nothin' gunna get yuh while ah'm here." *This city boy's been through too much in too little time. Too much killin' an' now he's got these guys to baby-sit.* "Hey, tell me 'bout one of you's dates with Kathy Lee." John never met Kathy Lee, but he felt like he knew her all his life from all of Matthew's stories. He listened to Matthew read his parent's letters and he even began to feel like a family member. "What?" Matthew's eyes popped open, surprised by John's suggestion.

"How come some fine lookin' lady pick't an ugly white dude like you?"

Matthew first responded with one raised eyebrow, but then grinned. He understood what his friend was doing and he answered in a low voice, "Thanks, I get what you're doing...I'll be all right, just got the shakes a bit." John replied with, "Don't we all," But he stayed close to Matthew until the mortar rounds ceased to fall.

Walstein sat off by himself, folded up into a ball and having experienced his first enemy fire, he felt very alone and an outsider. He was now too scared to sleep or do anything else, so he watched as Farm Boy and John finished washing out their socks and listened as Jose hummed an unrecognizable tune. Walstein pulled out his wrist watch, looked at the time in the glow of Base Camp's fires and put it back in his left shirt pocket. *It's going to be a very long night.*

Matthew studied Walstein for a moment and remembered what it was like to be the new guy. Except in his case, he had Jose and John to talk with. *I'd better talk with him, tough enough over here already without having a friend to share in the misery. After all, I am his squad leader...*He grabbed up his rifle and staying in a low crouch, Matthew made his way over to Walstein's side. "Got your gear ready?" Startled, Walstein hesitated and then replied, "Yeah, it's done." Matthew looked at the man's rucksack and weapon and then asked, "So, where are you from?" That's all it took and for the next twenty minutes the two men talked about their homes and end up with Matthew explaining the reasoning behind the new guy treatment.

"I thought they disliked me because I'm Jewish."

Matthew laughed and then said, "Nah, look around you...we got it all out here. We got Whites, Afro- Americans or Blacks, Mexican-Americans or Chicanos, American Indians, a couple Japanese-Americans and 2nd platoon even has an Alaskan Eskimo. We got Christians from different protestant factions to Roman Catholics, several Muslims, two or three Mormons an' even a Jehovah Witness who couldn't escape the draft and soon developed a fondness for M-16s and beer. Add in your own Jewish faith, a few agnostics and one or two straight out atheists, and then toss in all those Buddhists we're fighting...well I'd say we've got quite a smorgasbord of religion on this hillside."

"Has anyone thought to have a nice quiet sit down meeting to discuss their differences?"

Walsten asked. But Matthew shook his head in response, "It wouldn't work. Capitalists against communists, neither side wants to give an inch." Matthew slapped Walstein on the shoulder, "You okay now?" Walstein nodded his head, "Yeah, thanks for talking to me."

95TH EVAC HOSPITAL, DANANG, SOUTH VIET NAM, MAY 14TH, 1969, 2142 HOURS

Baxley lay on his stomach and his mind began to reel on fast forward like a movie projector out of control from the effects of the morphine drip administered by the nurse. From the other side of the curtain, he listened while the doctors reviewed his X-rays. Unable to move his legs or feel anything below the waist, his heart jumped a beat or two when he heard one of them use the word, "paralysis". No, I can't...I won't be paralyzed. I'd radder be dead dan live wit'out...mah legs. Even his thoughts were slurred by the heavy drugs and Baxley began to pray for the first time in his life, when the doctors opened the curtains and approached his bedside. He struggled to escape and wrestled with his arm restraints, but is forced to cease by a very strong nurse. The doctor then reached over and upped his morphine drip, which caused a cloud of euphoria to fill his mind. His last rational thought was to ask God's forgiveness.

INSIDE AP BIA MOUNTAIN, MAY 14TH, 1969 2200 HOURS

Day or night...what hour is it? Que had lost track of time. The hospital was cramped with 78 wounded men who lay upon a cold stone floor. The bloody mats had to be removed and there were no others to replace them with. Their fear filled eyes followed him about the room, each man silently begged for some degree of hope and he could only offer them a moistened rag and a kind word. Before midnight, over worked orderlies would move most of them out through the tunnel for a long painful trip to Laos. For the others, they would end up in the side room and await a mass cremation, when time and safety allowed and Que knew it would have to be soon because the foul stench of decay had nearly become overpowering.

Que knew they needed fans down here and generators, but ammo, water and food were the priority. Anything else, including medical supplies would have to wait until the battle was over. Sleep deprivation affected his mind now and he couldn't even remember when he'd eaten last. Yet still the wounded continued to arrive at a steady pace. Que hadn't seen the doctor all day and one of the nurses had collapsed unconscious several hours earlier. Fresh water was nearly gone, clean rags were all used up and they were forced to use soiled uniforms from the dead, cut up into bandages for the new arrivals.

No one had expected a battle of such degree and the tunnels did not allow for much storage space. Ointments and salves, what was left of them, were smuggled away for the officers to use, but not before Que objected and received a split lip for his impudence from a stiff-necked major. Que knelt beside one soldier with a gruesome stomach wound and tenderly washed the dirt and grime away. While doing so, he watched as the Angel of Death crept into the cavern to claim this man. Unsteady, Que stood to his feet and summoned two orderlies over to remove the man's body. But before they can move the dead man, a wave of dizziness caused Que's legs to wobble. Unable to stand, his heart racing, Que fell forward. A thick blanket of darkness had smothered him into unconsciousness and he collapsed upon the body of the dead man.

.

12 – I NEED MORE MEN

2ND SQUAD, A SHAU VALLEY, MAY 15TH, 1969 1019 HOURS *DAY- 6*

A flight of Marine F-4 Phantoms appeared overhead and made a low ear-bursting run on the mountaintop from 10,000 feet. One-by-one they dove on the summit and dropped 1,000- pound bombs from only 500-feet over the enemy's stronghold and within seconds, thunderous explosions caused the earth to rumble and dance. From a distance it nearly resembled a volcanic eruption as flame and earth burst forth in all directions. Numerous NVA tunnels collapsed and buried dozens of soldier's alive inside. From nearby firebases, 155 mm and 175 mm howitzers then attacked the mountainside with a massive barrage to keep the enemy busy inside this perilous ant hill, while three companies of weary men make their assault on Hill 937 for a sixth straight day. Within a matter of minutes, D Company found itself besieged under heavy machinegun fire when they come within sight of the enemy's first line of wood, rock and dirt bunkers.

These bunkers are old and the tunnels behind them older than most of the soldiers using them to stand-off the American invaders. Great care had been given to camouflage them, surrounding them with deadly and disabling traps and set inter-locking fire in place for the dozens of light and heavy machineguns protecting Hill # 937.

The new men making this climb, who had not been in combat before and had slept through their intelligence briefings due to the country's sweltering heat and hard labor from their first step off the helicopter, are now startled by the heavy concentration of enemy fire sent their way. When they view their first bunker in the distance, they're amazed to see these fortifications were actually made of rock, log and dirt. Some didn't know what to expect, but others, who had seen the French fortifications around Danang, had expected World War II-style concrete and steel rod bunkers. These innocent ones who had grown up on World II movies of the Army in Europe and Marines island hopping, wondered why it has taken a modern American army so long to breach these *Lincoln Log* jobs.

Matthew's mouth was utterly dry and he was reminded of those painful moments only a month ago, when they climbed that other mountain. He licked his cracked lips with a parched tongue and struggled to build up some tiny bit of saliva to comfort his dry mouth. He attempted to be heard over the sound of gunfire, his own voice cracking from fear and strained nerves, when he shouted out an order for his squad to follow him up the ridgeline. "Keep movin'! Don't stop, or you'll end up dead…Keep movin'. Jose, keep your head down or I'll knock it off myself!" Matthew leaned forward to maintain balance and he often dropped to all fours when the slope angle increased.

Campbell's 1st platoon was spread out in a staggered line formation when they came face to face with their first enemy bunker, which held an NVA .51 mm gun crew. Several heavy bullets raked the dirt hillside directly in front of Matthew and it forced him to jump to the right. Adrenaline gave him the speed of the superhero *Flash* as he sought cover behind a small outcropping of rock. *I need better cover than this!*

These jolts of adrenalin surged through him as the rapid fire shooting continued, which caused his upper body to tremble. An undistinguishable yell from deep within his lungs erupted from his lungs and out his mouth in a tension breaker, while enemy machine gun fire zinged over his position and bounced off the rock in front of him.

He tried to think, *what am I gonna do?* But his brain seemed to be locked in stall mode as bullets pulverized the rocks in front of the squad, forcing everyone to remain undercover. Flashes of memory appeared in scenes displayed from earlier action on Ngai Mountain and the faces of the dead men he had killed glared at him. In mere micro-seconds their smiling faces and cackling laughs were transformed to eyeless skulls, who screamed at him with taunts and threats. He had to shake his head hard to clear his mind of those devilish images and then refocus on his current situation.

At Matthew's right, John crawled upward for better cover, while heavy machinegun rounds and fully auto AK-47 rounds impacted near him. To Matthew's rear, Jose and Farm Boy crawled on their bellies to reach a position of momentary safety behind an uprooted tree. This gave Jose his first chance to bring his sixty into play and rake the bunker with well-aimed short bursts.

"Matt! What do you want us to do?" Farm boy yelled out. He was frightened by the heavier machinegun cutting deeper and deeper into their protective cover. He knew with that kind of firepower it wouldn't take long to turn their tree trunk into a pile of matchsticks and they'd be left sitting there in the open.

I should be doing something, but what? Matthew asked himself.

The rest of the platoon was in the same fix and Campbell was tied up with 4th squad in an attempt to take out a nearby light machinegun bunker. The NVA had placed two light machinegun bunkers, one on each side of the heavier 51mm weapon, as support and this had kept the other companies from breaching through the first line of enemy bunkers.

Army Intelligence had not realized Hill # 937 was completely encircled by such bunker layouts. Such instructive ways of warfare were taught to the North Vietnamese and Viet Cong by the Chinese and Russians, but before that it was the French and even before that- by the Americans, to combat the Japanese in World War II. Now it was coming back to bite the American soldier in the backside.

One man from 4th squad was wounded by a piece of shrapnel to the leg when an RPG exploded below their position behind a deadfall. With a battle dressing wrapped around the wound, the man was left to crouch behind a black smoldering log, as 4th squad continued to inch forward on their bellies. Between bursts of gunfire, Matthew heard the tension filled screams of the men below and above. *Better to scream than pee in your pants, I guess.* He reached down to check his own pants, relieved to find them dry.

Due to the heavy bombardment of artillery and air support, the slopes of Hill # 937 are littered with uprooted trees, most of them still smoldering from the recent bombing. These natural barriers offered 1st platoon some degree of protection as they make their assault. The recent rain had caused further erosion, providing shallow pockets underneath exposed tree roots, and within minutes of making the climb the men had become filthy, their bodies and uniforms layered in grime and mud. This also provided a natural camouflage as man and mountain become one.

While 1st and 2nd platoon moved up the hill, 3rd platoon came up behind in reserve to prevent the NVA from out-flanking the two other platoons to catch them with a rear end action.

Matthew heard Sampson yell at someone, "We're going to hav'ta blow everyone of those bunkers to take this hill." Sampson's last contact with Battalion revealed all three companies were meeting heavy resistance and one RTO reported Blackjack was on the verge of firing his Battalion Intelligence Staffs for "total and utter incompetence."

With the exception of those smoldering stumps and downed trees, the hillsides are now bare of all undergrowth. Only blackened earth and deep mud now cover the mountain, where once grass and low shrubbery had thickly grown. Hill #937 was dead, a victim of war like all the bodies lying on its scarred surface.

Matthew lay on his backside and cautiously took his canteen out. He kept his head down and took a lengthy gulp to force his throat open. *Stuff tastes better everyday.* He then watched John change rifle magazines and popped his own out to find only one bullet remaining. *Wow! Don't remember shooting that much.* He slapped in his last 30-round banana-clip and glanced about to see what his options were. *I've got us into a real mess here and I got to make some choices before I lose a man…or I get my own head blown off.*

"You okay, Matt?" Farm Boy shouted out. He hoped he could be heard over the sound of battle and Matthew was only 20-feet from him.

"Stay put!" Matthew hollered back. *Yeah, I'm just fine!* Then when he heard a lull in the shooting from the main bunker above them, Matthew cautiously raised up to observe the situation. In doing so, he saw the NVA gunner sight in on Walstein and ducked back down as a short burst of heavy fifty-one mm bullets struck the log Walstein was hiding behind. It hit with such force the huge rounds actually began to push the huge log back against Walstein. He had nowhere to go and the tree was being shredded by a 51mm ban-saw.

Walstein released a fearful cry, "Help me!" He hoped someone in the squad could hear him and thankfully, John did.

"Matt, Walstein's in big trouble!" John yelled out.

Yeah, I know. So what am I supposed to do? Knowing the new guy's protective cover is on its way to becoming a pile of kindling, Matthew locked eyes with John and saw him point to Matthew's shoulder. "What?" Only then does he remember his M-79. "I'm glad you're thinking right!" Matthew muttered and confirmed it was still loaded with a WP round. He took two rapid breaths to steady his nerves a bit and sprang up into a low crouch, behind his dwindling mound of rocks and dirt. It took him a half a breath for a quick aim and then he fired off the grenade. After the 40mm round exploded out of his M-79 he dove back down. It only took a couple of seconds for the WP round to rocket upward and it made an arc of 15-20 feet above ground before it spiraled downward and struck its target. The bunker exploded in a white and grayish cloud, then a growing flame, followed by the screams of the men trapped inside. Matthew knew it was the enemy, but it was a still sickening sight and he turned away.

"Get me out of here!" Walstein hollered. The log he was behind was now being eaten up by NVA light machinegun and AK-47 rounds. They came closer and closer to hitting him and he was growing more terrified by the moment.

Buried deep into the hillside, the heavier bunker, constructed of a dozen logs, dried mud and covered over with dried grass and brush, offered no protection against the power of a fiery blast furnace a WP round offered. Not wanting to join his comrades, a young North Vietnamese corporal spotted Matthew and began to swing his gun around toward the American. But he was too late. The 40mm grenade impacted two feet below the bunker opening and exploded. A bright searing heat wave blasted through the bunker and most of the NVA didn't even have time to scream when the burning phosphorus struck like boiling acid.

When they saw the bunker burst into flames, Jose rose up to his knees with his 60 in his hands and raked the bunker ruins with an extended burst. Farm Boy supported him, but then moved to the smaller bunker to assist, John, who was had his M-16 on full auto and the light machinegun bunker was soon silenced.

Walstein was up on his wobbly legs and he stumbled forward for better cover. He dove behind another blackened log, larger than the first one. His hands were sweaty and clammy and he trembled from adrenaline rush, as he tightly grasped his rifle stock and fought to control his nerves. He can't understand why his body is shaking so much, but he was glad to be alive.

Matthew suddenly heard an animal-like scream come from within the bunker he had blown up and the sound sent a cold chill through him. He pulled the pin on a hand grenade and rushed forward to lob it inside. He wanted to ensure the job was done. John was right there beside him, he emptied his rifle into the bunker to quiet those awful sounds and release their lost souls.

For a long eerie moment, Matthew and John stood there in silence and watched the flames burn until only a smoldering ruin remained. Matthew stepped forward and pushed a burning chunk of ember aside with his rifle and peered inside the simmering debris. Never before had he witnessed such grotesque carnage and the thought he had caused this scene made his stomach churn. It would be forever blazed into his memory.

"Can I see?" Walstein asked. He had crawled forward to view the damage. "Yeah, take a good long look," Farm Boy said. He then grasped Walstein by the upper left arm and pulled the new guy back before he could see anything. "No, not now…Later, dude. We got more work to do, there's a lot more bunkers up above."

John started to say something to Matthew, only to find his buddy had disappeared behind the bunker. He told Jose he would be right back and while he watched out for snipers and staying in a low crouch, he made his way back through the debris and smoldering growth and found his friend. Matthew was lying all curled up in the dirt and mumbling incoherently.

"Matt, you okay?" John asked in a worried voice. He then shook him by the shoulders when he failed to get a response. But that didn't work either and the glazed look in Matthew's eyes frightened John. Unable to think of anything else to do, he slapped Matthew hard across the face and it worked a bit too well. John suddenly found himself looking down the barrel of Matthew's rifle and his friend still had that crazed look on his face.

"You wanna die too? Do yuh?" Matthew asked in a growl-like voice, but then he slowly lowered his rifle when he finally recognized John's face.

"You back wit' me, buddy?" John asked. "Yeah, I guess so...just freaked there for a moment."

With grenades tossed into the two smaller bunkers and other squads moving up, both men inserted full magazines in to their rifles and Matthew gave the signal for the rest of the squad to move upward. They were ready, anything to leave the stench of death behind.

Except for Walstein. He wasn't too sure about leaving yet. The sudden realization that he had soiled his pants in his first firefight was embarrassing. In hopes that no one was watching, Walstein grabbed a handful of mud and wiped it about his crotch area. Satisfied his episode was well concealed, because everyone had muddy pants, Walstein began to climb when he suddenly caught sight of an NVA soldier. The man had popped up out of a spider hole like a Jack in the Box toy. Without thinking, he acted completely from countless hours of stateside training Walstein quickly raised his rifle to his shoulder, took aim and snapped off a three-round burst. The man's head jerked backward, dropped his AK-47 and died. Feeling a sudden coldness pour through him, Walstein stood straight up, exposed himself to enemy fire and stared down at the body. Matthew, who saw Walstein endanger himself, leapt down the embankment, reached his side and threw him hard to the ground.

"Walstein, you freakin' bonehead, you're making too big of a target out here!" Matthew backed off when he saw the kid's teary eyes. "Erwin, this is a war an' people get killed. We all go through this, but you don't have time to dwell on it now. We're in the middle of a battle and your squad needs you. So, suck it up an' keep going." Matthew shook him by the shoulders, "Are you listenin' to me?"

Walstein mumbled back, "Yeah...squad needs me," But his eyes looked better and Matthew led off with the new guy at his footsteps.

CAMPBELL'S 4TH SQUAD

Meanwhile, Campbell and Waters' 4th squad were in a tight situation. They had two wounded men on they're hands and they're stuck right below two side-by-side light machinegun bunkers. Campbell's M-79 was all but useless because of the outcropping terrain, but he inserted another HE round anyway, while Waters assembled a LAW.

They had one chance and it was a foolhardy one at that, but Campbell couldn't think of any other option at this point. "You ready?" Campbell asked. He saw the LAW was now fully assembled.

"Let's do it before I lose my nerve," Waters replied. Campbell glanced at the squad and then shouted, "Now!" Both men popped up and stepped out, which exposed them selves to the bunker's fire, while the remaining members of the squad offered supporting fire. Before he could fire, Waters went down with an AK-47 round to the upper thigh. He screamed in pain, dropped the LAW, grabbed his leg and tumbled down the embankment.

Unaware Waters was hit Campbell fired off his M-79 and dropped back down, while NVA bullets filled the space where he had stood only seconds before. When he turned, he spotted Waters lying on the ground below, holding his hand pressed against the wound to stop the flow of blood. Campbell ignored the explosion of his HE round and crawled down to Waters' side, pulled him behind a stone outcropping and inspected his wound. When he opened his medic bag, two bullets struck a nearby boulder and rock fragments hit Campbell in the face. He shrieked out like a cat with its tail stuck in the door, while hundreds of burning needles stung his face. Campbell fell backward, his eyes clenched shut and he rolled onto his stomach with both of his hands over his face, as warm blood trickled through his fingers. But upon realization he hadn't been shot, Campbell began to painfully wipe the rock splinters from his face. Once he was able to see, he put aside his own misery and went back to work Waters' leg wound.

"Sarge, you look a whole lot worse than I do," Waters said.

"Shut up!" Campbell shot back. He broke open a first aid packet, removed a field dressing and wrapped the wide bandage around Waters' leg. He tied it off with an old-fashioned square knot.

"Bullet went clean through, you're lucky." He used Waters' pants belt to hold the bandage in place and a second dressing to wipe his own face. He was a bit surprised to see the amount of blood on it when he pulled it away. "There's no morphine, no medic an' I got 'a get you back down before you bleed to death."

"You sure ain't gonna win any beauty contests with that mug of yours, Sarge. But I'll always be grateful," Waters said through clenched teeth. "Can you see all right?" Waters asked.

"You keep talking, I might leave you here," Campbell said. He looked around and found a small stick and wiped it off before placing it in Waters' mouth, "Bite down hard, this is gonna hurt...a lot." Campbell then picked up the unused LAW and after some brief time of thought, he elected to nail the other bunker to the left. That way he was only exposed on his upper body when he took the shot. He then gave Waters a single nod, inched his body up the dirt knoll and when he was ready, he rose up, aimed the LAW and fired the thing. He then dropped back down and heard the explosion. First it was the blast and then he felt the earth shake beneath him. Right afterward, debris rained down upon him and Waters. Not one to waste time in to examine his work, he yanked Waters over his shoulder in to a fireman's carry and hustled down the hill sidestepping to rejoin with the rest of the squad.

With a vengeance, the other bunkers in the immediate area opened up, but smoke from the burning bunkers obstructed the NVA's view for the moment and Campbell reached an uprooted tree. There he dropped Waters to the ground with a resounding *thud!*

D COMPANY'S THIRD PLATOON

Captain Sampson saw the tough spot his 1st platoon was in and ordered his 3rd platoon in. "Lt. Olson, move up and assist Campbell. We've got to take out those other bunkers!"

Frightened and tired men began to climb out from behind cover and move up the slope. Startled by the lack of men, Captain Sampson counted their numbers a second time in disbelief. "I've got to have reinforcements," Sampson said. His new RTO nodded in silent agreement and he handed the handset to Sampson before he even asked for it.

Moments later, "Yes, sir, I do understand everyone is screaming for replacements...Out!" Sampson exclaimed. He stared at the handset for a moment and then slowly handed it back to his stone-faced RTO. "The whole battalion is losing men on this accursed operation and this hill has become a killing ground for the men of the 101st."

BATTALION COMMAND POST, A SHAU VALLEY

The Battalion Commander chewed vigorously on an unlit cigar, while he paced back and forth the length of his Command tent and contemplated his next action, "If the Division wants this hill so badly, they've got to send me additional troops. I have to have more men," Blackjack said. He then stopped in front of Major Riggsbee, his adjutant, "For the life of me, Fred, I can not see why this minute speck of firmament can be worth the number of casualties we've received here." Major Riggsbee agreed with him with a nod of his head. Outside, a steady flow of helicopters continued to land and lift off with ammo and supplies. They carried supplies in from Firebase Blaze and transported the wounded back. While he listened to the steady *whump-whump* beat of rotor blades,

Blackjack made his fateful decision and ordered, "Get me Brigade." The corporal who manned the radios didn't reply, he simply did his job. A moment later, "That's right, General. I need additional manpower and as fast as you can provide them. At least one more battalion and I'd prefer two, if Command wants this hill taken." Blackjack stopped talking while he listened to the General and then added his response, "It's like trying to dig gophers out with a spoon, sir. This hill has more tunnels than we ever suspected and I'll give the enemy their due, Sir, the 29th NVA are not giving us an inch without us bleeding all over it." After a couple more words, Blackjack signed off and handed the microphone back to the corporal. He then gave Major Riggsbee a stern look and said, "It's on record now. They're the ones who have to make the big decision to either support this operation with additional manpower or withdraw my battalion before it's been cut to ribbons."

Riggsbee added his support, "You made the right call, Sir." But Blackjack looked doubtful. "Calling in the cavalry isn't something to boost an aging colonel's record, Major, but I value the lives of my men over some general's star." Blackjack looked down at his boots and nodded his head several times, as he reaffirmed himself with his decision to call for help. "Wish they'd given this assignment to some other unit. I really hate this A Shau Valley, it's cursed and everyone in this country knows it."

D COMPANY, 1ST PLATOON / 3RD SQUAD

Reynolds' squad wasn't in very good shape, not with one man wounded and the bunker above them still coughing out fire like a dying man in a smoker's cancer wing. They were pinned down by sniper fire and a small rocky ridge separated them from Campbell and 4th squad. Reynolds also wondered where 2nd squad was and if they could help get his squad out of this fix.

"Rogers, keep your head down!" Reynolds warned one of his men. The men wanted to fight, but they were trapped between two bunkers and Reynolds was down to one LAW. *I've got no choice but to keep my men undercover 'til night comes. Maybe then we can fall back. Only hope Tommy doesn't bleed to death before then.* Reynolds gazed compassionately into Tommy's face. He tried to ignore the man's bloody chest bandage and asked the boy, "Need anything, Tommy?" *What a stupid question.*

"R an' R in Haw...Hawaii might do," Tommy replied through clenched teeth.

Reynolds caught sight of Rogers, who popped up again to fire off a quick shot and started to yell at him, "Get down you..." Reynolds voice froze mid-sentence when a burst of enemy fire rang out and Rogers tumbled down the embankment with a bullet wound to the side. There was nothing Reynolds could do for him; it was too risky for anyone to reach the wounded Rogers until nightfall.

2ND SQUAD

Matthew wiped mud off his face for the third time in the last twenty minutes and then glued his left cheek to the mountainside. He was holding, waiting for some signal from Campbell. Like him, the members of his squad lay with their stomachs pressed against the steep hillside, while they listened to the light machine gun bullets zing by overhead and the sporadic heavier machinegun fire whistle over the top of them. Another foot higher and they would all be dead. *We've taken out one bunker, one spider hole an' still another bunker has us pinned down before we could climb twenty feet. Where's Campbell?* Matthew asked himself. *Could be a big mistake gettin' too far up this hill, not havin' any support to watch our flanks. But we might have gotten ourselves stuck here with no place to go but up.* Matthew turned his head to talk with John, "We've got to hold here 'til the other squads move up. Don't want to expose our flanks. Okay with you?" John glanced around and then answered, "Ah sure don't feel like goin' anywhere." He then passed the word on to the others. "We hold here."

The five of them lay spread out with Matthew at the highest point, John a couple feet below and to the right, Walstein to John's left, and Jose and Farm Boy below them. They kept talking as the minutes passed by and it helped them from losing it. Matthew was concerned one of them, maybe, him, might crack up and go off running off down the hillside and get zapped in the back by a sniper.

"Kind of reminds me of that old John Wayne movie, you know? The one where those crazy gung-ho gy'renes plant the flag on top that dead volcano," Farm Boy said. "First movie I ever saw where the Duke got wasted." Farm Boy added. His voice was strained from the tension and he had to clear his throat a few times.

"Sands of Iwo Jima," Walstein said. He then cautiously glanced from side to side and tapped his index finger on his rifle's trigger in hopes that sniper might pop his head up again.

"Sands of what?" John asked.

"Sands of Iwo Jima…Wayne got killed on some Japanese Island only minutes before they raised the flag," Walstein answered.

"You guys keep talking an' that's how you're gonna end up. Keep your eyes open, this place is lousy with spider holes," Matthew warned them.

"Yeah, like with the Duke. Some Jap popped up out of a spider hole an' nailed him," Farm Boy said.

"I said shut-up!" Matthew ordered in a deep growl. He couldn't believe them. Here they were pined down by enemy fire and they wanted to talk about a John Wayne movie. For added discomfort, smoke began to blow down the hillsides from all the bombardment and the stench of sulfur made it hard to breathe. This forced the men to cover their noses and mouths with their mud-caked towels.

"I ain't ever gonna play king of the hill again," Farm Boy said.

"Yeah, no more kid's game after this. Never be the same," Walstein said. His eyes began to water and as he wiped them with his towel, he felt like he had scratched his eye balls with glass.

1ST SQUAD

SPEC 4 Jackson's 1st squad scored a victory over one bunker, only to find a second bunker less than 20 yards up the hill and now they're pinned down once more.

"Man, I'd give my '57 Chevy for a flame thrower. I'd fry me some gooks with one of those things," PFC Olgers said.

"You'd never lug it up the hill, Olgers. You're the one who's always complainin' 'bout how heavy your pack is. Maybe the Colonel will get you a mule to carry it for you," PFC Jeffers said sarcastically.

"You two can both shut-up," Jackson ordered. Flamethrowers? What I need is another LAW...or maybe a howitzer.

2ND PLATOON

With all of 1st platoon pinned down and waiting for help, SSgt. Franklin's 2nd platoon now found itself in the same predicament. All four squads were pinned down, even after destroying two bunkers and killing six snipers. In repayment for their gallant actions, the NVA had wounded six Americans and one them now lay in serious condition and there was no way to get him back down the mountain. "I'll get you out, I promise," SSgt. Franklin said to the wounded men. *Now I just have to keep the rest of my men from getting shot up. This place is a nightmare come to life and it's only worth the mud I hold in my hand.* SSgt. Franklin shook his head in disgust and threw a handful of dried mud and blackened ash down at his feet. He needed to come up with some options and his time had run out, his men were dying.

D COMPANY

When Lt. Olson led his platoon upward, Captain Sampson and his RTO followed only a few footsteps behind. When they bypassed a smoldering deadfall, a sniper's bullet caught Sampson's RTO in the arm and he spun to the ground. Though only a flesh wound, the gash needed to be bandaged and Sampson was ready to oblige with a battle dressing. "Looks like you'll be collecting your second Purple Heart and I hope it's your last."

The RTO clenched his teeth and then replied, "Me too, Sir." He tried not to cry, but it stung like a hot branding iron. With the bandage tied off, Sampson pulled the radio off the man's back and handed it to the nearest soldier, "Looks like you're my new RTO," Sampson ordered.

"What...Me, Sir?" The young PFC asked. "You're it, son. Here you go." Captain Sampson helped the youth drop his rucksack and pull the heavy radio pack on. He then grabbed another PFC and handed the RTO's rucksack to him, "You carry it for him for now."

With an unhappy expression and other PFC replied with a sorrowful, "Sure, Captain."

When his new RTO took the radio off Captain Sampson, he gazed back with a look of apprehension at the wounded RTO. Captain Sampson saw the look in his eyes and grasped him by his left arm, "No time for complaints. You carry the load and I work the radio, okay?" With apparent reluctance, he replied, "Yes, Sir."

Lt. Olson crawled down the hill to reach Captain Sampson, "Captain, this hill is crawlin' with snipers, like one big ant..." Olson's mouth hung open. He spotted movement in the dirt behind Sampson and burst forth with, "Down!"

Lt. Olson brought up his rifle and fired off a short burst directly over the captain's head. Captain Sampson, who had crouched down and brought his rifle up, now brought up one hand to cover his right ear. The noise from Lt. Olson's rifle firing so close to his ear had nearly deafened him. But after the shots were fired, Captain Sampson jerked around in time to see an NVA soldier fall backward with gruesome wound to his head. Lt. Olson had seen him pop up and nailed him before he could kill the captain. "Thanks," Sampson said. He dropped to his right knee; clearly rattled by the thought of how close he had come to dying. He looked up at Olson and repeated his thanks and then added, "My wife thanks you too."

Lt. Olson grinned and said, "She's welcome too...Now can I pick up my toys an' go home." Olson didn't wait for a reply. He only tossed a hand signal to his 1st squad and shouted, "Keep moving up." Then he followed it up with an order to his 4th squad, "Guide to the right, don't bunch up and watch out for those spider-holes!"

Captain Sampson studied the line for a moment and realized they were getting spread too thin. He needed to change his orders, "Lieutenant, leave one squad with me and take your other men up to help bail Campbell out. Then withdraw both platoons back to this position, we'll hold here for tonight. I'll send a runner to locate Franklin, but the company will position itself along this line and go no further today." Sampson made a sweeping hand gesture to show Olson where to position his men, "Then we'll get our wounded back down the hill. Okay?" Lt. Olson answered with, "Yes, sir... I'll get it done."

2ND SQUAD

Between 2nd squad and the next bunker lay only a bare mountainside of thick mud, which made it an easy kill zone for the enemy. Two snipers kept Walstein and John busy, leaving Jose to grumble because he was unable to get a shot off without exposing himself. "Hey, Walstein, role over here an' trade places wit' me," Jose pleaded.

"Stay where you're at, Jose," Matthew ordered. "We'll need that sixty soon enough, but for now keep your pointy head down." Matthew looked back down the hill and for the first time in what seemed hours, he breathed a sigh of relief when he spotted Lt. Olson's men below. The man on point waved his arm at Matthew and shouted, "Fall back- fall back!"

Matthew yelled back, "We need help!" But his voice wasn't loud enough to be heard over the heavy machine gun fire. He waved, but the guy only waved back and began to move off. *Doesn't that guy see the situation we're in? To go up the hill is sheer suicide an' to go back down exposes us to that bunker's guns.* While Matthew thought over his options, the men from Olson's platoon had moved off to contact the rest of Campbell's men.

"Matt, why'd those guys take off," Farm Boy asked.

"Great, looks like we're here 'til dark," Walstein added.

"Did any of you'se see who dat was? We get back, ah'll give him a..." Jose shut up when he saw the hard look on Matthew's face.

"He doesn't see the mess we're in," Matthew said. "From down there we probably look like five guys taking a break. Now stay low an' keep your eyes open."

CAMPBELL'S 4TH SQUAD

While readjusting Waters into a more comfortable position, Campbell made eye contact with Olson's men and heard the order to fall back. He turned to his own men, and briefed them on his plan to withdraw, "Wait for my covering fire an' then hustle down the hill at a dead run. Zigzag, you'll make a harder target to hit an' the first twenty yards is gonna be rough. But after that you'll be out of sight."

Campbell then picked up his M-79, wiped the mud off it and inserted a WP round. He also removed two hand grenades from his harness suspenders and figured he was as ready as he was going to be. "I'll handle Waters, you guys beat feet when these grenades go off," Campbell said. He then took in a deep breath, exhaled and shouted down the hill to Lt. Olson's men, "Cover us!"

The men waved back that they understood and assumed positions several feet apart to provide fire support. Campbell pulled the pins on the two grenades, took two deep breaths to settle his nerves and then hurled them in quick succession. He immediately afterward grabbed up his M-79 and fired off the WP round toward the bunker above. Though the grenades and 40mm WP round were short, the explosion and bright flash of the Willy Peter round temporarily blinded the enemy. When Campbell heard the explosions, he yelled to 4th squad, "Go-Go-Go!"

Four riflemen jumped to their feet and began descending the hill in five and ten foot leaps. One man tripped in the mud and tumbled nearly 15 feet before bouncing to his feet again. Campbell almost yanked Waters' arm out of the socket when he jerked him up and pulled him over his shoulder. Like the others before him, Campbell ran downhill in a zigzag pattern and reached his goal with Waters cheering him on between painful grunts, "Go right, no right! Now left...run-run-run!"

Lt. Olson's men watched Campbell carry Waters down the hill and they thought it was a stirring sight, which caused the men to expose themselves so they could focus their fire on the nearest bunker in an exchange of raging fire power.

Lowering Waters to the ground, Campbell collapsed and gratefully accepted a canteen to refresh himself, "So, what's going on?"

A PFC answered him, "Lieutenant Olson said to find you and bring you back down. The CO is setting up a NDP down there." the man pointed down to a rocky embankment far below.

"What about my other squads?" Campbell asked between gulps.

"Found one, gave 'em the order to fall back," the soldier said.

He took another long drink, had a look around and then ordered, "Okay, let's get a stretcher for Waters here. You guys take him down while I find the others." Waters had nearly drained his own canteen by then and he watched as his men prepared a stretcher for him. The soldiers then made their way to Captain Sampson without anymore casualties, while Campbell went off to find the rest of his troops.

3RD SQUAD

Sgt. Reynolds was relieved to hear the order to fall back and hoped to find Rogers alive. He looked to PFC Hately, "You go down and check on Rogers, if you find him alive sing out and I'll send another man down to help you carry him out." When he crawled out of a shallow hole, a bullet zinged past his head and impacted in the dirt a couple feet in front of him. Another bullet struck the dirt behind him and gave him all the incentive he needed to start running for his life. Reynolds shouted the order, "Get moving, you idiots...I'm sure not waiting for yuh."

Resembling alpine skiers, the men jump down the hill by using the mud to go from side to side and escape the enemy fire. Somersaulting at least twice, Reynolds finally reached the bottom of the ridge in time to see PFC Hately half-dragging and half-carrying the wounded Rogers down the hill. Several times they dropped and slid on their butts, but by then they're out of sight from the enemy's guns. Reynolds rushed up and helped Rogers stretch out on the ground. His shirt and pants are soaked in blood and Reynolds knelt down to offer a few words of encouragement. "You're one stupid kid, but it looks like a tough one ta kill." After a moment of examining his wound, Reynolds added, "You're going home...just stay alive until I can get you to an Aid Station...okay?"

Between gritted teeth, Rogers whispered, "Sure...Thanks, Sarge."

Reynolds patted him on the shoulder, gently and said, "No morphine here, so you gotta deal with the pain," PFC Hately gave Rogers a stick to bite down on. Reynolds then turned to count his men and once satisfied everyone had made it, he ordered them down to the company's new position. "Let's get everyone moving."

1ST PLATOON

His uniform tattered and his face crusted over with dried blood, Campbell dropped down into a hole beside Sampson to report in, "We're bruised, battered and all shot up, Captain. This place makes Ngai look like a walk in the park."

Campbell glanced around to see how many of his men had made it back. "What happened to your face?" Sampson asked.

"Rock slivers, but I'm okay, sir." Captain Sampson nodded and then asked, "Are all your men off the hill?"

Campbell answered, "Not sure. We ran into a nest of bunkers up there. It seems like the NVA got them set up in a staggered line and it gives them a good field of fire. Only way to take them out is with LAWs an' these," Campbell held up his M-79, "...if we can get close enough."

Captain Sampson gestured to the line of soldiers nearby, "Account for all your men, put them into position and then check back in with me."

Campbell looked up the mountain and then replied, "Yes, Sir." He then climbed out of the hole Captain Sampson had acquired for his CP and walked over to where his men were digging in to the right of 3rd platoon. He found everyone except for 2nd squad and he turned to look up the hill again. They were nowhere in sight and it worried him greatly.

Captain Sampson was helping widen the hole they had dug, when Campbell reported, "Sir, my second squad is unaccounted for and I request permission to go back up the hill."

With some hesitation, Captain Sampson agreed, "Okay, but take one of Olson's squads with you and give the rest of your men a well-earned break. Make sure you take a LAW with you, they may be pinned down."

Campbell was grateful, "Thank you, sir." He then walked over to brief Lt. Olson and once he had his men, he started up the hill with six fresh men. This would be a search operation and Campbell wanted to locate his lost boys or find their bodies.

2ND SQUAD

"We move an' it will be like a turkey-shoot for that gunner up there. No, we gotta have cover fire if we hope to get out of this mess or we wait until dark," Matthew said.

"Matt, let's get this over wit' right now an' charge dese dudes!" Jose said. He started to rise, but Farm Boy jerked him back down by his canteen belt, "No heroes today, Amigo. We wait like Matt says."

Jose unleashed a mouthful of street-Mex at Farm Boy, but Matthew shouted him down, "Cool it, Jose!" And Jose responded with a hard look of silent defiance.

The tension in the squad was broken when they soon heard Campbell's strong bellowing voice from below, "Kendall, can you hear me?"

Matt waved his right hand and shouted, "We're pinned down from above, Sarge. We can't move up or down." The situation may be dire, but Matthew felt a whole lot better knowing Campbell was close by.

Studying the problem, Campbell could see 2nd squad was wedged into a small pocket a few yards above a burned up bunker, flanked by snipers and under the guns of another bunker 50 feet up the hill. *They're up a creek an' I'm down here with the only paddle.*

Campbell spoke to Lt. Olson's squad leader, "I've got to get close enough to nail that bunker with this LAW." He held up the weapon and wished he'd brought another LAW in the event he couldn't get the job done with the first one.

"Your men will give me covering fire while I run up to that overhang." With a bruised and bloody hand, he pointed to a large rocky ledge that could possibly protect him from enemy fire. "I won't have time to watch for snipers, that's your job…Understand?"

The squad leader replied with a simple, "Can do." The man turned to his 60-gunner, a large white kid with huge biceps and ordered him into position. His job was to keep the bunker busy while the riflemen concentrated on sniper activity.

"Kendal, can you hear me?" Campbell shouted up the hill. "I can hear you," Matthew yelled back. "Toss a couple frags up the hill in 30-seconds, I'm coming up."

Matthew looked to John, "You got any grenades left?" To answer, John pulled one grenade off his suspenders and gently tossed it over to Matthew. "How about you, Jose, got any grenades left?" In response Jose lobbed his last grenade up to Matthew. He pulled both pins, but kept the handles compressed. He then shouted down to Campbell to see if he was ready?

"Do it!" Campbell hollered back. Hearing the grenades explode, Campbell took off running uphill, while the 60-gunner cut loose on the enemy bunker. He didn't have time to run a zigzag pattern and running uphill was tiring enough. Below him, the men began shooting at possible areas where a sniper might be hidden. And just before reaching his goal, one sniper did pop up from out of his spider hole only to get shot before he could take aim on Campbell.

Campbell's heart rate surpassed the 120 beats per minute mark climbing the embankment at a run, when he dove behind the rock outcropping. An enemy machine gun burst raked the stone face only a foot above him. Sweat poured and his breathing labored, Campbell rolled over to his back and began assembling the LAW. He promised to get himself in better shape if he ever survived this operation. With his hands shaking, it took him ten seconds to get the LAW ready to fire. He looked across an open span of hillside and saw Matthew, who looked back down at him in anticipation, "Kendal, you've got to keep..." Campbell ducked down as the enemy machine gunner raked that same ledge above him. He stayed on his back and held the LAW down beside him, but Campbell continued shouting, "Keep that bunker busy, Kendal. Hit 'em with everything you've got."

Matthew looked to his people, "Any grenades left?" Walstein said, "I got two left." Farm Boy replied. "I still got one." Matthew then ordered, "Get 'em ready. On my call you toss them up the hill as far as you can. Then we all open up to give Campbell some covering fire." Matthew saw them ready the grenades and then looked to Campbell. "Ten seconds!" Campbell nodded that he understood and took that short time to get his breathing under control. He didn't want to blow this shot.

"Now!" Matthew yelled and he watched Walstein and Farm Boy overhand their grenades up the hill. As soon as Walstein tossed the first one, he took the second grenade in his throwing arm and gave it his best toss in hopes he could drop it right into the lap of the NVA gunner.

Right at that moment, a sniper fired off a burst and the bullet impacted the dirt only a few inches from where Walstein lay. He had exposed himself to take the shot and the sniper had given Matthew the opening he needed and he dropped the man with a burst to the chest. Though the grenades were short, the explosions of dirt and the combined fire support from 2nd squad and the men below, gave Campbell an opening to launch a single projectile launched from the tube. Three seconds later, the rocket impacted on top of the bunker, causing a loud fiery explosion.

"Get your butts moving!" Campbell bellowed. He waved his right arm to guide the men down the mountain before he began his own descent. With the men below providing covering fire, 2nd squad pushed themselves off the side of the hill and proceeded to leap their way down. A moment later they lay on their backs, struggling to breathe, while Lt. Olson's men kept watch. Campbell knelt beside Matthew and shared his canteen with his squad leader. For a brief moment they shared a kinship in gratitude for surviving another close call.

"What happened to your face?" Matthew asked. "Later," Campbell grumbled.

Pouring some water over his head, Jose grinned at Campbell with that Cheshire Cat-like smile of his and said, "Now Ah'm gonna name mah second kid after you…Michael Campbell Martinez."

Farm Boy laughed and said, "Now that's a name for you."

Jose sneered back at him, "Don't knock it, Farm Boy. Lots of good Scot-Mexicans where I growed up." Jose doused himself with another splash of water.

"Let's go, I want to make it down the hill before it gets dark." Campbell led off with two squads of jittery men following behind.

D COMPANY

Captain Sampson sent SSgt. Franklin down the hill with the wounded and with orders to find whatever replacements he can beg, borrow or steal, "Get me some men, even if you have to kidnap some clerks from Battalion." With today's action, D Company was now sitting at 55% strength. Unknown to Captain Sampson for the moment, A and B Companies were also down to 50% strength. The 29th NVA continued to chew up the men of the 3rd Battalion and only parts of the 1st defensive line of bunkers had been breached.

INSIDE AP BIA MOUNTAIN, MAY 15TH, 1969 1928 HOURS

Que slowly opened his eyes, surprised to find himself lying on one of the hospital's grass mats. He was surrounded by the moans and cries of the wounded, and he worked his way up to a sitting position and checked his pulse. *Slow, but that is understandable.* Cautiously, he stood to his feet and fought off a sudden wave of dizziness. He had to reach out and grab the cavern's stone wall to steady himself and his stomach continued to complain. When he saw Que was back up on his feet, the doctor approached and said, "How do you feel?"

Que straightened up and replied, "I am ready to resume my duties, sir." The Doctor nodded his head and replied, "Good, we need our beds for our valiant soldiers. Wash your face and then begin checking on your patients. You might find some food by the tunnel entrance…eat now because I don't want you passing out again." He then walked off.

Que found a sticky rice ball and quickly consumed it. Afterward, he licked his fingers and made sure he had accounted for each kernel and he even looked to the ground to see if he had dropped any rice. The urge to take a second rice ball was strong, but he knew the food should be kept for the soldiers. One of the orderlies brought him a pail of water and he tried not to concern himself with its reddish color as he washed his face with it.

CAMP EAGLE, BRIGADE HEADQUARTERS, MAY 15TH, 1969 2234 HOURS

Reviewing 3rd Battalions request for more men, the Brigade Commander held another paper showing how all available replacements had been sent into the A Shau Valley. *Division has made their decision; we are to take Hill 937 at all costs. Additional units will have to be sent in immediately.* Clerks were put to work and new orders sent down the pipeline. Two more battalions of the 101st would be sent in and before midnight, a South Vietnamese ARVN Battalion was reluctantly provided by the area commander.

Speaking to his inner staff, the Brigade Commanders voiced his fears, "If everything functions correctly, which of course it seldom does in operations such as this, the supporting battalions will arrive in the A Shau on May 18th. Until then, the 3rd Battalion will have to do with what they have. But, can a single battalion survive? It would be a major victory for the NVA if they were to launch a counter-offensive and force our men off that hill. As you men know, the war here in Viet Nam is not going well. A major defeat would only make matters worse back home. The battle for control of the A Shau Valley has caught the attention of the press corps; especially with the high numbers of wounded and dead coming from the battlefield. Against my requests, some of the correspondents have received permission from MAC-V (Military Assistance Command-Viet Nam) to cover this operation. This will allow the American people direct access to the battlefield itself, an unwise choice for MAC-V to have made. In a war such as this there are battles which cost dearly in lives and equipment...I do not believe the American people will understand this one."

3RD BATTALION CP, A SHAU VALLEY

They began to arrive by Huey directly from Phu Bai and a reporter of national fame was the first to step off the bird. In front of him on the dirt helipad was a row of 16 full body bags. He turned to a stunned colleague, who blurted out the question, "Is our involvement over here worth this?"

13 – TRAPPED IN HELL

2ND SQUAD, A SHAU VALLEY, MAY 16TH, 1969, 0624 HOURS *DAY 7*

With only three hours of sleep to get by on, Matthew found it extremely hard to stay alert. But a long night of sporadic sniper fire had kept him and the others from drifting off to sleep. With the exception of course being Jose, who fell asleep shortly after midnight and remained unconscious till he was awakened at 0600 hours. Jose sat in a hole partially filled with murky water and stretched out his arms and took in a lung full of air.

"Man, I feel *sooo* good!" Jose looked at Farm Boy, added that big teethe full mouth grin of his and said, "I had the mos' fantastic dream, could almos' touch…" He stopped when he saw the sour expression on Farm Boy's face, that and his two very droopy and bloodshot eyes. "How come you don't wake me up?" Jose asked in that all innocent tone of his.

"Wake you? I tried to wake you…for six hours I've tried to wake you. But you'd jus' mumble something in Mex and roll over." Farm Boy was clearly not happy.

"Sorree, Man. Ah don't 'member nothin'," Jose said. "Anything' happen las' night?"

Matthew stood over Jose and asked, "Where were you, on a different planet?" Matthew then jumped in between Jose and Farm Boy.

"That jerk slept all night long. I couldn't wake him up to relieve me," Farm Boy said and then he turned away in frustration and pulled his canteen out. After he swallowed a couple sips, he lifted his canteen over his head to let a stream of water wash down his face.

"Careful with that water, we may have to go another day or more before we get any more. If it rains again, open your mouth an' hold your helmet out too," Matthew said, and then he turned to Jose and shook his head in dismay for his friend's poor behavior. "I should put you out on point for this… maybe give your gun to Farm Boy. This poor guy stayed up all night and still has a full day ahead."

Jose held out his hands wide to signify he wasn't responsible and said, "Aw, Matt…Ah was asleep."

Matthew gave him a hard look. At this moment he was the squad leader and not his best buddy. "How do you sleep so hard out here with all the shootin' going on?" Matthew asked. He was now helmet to helmet was his little buddy, a glare to his tired eyes as Farm Boy looked on.

Jose backed off, gave him a wide-eyed look and tilted his head, "Matt, where I grow up the whole neighborhood is one big battlefield. Every night someone getting' shot at."

Matthew considered that and knew it to be true, "Will, what do I do about Farm Boy? Let him carry your pig for a change?"

Jose gasped and now wide-eyed, he grasped his M-60 and pleaded, "Matt, you can't take mah baby 'way from me...we's familee." But Matthew waved him off, "Forget it, but you owe Farm Boy big time."

Jose agreed and said, "No problem, I take care of 'im...any word on us goin' home?"

Matthew furled his forehead and replied, "We won't go home until we post our flag on the summit an' this hill's covered with dead NVA." He then climbed out of the hole, wiped the mud from his hands and added, "...with a couple of our bodies thrown in for posterity." Jose studied the length of his M-60, wiped it down tenderly, while he said, "Like thu man at the airport said, 'Welcome to Vietnam'." Jose grinned for effect as he whispered to his pig.

"I'll leave you here to make up with Farm Boy, I've gotta go see Campbell."

After Jose watched Matthew walk off, he turned back to address Farm Boy, "So, anythin' happen las' night?" Jose still had that silly grin on his face and for a brief moment Farm Boy seriously considered knocking it off. Instead, he turned his back on Jose and curled up in the hole to catch at least a few moments of sleep. Jose let go a sigh of wonder, glanced about and did his best to ignore the shaking of the head and raised eyebrow look of judgment John was giving him.

The men had given up on any attempt to stay dry. Murky water, thick pudding-like mud had become part of their lives. Many of them suffered from early signs of trench foot and jock rot, along with insect bites, nausea, headaches and joint and back pains from too much moisture. They also carried with them a distinct hatred for this accursed mountain. But for Jose, he simply shrugged his shoulders and climbed out of the hole.

Once he had made sure his M-60 was dry and wrapped up in his poncho liner to keep the rain and mud off of it, he ambled over to John's hole and slid in beside his buddy, "Hey, anythin' happen las' night?"

After he had listened to the entire exchange between Jose, Matthew and Farm Boy, John shook his head in amazement and slapped his friend on the shoulder, "You is really somethin' mah bandito buddy."

Jose grinned in response and said, "The ladies back home all tell me that too, but let me tell you'se 'bout mah dream. Las' night ah see my mother in my dreams an' she called out to me. If it wadn't been for dat good lookin' girl...ah might think it serious."

John gave Jose an odd look, "You dreamed 'bout a good lookin' babe? Who didn't?"

Jose agreed with him. "Yeah, guess so, but she's was in dis go-go outfit, you know...tall white boots...Anyway, she's was sittin' in dis primo 1961 Impala, low to the ground wit' sweet lookin' chrome mags. A cool dream, but don't know why my mother was in it?"

John smiled and said, "Probably to warn you 'bout sweet lookin' babes an' 1961 Impalas." He still felt a bit groggy and wished his friend would get to the point.

After a few more minutes of jabber, Jose could see how bored John was and decided to return to his hole and leave his friend to nod off for a few moments. He pulled out his Colt .45 and complained, "Awe, man, it's got mud all over it." He reached into his shirt pocket and pulled out a filthy toothbrush with bent-over bristles. He held the toothbrush in his teeth, while he broke the pistol down and used the toothbrush to clean each part until satisfied. Beside him, Farm Boy gave up trying to sleep and dug into his field pack for a can of pear chunks. With Jose's eyes following his every move Farm Boy opened the can and took a couple of bites. When he saw the sorrowful look in his hole-mate's eyes, Farm Boy broke down and asked, "You want half?"

Jose pulled out his plastic spoon. "Thought you's mad at me."

Farm Boy shook his head, "Do you want half or not?" Farm Boy said in perturbed tone. Jose grinned, "Okay." Jose accepted the can and finished off the rest in a single gulp. Breakfast was now out of the way.

It had taken Farm Boy a short time to learn when and if Jose's smiles and grins were sincere. It was by watching his eyes and the tilt of his head. The eyes would almost twinkle when he was being sincere and he titled his head to the right, otherwise one should count their fingers and keep their C-rations a safe distance away from this Los Angeles Chicano ex-gang banger and now reformed Catholic. But in combat, Jose was a natural warrior and willing to risk his life for anyone wearing a 101st Screaming Eagle Airborne patch.

1ST PLATOON

Campbell's voice carried with it an air of apprehension as he briefed his squad leaders, "According to Battalion, Air Force flyboys will commence their run on the mountaintop at 0700 hours; that's thirty minutes from now.

Following their bombardment, the artillery boys will lay down a heavy barrage. Then at precisely 0730 hours, we move up the hill as a Battalion…again. Now I'll add a bit to those orders. With the stiff resistance we've been hitting, I'm not too sure we can take this hill without a lot more help." He didn't like sounding like a defeatist, but this operation was wearing him down and he could see the same thing in the eyes of his men.

He studied the faces of the soldiers in front of him. He knew these men, mostly boys, had not received enough rest since their last major operation and all the patrol work they had been assigned. He tried to compare them to a football team; playing their 9th quarter in a grueling football game, or baseball; 25 innings in a championship. But in this one event, they killed the opponent and that was also bleeding the men of their humanity, he could read it in their faces. He was glad he didn't have a mirror, he would hate to see his own reflection and what this latest battle had done to him.

"All three companies will hit the first bunker line at the same time, but coming from three separate points on this map." He pointed down at a topographical map, illuminated by a cigarette lighter's flame. "As far as I know, the other side of this place could have a four-lane highway running to the top and bringing fresh troops in, and possibly a North Vietnamese USO Show with Hanoi Hannah as the star." There were no laughs, the men were too tired for jokes and they had a long day ahead.

"Lieutenant Olson brought a few replacements back and thankfully half-a-dozen LAWs. Make sure your men stretch their ammo and water, looks like tomorrow before we can get any more supplies. But, we'll probably get more rain at least. And no more chow."

Jackson briefly held up a hand and asked, "What about those replacements that came in?"

Campbell replied, "Franklin got them. His platoon is the shortest right now. Rumor has it Brigade is going to commit additional units, but by then we'll probably be sunning ourselves on the summit. So, any more questions?" Campbell waited, but there were no hands and only blank expressionless pasty white faces covered in streaks of mud, with bloodshot eyes ringed in black soot. Every man was covered in dried mud, their uniforms soiled from seven days of wear and no one wanted to waste their drinking water to wash up. When the rain came down hard enough, they washed off but within the hour they were using the mud again to keep the mosquito bites to a minimum. Malaria was a big scare and some of the men were placing bets on who would come down with the first case.

With Waters out wounded, SPEC 4 Bradley was assigned to the job of 4th squad leader. Only in country for four months, he was looking a bit shaky with the added responsibility.

"Here's how we stand…First squad has five men, 2nd squad is down to five men, 3rd squad has six and 4th squad is now at five. The platoon has lost 12 men, including Lieutenant Sinclair, since we entered this lovely tropical valley. We've got twenty-one men to make up this platoon an' word is the whole battalion is in the same shape. From 109 enlisted men and four officers, D Company is currently sitting at 64 enlisted and two officers. Six of these are new men with no combat experience. So, basically we've taken a real shellacking."

Matthew didn't hold his hand up, but he asked, "You have any good news?"

Reynolds piped in with his sarcastic wit, "What do yuh mean, Matt that was the good news."

Campbell quieted them down, shook each of their hands and ordered, "Okay, go get your men ready for war."

3RD BATTALION

When 0700 hours arrived the men of the 3rd Battalion duck deep down into their holes and placed their hands over their ears when the deep thundering roar of jets fly directly overhead. Seconds later, the entire mountain shook and rumbled under the massive explosions, which sent huge bellowing plumes of black smoke and fiery debris skyward for hundreds of feet. Some of the same debris rained down upon the American positions and then for a brief few moments, an ominous silence prevailed. But then the artillery opened up with 155 mm and 175 mm howitzers. Inch by inch Hill 937 was being reduced by a constant pounding, but still the NVA fight on and the haggard Americans are forced to dig them out from every accursed bunker and spider hole.

2ND SQUAD

Matthew was speechless when he looked up the mountain and observed in awe as the fiery explosions from the American artillery continued to blast the summit away.

"Ain't no one gonna be left after dat," Jose said in a loud voice.

"Don't bet on it," Farm Boy said in despair. He and Jose are bunched together, hands over their ears as the explosions continued and the air turned an ugly brown. Within moments the foul smell of sulfur drifted down over the mountain sides, burning eyes and causing a bad taste to everything until the next rain.

"Yeah, we've blasted that hilltop every day and still those little yellow men wait to kill us. Bombs can't reach them deep down inside, it's gonna take us grunts to dig them out," Matthew said. He was bitter and it came out in his voice and the deep crazed look in is narrowed eyes. When he heard the order to move out, Matthew looked to his squad, sighed deeply and issued the command, "All right, let's go. Quicker we get this done the quicker we can climb the next mountain…and the one after that."

John adjusted his gear and then lifted his rifle up. He then looked at Matthew and said mockingly, "Matt, you sure ain't no 'Remember the Alamo', or 'Remember Pearl Harbor' type, are yuh. All we get is a tired ol' 'Let's go'. You got to fire us up, boy, give us that old Airborne shoot'em-up, chew 'em-up and run it up the flag-pole try."

"John, shut-up and move-out. I'll do my Uncle Sam impersonation when we take the summit." He then glared at Jose, who was once again playing out his bandito act. Jose was making sure the two ammo belts he had crisscrossed his chest and a third wrapped around his waist. He also had one belt in his weapon, which was well seeded before he stepped off and began the climb.

Farm Boy, moved his weapon's selector from safe to semi-auto and then used his rifle butt to push himself up with. "Times like this I'd rather be back feeding my hogs," he said to no one particular.

"Me too, ah like pigs and a whole lot safer d'an d'is place," Jose said.

"Jose, the only pig, besides that one you're carrying, you've ever seen was wrapped up in some meat department," Farm Boy said. Then he fell in behind his gunner.

"So what, we leave here maybe you'se teach me how ta feed 'em?"

Farm Boy couldn't help but chuckle at the thought of Jose feeding his pigs. "First, we get out of here alive an' I'll buy you you're very own porker." Farm Boy then reached up and casually pushed Jose upward, it was time to climb again and Jose always needed a good nudging to get him going uphill.

Walstein stepped out of his hole and began to trudge up the hillside with his head in constant motion. He reminded Matthew of a turkey, especially the way he turned slowly from right to left and back again. He had learned all-to quickly that in this kind of combat the enemy could always be behind you and ready to spring up from out of a spider-hole.

Several shots rang out from above and Matthew shouted, "Hit the dirt!" He looked to his left and spotted several men from 4th squad firing down into previously exposed spider holes and relaxed a bit, *better to waste a round on an empty hole then have some sniper spring up behind you.* A moment later, both he and John fired into two known holes. *This place is turning me into a…*Matthew felt his left eyebrow twitch nervously, *great, now I got a twitch.*

As the dead soil sloshed beneath their boots, overhead a flight of Cobra attack helicopter arrived on scene to give the men a sense of security. Matthew climbed over a large outcropping of burned tree roots and followed the men of 1st Squad. They soon came upon the bunker Matthew had destroyed the day before with the WP round. He avoided looking in; the scene was still too fresh in his mind and the foul odor still lingered. But John, he gave the rubble a good once over in the event the ruins might be holding a new occupant.

Due to the natural rock formations and curvature of the hill, the platoons soon began to split up and the squads separate, while the men, now bent over at the waist due to the steep incline and the weight on their backs, continued to climb ever upward. The shout of, "Grenade", goes out only mere seconds before an RPG sailed overhead and exploded 20-feet behind 3rd and 4th squad. "Hit 'em--Hit 'em hard!" Campbell yelled.

While the men of 1st and 2nd squad send a hail of lethal fire at one heavy machinegun bunker, the men of 3rd and 4th squad send out a wave of lead against the nearest light machinegun emplacement. Second squad lay a short distance below the heavy machinegun bunker and while 1st squad and Matthew's men exchanged semi-auto shots with the enemy gunner crew and three NVA riflemen, Matthew needed cover fire, while he unlimbered his M-79 over his shoulder and loaded a round of High Explosive. He then warned the others to get ready. The 40 mm grenade exploded right in front of the bunker and sent forth a plume of black smoke upward and showered the area with mud and wood chips from the bunker's logs. One man from 1st squad received a minor wound when a large wooden splinter over four-inches in length pierced his upper right arm. He bit down on his other hand while a buddy pulled it out and wrapped the arm in a battle dressing.

Now lying on their sides, John and Walstein were the only two within range and they had grenades ready. As several men emptied their magazines into the bunker opening, both John and Walstein quickly rose up on their hips and lobbed their fragmentation grenades toward the bunker opening. When black and gray smoke from the explosion cleared, a lone NVA in a smoldering uniform stood out front of the collapsed bunker. Apparently wounded and dazed by the blast, he then saw the Americans and made a mad dash up the hill to escape. But John was ready. He sighted in on the man and dropped him mid-stride with a short burst of full automatic fire.

Under Campbell's strict orders, they waited until 3rd and 4th squads had cleaned out their own bunkers and only then, did they begin to move upward. But once 2nd squad moved off to the right and 1st squad went to the left of the burned out heavy machinegun bunker, Matthew and his 2nd squad walked right into a trap between two side-by-side light machinegun bunkers, supported by three spider-hole snipers.

Suddenly, the air was filled with the sounds of rapid firing light machinegun fire, punctuated by the heavy roar of yet another heavy machine gun crew further up above. They had climbed right into the open end of a well-placed U-shaped ambush. Now it was a duel, Jose's single M-60, supported by four M-16s on full auto. Matters only worsened when the snipers started to pop up, took quick aim and fired before they dropped back down into the safety of their holes.

D COMPANY

All three platoons are heavily engaged and momentarily pinned down by a heavy concentration of interlocking fire from a dozen or more bunkers, entrenched riflemen and spider-holes. Two more men from 2nd platoon go down when RPG shrapnel caught them both in the legs, but they are not the last.

"Medic-Medic!" goes out in all directions for more than half-a-dozen wounded men and with the company down to a lone medic, he became a quick target for snipers. When the exhausted medic from a south Texas hamlet ran to the aid of the nearest wounded man, he took a painful zap to the right knee by an AK-47 bullet and tumbled face first into the mud. He rolled to his ride, clutched his right knee and watched in horror as the mud around his wound turned the color of blood. He bravely bit off the scream, but his medical services were now all but rendered useless. In revenge, SSgt. Franklin spotted the shooter and took him out with a single well-placed shot.

"Help me...Oh, God I don't wanna die. Please, someone's got to help me..." A wounded man cried out and the medic, dragging his useless leg behind him, fought to reach his side but he soon passed out from loss of blood.

2ND SQUAD

With the help of 1st Squad's firepower, Matthew's squad was able to retreat back down to the bunker ruins below. His own heart racing, blood surging, Matthew kicked aside a smoldering log to look deeply inside to ensure everyone inside was dead. They were. The blackened bodies of three men were covered by debris and smoldering ruin and their stench brought tears to his eyes. But with no other place to go without exposing them to enemy fire, he ordered the squad to position themselves around the bunker's exterior wall. The slower thumping rotation burst of a 51 mm heavy machine gun fire raked the blackened logs only a foot or so above

Walstein's head and he dove down as splinters bounced off his helmet. He screamed out when he caught one splinter in the shoulder, but while he lay in a prone position, John was able to jerk the one-inch splinter out.

"Aren't you going to bandage it," Walstein said in disbelief, when he saw that John was done.

"Too small for a battle dressin', but Matt can kiss it for yuh if yuh want…We cun put a band-aid on it later."

Walstein snarled in response, but then he felt the heat of the smoldering ash through his muddy uniform and jumped into a crouching position. But when he did, he grimaced from the pain from his minor wound.

Jose propped his gun up on top of a scorched log, pulled his next to last ammo belt over his shoulder and seated his first round. Once he was ready, he spewed out a 20-round burst up the hill. To his satisfaction, he heard a scream and saw a lone figure drop over the lip of the bunker above and he shouted, "That's one!"

Matthew shouted. "Keep that gun busy, Jose! You gotta make up for all that sleep you got last night, but short bursts."

Farm Boy held his nose, while he helped Jose. "Man, this place really stinks!"

Walstein, without a smile, asked him, "Worse than a hog pen?"

Farm Boy snarled at Walstein and said, "Ain't no pig that smells this bad!"

Matthew grew weary of the conversation and said, "Complaint department is up the hill. Now shut-up and keep your eyes up for snipers. They might make a suicide run at us."

1ST SQUAD

"Johnson, move up an' get a shot off!" Jackson ordered.

PFC Johnson, the man with the M-79, shouted back, "I'm movin' already! Yuh got some kinda date or somethin'." He crawled on his belly and used roots and muddy dirt mounds to cover him. Once Johnson had worked his way into a better position he hoped he was now close enough to take a shot. Two rounds had already fallen short, but the last shot was closer than the one before. *I get any closer I can hand deliver this thing to them. Avon callin'!*

"RPG!" A soldier yelled. An RPG grenade exploded some 15-feet below Johnson and a small piece of shrapnel cut deep into his cheek and opened a hunk of flesh below his right eye. His eyes clenched shut, he bit off a cry and very carefully removed the hot metal. He then wiped the blood of his cheek with a filthy shirtsleeve. *Man, would mom give me grief over doin' that.*

"You ain't that good lookin' anyway, Johnson." The remark caught Jackson off-guard and he turned to focus an icy glare on the big mouthed man, who was smiling up at Jackson and seeing the contempt on his squad leader's face the smile instantly disappeared.

"Hey, I didn't mean anything by that." But before Jackson could reply, PFC Johnson's M-79 round exploded right in front of the bunker's exterior logs. A searing wave of fire poured into the bunker opening, which set the fortress aflame and killed the men inside instantly.

"Nice shootin', Johnson," Jackson shouted. He forgot all about Mr. Wise Guy's remark for the moment, but before anyone can celebrate the moment, four NVA jumped up from a hidden trench and charged 1st squad with fixed bayonets.

"Look out!" Jackson yelled. He sprang to his feet, lifted his own rifle up to waste level and fired off an extended burst on full automatic. The NVA ran right into a wall of fire, which drove their lifeless bodies backward against the hillside.

"Why didn't they surrender?" One young man asked in a squeaky voice. He was a new guy with less than two-weeks in country and his name was PFC Tommy Littleton.

"Because they're soldiers, kid and they've probably been told to fight to the death. Remember, we was told they were a bunch of wimps, so imagine what they were told 'bout us." PFC Scotty O'Brady said.

"Littleton, you're wounded." Jackson said. He was the first to notice the crimson red streak running down Littleton's arm. "No problem, I can hack it." Littleton said.

"Fine, but put a dressin' on it an' let's move on. Infection can kill you too." Jackson looked up ahead, saw the terrain and decided they'd take five minutes here to get Johnson and Littleton bandaged up.

1ST PLATOON

With his entire platoon committed and each squad already in big trouble, Campbell was unsure on where he should be at any given moment. To his left, SSgt. Franklin's platoon was fighting to reclaim some of the same ground they had seized yesterday and further over, Lt. Olson's men had become pinned down by a series of light machine gun bunkers, entrenched rifleman and all with deadly interlocking fire.

"Sarge," PFC Osgood shouted out. "1st squad's passed the first line!" Campbell crawled over to where Osgood lay and through the smoke coming down the mountainside he could make out Jackson's squad slowly moving up.

"At least someone's makin' some headway." Campbell said. A wide-eyed Osgood nodded back in agreement and wiped some of the smoke from his eyes.

The smoke from all the bombing and artillery made it hard to see and breathing became more difficult as the day wore on. Campbell hoped for more rain, but he knew the rainfall would make climbing more difficult. *In either case, we're gonna have problems. This mountain just doesn't like Americans!* When Campbell realized he couldn't see 2nd squad anymore, he left PFC Osgood behind for the moment, grabbed his less than anxious RTO by his harness and went off to locate them. *That squad of mine is like a wayward child, always wandering off in getting into trouble. If it wasn't for the fact they're all a bunch of heroic idiots I'd brain the lot of them.*

Five minutes later, he found them and they were in trouble once again. "Kendal!" Campbell shouted.

"What?" Matthew yelled back in anger. *What's he want now? Can't he see I'm a bit busy right now and someone's trying to kill us.*

"Hold right there, I'll be back with some help."

Matthew shouted back, "You do that." Matthew then pulled the pin on a hand grenade. He didn't even bother to look, but lobbed it over his head as hard as he could and up the hillside. He then curled up like a ball. Unfortunately, when the grenade exploded, it was still a good fifteen feet short of the bunker.

Debris showered down upon the squad and Jose growled at Matthew to stop. "Would you'se quit doin' dat! Dey don't like it."

Matthew snarled right back, "It keeps their heads down. You got any better ideas?" Jose suggested a white flag and a nice peace treaty, but Matthew replied with another grenade over his shoulder and up the hillside.

Nerves were strained because they all realized this was a replay of the day before. They couldn't move upward or downward, snipers had both their flanks zeroed in and only the uprooted trees and a single rocky ledge protected them at the moment from the NVA's 51 mm weapons.

A few moments later, Campbell returned to his 3rd squad and nearly got zapped when a string of machinegun rounds stitched a stretch of muddy earth only a few feet away from his left boot. He ended up with a somersault into the side of a startled Reynolds. "No visitors!" Reynolds said in a poor attempt at jest, as he helped Campbell to his feet.

"Second squad's in trouble...again," Campbell said when he came face to face with Reynolds' mud-caked face.

"Who ain't," Reynolds replied and he gestured to his own men and their predicament. Campbell nodded his head in agreement to show he understood and left Reynolds there to trade off fire with a bunker and a trench full of riflemen, while he took off in a low crouch for 4th squad.

When Campbell rounded a pile of smashed and uprooted trees, he found the 4th Squad outside a burned out bunker. They were preparing to advance up the hill through a rugged natural culvert and Campbell stopped them. "Hold on, I got another job for you, guys," Campbell said to them. He then had his RTO, SPC Haggerty, get on the radio and advise SSgt. Franklin he was forced to pull his 4th squad out of the line to rescue his 2nd squad. "Tell' em to watch his right flank until I can move my 4th squad back into position. I'd hate to have some NVA sniper move down and take pot shots at them."

Suddenly, the air was filled with the loud *whoop-whoop-whoop* sound of helicopter rotors and Campbell flipped around on his back and saw two Cobra gun ships hovering less than 200 feet above them. The heavy updraft off the rotor blades caused the air along the mountainside to explode outward and drive it in all directions, but the men didn't seem to mind a bit. This kept the enemy from targeting them, even if it was brief.

Campbell quickly crawled over beside Haggerty and ordered him to contact the lead Cobra to request their assistance, "Tell them I got a squad in trouble." Haggerty replied hurriedly, "Doin' it right now, boss...trying' to find their frequency."

2ND SQUAD

"Has anybody got any more grenades left?" Matthew asked in a raised voice.

"No, but ah still got dat little white flag," Jose answered.

"Can it, Bandito!" John said. He followed that up with a handful of dirt he tossed at Jose.

"That's enough," Matthew ordered. "The enemy's above us, so focus your anger at them an' not each other."

Jose began to apologize, "Aw, Matt, I was jus'..." and stopped in mid-sentence. He suddenly heard and then saw first one and then a second helicopter swoop down from above. Matthew was reminded of films he'd seen of beautiful American eagles as they swept down from above for Alaskan river salmon.

"Yeah!" Matthew shouted and he waved a clenched fist. His shout was seconded by Farm Boy and then the others enthusiastically joined in. Walstein held his helmet down in fear of the concussion to come and he began yelling, "Get 'em--Get 'em--Get 'em!"

The weapons officers aboard the Cobra gunships sighted in on the three bunkers and released Hell upon the mountainside. Matthew and 2nd Squad ducked down deep in their shallow holes and held their helmet tightly over their heads, while quad-60s and 40mm grenade rounds shot out from the two hovering birds. The American soldiers were too close to the enemy for the Cobras to use missiles, but the other onboard armament was doing its job quite well. The Cobra gunships had caught the NVA gunners by surprise and they were dead before they could even take aim on the American birds. Tracers; bright flashes of sunlight, burst forth from the lead Cobra's quad-sixties and shredded the front of the 51mm bunker like it was made of papier-mâché. The other support bunkers were silenced too, but before anyone could thank the pilots, another heavy .51mm machinegun opened up on the Cobras and forced the helicopters to take evasive action. Several enemy rounds impacted on its tail section of one bird.

"They're nailin' one of the Cobras!" Farm Boy shouted in alarm. When they reached a position below 2nd Squad, Campbell and Haggerty waited to see what the Cobra pilots had in mind. *The slope's real steep through here an' 2nd squad's too close to that enemy gunner for those pilots to use their missiles*...Or so Campbell thought.

The second Cobra lifted and flew a wide circle to avoid being hit and then dove on the hillside from several hundred feet back and popped three missiles in rapid succession.

When Matthew saw the missiles fired, he screamed at his men, "Dig for China and don't look up!"

Once again the terrified men of 2nd squad pulled their helmets down, held their breath and glued themselves to the bottom of their holes. When the explosions began, Matthew knew the blasts would obliterate the fortification into permanent silence and might bury them too. When an eerie silence followed, the men of 2nd Squad cautiously stood up, pushed the dirt and debris aside that had fallen on them and held their rifles ready. They all watched in stunned silence as black smoke plumes geyser upward from secondary explosions, as NVA explosive rounds detonated and debris continued to rain down upon the hill.

"Now's its mah turn," Jose said. He brought his gun up, positioned it between tree roots and zeroed in on a trench of shaken-up riflemen. With an extended burst, he raked the trench line.

"Yeah-yeah-yeah!" Farm Boy yelled with enthusiasm. He used his one hand technique to fire his rifle on semi-automatic to support Jose's attack and still keep the ammo belt flowing freely. The sudden Cobra attack created mass havoc for the enemy and several NVA left good cover in an attempt to escape up the hillside. They never made it, cut down by either

Jose or one of the others. Thanks to the air support, 2nd squad was on the move again.

D COMPANY

Down the hill, Captain Sampson was on the radio with Battalion, "We're meeting stiff resistance up here and most of my men are still engaged with the first line of bunkers...Over." There was a pause as Captain Sampson listened to Blackjack's reply. "Yes, sir, only two squads have reached the second line of fortifications and that was due to close air support by Cobras gunships...Over."

At the other end of the radio contact, Blackjack told Sampson, "Your orders are to keep moving up the mountain, do not stop...Out." Blackjack then had his RTO break off contact.

"What does he think we're doin' here...sightseeing?" Sampson dropped the handset and stared off into space. His RTO remained quiet until a call came in from SSgt. Franklin, who reported they were in dire straits again. Captain Sampson contacted Campbell by radio and issued him new orders, "I need you to bail Franklin out. Take three squads with you, but leave one to cover your right flank...Over."

Campbell asked, "What's he facing? Over."

Captain Sampson waited a few seconds and then replied, "Bunker complex...Over."

Campbell knew that, but he had hoped there would've been some word of enemy strength or possible offer of air support. "Okay, on my way...Out." He handed the handset to a sullen RTO Haggerty. "You know the saying, Haggerty, 'Ours is not to reason why....'"

His RTO gave him a raised eyebrow and said, "Sarge, whoever said that had to be an officer." Haggerty then spit into the mud beside his right foot. To make matter worse, it began to rain hard again and Haggerty could only shake his head in frustration.

In a fierce firefight that lasted for over two hours, seven undermanned squads of men were able to rescue SSgt. Franklin's platoon and seize the enemy position. The action resulted in 14 NVA dead and three NVA wounded prisoners. Franklin's platoon suffered three WIA and one KIA; PFC Walter C Edgewater, a blonde haired 19-year old kid from Maine.

3RD PLATOON

When Lt. Olson's 3rd platoon reached the second line of enemy bunkers, they uncovered a hornet's nest of five light and heavy machinegun bunkers and a company-sized force of entrenched riflemen mixed in between them. 3rd platoon was brought to an abrupt halt and forced to dig in. But they didn't retreat. Over the next three hours they moved ever upward from rock to rock and tree stump to blackened log as the men inched their way forward. But the enemy's stiff resistance is costing the platoon greatly in men and equipment.

Lt. Olson knelt beside his wounded RTO, who had taken an AK-47 bullet through the leg and had two-battle dressing wrapped around the wound to staunch off the flow of blood. He nodded his head in an understanding way and then advised him to make contact with Captain Sampson, "Contact the CO, pass on how I'm out of LAWs, nearly out of 40mm rounds and grenades, and we're running low on ammo. Very soon we will be down to using clubs and then the issue will be in serious doubt."

D COMPANY

When Captain Sampson got that message, he had already recently received similar messages from both Campbell and Franklin. He wasn't sure what his options were at this point and his voice was strained to a tone of near madness when he turned to his surprised RTO. "Supplies? Supplies!? My men are running out of bullets and if I don't get them resupplied we ain't goin' nowhere but Hell!"

The RTO hoped to calm his CO down and replied uneasily, "Maybe they expect us to use mud balls...Sir?"

For a solid five-seconds Captain Sampson glared at his frightened RTO and then he broke into a smile as he shook his head, "According to what certain officers believe, you're only a dumb enlisted man and incapable of understanding the complicated inner workings of a military operation of this size. I on the other hand am an officer and a gentleman who believes with a lot of you," Sampson raised his voice, "...that they've sure got things pretty screwed up around here." Sampson actually laughed when he saw the look of relief on his RTO's face. "It's okay, son. They may kill us, but they can't eat us. Most Buddhists are vegetarians."

His RTO replied with a courteous, "Yes, sir." He really liked his CO.

2ND SQUAD

His hands caked in new mud and trembling from adrenaline, Matthew checked his ammo pouches and was surprised to find he had only two magazines left and only five more loaded ones in his field pack. *I'd better cool it, only seven mags left and we still have a lot of mountain to fight.* With his thumb, he switched the rifle's selector from automatic to semi and then ordered his men to do the same thing. He then pulled the loaded mags out of his pack and stashed them into his pouches. "We have to make our ammo last, probably won't see resupply 'til morning. How's your ammo, Jose?"

Jose pointed at his pig, "Dis belt an' Farm Boy's."

Matthew nodded and said, "Short bursts, make it last." He then addressed the squad, "Okay, we move to the right ten-yards an' then up at a steady climb." Matthew started out on point and remained in a low crawl, one hand holding his rifle up above the mud and his left hand used to brace him-self against the muddy hillside. Rain continued to fall and it made the hill sloppy. Matthew's left hand sunk more than two-inches into the mud and he knew it was only going to get worse. It continued to be a constant battle to keep the rifles in good working order. Grime and mud was coating everything and the M-16 was not the best military rifle for these conditions, but the men did their best and that meant constant maintenance, and still watching out for the enemy.

John fell in behind Matthew. Before Farm Boy could move, Jose reached over and relieved him of his belt of ammo and swung it over his shoulder, "I want it close. Case you slip an' fall down thu hill. Ah know how you Farm Boys are…clumsy-like."

Farm Boy Andrews replied with, "You're all heart, Jose."

With a tired grin, he said, "What's heart got ta do wit' it, you'se clumsy." Jose then presented his famous teeth that were now darkened by grit.

"I hope you get cavities," Farm Boy replied.

Walstein waited for his turn and then he stepped off, but he continued to keep watch for 360-degrees. With the squad dwindled down to five men, Matthew was forced to put Walstein, the newest member, on tail. He needed John up front in the event he went down and John had to take over. Jose and Farm Boy had to handle the M-60. But so far Matthew had no complaints with Walstein; he had done his job and even saved his hide once from a sniper. He hoped he could live long enough to turn Walstein in for a Bronze Star, but that was for later. Right now he needed to concentrate on this accursed mountain. In a single line, spread apart by at least two-yards, the squad cautiously crawled up the hill. Each man struggled with his own fear, wondering if the next bullet would have their name on it.

4TH SQUAD

When Campbell joined up with Bradley's 4th squad, he found the men crouched over the bodies of several NVA. They had collected a handful of documents and personal belongings. Bradley looked over his shoulder to acknowledge Campbell with a tired voice, "Four more for the body count, Sarge." Before Campbell could reply, he surprised the men when he suddenly grabbed a man from 4th squad, swung him around and hurled him down the hill several yards. He was in the wrong spot at the wrong time and would've been killed when Campbell spotted a light machinegun open up. He hoped he had moved in time to save the man. A deadfall had hidden another bunker and the gunner was apparently waiting until he had enough of the enemy under his gun before he fired.

Campbell brought his shotgun up and fired off three quick rounds. Two other squad members left cover to run, almost skiing down the hill after their buddy and pulled him behind a still smoldering tree stump. They verified he was still alive by one of them waving their hand and making the "okay" gesture.

Campbell didn't have time to be thankful, for he was taken off guard when another man from 4th squad lost control and began to stomp his feet in the mud and shout, "No more--No more! I can't take no more..." He threw his rifle down and began to walk away from cover when Campbell grabbed him by the canteen belt and jerked him to the ground. A wrestling match resulted. The man fought like a barroom brawler to get away, but Bradley entered into it and between him and Campbell's headlock, they were able to secure the terrified man between them. Suddenly it was over and the bruised up man broke into a childish sob. Campbell released his hold around the young man's neck, pulled out his canteen and poured water over the kid's head. "It's okay, kid. You just rest up for a minute, you'll be all right."

The young man blew his runny nose and wiped it with his sleeve. Teary-eyed, he then looked up into Campbell's eyes, "Sorry, Sarge...Guess somethin' snapped."

Campbell shook his head, "Don't sweat it. Between this heat and all...well, my own nerves are stretched pretty thin too." Campbell watched the kid take a long gulp from his own canteen. "You ready to go?"

The man nodded his head and answered, "Yeah, I'm okay." Campbell handed the kid back his rifle, which needed to be cleaned off and turned to Bradley, "Move your squad to the left, try to link up with Franklin's 1st squad."

Bradley replied with, "Gotcha." Shaking from fatigue, Campbell then signaled for Haggerty to follow and the two of them left 4th squad to find Captain Sampson.

2ND SQUAD

Matthew felt as if he had just played a 6-quarter football game, going both ways, as he crawled uphill on his stomach. He spat mud out of his mouth and wiped the rain and grime from his eyes. They bypassed another burning bunker and didn't bother to look inside to verify a body count. He knew he was tired and probably making mistakes, but he didn't have the grenades or the ammo to waist on possible things. For five minutes he climbed and pulled himself upward by several tree roots and by digging his hands into the hillside. More often than not the mud went up past his wrist. His goal was a large dirt berm up ahead, one he hoped would offer him and his squad enough cover to grant them a moment of rest. While overhead, the air was filled with bullets of all sizes going both ways and flying hot shrapnel with, "Made in the USA" and, "Made in the USSR" imprinted on it. *Maybe we should bring all of the world's arms dealers over here and let them shoot it out.*

With one last tug, Matthew crested the berm and he peered over it and the scene above caused a "Dear God…" to escape between his cracked mud-caked lips. Nearly 35 yards of open space, all of it mud in the form of a small plateau, with a gradual incline, held by to two large bunkers. The bunkers themselves were separated by an estimated 20-foot long trench and it was filled with NVA riflemen. *No way! There is no way.*

Matthew cautiously and silently, inched himself back below the crest and he signaled John to join him. For now, a few hundred pounds of dirt and a clump of small boulders were the only thing to prevent the enemy from seeing them.

"What yuh got, Bro?" John asked in a whisper. He had seen the mournful look on Matthew's face and knew something bad was ahead.

"Your worst nightmare," Matthew whispered. "Two bunkers, the one on the right with a fifty-one and they got a trench between them plumb full of little men with rifles. No way we can take this on…not unless we can get those Cobras back."

John looked at him in silence and then said, "But we ain't got no radio."

Matthew nodded his head, "I'll send Walstein down to find Campbell an' let him make the decision."

John looked back up the hill and then at Matthew, "What about for now?"

Matthew didn't answer right away, until John repeated his question and Matthew replied, "We pull back down and take cover around that bunker below. That way we can still cover Jackson's flank."

While Matthew briefed Walstein, John pulled himself up to take a quick look and began to think Jose's white flag might not be such a bad idea. *We need an air strike on that place. Dis is a job for duh Marines.*

"Now if you can't find Campbell, try to locate Captain Sampson." Matthew went on to describe the bunker complex above them so Walstein could fill in the higher-ups on what waited above them. He even drew a diagram in the mud of the fortifications so Walstein would have a true understanding of what lay ahead.

"You've made my mother a very happy woman," Walstein said.

"Why's that? Matthew asked?"

Walstein answered, "A lot of heroes would've tried taking that place out an' probably got us all killed. My mother will now send you a box of homemade cookies."

Matthew smiled and suggested, "Chocolate chip?" Walstein shook hands with Matthew to seal the deal and began climbing down the hill alone. He only got about ten feet before Matthew ordered John to accompany him, "Two of you have a better chance of making it."

John understood. "We'll be back, Matt," John then turned to leave.

Watching the two men go down the hillside, Mathew's stomach began to rumble as another wing of butterflies gave erratic flight. Out of sight from the rest of the platoon, Matthew, Jose and Farm Boy were all alone with an estimated 20 or more NVA only 50 to 60 feet above them.

"Matt, how long we been up here?" Jose asked in a low whisper.

"Lost my watch, but it feels like mid-afternoon. It's hard to tell with all this rain."

Jose then asked in a nervous voice, "So, what we gonna do now, boss?"

Matthew clapped him on the helmet, "We plant it here until help comes."

Farm Boy then asked, "You got any water left, Matt?"

Matthew took his canteen out, shook it and answered, "I'm on my last canteen, 'bout a third-full."

Farm Boy added, "I got maybe a good gulp left myself."

Matthew then asked Jose, "How 'bout you, Amigo?"

Jose shot both of them dirty looks and replied in a snarly tone, "None of your business, Mister white-man."

Matthew grinned at him, which wiped some of the mud off his face that cracked with his smile and asked again, "How much water, Jose."

Jose sheepishly answered, "Half-full canteen, but it's gonna cost you big for a drink from my water bucket."

Farm Boy was astonished. "You'd make your friends buy water from you?"

Jose grinned in response, "Only thu dumb ones. Jus' wish you white boys knew how to save water. Now Chicanos, we know how to go wit' out water for days."

Matthew held his hand out, "Okay, you give me your canteen and demonstrate this amazing talent?"

Jose pulled out his canteen and allowed both Matthew and Farm Boy to take a swig before he placed it back in its holder. "You funny man, Amigo," Jose said.

Matthew then advised, "Now keep your heads down. I'll watch up ahead… Jose, you've got the left flank an' Farm Boy, you have the right. No shooting unless you have too. We don't want the NVA knowing we're down here. They'd roll right over the top of us and I sincerely doubt they're in the prisoner taking mood right now."

Jose clutched his pig, "Ah'd get a few of 'em."

Matthew shook his head at Jose again, "But we'd still be dead, Amigo." He then gave his friend a wink and turned to look up the hill. *Lord, keep us safe…And Lord; help me keep from losing my mind. I feel like I'm in the outer fringes of Hell and its trying to suck me in.* "If the rain picks up again try to collect some in your helmets, but wash them out first."

"It's clean mud," Farm Boy replied.

Matthew shook his head, "Mud I can stand, not your sweats and when was the last time you washed your hair?"

Both Jose and Farm Boy remained silent, continuing to observe the surrounding hillside and hope for ten minutes of a downpour to refill their canteens and cut the two to three inches of filth off their battered and bruised bodies.

D COMPANY

Nearly a long and tiresome hour passed before Walstein and John spotted Campbell at the company CP with Sampson. They were really glad to see Sgt. Campbell and even the CO. The Command Post was a large crater made from either a bomb or a large 175mm artillery round and it was now filled with six to eight inches of filthy brown water covering the men's boots and partially surrounded by a mixture of rocks, a two-thick sandbag wall six-feet high and piled logs. There were shelter halves to keep the wounded dry too. John and Walstein jumped in beside them with a splash, only adding to Campbell and Sampson's foul mood, which only grew worse when John and Walstein filled them in on 2nd squad's dilemma.

Captain Sampson tried to listen to both John's report and a busy radio. He glanced repeatedly to Campbell and then finally ordered his platoon back up the hill, "See what's up and advise me what you need."

Campbell replied, "Yes, sir." He grabbed John by the arm, "C'mon, show me where your fearless leader is goofing off, again."

John pointed to some open ammo crates and said, "We're down to half-a-dozen magazines and no grenades, Sergeant."

Campbell glanced over at Captain Sampson who was busy and then told John and Walstein to steal what they could carry. "But hurry, that's all the company has."

2ND SQUAD

Matthew felt like hugging Campbell when the big man suddenly appeared and said "Okay, show me what you got." A moment later, with his helmet off and hair covered in mud for camouflage, Campbell cautiously peeked over the crest and observed the bunker complex and then ducked back down. "Yeah, this is going be a real bugger," he whispered.

"Nothings come easy since we landed in this hellish valley," Matthew complained. He then added, "It's those men in the trench who pose the real threat. Between them, they have a field of fire covering nearly 360 degrees."

John was the one to ask, "Can you pull Jackson over or get us those Cobras back?"

Campbell shook his head, "I doubt it on the air power, but maybe on Franklin...though I sure hate to leave our right flank exposed. Let's head back down and have a chat with the Captain." Campbell slid down the hill on his butt and was just about to spring to his feet when a bullet struck the stock of his M-79 and drove the weapon into his side. Down he went head over heels for nearly ten yards before he could stop himself in the sloppy hillside mush.

Seeing where the shot came from, Matthew fired off a quick burst and dashed over to where a man was attempting to slide back into his spider hole. Thinking the sniper had killed his friend Matthew threw the grass mat back to expose the wounded man completely. He then stood over him and coldly emptied the rest of his magazine into the man. Right then another sniper opened up and two bullets missed Matthew by mere inches and without any knowledge of the near death experience, he went running down the hill to reach Campbell's body.

"I thought you were dead," Matthew said when he saw Campbell pick himself off the ground with Haggerty's help.

"Close...too close," Campbell said. He then showed Matthew his damaged stock. "I'm learning to really hate this place."

With a hopeful gleam to his eyes Haggerty asked, "We going back down the hill, now?"

Campbell shook his head and with a determined look on his face he pointed up the hillside. "No, I'm getting' real tired of climbing this stinking hill an' fighting over ground we already took the night before. Get on the radio an' advise the Captain we need at least three...make that four LAWs or another air strike."

Dismayed, Haggerty delivered the message and then turned to Campbell, "CO wants you down at the CP."

Weary from all the footwork in the mud, Campbell turned to Matthew. "Hold here and dig in, I'll be back."

D COMPANY

As darkness descended over the valley, 1st platoon dug in along a staggered line to match up with Franklin's platoon of worn out soldiers and then match up with Olson's bedraggled troopers. Lt. Olson left Franklin in charge of the line and climbed down the hill to meet with Campbell and Captain Sampson. "That's the way it is, Sir," Campbell said. He wiped the weariness from his eyes and smeared filth over his eye lids and forehead. "We got to have LAWs an' that bunker complex up there is a real beast even with heavy weapons."

Captain Sampson inspected his sergeant and he couldn't help but notice the strain the man was under. "Not much chance on an air strike, Sergeant, everything is tied up." Captain Sampson then asked, "Show me where the company is?" A topographical map was laid out across a blackened log and it displayed Hill # 937.

Campbell replied, "Sir, I really hate maps. You'd better have the lieutenant show you."

Lt. Olson smiled at Campbell and reached forward to use his finger to draw out a line representing D Company's forward position. "I want your opinions. Do we pull back?" Sampson asked.

Campbell didn't wait for Olson's reply, "No, sir. We don't want to lose any more real estate. Too many of our troops have paid for that ground already."

Lt. Olson agreed, "We're paying too high a price as it is for this mountain. Those bunkers have my men pinned down and I know Franklin's in the same shape. We've got to have heavier weapons to take them out or fly back to Eagle Camp for a hot shower and a good meal."

Captain Sampson thought about what the two of them had said, but even more what was in their eyes; they wanted payback. "All right, I'll advise Battalion of our situation. Get the wounded rounded up and brought down here. Later, we'll take them down the hill and the men carrying the stretchers can bring supplies back up. Everyone gets one canteen filled up and make sure they know it has to last. Are there any questions, gentlemen?"

Campbell said, "Ammo, sir and grenades." He lifted his four remaining shotgun rounds out of his pouch to show how low he was.

"All right, once we get the wounded moved out I'll move my CP up to your line at 2330 hours. Advise the men taking the wounded down to leave most of their ammo with the company, in the event we get attacked." Campbell and Olson both answered with a tired sounding, "Yes, sir." They both climbed out of the hole and began the wearisome and dangerous trek back up the hill.

1ST PLATOON

"We're staying here for the night. Fifty-fifty watch until 2100 hours, then we go on 100% alert," Campbell told his men and then told Jackson his squad's assignment, "Jackson, your squad is assigned stretcher duty. Get an empty canteen from each man in the platoon and fill them up at the base camp. When you get to supply, make sure you pick me up some shotgun ammo. I want a new M-79 and equal HE and WP rounds...also, lots of grenades. But most importantly, bring us back some LAWs."

Jackson stared back at him in silence for a moment and then asked, "What about the donkey?" Campbell gave Jackson a funny look and asked, "What donkey?" Jackson pointed down the hill, "The donkey I'm gonna need to carry all that crap back up this hill...Sergeant."

2ND SQUAD

Matthew dug deep and fast. He hoped to use the strenuous work to bleed off his tension, but stopped when he glanced up to watch the wounded men leave. Most could walk, some needed the help of another, but others were carried down the hill on hastily built stretchers. The one dead man was wrapped into two ponchos and carried down with the wounded, but last in line. By the time they got ready to leave, another squad from 3rd platoon had to be pulled off the line to help SSgt. Franklin with the detail. It was not an easy climb in either direction because of the muddy hillsides. At any moment the ground could give way under a soldier's foot and he would end up falling several yards or more down the hill. More often and not, it was stump, blackened log or a boulder that stopped a man and it was abrupt.

"We sure look like we've been whipped," Farm Boy said.

"Not whipped, but we've been in a tough fight," Walstein added. It was his turn to keep watch while John slept, but the time for 100% alert was approaching rapidly.

Whipped...fight...I feel like I'm already dead, Matthew thought. *How many more hills after this one, how many more men must die an' how many more must I kill before this ends...And will it ever end?*

D COMPANY

With the wounded men on their way down to Battalion Aid, D Company had only 58 fighting men left on the line. A Company was reduced to 54 men, B Company had 57 and C Company was guarding the Battalion's perimeter with 78 men. The 2nd Battalion now had only 247 combat soldiers on Hill # 937 and they were out numbered by the NVA by better than five to one odds and the enemy still held the high ground.

Later that evening, Captain Sampson was advised by Battalion, "Artillery will be using CS gas for the morning bombardment." Sampson couldn't help but wonder, *Gas? Tear Gas? We want bombs!*

It was shortly after midnight when SSgt. Franklin returned with supplies, a few new replacements and even some chow. Once the LAWs and badly needed ammo was handed out, hungry and thirsty men were grateful to see the cases of C-rations. Many a man commented on how good it felt to taste the sugary juice from a can of fruit cocktail run down their parched throats.

With the company on 100% alert, Captain Sampson briefed his platoon commanders on the morning's plan of attack, "From 0800 to 0925 hours, artillery units will bombard the hillsides above us with CS gas and explosive rounds. This will be followed by an air attack on the summit. We will then attack at 1000 hours for an all-out assault to reach the top." Sampson stopped for a moment and released a weary sigh. Like the men who set before him he was growing tired of Battalion's so called all-out attacks, but now headquarters staff had come up with something even better.

"Listen to this one, Battalion has issued orders for the men to stop for nothing on this attack...not even the wounded. We are to take the hill at all costs, we'll come back to check on our wounded comrades once the hill is secured." Campbell stared at Sampson in disbelief. Both Olson and Franklin had looks of shock on their faces.

"That's the order, gentlemen. But in my company, I refuse to punish any man who stops to assist one of his wounded buddies. And if I see or hear of someone deserting a wounded man without making sure he's fit to leave behind with a loaded rifle in his hands, he'd better hope I never get my hands on him. This mountain has cost us enough. Now go brief your men, we'll have another meeting at 0700 hours."

Ten new guys, the ones who had come up with Franklin, were grouped off to one side. Between the staggering number of wounded cases and the stacks of body bags, they were pretty shaken up when a lieutenant told them to follow SSgt. Franklin up the hill. Sampson gave five of the men to Campbell, two to Franklin and three to Lt. Olson.

"Welcome to D Company, men. Keep your eyes open, your mouths shut and listen to your squad leaders," Captain Sampson said. He gave them a final look over, a silent nod and turned away. Although he needed the men, he had silently wished they hadn't sent any new replacements in unless they each came with a company of men attached. *More lambs...more men to be sacrificed for Hill 937. What useless slaughter!*

2ND SQUAD

Using a scraggly looking toothbrush to clean his rifle bolt with, Matthew glanced up when he saw Campbell approach with a new man; a black guy. "What's up?"

Campbell replied, "New man," and then introduced him. "PFC Monroe, this is Kendal, your new squad leader." Monroe stood there in the dark and looked at Matthew.

"Take care of him, Matt. He's greener than grass. I've got two LAWs for you an' plenty of ammo. But tell Jose to keep his bursts down, may be awhile before our next supply shipment. And one canteen of water for each man, they'll make it last or eat mud."

Matthew nodded his head and then asked with sarcastic wit. "What, no mail?" Campbell ignored the question. They wouldn't see mail until they got back to Camp Eagle.

"Squad leader's meeting in one hour. Leave your mouth here." When Campbell walked off into the dark, Monroe quickly stepped down into Matthew's hole and dropped off his new field pack.

"We're a small squad, only six of us now counting you." Matthew pointed to the next hole and said, "That's John Adams and Walstein over there and the next hole after is Jose Martinez and Farm Boy Andrews on our 60. You'll team up with me for now, but tomorrow you'll sleep with Walstein."

Monroe replied with a courteous, "Yes, Sir." Matthew shook his head, "Don't sir me. It's either Kendal or Matthew or Matt. I'm only an E-4. Campbell was our squad leader, but with the L-T out, he took over the platoon."

Monroe glanced around in the darkness and then asked, "What do you want me ta do?" Matthew put is rifle together and then replied, "Help me get this ammo divvied up first off and make sure every man gets four grenades, too."

Before leaving for the squad leader's meeting, Matthew learned how Curtis Monroe was from Birmingham, Alabama and had been in Vietnam for a total of seven-days. When Monroe told Matthew how the heat in Nam reminded him of Birmingham, Matthew promised himself right then to never to visit Alabama in the summertime.

1ST PLATOON

At the squad leader's meeting, four droopy-eyed young men listened as Campbell briefed them on the coming operation. It was Jackson who spoke up first, "What do they expect us to do, Sarge? With C Company in reserve, there's..." Jackson did a mental recount on the numbers Campbell had just given them, "...there's only 169 of us left in this battalion to attack with."

Campbell gave him a hard look, "They expect us to obey orders, even if that means to abandon our wounded. Now listen, I don't like it either so make sure every man we leave behind has a loaded rifle in his hand, his canteen and any first-aid we can provide. But D Company will do its duty; we will climb. Got it?" Campbell looked at each man to make sure they understood their orders. "C Company will be pulled from perimeter duty and pushed into the attack. The CP has enough people to handle their own security now. When it starts to get light, put the men back on fifty-fifty watch, try to catch some Zs before the attack begins. At least up here we can see the sun again...if the clouds ever clear. I don't wanna go back down into that valley, it's like walking through Hell and the NVA are the demons who torment us."

Campbell stretched his leg out and Matthew could hear the crackling noises his knee made. "Last thing...spend some time with your new guys an' get 'em ready. We'll have another meeting at 0600 hours. Are there any intelligent questions?" There was none and the meeting broke up.

2ND SQUAD

While Matthew was away, John slid in beside Monroe and introduced himself, "Hey, Bro." John brought his hand up for a quick dap and Monroe only looked at him with a confused expression on his face. The light from the fires burning on the hillside provided enough illumination to see for about two-feet and the occasional mortar flare illuminated the hillsides. This gave the men an eerie light to see by as monstrous shadows were cast over the hill.

"Hi, ah'm Curtis Monroe from Alabama." Monroe's strong southern draw almost made John smile as he remembered Jack Waterford's strong southern accent.

"From the deep dark South, huh? Well, what's happenin' back in thu world?" To which Monroe replied in confusion, "The World?"

John grinned, "Back in the USA...we calls it thu world."

Quiet at first, Monroe then answered, "Not much...Ah don't know much 'bout those things. Work't in mah dad's gas station, fixin' tires an' such. Weez got a two-pumper, hope to get a tow truck next year with my GI pay." Monroe picked up Matthew's shovel and started digging to make their hole wider for two men.

"Did you finish school?" John asked.

"Nah, Lef' afta thu sixth grade ta help mah dad. Did yuh?"

John grabbed up a spare E-tool and began helping Monroe shovel. "Ah got my GED, but someday...maybe college."

"Where you from?" Monroe asked.

"Washington, D.C." John threw a shovel full of mud over his shoulder.

"Ah heard it a nice place, lots of white statues."

John shook his head, leaned on his shovel and said, "For uppity white people. For Blacks, its jus' poor."

Monroe glanced over at John, "Matt seems like a nice guy."

John nodded his head in response and said, "Pure gold, Monroe...He's mah best friend."

Monroe went back to shoveling. "Must be a nice guy then," Monroe said as he glanced up and gave John a smile and continued on with his dirt work. John was about to leave when a flare burst overhead and he noticed a small silver cross hanging from Monroe's dog tag chain.

"You a Christian, Monroe?"

He grabbed his cross in his right hand and said, "Yup! Southern Baptist."

John replied, "Don't know much 'bout Baptist. Is they protestant?"

Monroe chuckled. "Sure am. You a Christian too?"

John answered, "Yeah, pretty new one too."

Monroe put his cross and dog tag chain back under his camouflage fatigue shirt. "Well, you'se get you'self kill't over here an' you'se be wit' thu Lord. But ah surely do t'ink some d'ese men over here got a surprise a cumin'. Surely do."

Matthew came running up, jumped into the hole, shoved both men aside and then ignored Monroe, as he looked at John and in a whisper of a voice blurted out, "You ain't goin' to believe this one.

INSIDE AP BIA MOUNTAIN, MAY 17TH, 1969 0108 HOURS

The number of wounded coming in had dropped off slowly, but Que knew the fighting was still going on from the sound of gunfire. Upon asking, he was told how most of the tunnels were destroyed and as a result, they couldn't get the wounded into the hospital. Orders soon came down, all the remaining wounded were to be moved tonight and the medics and nurses would be moved outside to treat the wounded where they fell. This terrified Que at first, the thought of going into battle sent a surge of cold fear through him. With dreams of becoming a doctor someday, Que knew nothing about the art of war. He'd never fired a gun, thrown a grenade or actually hurt another human being in anger. *What will I do if I'm forced to take another's life? Can I? Will I?* Que's thoughts only added to his confusion, *Medicine...medicine is what I know, but to kill...*

14 – AND THE RAINS CAME

D COMPANY, MAY 17TH, 1969 0422 HOURS *DAY 8*

Shortly after midnight someone pulled the plug from the heavens and a deluge of heavy monsoon rains poured forth upon the A Shau Valley. For four hours the steady downpour soaked the men of both armies and transformed the hillsides of Hill #937 into a thick pudding-like mud. In some places the brownish goop was mid-calf in depth and the foxholes became uninhabitable, with the murky waters rising above the edges and driving the soldiers out of them. For men wearing the same uniform for the last eight days, they resembled poverty stricken street urchins of a European country at the end of World War II. Their ratty jungle fatigues, covered with C-ration juice stains, dried blood, blackened ash and grime and mud, literally hung off their wet bodies in tatters. Even as the rain-washed away some of the dried mud and soot, the blood stains remained and new mud was splashed upon them as soldiers made their way from cover to cover. Within the first hour the men had stopped using their ponchos for shelter because the wet shiny surface made too great a target for enemy snipers and the humidity underneath made the air stifling.

As the tempest slowly moved across the valley, the men of D Company remained snuggled in their newly dug holes and listened while rain pellets struck their helmets. It doesn't take long before their new holes fill up and once again the men are forced to use helmets as bailing buckets or they move off to dig yet one more hole. But for some, they've given up and utterly depressed, they remained in those newly formed ponds as the waters continued to rise all about them.

2ND SQUAD

Since 2240 hours Matthew has been wide awake, alternating his routine between watching the surrounding hillside for the enemy, bailing water with his helmet and taking a brief moment to glance over at PFC Monroe. Matthew fought with a deep depression and he turned to thoughts of his own death, *Today's the day, I feel it…I'm gonna buy it. That golden bee-bee is gonna zap me an' someone's gonna zip me into a body bag with a few kind words. I'm finally coming home, mom and dad…*

Disgusted by his defeatist thoughts, Matthew dipped his helmet into the waters about his knees and went back to bailing, while streams of muddy water poured into the hole he shared with Monroe. He was losing the battle and could use Monroe's help, but someone needed to keep watch and it was Monroe's turn. *Yeah this was sure a great idea. Never took a moment to consider their emotional needs, never wondering how bad this will hurt mom when I got killed. Yeah, I was sure the bright one to volunteer…boy, was that ever lame. Now I'm sitting a top this hill, 5,000 miles away from my girl. This is glory? I, the avenging angel…what a joke!*

When the rains began to slacken off, the men faced a new danger; rivers cascading down the hill turning into rushing waterfalls, and then walls of mud begin to come at them from above. The hillsides, now empty of trees and growth, had given way and thick walls of mud, filled with debris, began to landslide down the hill in slow waves from above.

"That's it!" PFC Edwards, a man from Franklin's 2nd squad, shouted. "I've had it- had it –had it!" He began to rave, while he splashed about his hole with his bare feet. He then leapt out, tossed his rifle down in the mud and took of at a dead run downhill. But He slipped, fell on his behind and began a long slide. This gave time for two of his squad-mates to soon catch up with him. They grabbed him by his arms, lifted him up and dragged him back to their position. By the time they got him to his foxhole, the man was weeping and muttering incoherently. SSgt. Franklin, tired of the battle and the rains himself, and seeing so many of his men go down, only shook his head and ordered the men to take the soldier back to the first aid station so the medics could treat him.

"He's no good up here in his current condition…see what they can do for him. But you two get back up here ASAP! Remember your pass words, or you'll end up dead and I need you."

2ND SQUAD

Matthew took a brief break and leaned back against the wall of his hole and looked above to the brown sky and whispered a prayer to God, "Lord, I've made some really stupid decisions since Luke's death and could really need your help. I've done so many…crappy things since coming here and I've had to kill a lot of men, but worst of all was my faith…I began to doubt you really cared…again." Matthew let the rain wash the tears away. "Forgive me, God." Matthew waited, in hopes he might hear an audible word from God, but the night remained silent and very wet. He shook his head, wiped his face to leave it covered in streaks and put his helmet back on. "It's your turn, Monroe…I'll keep watch."

1ST PLATOON

Shortly before 0500 hours, the rain stopped and almost immediately afterward, the jungle heat began to rise up the hillsides from the valley floor. Everything was wet or clammy and the humidity was so thick a few of the new men became ill. Instead of rain the men are now wiping away sweat as they watched dumbfounded when patches of steam began to rise and form a thick mist. The stench of mildew and the foul odor of filth emanates from their uniforms, now intermixed with the smell of death and decay. For some of the men, those who begin to loose their grasp on sanity, they envision themselves on either another planet or the vile plains of Hell itself. But soon the sounds of war return and the eerie silence is broken when a shot rang out from a man in Jackson's squad. He had spotted a careless sniper and his shot was answered immediately by more than a dozen AK-47s. A fire-fight was then on between the men of 1st platoon and an unseen enemy, hidden by mist and darkness, from above. Within seconds the hillside is lit up with the bright luminous glow of tracers going back and forth between the two forces.

"Cease fire--Cease fire!" Campbell ordered and all too soon the spooky silence returned to haunt the weary soldiers of the 1st platoon.

2ND SQUAD

Matthew looked to his right and noticed Monroe braced against the rim of their hole, his helmet back on his head and rifle ready. They exchange nods; an acknowledgement the fight was over for the moment and they were both okay. "What now?" Monroe asked in too loud of a voice.

"Sh-h-h, you're too loud. Whisper or you'll get an RPG in your lap," Matthew said. He then moved closer to Monroe, "We wait for now." Matthew looked away and checked to make sure all his men were okay and was glad to see no one had gotten hit in the fire fight.

"Cun we talk a bit?" Monroe asked.

"Keep it low...what's on your mind?"

Monroe hesitated and then said, "Wonderin' 'bout death. Ah cun see it in your eyes, you'se been doin' dis for 'while an' ah was wantin' ta know what's it like to face your enemy?"

Matthew thought about his response and then answered, "I don't think about it...but I'd be lying to you if I told you I wasn't scared. Up here everyone's frightened...if they're not, they're fools."

Monroe asked, "What 'bout killin'?"

Matthew tensed up, but relaxed somewhat when he realized Monroe was only asking a question and not making an accusation. "Some men think nothing of killing and they look at it like killing a rabid dog. Others don't want to pull the trigger again and those guys end up endangering their squad. I guess I'm somewhere in the middle. Don't enjoy it, but I got a job to do and so do you. We're not murderers and don't let anyone make you think you are for doing your job." Matthew took a glance up the hill and looked back at a quiet Monroe, "Does that answer your question?"

Monroe slowly nodded his head, "Yup."

1ST PLATOON

By 0600 hours a gray dawn hung over Hill 937, when Campbell met with his four- squad leaders in a small hallow. To a man, they all look like some hideous mud demons and only their weapons are kept reasonably clean. Playing the role as host, Campbell tossed to each man a can of fruit. Matthew studied the can of fruit cocktail for a moment, lost in thought as he stared at the green can and wondered about the people who had picked the fruit and made the can itself. He sighed, pulled his dog chain out with a P-38 can opener on it and began to open the C-ration delicacy. He didn't bother with a spoon, but finished it off in four gulps. Between the rain, mist and heat, Matthew began to pick up a sore throat and a case of sniffles.

"Okay, breakfast has been served so let's get down to business." Campbell suddenly broke into a grin, which surprised his squad leaders, "Man, we look like a bunch of real slobs."

Jackson pointed out, "Sarge, I had trouble getting over here. Mah boots kept sinkin' in and it getting' tougher an' tougher to pull 'em out."

Campbell shook his head, "I can care less what your boots and uniforms look like right now, you just keep those rifles clean. Now the big cheese wants that summit taken today. We've heard it before…and again, 'at all costs'." Campbell shook his head in frustration. "We can expect a barrage to last from 0800 to 0925 hours. This hill is gonna shake, rattle an' roll an' we'll probably be all deaf before it's over and put in for medical discharges." He looked into their faces, caked in dried mud and their deeply recessed and black rimmed eyes returned an almost lifeless stare. *These boys are too young to have that look!* "For an added gesture, they're gonna use CS gas to drive the enemy out of their holes. So keep your heads down or you're liable to get a strong whiff of the stuff yourselves. Then we launch at 1000 hours and once we start climbing, we don't stop. We're to leave our wounded behind, but like I said before we make sure they're bandaged up got a loaded rifle in their hands and a canteen. Every man is to carry as much ammo an' grenades as he can haul, because there won't be any resupply until we've taken this anthill. After we take it, we can collect our wounded up an' count our dead.

"D Company will move up together, holding a line formation as long as we can. Any...smart questions?" There was none so far. "Okay then, get your men to eat something so they don't run out of energy half-way up and check their supplies. Captain Sampson has ammo and grenades, maybe some LAWs and M-79 rounds, so send a runner for what you need. That's it, good luck." Campbell shook each of their hands and then watched as they drifted off like dead men walking. Between dried mud and lack of sleep, the four of them suddenly reminded him of ghoulish creatures from some black and white gothic painting. *Maybe Dante's Inferno?*

D COMPANY

At exactly 0830 hours, the Air Force, late as usual, announced their arrival with F-4 Phantoms strafing the second bunker line. A second run of Marine F-4s dropped 250-pound bombs upon the summit that sent vibrations down through the mountain. The hillsides gave way, which created mudslides and several more tunnels collapsed, which trapped and killed several of the NVA. Cobra gunships then entered the picture and they launched rockets against visible targets and pounded the hilltop with 40mm grenades. Within moments of the attack the air became filled with blackened clouds and the pungent odor of sulfur and the stench only worsened when the heavy artillery opened up from nearby firebases.

The 3rd Battalion is then caught by surprise when almost incoherent screams comes over the radio; CS gas rounds had landed right on top of A Company. Men abandoned their positions to escape down the hill and getaway from the gas. Some of the soldiers fell face down on to the mud and began long slides, cutting a shallow furrow as they went, only to collide with deadfalls and some of the soldiers were knocked unconscious. Others lost their footing, rolled or somersaulted and landed in muddy heaps. If it wasn't so serious, Captain Sampson would have broken out into laughter, but he shook his head in frustration when he saw several loose M-16s go flying; one sunk in a large puddle and another smacked against the stump of a burned tree and broke its stock. Disgusted with the whole mess, he turned to his RTO, and asked, "What else can go wrong?"

At 0940 hours a flight of rearmed Cobra gunships returned to rake the hillsides and they come under attack by a heavy concentration of machinegun fire from hidden bunkers. Within moments, the Cobras are driven off. "Looks like the occupants have decided not to vacate the premises as the big brass expected," Sampson said with a strong note of sarcasm.

At 0953 hours the hillside fell silent and in seven minutes the men of the 2nd Battalion would once again launch an all out attack. They waited, each man nervously fingering his weapon, staring at one another and wondering if this might be his final day on this earth. They waited for the order to move out and the men take this brief moment of time to utter a final prayer. For some, they're busy rubbing a rabbit's foot, fingering a special lucky piece or thinking about a loved one back home. They adjust a chinstrap for the tenth time and recheck a rifle, or they reposition their field pack to a more comfortable position. All this was to help pass the time and keep their nervous hands busy. It's a tough time for the smokers, men who haven't had a smoke all night for the newcomers or all week for the ones who have been here from the beginning. There was always that one or two who would sneak a smoke in the bottom of their hole, until the rains filled the foxholes up and there was no longer any place to hide the flash of a match or the burning ambers of a lit cigarette. Some chomped down on cigarette tobacco or they chewed tasteless chewing gum, anything to keep their teeth from chattering as the jitters hit. This is white knuckle time and for the newcomers, it was also upchuck--a time when a nervous stomach revolted.

When Sampson's watch struck 1000 hours, he raised his hand to signal to his platoon leaders and shouted at the top of his lungs, "D Company... Move out!" He stood there and watched his men step off and a sense of pride shot through him for these brave soldiers he commanded. But then he followed soon afterward with a reluctant RTO right behind him.

2ND SQUAD

"All right, we got people waiting on us," Matthew said. His teeth clinched, he leaned forward and began to climb up the mud and slime of the hillside. His squad was covered in it as they stepped out of their holes; a natural camouflage. They're a bone tired, knuckle dragging bunch and each step upward brought with it a grunt of complaint from one of the men. But still they climbed.

Before he jumped off, Matthew advised his squad to switch their selectors to *auto*, "Time to rock an' roll and party-down." Up ahead lay the bunkers destroyed in earlier action and each one had to be checked out for snipers and being cautious, Matthew fired off a short burst into the blackened rubble of the nearest bunker. Monroe was caught off guard by the carnage inside, his first taste of war, and it took some effort to keep from vomiting.

"You'll see worse before this is over," Matthew said to him. "Now keep moving...snipers love stationary targets."

A frightened Monroe replied, "Yes, Sir."

At 1004 hours: an NVA bunker concealed deep inside a pile of fallen trees opened up on 2nd squad. The men dive for cover and returned fire, until Matthew used his M-79 to drop a 40mm HE round in the middle of enemy's position. Second Squad then took a breather below the burning bunker and Matthew had the men hold, while he crawled up to check on the huge bunker complex still in their path. His heart raced at better than 130 beats-a-minute when he cautiously inched over the berm of mud for a quick look-see and was stunned by the site before him. *Wow! They actually hit something this morning.* The larger bunker to the right had completely disappeared and the area where it had been holds a blackened crater. Though damaged, the bunker to the left was mostly intact and he spotted movement in that side of the trench line, too. In the clearing in front of the enemy emplacement lay the bodies and remains of several NVA. No one in the enemy position had attempted to recover their dead and it made Matthew wonder why they hadn't. *Don't they care about their dead the way we do about ours? Is it a Buddhist thing or maybe its just they knew we were coming and didn't want to risk being exposed?*

Matthew ducked back down behind the berm of soft mud, rolled over on his back and glanced around to identify any cover his men could use as they made their attack. To his right was a large outcropping of blackened rocks, with rivets of muddy water pouring over them. That would do well for Jose. *I should be able to take that bunker out with a LAW...if Jose can keep 'em busy.* He slid back down the hillside on his backside, holding his weapons up, but stopping before he bypassed the squad had quickly turned into a problem. The muddy surface had transformed the hillside into one giant slide and it took John's quick movement and a strong right arm to bring him to a gradual halt.

Dragged in beside John like a hooked halibut, he swept some of the mud off his face and then turned to his squad, "You guys follow me up, but stay low. I don't want them spotting us until I can get a LAW off."

Matthew rapped his knuckles on Jose's helmet, "Wake-up, Bandito, there's a pile of rocks to our left. You get behind it an' wait for my signal. Rake the trench first and I'll take the bunker. The right bunker is already gone, bombed or hit with artillery. But we don't advance until every thing up there is dead. Got it?" Monroe was the only one to nod his head; the rest only stared back at Matthew in blank expressions and waited.

"Farm Boy, you make sure you keep the snipers off Jose's backside. Watch out for spider-holes to your right flank and behind you," Matthew reminded him.

"I got him covered, Matt."

Matthew nodded in turn and then removed the LAW from John's pack. He quickly glanced at each man, provided a brief grin of reassurance and then led the squad forward with everyone crawling on their stomachs. They had to pull themselves upward through mud six to eight inches deep and the going was tough, as they now resembled swamp critters swimming through a Louisiana bog.

1ST SQUAD

Jackson moved his squad up a deep culvert to position themselves for the attack on the bunker complex. When he spotted 2nd squad, Jackson stopped to see what Matthew had in mind. From his vantage point, Jackson could see at least five NVA riflemen sitting in the trench busily bailing water out of it. Another two or maybe three men were in the one bunker and on watch. Jackson positioned his men on the lip of the culvert and waited for Matthew to make his move. When Matthew did, he would now be in position to provide supporting fire.

2ND SQUAD

Matthew had to really scramble up the hill like a six-legged mountain goat to keep the LAW out of the mud. But when he slid the assembled LAW over the crest of the berm and sighted on the bunker's opening, the weapon was mostly dry and very ready to do its job. With so much mud, Matthew's helmet was well-camouflaged and he did not think the enemy would even notice him. Then with a quick glance to ensure his squad was ready, Matthew took a final sighting and signaled for Jose to begin firing. Hearing the first shots, Matthew compressed the trigger that launched the anti-tank rocket forward. The blast left a bright flash in its wake and the rocket sailed through the air to pass right by the startled NVA riflemen and impacted the bunker a foot from the bunker's machine gun opening. It didn't matter though. A fiery explosion sent logs flying and threw one burning man for over 15-feet outside in the deep slime. The anti-tank round had reduced the small fortress to a pile of kindling wood, now blackened by only smoke and smoldering in small flames because of heavy rain. But with the sound of the explosion, Jose turned his baby loose on the bunker to ensure it was assuredly dead, before re-aiming on the trench line.

Staying prone, John fired off several short bursts with his M-16 and then stooped to lob a grenade. Over 25-feet through the air, a personnel best uphill, it landed on the forward edge of the trench and exploded. John then lay on to his back and quickly changed magazines. Afterward, he rolled back over to the prone position and along with Monroe, Farm Boy and Walstein they continued to lay down a fierce fire storm of lead between the rain drops.

Walstein had a moving target, a lone NVA shaken from the blast and bleeding from his eyes and nose, who staggered toward him. Unsure of what to do because the guy was unarmed, Walstein lifted his head up and shouted, "Put your hands up! Get your hands up, you stupid gook!" But the

NVA kept coming toward him as if he was drunk. To Walstein's shock, a sudden burst of AK-47 fire cut the man down from behind. Another NVA, who was hidden behind a large stump, shot his own man to get a clear shot at the Americans. Shot in the back, the dying NVA was driven forward to land only a few feet in front of where Walstein lay.

For a long few seconds, Walstein saw the man's chest rise and fall, and he rose up to crawl forward to reach the man. He was in the process of pulling out a battle dressing in an act of compassion, when for his effort, the NVA rifleman behind the stump stood up and shot Walstein in the stomach. Shocked and holding his stomach wound, Walstein tumbled backward a few feet to land on his back and there he lay silently, a stunned expression on his face. *Feels so strange…so warm…no pain…no pain.* The man doesn't get a chance for a second shot, Jose blasted the stump and killed the shooter with a quick five round burst. Farm Boy left Jose's side and made a dash for Walstein.

"Cover us, Jose! We're goin' in." Matthew shouted. Leaving Farm Boy with Walstein, he then led John and Monroe against the trench line. With fire support from Jackson's squad, Matthew's people moved across the clearing, firing their rifles from the hip and finish off three more NVA soldiers.

"Reload and secure the area," Matthew ordered, as he fought to breathe.

Lifting his 60, Jose noticed Jackson's squad and alerted Matthew, "Matt, Jackson's comin' in."

While 1st squad checked out the area for snipers, Matthew went to check on Walstein. Farm Boy had him stretched out on his side and was speaking to him in a calm voice, "Yup, looks like you took one in your right hip, took part of your gut too so you might have to hold off on the belly bombers back home for a while. Now hold still while I get a dressing on it."

Farm Boy used his survival knife to cut Walstein's pants away from the wound. Then he pulled out a battle dressing, pushed a small piece of intestine back inside and sprinkled some sulfur powder on. He then told Walstein to apply pressure on it, while he secured the bandage around his waist. Walstein bit his lip to stifle out a cry when Farm Boy forced the end of the bandage under him to bring back up on the other side. Then in a painful plea, he asked, "Am…Am I gonna die?"

Farm Boy looked him in the eye, "Probably someday, but not from this bug bite. Don't know 'bout your dancing days though…Hey, do Jewish people dance?" Seeing the painful expression on his face, Farm Boy ripped a pocket off Walstein's shirt and folded the somewhat cleaner, but soaked side over before inserting it into his mouth, "Bite down, it'll help."

"Let's move him over to the bunker, we're too exposed out here," Matthew ordered.

Farm Boy nodded his head and warned Walstein, "This is gonna hurt, buddy, but we'll make it quick." He picked Walstein up by the shoulders and with Matthew's help carried him over to the blackened bunker. Teary eyed and curled into the fetal position with his hand pressing down on his bloody bandage, Walstein's mouth began to bleed when he bit down. Matthew knelt down beside Walstein, lifted his head up and let him take a couple sips from his canteen.

"Erwin, don't swallow, just rinse your mouth out and spit." Matthew waited until Walstein did like he was told. Orders were to never give water to those soldiers with stomach wounds and Matthew figured it had something to do with bleeding control, since he slept through the rest of the briefing. "Look, I got to leave you here. We'll brace you up against this bunker an' leave your rifle with you." Matthew saw the terrified look in the man's eyes, "Hey, we have to go on. You heard the orders, but no canteen. You'll have a fresh magazine, but you have to stay awake or some commie is gonna sneak in here and cut your throat." He saw the watery mournful eyes and tried to reassure him, "I'll be back for you, I promise you that."

Sucking in a deep breath, Walstein exhaled and blurted, "You can't leave me...I'll bleed to death!"

Matthew shook his head, "You won't die, you just have to remember to keep telling yourself that. Hear me, Erwin? Keep repeating that over an' over, and don't fall asleep." Not only pain, but Walstein's eyes now displayed the anger he felt right now toward Matthew.

He stuffed the pain as best as he could and his teary eyes turned cold with thoughts of betrayal as he glared at Matthew, "Yeah, leave the Jew boy. I got it...Jus' hope you get yours too." Walstein turned away and spat blood on the ground. Matthew pulled Walstein's canteen out of its holder and removed two full rifle magazines from the wounded man. "Get mad...get real mad, and you just might survive this...Jew Boy."

Farm Boy handed him his rifle after sitting him up against the only surviving bunker wall. "Safety's off, just point and shoot. But make sure it's the enemy you're shooting at."

For a brief moment, Matthew wondered if Walstein was going to turn his rifle on him, but the tension ended when Jackson walked up. "Looks like we're climbing together, Kendal. Couldn't get any farther unless I move to the right another 100 yards or so an' that's too much open space to cross."

Matthew looked at Walstein, stood up and nodded, "Sounds right, let's get out of here." Walstein watched the men leave and once they were out of sight, he burst into tears. The pain was nearly unbearable and several times he considered ending it with his own rifle, but it was his faith that prevented it. And the anger he had for being abandoned also helped him stay alive.

Matthew hated calling Erin that name, but he needed him angry and if directing it at him would work, he could handle it. Now he needed to refocus on the climb and his orders to secure the summit. At this point, He felt those orders were for him personally, it had come down to a battle between him and Hill # 937.

For the next ten minutes or so the two squads stayed together until they cleared a narrow ravine and then they split up again with Jackson taking his men to the right. Less than a minute later, 2nd squad ran into a large well-camouflaged log bunker manned by six NVA. Matthew and his men go flat when machinegun fire passes overhead. For the next hour the two sides exchanged fire, with neither side giving up an inch. Matthew used a scorched four-foot tall stump for cover and emptied one magazine. But the rifle bullets simply burrowed into the large logs like two-penny nails. Farm Boy had the last Law, but he was unable to reach a position to fire it.

"Keep shooting! They can't fire if they're duckin' lead," Matthew shouted. He then began to change magazines.

"Look out, Matt!" Farm Boy yelled in warning. Matthew looked to his right and was startled to see an NVA soldier charging across the hill at him. The man was holding his rifle at the waist and his bayonet was aimed right at Matthew's head and almost on top of him before Monroe dropped him with a two-round burst to the chest.

"Thanks," Matthew muttered nervously.

Monroe tossed him a quick wave in return. The firefight continued, but Matthew knew they were using up their ammo too fast and they still had at least another 200 yards to go before they reached the summit. With a fast wave, he signaled Farm Boy to get closer and then ordered Jose to provide covering fire. Right then, Monroe spotted an NVA soldier preparing to fire off an RPG and yelled out a warning, "RPG!" The grenade sailed through the air and exploded on the ground only ten feet below Jose and Farm Boy. The concussion wave from the blast rolled Jose over onto his back and left him temporarily stunned. But Farm Boy wasn't so lucky- hot shrapnel ripped into his legs. With an ear piercing shriek, Farm Boy frantically crawled away from the impact point with only the strength of his two hands reaching into the mud for something to grip. His legs were useless and bleeding and he knew he was going to die unless he got help real fast.

"Jose…ah need help. Oh, God it hurts…Please, Jose…wake-up. Jose!"

With a number ten head banger, Jose slowly awakened and through the fog he began to hear his name called out. Shaking his head to clear it, he rolled over and spotted Farm Boy lying only a few feet away and there's blood all over the ground. "Hold on, man," Jose said. He glanced up the hill in search of help. But the squad was pinned down, "Looks like I got ta do dis mahself," Jose said. He began to crawl toward Farm Boy and the closer he got the more sickened he became by what he saw. He bit his tongue to keep from losing it and scaring Farm Boy even more. Farm Boy's right foot is nearly severed at the ankle and bone is sticking out below the knees of both legs.

His mind racing, Jose yanked Farm Boy's pants belt off and then his own to use them as tourniquets. He wrapped them around the upper thighs, cinched them tight and tied them into place.

"Jose, we need that LAW!" Matthew shouted.

"I'm busy, come get it yourself," Jose growled back. With Matthew and John providing covering fire, Monroe low crawled over to where Farm Boy had dropped the LAW. Fighting to ignore the bloody mess where his new friend lay, Monroe climbed back up to where Matthew waited. A split second later, the bunker exploded in a fiery blast of black smoke and bright yellow and orange flames. Matthew, John and Monroe approached the dying bunker while firing from the hip. The bunker dead, they returned to help Jose with Farm Boy.

"It hurts…it hurts! Oh, God someone jus' shoot me," Farm Boy begged through clenched teeth.

"Shut up, Pig Farmer an' press down here," Jose said. He wrapped a second and then a third battle dressing around his legs. "Matt, we got to get 'im down the hill, he'll bleed to death if we don't."

Matthew looked down the hill and then back at Jose, "You know the orders, we keep goin'."

John stepped up, "We can't leave him here." Matthew turned away, but then John grabbed him by the arm, "We take him back, Matt, or he'll die for sure."

Whirling around, his face full of rage, Matthew glared at John, "You think I wanna leave him here? You think I get a kick out of leaving Walstein back down there? I got orders, I got…" Matthew's voice ground to a halt. He was unable to respond further to his friend. John remained quiet, seeing the inner turmoil his friend was warring with.

For a brief moment the two men simply stared at each other and then John responded in a low whisper, "Sorree, Matt."

Matthew glared at John, but then his eyes softened, he nodded and released an audible sigh. Matthew looked down at Jose and muttered quietly, "We climb." Nearly unconscious, his bleeding down to a seeping trickle because of Jose's quick action, Farm Boy was left with his rifle and two hand grenades. Reluctantly and nearly dragged up the hill, Jose left his friend and followed the others upward. Jose could see other wounded men being left behind, their buddies being forced ahead by sympathetic squad leaders or at rifle point.

Orders were orders, as foolish as they sounded and they were to be obeyed. More lives would be saved if the summit could be taken without having to force another climb. But that was hard to understand when you're the wounded soldier or the close buddy of one.

They're soon back on their bellies again, crawling past one rocky ridge and over another until stopped by a squad of enemy riflemen. Entrenched behind a log barrier, the NVA make a tough nut to crack without a LAW. As an alternative, Matthew lay on his back and thoroughly wiped mud and grime off another M-79 HE round before he loaded it. He then looked over at Jose and they exchanged a hard glare. Jose wasn't happy with leaving Farm Boy and he resented Matthew for having to do it. But Jose knew his job and he positioned his sixty sticking out between the black roots of an uprooted stump and began to hit the enemy position with shot bursts. Matthew popped the 40mm round off, but it fell short. So Matthew loaded a second round and fired it off at a higher angle. This one was dead on and it exploded inside the trench. The blast blew three men right out of the trench and they made a splat-like sound when all three landed in the mud and remained motionless with lifeless dark brown eyes staring at the sky.

Venting his anger, Jose continued to hit the trench until Matthew ordered him to cease fire. "That's enough, Jose!"

Jose yelled, "don't you mess wit' us!" Up the mountain he waved a clenched right fist of defiance. Moving forward, Matthew had a grenade ready if need be.

When he reached the trench, he counted three bodies outside and two more were found on the bottom of the hole. "Five dead," Matthew whispered, so only he could hear.

Cautiously, he slid into the trench, which was nearly 15- feet long, four to five feet deep and four feet wide. It appeared to be safe now. "Looks clear!"

Matthew laid his rifle aside on a relatively dry piece of debris and knelt down to search the bodies for any documents they might be carrying. A sudden noise to his right jerked him upright and much to his surprise the ground began to move. A small landside from the explosion had come down to his right and it was then he noticed a previous slide had covered a piece of canvas draped over a tunnel entrance. *Tunnel!* The flap slowly moved aside and Matthew spotted the tip of a bayonet emerging. Before he can grab his rifle, an enraged NVA burst out and charged right at him with his hands clutched around an AK-47 with a fixed bayonet aimed right at his chest. The

NVA was bleeding from his eyes, ears and nose, the result of concussion and he locked eyes with Matthew. The enemy soldier released a loud shriek and made an extended thrust with his bayonet.

Training took over and Matthew sidestepped the lethal move, grabbed the man's rifle barrel with his left hand, lifted upward and in doing so clutched the stock of the AK-47 with his free hand. He lifted up first for leverage and then drove the rifle butt into the man's stomach. The move forced the man onto his back against the side of the trench and Matthew followed up with a leg trip. In the process of falling the man let go of his weapon, but Matthew lost his balance and the two men ended up tangled up on the bottom of the trench. The NVA's blood splattered hands were now locked around Matthew's throat. His air supply cut off, Matthew brought both of his fists hard against the man's ears and then in a downward swing against the man's wrists. The move broke the soldier's hold and then Matthew used a Judo blow and delivered a second downward strike against the man's collarbone, and the result left the man slumped to the side. This allowed Matthew to get out from under him and use a knee thrust to the man's jaw and render him unconscious.

When John arrived and saw that Matthew was all right, he fired off a burst into the tunnel opening and then followed it up with a grenade. When a cloud of dirt from the muffled explosion cleared, Matthew looked up at his friend, "You took long enough."

"Looks like thu little guy almos' beat yuh, Matt."

A tired grin on his face, Matthew answered, "He's one tough little dude." Matthew noticed Monroe and Jose, when they dropped into the trench.

"Spooky thu way those guys jus' pop out of thu ground," Monroe said.

"Check your ammo," Matthew ordered when he pulled himself to his feet. "Five mags, plus thu one ah got here an' two grenades," John said.

"Four magazines," Monroe said, "...one in mah rifle an' three grenades."

Jose answered, "T'is belt an' the one across mah chest," Jose said. "I've got four grenades an' 'bout twenty-one rounds for mah forty-five." Matthew patted his rifle pouches, "Okay, I got three mags, three grenades, an' six HE and one Wiley Peter left for my M-79. Not much for this so-called all out attack." Matthew glanced around before he continued, "I'll lead off, Monroe next, then Jose...and John, you bring up the rear." Matthew stopped for a moment as the four of them listened to the war around them. The mountainside sounded like a huge shooting gallery, with light and heavy weapons dueling it out.

"Don't know how much farther we can go without..." Matthew stopped when John let out a warning, "Look out!" The NVA soldier, who was now conscious, reached out for his AK-47 as he tried to stand. But John was faster and was forced to kill the man with a two-round burst. For some unknown reason they had all forgotten about the man. Exhaustion had led them to lose grip on important things like tying up a prisoner. Shaking his head, Matthew turned away and led the men upward, one backbreaking step after another as the shooting continued.

1ST PLATOON

The platoon was in bad shape: First squad had one man wounded, 2nd squad had two wounded and 3rd squad has lost one man. In 4th squad, Bradley was down with a bullet to the shoulder. No one wanted to leave him, but he ordered them up the hill by gunpoint and when they left him 4th squad was down to four men.

D COMPANY

Sgt. Campbell, with a ragged and slop-covered Haggerty following behind, left Captain Sampson's CP and worked his way over to join up with his men. To their left, SSgt. Franklin's platoon has been shot up pretty badly. Above the 2nd bunker line, Franklin was locked in a fierce battle with several trenches filled with rifleman below the summit's outer rim.

Lieutenant Olson was down. He had caught a bullet in his left leg and was left sitting beside a destroyed bunker. But he sent his RTO forward with a 15-member platoon. Shortly after they left, Lt. Olson nailed a sniper who popped up less than ten-feet away. Unfortunately for the NVA sniper, who was caught facing away in hopes of zapping one of Olson's men in the back as they climbed, Lt. Olson was a crack shot.

Studying the hillside through binoculars and counting the bodies of the enemy and his own men, Captain Sampson turned to his RTO, "Looks like we need to take over 3rd platoon."

His RTO could only answer in a tired voice, "Yes, sir." Then with a shrug of the shoulders and a strong right arm, he hefted the radio pack and fell in behind his Company Commander. *They keep knocking these officers and NCOs off and I'm liable to be the CO before this fight is over.*

2ND SQUAD

"Kendal!" Campbell shouted to get Matthew's attention. In hearing his name between explosions and rifle fire, Matthew let out an exhausted sigh and stopped to look back over his left shoulder. He spotted Campbell and Haggerty, but they weren't alone. Matthew spotted a sniper emerging from a spider hole only a few feet below them. With an SKS rifle in his hands, the sniper appeared to have either Campbell or Haggerty cold.

"Sniper behind you!" Matthew hollered out. He flipped over on his back in hopes of getting a shot off, but the two men blocked his view for a clear shot. A single shot rang out, but Campbell had dropped to the ground with Matthew's warning and the bullet missed him by mere inches. While the sniper snapped the bolt back to seed in another cartridge, Campbell brought his shotgun into action and gave the man a taste of double-ought buckshot. Haggerty, trembling from nervous reaction to how close they had come to filling a body bag, was looking around to make sure there wasn't another sniper in the immediate area.

A small mudslide came down and trigger-happy Haggerty emptied nearly half-a clip into the mud and all Campbell could do was shake his head. He knew everyone was getting a nervous twitch on this accursed mountain. Moments later, Campbell and Haggerty reached 2nd squad, "This …all you got left?" Campbell asked in labored breath. He was growing very weary of climbing this blasted hill and his filthy face displayed his bitterness for this whole operation.

"Me an' them…that's it, boss," Matthew said. "We left Farm Boy and Walstein below as ordered," Matthew added coldly. But then turned his anger away from Campbell and asked, "How's the rest of the company?"

Campbell loaded another shotgun round into his weapon to keep a full load. "We're shot to pieces. You got much ammo left?"

Matthew patted his pouches and replied, "Not much." Then frustrated with this whole operation and leaving his two men behind, he lashed out again at Campbell, "Sarge, this is plain suicidal! We can't take this hill with what's left of us and before long we'll be throwing mud balls at them or swinging clubs. We might as well challenge them to a game of soccer up on the summit and the winner gets to leave this place."

Campbell was disgusted too, but he was also a platoon commander and kept his feeling pretty much bottled up. "Charlie Company is on the way up." He didn't like the way his men looked and it grieved him to see the condition they were in. Especially his new squad leader. *He's gained at least ten years up here. Ngai took it out of him, but this place is bleedin' him dry.*

"You want me to join up with either Jackson or Reynolds?" Matthew asked, while keeping his eyes forever moving in search of the enemy.

"Yeah," Campbell replied, "work your way over to Jackson. I'll have Reynolds team up with Bradley. But hold the line right here until I get back to you."

Matthew nodded his head and answered, "You'll get no argument from me."

Campbell began to move away, but then he turned, "Oh, thanks for the warning."

Matthew dropped his shoulders, picked up a handful of slop and grinned, "You're welcome." He then remained crouched there on the hillside, the mud dripping off of him and watched as Campbell and Haggerty vanished over the next ridgeline in search of 3rd squad.

Matthew didn't know such conditions were possible; fighting the mud, rain and an enemy that wouldn't give up. But he was reminded of the Solomon Island Campaigns in World War II and what the Marines and Army endured. *I wonder if they had to climb many mountains like this place. I know I'll never make fun of a combat Marine again.*

"All right, let's go find Jackson and dig in." Matthew led off, crawling to his right with the others following in his path. Above them, an enemy soldier spotted them and lobbed a Chinese pineapple grenade down the slope toward them. No one saw it coming until it landed at Matthew's feet.

"Grenade!" John shouted and he jumped clear. Monroe rolled to his left, squirming behind a small rock outcropping and began shooting toward the trench where the grenade had apparently come from. For Matthew though, he simply froze. In his exhaustion, he stared blankly at the grenade and looked as if he was waiting for death to close its arms around him.

Later and for years to come, he'd wonder about his lack of action and how he could have changed things if he had jumped clear or taken a chance and tossed the grenade elsewhere. But these next three seconds would haunt him for the rest of his life

Jose, the closest one to Matthew, saw the grenade at Matthew's feet and reacted quickly. He shoved Matthew down the hill with a hard body block to the legs, yanked off his helmet and holding it in both hands, dove on top of the grenade. The explosion nearly ripped Jose in two and the concussion wave hurled him into the air for over 5-feet and several feet down the hill. When the smoke and clouds of dirt cleared, NVA riflemen opened up on 2nd squad from several positions up the hill.

Semi-conscious from the blast, Matthew laid on his side while enemy bullets impacted the mud closer and closer to him. Fighting through a fog, the sky seemed to whirl around him and he felt he was trapped inside some kid's toy top. For one brief moment he can't remember where he is until he felt John grab him by the right foot and drag him out of the line of fire. The upper ledge of a large depression provided the only cover for the squad and here they waited. Matthew's head cleared and he saw Jose lying there, bleeding profusely from countless wounds about the stomach, upper legs and chest, his face and arms. He couldn't leave him out there exposed and he crawled over to Jose's side.

John and Monroe returned covering fire, while Matthew dragged Jose back below the upper ledge and was nearly hit half a dozen times while he did it. Jose was only semi-conscious and didn't even utter a complaint, but he was letting out a soft moan. Matthew yanked out a battle dressing and gently placed it upon his friend's chest, followed by a second dressing to his stomach. "I need more bandages!"

John lay prone on the other side, blood trailing down from a minor scalp wound from the blast. He attempted to shove Jose's intestines back in until Jose finally screamed for him to stop. Somehow, Jose rallied briefly and he grabbed a hold of John's left wrist, "No…no more." He then glanced from John to Matthew and laid his free hand on top of Matthew's arm. With one side of his face nearly gone, the other eye only partially open, Jose whispered a farewell, "Sure…sure gonna miss…guys, but…but time ta go… some… one callin'…Amigo*ooo*…" E-4 Jose Martinez died in the arms of his two best friends.

"Jose?" Matthew stared at his friend and then realized he was dead. "No-o-o-o!" Matthew cried out and began shaking him frantically to get his friend to wake up. But John grabbed Matthew and jerked him away and then held him in a tight bear hug as Matthew wept like a small child, the two of them unable to hear the war around them as deep grief consumed their thoughts. The last eight days had been tough on Matthew and the loss of Jose had turned him into an emotional basket case.

"Go ahead, Matt, let it out," John was crying too, but he continued to hold on to Matthew.

Emptying one magazine, Monroe crawled over and picked up Jose's 60 with a half-full belt of ammo hanging from it. He rose up to a low crouch and cut loose with a long extended burst that caught three NVA who had made the mistake of putting their heads up at the wrong moment.

"Matt, we got to go on, we still got a fight goin' on here," John said as he brought his canteen up and splashed some lukewarm water over Matthew's face.

Matthew appeared to wake up and began to wipe his face with his left hand, while he slowly nodded his agreement. Still, he didn't want to leave Jose.

"We got ta leave 'im here for now, but we be back for 'im later." John reached down and pulled Jose's .45 pistol out of its holster and handed it to Matthew, "He'd want you to have it."

Taking the pistol, Matthew slid it under his pant's belt and retrieved the two extra .45 magazines. "Viya con Dios, mi amigo. I'll be seeing you real soon." Matthew then looked up to the sky and raised his right fist.

Shaking it angrily, he asked with contempt, "Why? Why do you have to take the good ones?" He then gasped in a lower voice, "Curse you, God!"

Matthew then went back to war. He grabbed up his M-79, made sure it was slop free as possible and loaded it with a round of HE in the event he needed it. A part of him wanted to charge up the hill, to kill the men who had killed Jose. But he was the squad leader and still responsible for his two remaining men--John and Monroe. "We'll leave him here. Too slow carrying him and too dangerous to pull him down with us," Matthew said in a strained whisper.

"He'd agree wit' you, Matt," John said. He then took out his poncho to wrap Jose's body in it. Then both John and Matthew took a moment to lock this location in their memories and they vowed silently to return to this spot for their buddy.

WILLIAM CASSELMAN

15 - RENAMED IT HAMBURGER HILL

HILL 937-A SHAU VALLEY, 2ND SQUAD *DAY 8 CONTINUES ON* MAY 17TH, 1969 1728 HOURS

Ammo and grenades nearly exhausted, water in short supply, their uniforms in sopped and in tattered condition, and their bodies too worn out to think straight, the three surviving members of 2nd squad was unable to go on. Frustrated and exhausted, they cautiously slide down the hill one at a time to the next trench-line below. There, Monroe was alert enough still to quickly grab-up two operational AK-47s and magazines of ammo for the weapons. If the need arose, they could fight the NVA with their own weapons.

While Matthew kept watch with Monroe, John made a second trip down below to check on Walstein and Farm Boy. "If you can, move Farm Boy over to Walstein's position. That way they can cover each other's back an' they're closer to C Company's lines," Matthew suggested.

"Why don't we jus' bag it, Matt?" John asked. "Three of us can't hold here fur too long."

Matthew shook his head and had that stubborn look to his eyes, "No, we're not gonna lose this line. I'm getting' real tired of taken back ground we already bled over...Jose died up there and he didn't die for nothing." Monroe dropped the two AK-47s, four 30-round magazines and a Chinese pineapple grenade at Matthew's feet. "Everythin' else ah'll bust up."

Matthew looked at the foreign weapons and said, "This will do...it's gotta do." He then focused his attention on the Chinese grenade and thought of Jose's sacrifice. *For me! He saved my life because I froze.*

D COMPANY

Captain Sampson, now in command of Lt. Olson's 3rd platoon, spent nearly an hour in a shoot out it with two bunkers before four well-placed grenades ended the fight. A lull in the fighting then allowed the wounded to be pulled back, but only a few yards. With too little firepower, D Company was rapidly reaching a stalemate with the elements of the 29th NVA positioned over them. Weary to the point of trembling, his stomach turned into one big knot, Captain Sampson dropped to the ground on all fours when a spasm of dry retching struck. His throat burned, his eyes watered and with some effort he pushed himself back in to a sitting position. He even ignored the deep mud oozing between and over his legs. Above him, a single F-4 Phantom came in from the west and it was flying in unadvisable weather. Captain Sampson watched with a blank expression on his face as the huge fighter-bomber began its strafing run of the summit with 20mm fire. But Sampson seemed oblivious to the Phantom's firepower. His nerves were strained to the breaking point and he simply sat there staring off at where the jet had flown from and he began to ignore his RTO's questions.

Twenty-five yards away, a young sniper concealed under an outcropping of thick tree roots, now blackened by artillery fire, sighted in on his target with an SKS bolt-action rifle. He had received his training from Russian advisors in Hanoi and had learned how to control his breathing. The 19-year old NVA sniper slowly and gently applied pressure to the trigger on his ancient Russian rifle and blinked as a single bullet exploded out the end of his rifle long barrel. Captain Sampson, sitting there in the mud and thinking of home, never heard the shot that killed him. He would also never know how his wife was killed the day before; victim to a drunk driver two miles off post. The sniper, who was in the process of chambering a second round to shoot the RTO, was killed only seconds later by the RTO emptying his M-16 into him.

Lt. Olson's senior squad leader looked down at Sampson's body, shook his head and with a sudden realization; he found himself in charge of Lt. Olson's 3rd platoon. He gestured to the RTO for the radio handset and while the RTO mourned his captain, he made contact with Campbell and notified him of Captain Sampson's death. "What do yuh want me to do now?"

Saddened by the news of Sampson's death, Campbell hesitated for a moment before he responded with, "We hold here, have 'em dig in and be ready for anything."

D Company, with no officers to lead them and running dangerously low on ammo and water, ceased its advance. Men, covered from head to toe with mountain slop and sweat, move about in slow motion as darkness begins to descend upon Hill 937 and a strange eerie silence descends upon the men. No one wanted to talk, to even whisper; it required too much energy. To look into the eyes of these men one would see little fear, for fear required emotion and these men have been nearly drained of all feelings. No one can remember how many men they've killed or how many men they had lost since Day-one. Body counts no longer matter. So they pass the time taking care of the wounded, keeping weapons clean and salvaging what, if any life they have left inside of them to press on. These are the only priorities. Battered and weary, these pitiful looking specimens of D Company now under the command of an NCO, come together to form a single line of defense stretched out over 75- yards. The wounded were brought down and placed under protective cover near one of the destroyed bunkers, but not the dead. They can't afford to get into a firefight for the dead, so Jose and the others must wait.

"Ah figure we gots maybe fifty ta sixty yards ta go. Dat's all we gots left, but not today...not today an' maybe not tomorrow," Jackson said. Then he added, "Ah jus' wanna sleep...Tomorrow...tomorrow we cun take thu top." Lowering his head, Jackson began to sob. The others nearby felt much the same way and no one took it upon themselves to judge Jackson, for too many of them felt much the same way. The killing, the muck and constant rain and the order to desert their dead comrades and abandon their wounded had sickened them. This was too hard for a lot of 18, 19 and 20-year olds to understand. This was not the Army they trained to serve in and confusion only made it worse.

2ND SQUAD

John, who now resembled a mud monster from some B rated black and white movie of the 50's, found Farm Boy semi-conscious and pale. The tourniquets had stopped the bleeding, but his legs were an unhealthy shade of white from the lack of blood flow. When John loosened the belts, Farm Boy let out a loud scream when the blood began to flow, and it could be heard all the way back to D Company's position and it frightened several of the young men. Twenty-some minutes later, John gently lowered Farm Boy down beside an equally pale-faced Walstein, who was going in and out of consciousness. He got them both awake with a couple face slaps, got them to take a drink of water and eventually left them to help each other before he climbed back up the hill to brief Matthew on their condition. When John arrived he saw the extra men, but was then shocked to hear this was what was left of D Company and it grieved him to know they had lost the CO and so many good men. "They're not doin' too good, Matt. We gotta get 'em back down thu hill 'fore Farm Boy loses both his legs an' Walstein just ups an' dies."

Matthew looked around in silence and then responded to his buddy, "Campbell's runnin' the company now and we're down to 30 men, John. Franklin's shot up. Lt. Olson's wounded an' Captain Sampson's dead."

"Captain Sampson was a good guy." John lowered his head and sulked. He thought about praying, but at the moment his faith in a caring God bordered on a fine line between belief in a Supreme Being and a fairy tale. Doubt made him uncomfortable.

D COMPANY

From one of the men came forth a light chuckle that slowly grows with intensity until PFC Louder was rolling on his back wrapped in belly laughter. Campbell, his face a mask of rage, stomped over to him and jerked the startled man to his feet and demanded to know what was so funny? "Men are dyin' up here, laughing boy and you think this is funny?"

Droplets of tears rolled down his cheeks as he said, "Don't you see it Sarge?"

Campbell asked, "I'm waiting."

PFC Louder wiped his eyes and answered, "No disrespect, Sarge, not for the wounded or the dead, but all of a sudden it just came to me."

"What came to you?" Campbell asked in a calmer tone. His earlier anger was giving way by just sheer weariness.

"I got this name... a name for this place...You see, Sarge, we've been ground up like hamburger...So, I say we should call this place Hamburger Hill. Even the mud looks like ground beef, especially with all our red blood mixed into it"

Campbell stared at the man for a moment, but then to Louder's relief he simply nodded his head and said, "Sounds 'bout right. But knock off that maniacal laughter, it puts me on edge."

The name, though unofficial, stuck, though PFC Louder would never get credit for it. But Hill 937 became known to the men of the 3rd Battalion and later to the world as "Hamburger Hill".

1ST PLATOON

Shortly after 2100 hours, another ferocious firefight broke out between NVA riflemen and scattered members of 1st platoon. Out of ammo for their M-16's, Matthew and John were forced to use AK-47s and the slow firing of the communist weapon surprised some of the Americans, who briefly thought the enemy had breached their lines. Within minutes the fighting intensified when a platoon sized force of NVA leave their trench and actually rushed down the hill shrieking and screaming like World War II Japanese troops on a Bonsai charge. They were attempting to frighten the Americans into retreating, but it didn't work. Though several of the enemy fell under a wave of heavy fire, a dozen or so NVA make it to the American's line and leap into D Company's position. The men are forced to go hand-to-hand with knives and bayonets becoming the weapons of choice. A rifle butt strikes out, a bayonet is thrust and one man swings his rifle like a Louisville Slugger. It is only a sample of what is yet to come.

The fighting remains intense with the only sounds being loud grunts, screams of pain and curses, and men wrestling in a death struggle over the bodies of the wounded and dead.

Unable to use his rifle in such cramped quarters, Matthew pulled out Jose's .45 in time to shoot two NVA at close range before pulling another NVA off the back of Monroe and clubbing him fiercely in the face with a pistol butt. He then looked up the hill, now illuminated by mortar flares and spotted another line of NVA climbing out of the trench directly above them.

That's where Jose is…They've got Jose! Matthew wasn't thinking about the enemy's strength now. He was more concerned about his friend. Caught up in the emotion and blood lust of the battle, Matthew jumped up on the edge of his foxhole and shouted, "You want a piece of me? Step up, Charlie and I'll take the whole lot of you on!"

Matthew remained on his knees and assumed a two-handed hold of his .45 and began firing at the NVA with Jose's pistol until he emptied his magazine. Then he side stepped an enemy bayonet and struck the young NVA soldier in the chest with his fist and knocked him to the ground. He glared down at the young man and yelled, "You can kill me, but you can't eat me!" Matthew grinned wildly, pulled his knife and dropped down on the man with his knees and stabbed him with his knife several times.

A shotgun blast exploded to Matthew's right and he felt himself jerked back as Campbell pulled him back down into the trench when another dead NVA, a victim to Campbell's shotgun, had fallen face first into the hole beside him. "Nice ta see yuh, Sarge," Matthew said. He sheathed his bloody knife and popped in a fresh pistol magazine so he could continue firing.

"Yeah, you too," Campbell replied. He had to reload and stood behind Matthew while he reached inside his ammo pouch and pulled out a handful of double ought shells. He quickly reloaded his shotgun with his last five rounds.

"Here they come again!" Jackson yelled when another platoon-sized force began their charge down the hill.

"I'm out'ta ammo!" A voice shouted out.

"Pick up an AK, use theirs." Campbell ordered back.

For a brief moment it looked very bad for the men of the 1st platoon. Vastly outnumbered and both 2nd and 3rd platoon already engaged, Campbell was about to order a retreat when C Company announced their arrival by sending out a lethal wave of hot lead that forced the NVA survivors to retreat.

"Charlie Company!" Campbell yelled out as the newly arrived Americans poured into the trench to drive the NVA back, until a ceasefire was ordered. When the count was made, 49 NVA soldiers were dead and D

Company miraculously listed only seven men wounded. But this reduced D Company strength to a total of 23 men and all of them about to fall down from exhaustion.

D COMPANY

"I'm Lieutenant Masters, who's in command here?" Lt. Masters, a brand new 2nd lieutenant, Class of 1968-West Point, asked with a note of arrogance to his voice.

Second lieutenants!

"I'm in command, Sir." Campbell said as he offered the L-T his hand.

"Where's all your officers, Sergeant?" Lt. Masters asked.

"They're either dead or wounded, Sir. Captain Sampson was killed by a sniper earlier today." Campbell was suddenly overcome by sheer weariness and forgot all about military courtesy when he plopped down on his butt with a *splat*.

"Are you okay, sergeant?" Lt. Masters asked. "Are you wounded?"

Campbell shook his head. "No, sir…but it has been a very long week." Campbell was helped up by two of the men standing nearby. "Sorry, Sir…no disrespect intended."

Lt. Masters gave him a casual wave to show he dismissed it. "Of course, Sergeant, I imagine the strain of command has been quite stressful."

Second lieutenants and this arrogant brat is actually sticking his nose up at me. In dismay, Campbell shook his head at Lt. Masters and then asked for his company's help in checking the enemy dead for papers.

C Company's men stepped up, helped with the wounded and removed the dead NVA from the trench. A couple of wounded prisoners were taken, the first ones as far as Campbell knew to be taken on this operation and he was sure Lt. Masters would take credit for it. But at the moment he really didn't care that much.

"They don't look like much," Lt. Masters said, as he watched the prisoners be led away.

"Sir, they've proven their metal up here. They're not Cong, but regulars and they know how to fight."

Lt. Masters looked at the prisoners going down the mountain and said, "Well, we sure kicked their butt today."

A weary Campbell could only shake his head again in wonder and reply with a quiet, "Yes, Sir." *This guy's gonna last about 24 hours at most and it may be one of his own men who shoots him. Guys like this love to endanger their command so they can receive the glory and get that next promotion. Why do they*

*even send second louies to the front? It's like dropping babes in to a pack of wolves.
Except these guys get good soldiers killed.*

Most of the men of C Company are new replacements and like their
platoon leader, this is their first taste of combat. The grizzly scene before
them is too much for a few and these innocents react by vomiting up their
last meal of C-rats. Lt. Masters ignored Campbell's unmilitary-like conduct
and appearance, mainly because he was stunned by Campbell's astonishing
report.

"You mean to say that this is all that's left of D Company?"

Campbell looked at his command, "That's right…twenty-three men
left, Sir. Rest are either wounded or dead."

It took Masters a moment for it all to sink in, but the lieutenant rallied.
"My orders are to help you move all the wounded down the hill. Later, we'll
recover your dead. Get your men ready to move out in five minutes,
Sergeant. They'll need to show us where the wounded men are." Masters
then changed that to 15 minutes after he looked over the condition of D
Company.

"Yes, sir," Campbell answered and then shouted to Matthew to come
over. "Kendal, show the Lieutenant here, where you left Walstein and
Andrews. Adams, you an' Monroe better go too." Matthew gave Lt. Masters
a quick glance, thought he looked a bit young to be an officer and pointed
off down the hill to the left. "We left them down that way, sir…you must've
just missed 'em on your way up."

Lt. Master said, "I'll assign one of my squads to accompany you."
Matthew dropped his tired hand and checked the magazine on his AK-47.

"Thank you, sir." Matthew said. He gave John a single nod and headed
off down the hill in front of the others.

The blank look in Matthew's eyes has John extremely concerned. It was
as if when Jose died, a good part of Matthew had died with him and John
was worried his best friend might not come back from this inner torture he
was putting himself through. Yet, John had committed himself to following
Matthew and he fell in behind his squad leader with Monroe right in step
behind him. The three survivors of 2nd Squad slowly made their way across
the muddy hillside, with a fully manned squad of extremely anxious, but
now nervous riflemen from C Company coming up behind them.

These new men, loaded down with ammo and grenades, and newly
issued, but already muddied-up field packs on their backs, wanted a taste
of battle and glory. Then they had a brief taste of it while rescuing D
Company and finding the deplorable remnants of 23 survivors. Second
Squad was clearly an example of what would happen to a highly trained
fighting unit on this hill and it frightened them. A few of these new men

were no longer so sure of what they truly wanted and decided they had better they keep an alert eye out for any sign of the enemy.

Walstein was sobbing when Matthew reached him. They had found him holding Farm Boy in his arms, alive but unconscious. "He's sufferin' so bad…Nothin' I could do," Walstein said. He struggled with his own pain, but compassion for his friend lessoned some of his burden.

"We'll get you down the hill, Erwin, you just hold on," Matthew said. He held Walstein's hand, while the men from C Company placed him onto a stretcher. The heinous wounds the two men had suffered startled the new men, but they did their job as Matthew instructed. The new squad leader kept quiet, knowing well enough to let the veteran issue the orders and he stepped in to help construct the stretcher. Monroe and John stayed on watch, with a special eye out for spider-holes. Matthew didn't like the idea of leaving Jose behind, but Sgt. Campbell had assured him they would be back for Jose's body. The important thing now was to get both Walstein and Farm Boy delivered to Battalion Aid.

Due to the slick mud and condition of the wounded, the going was slow, but by midnight they had reached Base Camp. The wounded were handed over to the waiting arms of a surgical team and the three men of 2nd squad thanked the men from C Company for their help. Afterward, Matthew, John and Monroe wandered over to the Battalion CP where they spotted Campbell leaving the massive green tent and they caught up with him.

"Colonel says we'll get re-supplied and fed tonight without any problems. We can expect new officers within a few hours and hopefully they're a bit more experienced than that glory seeking Lieutenant Masters," Campbell said. He knew Masters' type and new that man was going to get some of his people killed.

"What 'bout Jose?" John asked.

"We'll get him. This battle isn't over yet, they're bringing in more troops tomorrow for another big assault," Campbell said "

They should just nuke the place an' be done with it," Matthew said.

"Yuh got dat right," John agreed.

Leading the men away from the CP, Campbell spotted a cardboard sign near the trail leading up the hill and pointed to it, "Probably Louder's handy work." Made from a C-ration box, the sign had large black letters printed on it, which spelled out, *Hamburger Hill*.

Campbell stood there staring at it until a newsman with a camera guy in tow walked up and shoved a microphone in front of him, "What do you think of the sign, Sergeant?" Without a word, Campbell presented the newsman with an icy glare and walked off. Matthew, John and Monroe each gave the newsman a look of disgust and they followed their Sergeant back up Hill 937.

"Well, that went well," The newsman said to his long haired camera operator. "Count your Blessings, Dan. That guy could've made you eat that microphone." That night seven bodies were carried down the hill and Jose was one of them. His body was reportedly found shoved head first into an abandoned spider hole. By the looks of it, the NVA had taken out their revenge by inflicting multiple bayonet wounds to his corpse and disfiguring him. By the time Matthew, Monroe and John learned of how Jose had been recovered, they found him by the helipad zipped up into a mud covered body bag.

"Tagged, bagged an' ready ta go home," Matthew said quietly when he knelt beside the black body bag and swept some of the mud off. Monroe appeared with Jose's M-60 in his arms and as the other two watched, he laid the pig down beside the body bag, "Dis belongs ta you," Monroe whispered before he walked away. He knew Matthew and John wanted some private time with their friend.

With one trembling hand rested upon the body bag, Matthew whispered, "Thanks for my life, Amigo." He then stood up, saluted his friend with a crisp boot camp salute and turned to wander off.

"Adios, you little Bandito," John muttered before he rose to follow his friends. Twenty-two men of D Company, their faces pale with large dark circles closing in around bloodshot eyes and their filthy uniforms nearly falling off them, silently sit around a stack of C-ration boxes. Nearly every one of them have that same blank stare; giving nothing back, no emotion or feeling. Some would later call it the *thousand-yard stare.* Others would refer to it as the, *I don't care, I'm dead already* expression. Another news correspondent wandered over to interview a few of these men, but they wouldn't even notice him. Finally, one of the officers and an NCO from the CP came running over, "You mess with these men and they're liable to cut your heart out," the NCO warned the crew.

"They've lost too many friends…they need some time to themselves," the Captain added.

"But the folks back home deserve the truth!"

The Captain glared at the newsman and said, loud enough for the men of D Company to hear, "If you want the truth, mister. Then tomorrow you climb up that hill with these men. You'll find the truth, if you got the guts." The Captain looked over at the NCO, who was smiling at him. The NCO had been up hills similar to Hill 937 and knew exactly what these men were feeling. He was just glad he was working with headquarters staff now and wouldn't have to make that kind of climb again.

Filing his report, this same reporter who opted not to make the climb and made his camera crew happy with that decision, said to the nation, "These gallant fighters behind me now wear the mask of death. Although untouched by mortal hands, they have looked straight into the eyes of the grim reaper and have been forever marked."

When a man from D Company overheard this, he began to lift his rifle, but Sgt. Campbell saw it and called out, "Knock it off, ammo is too short to waste on idiots". Once re-supplied, D Company's new officers and replacements arrived to meet up with the veterans. Campbell, who was grateful to be returned to 2nd squad, promptly made Matthew his assistant squad leader. First Lt. Ruebal was assigned as the new commander of 1st platoon and Captain Louis replaced Captain Sampson as company commander. First Lt. Roberts was given command of 2nd platoon, which now included the survivors of 3rd platoon. D Company had been reduced to two platoons due to a lack of replacements on hand. Much to Campbell's delight, 2nd squad received four new men; PFC Habib, PFC Williams, PFC Sanders and PFC Razor.

2ND SQUAD

"Dey all look like dey come from thu same cookie press," John muttered, while he looked the new men over from boot to helmet. He almost envied them for how clean their uniforms were, but he knew it wouldn't last. One trip up through the mud would change all that.

"New meat for the butcher," Matthew added.

"Kendal!" Campbell hollered.

"Yeah, Sarge!" Campbell pointed over to where the C-rations were stacked.

"Get them all fed, re-supplied, weapons checked and briefed on what to expect on top of Fairy Mountain."

Fairy Mountain!? "You got it, Sarge." Matthew pushed himself off the ground and signaled for the four new men to follow him toward the supply tent. *New guys…I got no time for new guys.* The replacements seemed eager, maybe a bit too eager in Matthew's opinion. Razor, a black kid from Oakland began bragging right off, "Ah'm gonna kill me a whole bunch of those yellow skinned boys." After hearing it once too often, John and Monroe escorted Razor off for a little Brotherly chat. When they returned, Razor kept his mouth shut. But it wouldn't last because PFC Razor had a real attitude problem. Habib, of Arab descent, came from Central California. He barely talked unless asked a question. But Williams and Sanders behaved like a couple of stand-up comedians, only they couldn't decide which one was the dummy and who was playing the straight man bit.

Campbell made Habib the new 60-man and assigned Sanders as his assistant. Their first job was to reclaim Jose's 60 and clean it up, which got Campbell some dirty looks from Matthew, John and Monroe.

"Look, I liked Jose too. He saved my life, but they won't bury him with that gun and we're short weapons. I'd rather keep his pig with the squad, so get over it!" Campbell hoped for the moment that his explanation closed the matter. Much too every one's surprise, mail call finally made it to the A Shau Valley and Matthew received six letters from Kathy Lee and two from his parents. The replacements were all but forgotten for the moment as Matthew read the news from home. It provided a big boost to his morale and late that night, Matthew dropped off to sleep with the feeling he might just survive. But nightmares, the ugly ones with teeth, woke him up. Then the rain returned and everyone was awake with the valley floor becoming a lake.

INSIDE HAMBURGER HILL, MAY 18TH, 1969 0020 HOURS *DAY 9 BEGINS*

His medic bag open, Que inserted a handful of rags to use for bandages. Two canteens hang from around his shoulders by thin straps, along with a small coil of rope to be used for tourniquets. He also carried two knives on a rope belt and a pair of scissors. He walked over to a small table and reached into a cold cook pot to retrieve a handful of cooked rice. He molded the rice into small balls and followed this up by wrapping them individually into banyan leaves. He then secured them with thin pieces of twine. He then checked himself over, made sure he had everything and once ready, he departed the hospital and headed outside through a series of dark narrowed tunnels. Within moment of bypassing debris and fallen timbers, he found himself back in the open air and atop the summit.

Outside of his small knives, Que carried no weapon. His uniform consisted of a tan colored shirt, which is now blood stained and soiled by smoke and dirt. He also wears a pair of baggy tan colored shorts secured by a rope belt to hold his gear. On his feet he wore a ragged pair of sandals, commonly known to the Americans as Ho Chi Minh sandals. He wore no rank or insignia and his appearance resembled that of a simple Vietnamese farmer. He had once worn a used pith helmet with the red star on the front, but he had lost his during the early hours of the American's aerial bombing and had not taken the time to find a replacement. He could've taken one from a wounded or dead soldier, but he felt this was wrong and decided to go without.

Once outside in the fresh air, Que became lightheaded as his lungs filled with the fresh air and he found it almost intoxicating. The rain drove the smoke of the bombs and artillery rounds to the ground and Que found the constant downpour stimulating. He began to let it wash away the grime he had collect from spending so many hours in the tunnels. Que took one of the bandages out of his bag and used it to wash his face and hands, but then felt guilty for using it on himself and wrung it dry. He then heard his name called out and began to follow another young medic down a rocky path to where a sergeant directed them to a dry spot under an overhanging rock outcropping. "The night is quiet, so for the moment you won't be needed until morning…when the American devils come again to attack." Within minutes, Que was in a sound sleep; the first real sleep in many days for the weary youthful medic. Yet only 100 yards below this NVA position, the men of the 3rd Battalion are on full alert and it would be a short night for the combatants of Hamburger Hill.

16 – AT ALL COSTS...AGAIN!

"What we got us here is a real Texas-style gully washer," Captain Adrian Bronson from Dallas, Texas said as he entered the CP Tent and pulled off his soaked poncho. After eight hours of constant downpour the valley floor had transformed into an ankle deep quagmire. Some spots were even deeper. Before long, the thick-pudding like mud caused several soldiers to lose their footing and end up on their backside. It was also impossible for anyone to stay dry in this kind of weather; even the thick canvas wall tents of the CP and Aid Station soon developed hundreds of leaks. When the rain finally stopped, thick steam-like mist began to rise up from the ground and the humidity and heat quickly turned the valley into one giant hot house. Still, it was an unusually quiet dawn, almost serene, on the morning of May 18th, but it only lasted for a few brief moments.

Suddenly, dozens of UH-1 helicopters appeared overhead; their thunderous roar and steady *whomp-whomp-whomp* shattering the silence. They circled about and one by one they began to land throughout the valley floor. But they were only the first. Before long they appeared to be arriving like a swarm of locusts, dislodging troops and immediately returning to the Firebase Blaze for even more men. To the east, the 2nd Battalion of the 501st Infantry touched down and to the west, the 1st Battalion of the 506th Infantry arrived and later in the day, the 2nd Battalion of the 3rd ARVN Infantry would be brought in directly east of Hamburger Hill. With the additional units, the 29th NVA will soon find itself completely surrounded by more than 2,000 American and South Vietnamese troops. A massive airlift was underway with helicopter pilots making five or more roundtrips a day, ferrying men and equipment to Hill 937.

One correspondent was overheard as saying, "With all this activity, the military should position an air traffic controller on top the mountain. They'd be safe enough. Everybody knows that no one messes with the Federal Aviation Agency." A burley looking cameraman with a heavy red beard added, "Yeah, them an' the IRS."

2ND SQUAD

He was sitting in six inches of mud, his uniform soaked through and he was suffering from a bad case of jock and underarm rash, but Matthew looked relaxed for the moment. He was simply too bone tired to care about anything at the moment and said so to anyone within earshot, "Tired of climbing in this muck--I'm tired of crawling on my belly, tired of being thirsty, tired of my lips being chapped and my throat dry--I'm jus' plain too tired of that damn mountain." Matthew then said to John, "All I wanna do is go home to my Kathy Lee, hold her tight and never let her go." Matthew grabbed his nose and made a face, "Man it sure stinks around here. Didn't you take a bath last night?"

John gave Matthew a look of disbelief and then went along with it. "Naw, thu maid don't have any dry towels," John replied. He then squished a handful of mud through his fingers. "T'ink, back home women pay a fortune to do dis, make 'em look beeeautifulll."

Matthew then asked his buddy, "You got any dry socks, old buddy?" He had a hand full of mud in his hand when he slapped John on the shoulder in a friendly manner.

"If ah did, ol' buddy, it'd cos' you a month's pay ta get 'em." John looked down at his own feet and was afraid of what he might find when he took his boots off.

"Let's go over to supply, see if we can dig up some socks…maybe some underwear too," Matthew suggested. He then pushed himself up with some help from John and slung the two enemy AK-47's over his shoulder.

"You'se gotta be dreamin', boy. Shells for a 175 maybe, even a case of grenades. But socks an' underwear…nev'a!" John shook his head.

"What about Monroe?" Matthew asked.

"He's soun' asleep. That southern boy cun sleep anywhere."

Matthew stomped his feet and watched as water came gushing out, "I feel like a frog."

John smiled at his friend, "You do look soggy enough." Right then another flight of helicopters flew over them and in jest, John waved his M-16 at them and said to Matthew, "Sure are makin' a racket, jus' gonna ruin our deer season."

Matthew pointed to them, "Reinforcements, John. The 7th Cavalry has done arrived to save the day for you and me," Matthew said. He handed John one of the AK rifles. The two of them stopped off at the field kitchen to wash their hands, arms and faces in some hot water the cooks were keeping for just that purpose and then use their canteen cups to grab a cup of near boiling hot coffee.

"Nothin' like the smell of fresh GI coffee," Matthew said. With a metal dipper, he poured the steaming brown liquid into John's waiting cup.

"Hot chow," The pimply-faced young cook yelled out.

"Really?" Matthew asked in surprise. "T'ings lookin' up, buddy. Next comes thu USO show and Bob Hope," John said.

Following a meal of C-ration ham loaf and peaches, washed down by three cups of coffee, Matthew and John wandered over to the supply area. There they find a grumpy sergeant by the name of Wilky, who acted as if all the supplies personally belonged to him, and over the next ten minutes they ask, beg and finally horse trade an AK-47 for a few pairs of OD green socks. For a second AK-47, they left the car salesman of a supply sergeant behind and carried off a couple sets of boxer shorts and a tin of talc powder to help with Matthew's rash problem.

"Those supply guys must take a course in underhand dealing and a specialty in black-marketing," Matthew said. "You know he's going to get a fortune for those two AK's and he'll write the stuff he gave us as lost or damaged goods."

"Cost of doin' the war, Matt."

Back with the squad, Matthew carefully and somewhat painfully, removed his boots and was not happy at what he discovered. He had to scrape away the rotted socks with his bayonet and was a little weak at the knees when he found his how most of each foot had taken on a ghastly green color from the dye in the socks. But his toes were still a pasty white and all wrinkled up from all the moisture he had stomped through. For a moment there, Matthew wondered if he was going to be able to get his boots back on again.

When Monroe saw the condition of Matthew's feet, Monroe hustled over to the cook area and promptly returned a moment later with a large cook pot. Using the shavings from a block of C-4, he was able to get a roaring fire going and placed the pot over it. He then filled the pot with several gallons of fresh water he had sent one of the new guys for and waited for it to come to a boil. Several of the others helped by breaking up used ammo crates to provide dry wood for the fire. Then to all their astonishment, Monroe took a hold of Matthew's helmet, poured the water into it and cautiously dipped Matthew's feet into it one foot at a time.

"Use't ta do this for mah dad when he come in from workin' all day," Monroe said.

When Campbell heard about the footbath party, he dashed over and waited his turn right behind John. Before long, the other veterans of D Company were in line for hot water and soon a grateful bunch of weary vets were soaking their feet. Later, they used the last of the hot water for washing up with. Someone even came up with a couple cans of G.I. issue foot powder and a few bars of soap.

In Matthew's case, Monroe followed the foot washing up with a lengthy foot rubdown, while he dried out John and Matthew's boots beside the fire. "This is true happiness...Thanks, Monroe," Matthew said gratefully. He sat on a stack of wooden crates and carefully slid the dry socks on before pulling on his nearly dry boots.

Monroe had retrieved some more water and was waiting to bring it to a boil--it was now his turn.

"Monroe, they should promote you to sergeant for this," Campbell said as he rubbed his feet down. He had found several open soars between his toes and sprinkled foot powder on them.

For a brief moment the men forgot about the war, they kidded and joked with each other, and for those who had the habit they smoked C-ration cigarettes. The new guys also shared bits of news from home and afterward, they cleaned their weapons and re-sharpened the knives and bayonets.

While breaking down Jose's .45, Matthew looked up when Campbell knelt down to look at the weapon and asked, "Is that Jose's?"

"Yeah, any problem with me keeping it?"

"Don't see why not," Campbell said and then he added, "I'm sure gonna miss that little Bandito, he was one..." Campbell had to wipe the tears from his eyes and after a moment of silence he said, "I've written up a statement an' gave it to the CP, recommending him for a medal."

"No one to send it to, Sarge...but maybe they'll let John or I keep it for him?"

"Doubt it, but at least we know how he died, Matt." Campbell stood up and as he did, he failed to notice the look of surprise on Matthew's face. It was the first time he could remember that Campbell had called him by his first name.

"You okay?" John asked, when he dropped down beside his friend.

Ignoring the question, Matthew asked one of his own, "John, what's the first thing you wanna do when you get home?"

"Not sure, little foggy in thu future department...Hey, you notice how thu mosquitoes are leavin' us alone?"

"Yeah, they're over there, swarming around the new guys. Guess our blood's too thin for 'em now. Either that or our stench is driving them away."

"Wish ah had a sweet lady like your Kathy Lee waitin' for me back home." John had no girlfriend to write to, no one who cared whether he lived or died, with the exception of his friends here.

"She's out there, John. I can almost see her face when I close my eyes."

"Is she pretty?" John asked.

"A real looker, John…A real looker."

"Than you quit makin' time wit' my old lady an' send dat vision dis way. All I see if close mah eyes is burnin' bunkers and dead men."

"Yeah, I know what you mean," Matthew said. "Man, I hurt from my toes up. Can't remember ever feelin' this drained. How about you?"

"Once ah…yeah, that las' mountain they had us climb. Don't they has any flatland 'round here we cun fight over?"

"They save that for the 9th Marines," Matthew said.

The next few moments passed in silence, neither man saying a word while they both tried to settle in for a couple minutes of sleep. Try as they may though, each one had reached a point of deep exhaustion which actually prevented them from falling asleep. Between adrenalin rushes and fear of going back up that mountain, very few of the D Company veterans could sleep. After awhile of restlessness, they gave up trying, with the exception of Monroe, whom had his head rested on top of Matthew's leg. It's a troubled sleep though and twice Matthew heard Monroe call out Jose's name. No one else seemed to notice, everyone was lost in their own thoughts.

D COMPANY

As the hours passed by, Captain Louis noticed how the veterans seemed to keep a distance between themselves and the replacements. It concerned him and he sent for Campbell. RTO Haggerty found him stretched out by one of the NVA huts, writing a letter. "Captain Louis wants you."

"Okay." Campbell folded the letter up and placed it in to a plastic bag to keep it dry, before he dropped it down into his right breast pocket. A moment later Campbell reported to his new company commander, "You wanted to see me, sir?"

"Sergeant, I'm worried about our men, particularly those men who came down the mountain with you. They're behaving a bit strangely and I'm not too sure what to expect out of them when the order comes down to move out." Louis studied Campbell for a brief moment before he continued, "I need your opinion, sergeant. Do you think they'll go back up?"

The question actually surprised Campbell. It was not something an officer would normally ask of an NCO, as to whether his men would fight. Campbell never doubted it, but he wasn't sure how to answer his new CO.

"Sergeant, you can probably tell this is my first combat assignment. I'm a new arrival from Fort Benning, where I've spent my time as an instructor. The last eight days have left the 101st extremely low of company grade officers, especially those with combat experience. So, I need to know…can I count on these men?"

"Sir, may I be blunt?" Campbell felt too weary for games.

"You may consider this talk off the record."

"Thank you, Sir…In the last eight days these men have climbed up this hill a dozen times. They've watched their best friends die a gruesome death and we're even ordered to abandon the wounded and the dead to reach an objective we've been too undermanned to accomplish.

"My own squad went hand-to-hand with the NVA when their ammo supply gave out and we were forced to use the enemy's weapons to survive. Inch by inch they've taken ground and I've seen one man take on a heavy machinegun bunker by himself and in a separate action three men fight off a dozen NVA for rights of ownership.

"When I took over the platoon and then the company, I had a 19-year old kid leading my squad when it was down to him and only two others. Out of water, no ammo, these kids wouldn't quit. From 110 men, we made that last assault with 68 bone tired soldiers and only a couple dozen of us are left.

"We call this place Hamburger Hill now, Captain and the name fits. We've been ground up and spit out." Campbell stopped as he glanced around the camp and saw the new troops preparing for battle. "I guess what I'm sayin' here is yes, they'll fight. They'll fight because they don't know what else to do and they want to revenge their fallen comrades. They want to finish this job, Captain…but as to keeping away from the new guys. They've lost too many friends, Captain and they don't want to make any new buddies out here, just to see them die. When a friend dies out here, it takes a little piece of you with them and my men have very little left to give…but oh yes, they will fight."

Captain Louis didn't respond right away. He took a moment to think over what Campbell had said. "Thank you, Sergeant. You may return to your men now."

"Yes, sir," Campbell said and then he turned, flashed a quick smile at RTO Haggerty and returned to his squad.

Captain Louis summoned his platoon leaders an hour later. During the meeting of the three officers, Louis reminded Lt. Ruebal of how lucky he was to have Campbell in his platoon. "I've talked with the Colonel about getting him promoted and awarded for his actions for the last eight-days. It's hard to believe a sergeant commanding a company in combat."

"From what I've heard, Campbell deserves whatever we can get for him," Lt. Ruebal said in reply.

"All right, here's how it will play out. We will move back up the hill at precisely 1400 hours, rendezvousing with Charlie Company at their most forward position. Lt. Ruebal, your platoon will lead out with Sergeant Campbell's squad on point. I want an RTO with each platoon and have a man ready to back him up if your RTO goes down. We must, I repeat we must stay in radio contact at all times. Are there any questions?" Both lieutenants shot their hands up. They were both 90-day wonders and as green as the jungle growth they were sitting upon.

2^(ND) SQUAD

"Ah'm getting' tired of humpin' this hill an' killin' those little people up there. You think they'd let me sit dis one out, Matt?" John asked. "Say ah was sufferin from battle fatigue or somethin'.'"

"You're talking stupid, John. We owe it to those other guys and we owe it to Jose. We have made this climb and we'll make it again, John…for them…and for us."

"You soun' like John Wayne. But Matt, those was Marines, dey attack tanks with bayonets in their teeth. We'se Army Airborne!" John exclaimed. He then jumped to his feet. "Ah've had enough of dis, ah wants to goes home! Yuh hear me, Colonel? Ah wants ta goes home!"

Matthew leapt to his feet and wrestled John to the ground. He had to silence him before some officer heard him hollering and threw him in to the brig. "What's the matter with you? You wanna end up in some padded cell? Now calm down." Matthew removed his hand from John's mouth and let him sit up.

"Blowin' off some steam, Adams?" Campbell asked.

"Guess so, sarge. Jus' blew up."

"You all right now?"

"Yeah, won't happen again." John stood up, turned away from both men and he wandered off to be alone.

Campbell looked to Matthew, "Get 'em ready, Matt. Equipment check in ten minutes. L-T says our squad will be on point, we gotta be sharp. I'll be back in a moment. Want to check on a few things before we move out."

"Gotcha."

D COMPANY

At 1346 hours, Captain Louis, a small man from the State of Maine, ordered the company to move out. As an up and coming 1^(st) lieutenant, Louis served as an aide to a major general in Airborne. To assist him in his career, this same general got Louis a combat assignment in Viet Nam and right at this moment, Louis would have liked to have that same major general in front of him for a swift kick up his behind. His stomach felt like a bomb was going off inside as he followed Ruebal's platoon up Hill 937.

Behind Louis, Lt. Roberts and 2nd platoon stepped up on the trail leading up the hillside. A graduate of ROTC from Arizona State University, Roberts had attended the 90-day Officer Training Course and had served the last five months as a liaison officer with the South Vietnamese in Saigon. This was his first combat assignment and he sincerely hoped the enlisted men in his command could not hear his knees shaking and see his hand trembling. He also prayed that he would not embarrass himself when the first fire fight opened up.

D Company reached the first bunker line within the hour. It was taking less time to make the climb with the area secured from the earlier battles. Still, Campbell sent Matthew and John up ahead to check out the ruins and make sure the NVA hadn't snuck around C Company and placed a couple snipers in there to surprise the Americans.

So far, not a single shot had been fired and Campbell hoped they could reach the second bunker line without a fight and they did. Leaning up against a blackened log from a burned out bunker, Campbell breathed a sigh of relief. This same relief was echoed by the men of C Company, who were ordered to withdraw down Hill 937 for re-supply and a brief rest.

When the artillery barrage on the summit ended at 1500 hours, the NVA once again poured out of their tunnels like ants to enter their trenches and bunkers surrounding the rim of the summit. Hill 937 still had a sizeable NVA force waiting for the 3rd Battalion and Campbell knew this wasn't going to be any cakewalk.

2ND SQUAD

Matthew spotted movement in the next trench line above and signaled for John to halt. Without waiting for orders, he crawled forward on his belly, pulled a grenade off his suspenders, yanked the pin out and lobbed it up the hillside. Once the explosion cleared, Matthew moved up to find the trench clear and no bodies in sight.

"Must be nerves," Matthew told Campbell, when the squad leader showed up beside Matthew and John.

"We've got grenades, better to bag a sniper than get nailed in the back," Campbell reassured his two point men. He then turned to wave the rest of the squad forward. "Move up! Join on me."

Campbell then turned back to Matthew and John, "Orders are to get as high as possible by late afternoon, so we keep moving up." Campbell then popped his head up to see how far the next trench was. "Matt, when you get to that next trench, lob in a couple grenades for safety sake and hold there until we join you. If you spot anyone moving above you, get back here on the double and we'll camp here for the night. Looks like about thirty yards."

Matthew nodded his head and began to leave the trench on a stomach crawl uphill, while John followed right at his feet. Suddenly, Campbell reached out and tugged on John's boot, "No, stay here, I'm going up with Matt."

"You'se the boss," John replied as he dropped back down into the trench.

Matthew was surprised to see Campbell behind him when he looked back, but Campbell simply gestured for him to keep moving. They stayed clear of the slide marks, made previously by an earlier attack, in fear of booby traps, but Campbell and Matthew continued to snake their way upward a few cautious inches at a time.

They start and stop, and each time they glanced around for some sign of movement. Spider-holes were always a threat and this fresh mud made it difficult to see any earlier digging. Several times they lost their handhold and slid backward and it was a frustrating job. Twice Matthew's boot ended up in Campbell's face and the sergeant would simply shove Matthew upward. With erosion getting worse, several tons of mud began to slide down the hill in brownish waves as the hillsides fell apart.

Matthew suddenly shot his hand up and slid back down the hill to Campbell's position, "We got gooks up ahead and they're working on the trench. It looks like the rain an' mud made it rough on them too."

"Okay, we'll head back."

But as they began sliding back down the hill, the muddy surface beside Campbell erupted with the impact of machine gun fire. "Run for it!" Campbell yelled. He leapt to his feet and began to bounce down the hill like a downhill skier, with a startled Matthew right behind him.

While making their rapid descent, Matthew lost his footing and began somersaulting right past Campbell. Luckily, he landed in the trench with a *splat* right beside John, his face plastered with mud and his rifle covered in slop. Right behind him came an exhausted Campbell, who in his rush gained too much momentum to stop and ended up tumbling into the next trench. He landed right on top of a very startled Lt. Ruebal.

With the help of Monroe and Habib, Campbell was able to pry himself loose from Ruebal and help the stunned lieutenant to his feet.

"Sorry...*spit*...'bout that, sir." Campbell said as he continued to spit mud out of his mouth.

Ruebal didn't reply, but continued to wipe mud from his face. He spat mud from his mouth and wiped fresh parts of the hillside off his uniform. His mouth now clear, he gave Campbell a raised eyebrow and said, "It appears we'll stay right here, sergeant." Ruebal then turned to his RTO and sent the message back to Louis.

D COMPANY

The men of D Company began to dig in, widening the trench as Captain Louis held a quick officer's call. "We jump off at 1000 hours tomorrow. At 0800 hours the artillery will blast the summit for two hours, followed by all four battalions attacking at once." Louis unfolded a map showing Hill 937, "2nd Battalion will attack from here," He pointed to the northeast side of the mountain, "...while 1st Battalion attacks the south an' southwest sides. From what we've seen so far, they'll find themselves on their stomachs real fast and the going will be slow. I don't put much faith in the South Vietnamese, but they've been given the southeast side to secure. Any questions so far?"

"Sir, some of my men...they look like...well, ghouls." Lt. Ruebal said and then felt foolish for saying it.

"Lieutenant, they've seen their share of Hell. This isn't their first engagement, so be glad we got some veterans with us."

"Yes, sir." Lt. Ruebal wanted to kick himself for even bringing the matter up. He just felt nervous around these men and admittedly, felt a bit envious of their experience and yet the blank look in their eyes when they stared at him frightened him. He had heard the tales of officers being *fragged* by their own men and wondered if any of these soldiers were capable of such action in the current mood they were in.

"All right then...we climb and the order giving to me is that we don't stop for the wounded." Captain Louis saw the look of surprise on his two officers. "Yes, that's the order and apparently it was the order for the last attempt. From what Sgt. Campbell told me, they made sure their wounded were bandaged up and left with a loaded rifle in their hands. But they left them and continued to climb.

"The important thing is to take this mountaintop tomorrow and at all costs. The Communists are using this as a major propaganda victory, telling the world how they've held us off for nine days with only a small token force."

"Sir, that's the 29th NVA up there...not some token force," Lt. Ruebal said. He pointed back up the mountain with his left index finger.

"I know, lieutenant, but that's how the communists work...lies and more lies."

"We'll take the hill, sir," Ruebal said with enthusiasm.

"We'd better, lieutenant, or a lot of us are going to be riding a desk after this operation," Louis shot back.

Lt. Roberts struggled to hide his frustration. *Brave talk, Captain...but to abandon the wounded...Now that really is a morale builder.*

A thick moist darkness, accompanied by a heavy blanket of apprehension and fear, descended upon the A Shau Valley. Under the cover of night, several NVA snipers slip down the mountainside and began to harass the Americans with intermitting fire. D Company was on the far left, B Company held the middle and A Company was positioned on the far right. Held in reserve, C Company remained at base camp for now.

2ND SQUAD

His back against the side of the trench, Matthew stood in three inches of murky water and PFC Habib was to his right. They exchanged semi-auto rifle shots with NVA riflemen in the trench above. "Save your ammo, Matt," John suggested. But Matthew wanted these guys. His patience was finally rewarded when the NVA shooter popped up to take a shot and Matthew popped him in the upper left shoulder. When the man let out a cry, Matthew looked at John and said, "Lord said that patience was a virtue, looks like he was right."

"Lord nev'a meant it that way," John said. But Matthew frowned in response and went back to his shooting.

"Hey look!" Sanders shouted. Illuminated by a mortar flare, a wounded NVA soldier crawled out of his trench and shouted a challenge in North Vietnamese. Unarmed except for a large knife, he beckoned for Matthew or another American to come up and meet him.

"Watch this," Razor said as he raised his rifle to take a shot, but Matthew knocked it away, "No, leave him alone." Matthew felt a wave of guilt pour over him while he watched the man slowly step forward, his movements unsteady because of his wound. He fell twice, only to rise up and before long he was close enough for Matthew and the others to see his face and to recognize his agony his was under. But they could also see the hate burning in his eyes.

"He's just some punk kid," Matthew whispered.

"He's also getting' kinda close, Matt," John warned.

"But I can't...we can't, he's only a kid for God's sake."

"Matt, look aroun' you, we'se all just a bunch of kids. That's who fight dese war…kids!"

John raised his rifle, but Matthew forced it down, "I gotta save him, John. I gotta save this one," Matthew said. Then he started to climb out of the trench.

Thinking his friend had gone crazy, John grabbed him by the legs and pulled him back down. Fighting to break free, Matthew heard a shot and looked up in time to see the youth's face explode into a mass of gore. "Oh, God…not again…not again," Matthew moaned.

He dropped to the bottom of the trench and then suddenly, his body went rigid and his mind slipped into a dark void filled with images of Jose's death and the men he had killed.

Shoving the replacements out of the way, Campbell knelt down beside Matthew, "What's wrong, Matt? Are you trying to get yourself killed?" But Matthew didn't answer, he couldn't even hear Campbell. His mind was trapped in his inner Hell and he couldn't find an escape as the images taunted him. He saw Jose, wounded from the grenade, standing there in front of him and pointing an accusing finger, blaming him for his death.

Looking to John, Campbell asked, "What happened?"

"Ah don't know, sarge. He jus' sort'a flaked out."

Campbell looked at his squad and with the exception of Monroe; they all had their eyes on him and Matthew. "Quit looking at me, this hillside is still crawlin' with gooks. If you don't wanna end up in a body bag you'd better keep your eyes aimed out there!" Campbell growled.

Only John remained at Matthew's side, but even he continued to pop up for a gander at the hillside above and all around their position.

Campbell reached down and lifted Matthew's face up. He wanted to see his eyes. He then cupped a flashlight with his hand and waved the beam back and forth in front of Matthew, but all he got was a blank stare and barely a blink. "Matt, you gotta come out of it! Do yuh hear me?"

Nothing, only a face drained of emotion and eyes that offered no clue to what Matthew's mind might be going through. "I've seen it before, during my last tour. Matt's reached his limit and he can't take any more." Campbell turned to John and said, "You're my number two now. Watch over Matt when you can or until we move up, then the medics can have him when we're done."

"Leave him? Ah can't leave Matt…No way!"

"You'll do what I tell you to do, John," Campbell said sternly and then reached down to remove all of Matthew's weapons, including Jose's .45. "I don't know how or why, but Matt's gone over to never-never land. I've seen guys turn on their friends when there in this shape, thinking they're the enemy. So until the Doc can look him over, he's dangerous to all of us. But I'll check on him again later, before we move up." Campbell then moved back to his position at the other end of the trench. He didn't let on, but losing Matthew had shaken him up.

John kneeled down beside Matthew, "Talk to me...say somethin'." But Matthew remained locked in a state of silence, his eyes now locked on something far off in the distance.

Frustrated, John grabbed him by the shoulders and shook him violently in hopes of breaking him free of this strange sickness. "Matt, answer me! Wake-up, man...you gotta beat dis."

In a world without sound, a movie projector was running and showing a series of ghastly pictures with Matthew's mind as the screen. Faces of dead enemy soldiers fade in and out with gruesome clarity and they displayed their hideous wounds as horrifying evidence to the carnage of war. Then the faces of Captain Sampson, Isaac Washington, of Jack Waterford and Brodrick appeared, all mixed in with flashing images of Jose. Their eyes displayed that same thousand-yard stare and at one point all five of them line up shoulder-to-shoulder and point an accusing finger at him. Suddenly they then disappear and only one man stands in front of him--it's his brother, Luke.

A whisper shattered the silence, a voice he recognized and it is quietly calling out his name, "Matt, you gotta wake up." John's voice begins to break through the fog and as Luke's image fades away, Matthew's vision cleared and he looked into the wide and fearful eyes of his friend.

"Matt? Can you hear me?"

"Yeah...what happened, John?"

"Man oh man, you had me scared. T'ought you gone crazy on me, sarge t'ought so to...said you fried your brain."

Matthew reached down and brought up a handful of muddy water to wash off his face.

"You'se sure you'se okay?"

"Guess so, but it felt like I'd walked down the yellow brick road and the wicked witch was broiling me for lunch. But it looks like I'm back in Kansas, Toto."

Seeing Matthew standing, Campbell made his way over and gave him a good going over. Satisfied Matthew was back on track, Campbell returned his weapons to him. "You had me worried there, Matt. Most guys don't make a round trip so fast...if ever. They usually end up suckin' on their toes and singing silly songs."

"Guess when I saw that guy's head explode, my mind caught fire. Saw a lot of nasty pictures, Sarge…be real glad when we get off this hill. Place does strange things to people's minds."

"Me too, Matt…this mountain is haunted from 400-years of death. But for now, we have a war to fight. So you check the men out and get me a status on ammo, grenades and water."

At 0244 hours the rain returned, only a drizzle at first but soon a torrential downpour and within minutes it began to fill the trenches. Men frantically bailed the muddy waters out with their helmets. For it was either that or they would be forced to abandon the trenches and lie upon the hillsides, and become easy targets for the enemy above.

SUMMIT OF HAMBURGER HILL- 29TH NVA, MAY 19TH, 1969 0300 HOURS

The rice quickly ran out and the wounded men still begged for more as the last kernel was consumed. Frustrated with his inability to properly take care of the soldiers, Que returned to the hospital. He wore a rag around his face to lesson the stench as he made his way past the bodies of the dead that now overflowed into the main treatment room.

The doctor had ordered the bodies to be removed outside, but even the orderlies had been assigned to duties outside and so the bodies remained to foul the air.

Que saw that one of the nurses, a young woman from his old neighborhood in Hanoi, who used to have a friendly smile on her face whenever she saw him, sat on the floor in the deep cavern and wore a blank expression on her face as she tore up soiled uniforms to make bandages. She noticed Que briefly and before she returned to what she was doing, he saw her sunken eyes and the dark rims about them, and it saddened him.

Que knew she had to have removed the uniform articles from the dead and the last few days of experiencing the horrors of this war had cost this young cheerful girl her innocence and left her with a lifetime of nightmares.

He wandered into the kitchen area in hopes of finding some more rice and possibly some vegetables, but the kitchen was empty. An old weathered looking cook, her face an ocean of deep wrinkles and her arms and hands covered in many burns, shuffled up to him and told him they had no more supplies. Everything had been taken to Laos, in the event the 29th NVA would be forced into a retreat. Until then, the men would be forced to live on what they had in their own satchels. Que watched as the old woman, her body bent over from age and she wore several aprons about her, wander off. He wondered if she would ever see the outside world again, but then he remembered he had duties to perform and forgot about the old woman for now. He returned outside, gratefully relieved to be away from the dying and the foul stench inside the mountain.

Que began his search for the wounded and twice he carried wounded men back inside the mountain, but only far enough in to keep them from harm's way. They needed fresh air and only death awaited them in the deeper bowels of Hill 937.

Another man, an older sergeant who had once fought the Japanese in World War II, died from his wounds before Que could reach safety. So the man's body was left in a crevice for the time being and Que, his eyes moist with tears, looked upon the man one last time and presented a salute to him out of respect for the man's long and honorable service to his country.

Mud from head to toe, his clothes and flesh splattered with the blood of so many men and a few women who had joined the ranks, Que was utterly exhausted when he climbed back to the main tunnel to refill his canteens. There he learned how his friend, another medic, had died in a cave-in. *Such a loss, his wife and boy child will grieve much when they learn of this tragedy and I have lost a friend.*

Que set near the tunnel's entrance, wept for his friend and then thought of his beloved Hanoi. He recalled the fantastic smells of the nearby market, walking by the booths and choosing his personal favorites. He had loved haggling with the shop keepers over the prices and then he remembered the long bicycle rides through the city and the occasional long ride to Haiphong Harbor to watch the fishermen coming home with their hauls of bounty. *So long ago…so far…far away.*

Then the rain returned and Que knew the hillsides would be extremely hazardous for him. He examined his feet and knew his sandals wouldn't last another night. The rocky tunnels inside the mountainous terrain outside had torn the shoes up to where they barely cushioned his feet anymore. He would have to return to the cave of the dead and find some footwear, but the very thought of taking from the dead sickened him. He let out a deep sigh and rested his head against the rock face. He hoped that just for a moment, he could close his eyes and dream of a happier time, while outside, the rain increased until rivers of murky water began to wash down through the tunnel.

Several of the wounded men who lay about the cave floor, began to shout out in panic as the waters began to rise up around them and further down below, deep inside the mountain, the dark waters began to rise in the lower chambers and men became trapped.

Que's brief sleep ended when he was shaken awake by a sergeant, who told him his services were needed down below. Men were drowning and tunnels needed to be cleared in order for them to escape the rising waters.

"We don't need your services out here right now, Medic, the fighting has ceased for now. But you are needed below."

Groggy still, Que nodded his head to show he understood and he pulled himself up by a hand hold on the tunnel wall. He glanced toward the tunnel opening, took a final lungful of fresh air in and followed the rising stream of water down through the tunnels until he came to a work party. On the other side of a cave-in, he could hear the screams of the men trapped on the other side and as he grabbed a hold of a large rock he thought of the Americans and how much he hated them for all the pain they had caused. *I wish I was a rifleman, a soldier and I could inflict upon the American devils the deep avenging pain they have caused against my countrymen. To shoot even one of them would be an honor…but now I move rocks…for this is my duty. But damn those Americans!*

UPLAND, CALIFORNIA, MAY 18TH, 1969 1712 HOURS

Kathy Lee was in the kitchen, helping her mother with dinner, while in the background the stereo in the living room was playing Dick Clark's Top 40. Busy with tossing the salad, Kathy Lee suddenly stiffened up when the music was interrupted with a newsbreak, "With fighting drawing to a close on this 9th day of battle, the men of the 101st have once again failed to take control of Hamburger Hill. As more medivac flights are flown out of this infamous A Shau Valley, it has been reported more than 200 men have been wounded and at last count 30 servicemen killed in this battle for what has become known as Hamburger Hill."

The newscaster finished off by saying there would be an in depth story of the battle on the evening news and then his voice faded, as the radio station returned to the music of the Rolling Stones.

For the last few days, the American people were actually interested in the current happenings in Viet Nam. People, both pro-Viet Nam supporters and anti-war protestors from around the country were tuned into their radios and television for the up to the minute details surrounding this epic battle of Hamburger Hill.

17 – IN THE COMPANY OF FRIENDS

2ND SQUAD, HAMBURGER HILL, MAY 19TH, 1969 0400 HOURS DAY 10

Sixty-three minutes had passed by since the last shot was fired and each minute dragged by ever so slowly. Men's nerves were stretched tight and heart beats raced as they all waited for that first shot to ring out. No one slept, for to close one's eyes could mean a sleep of death and every man kept watch on his buddy's blind side and hoped their buddy was doing the same for them. For at any moment an enemy soldier might drop into a trench and end one's dreams with a silent slash of cold steel. But in this kind of warfare where a firefight can last only seconds or go on for endless hours, men begin to make mistakes and sometime these errors in judgment can be very costly.

Campbell quietly made his way over to Lt. Rebel's side and was a bit surprised to find him carefully and with some concentration, sharpening his bayonet on a small sharpening stone. "Sir, we haven't seen a flare over our area in five minutes...it's getting too quiet and I thought you might request some illumination for us."

Ruebal gave Campbell a thoughtful look, put his sharpening stone in his left shirt pocket, his bayonet in its sheath and then replied, "Yes, you're right, we'd better have a look." Ruebal turned to his RTO, who kept an eye to the left flank and extended his hand, "Make contact with the CP and then hand me the handset."

His RTO nearly jumped from being startled, but he replied with a quiet, "Yes, L-T."

Ruebal took the handset and then pulled a small folded up map from his canvas map case and dropped to the bottom of the trench so he could use the narrow beam of his flash light. Once he had his coordinates, he contacted the CP and requested two mortar flares above their location. Less than a minute later, two pop-sounds were heard overhead and the sky lit up with the fiery bursts of mortar flares hanging in the air. Each flare hung from a small silk parachute and drifted slowly to the ground, which allowed D Company a brief moment of a false twilight.

Before Campbell could even offer up his appreciation for the new lieutenant's having taken his advice, Reynolds was shouting out, "Here they come!"

Lt. Ruebal stared at Campbell, shook his head in wonder and began to ask, "How'd you know?" But Campbell was already on the run back to his position. Not that he could explain it so a new officer would understand it anyway. It was an eerie feeling that something wasn't quite right, a combat antenna of sorts that veterans developed and new guys could only look on in awe.

A large force of NVA had hoped to sneak down the hill under the cover of darkness and got caught halfway between their trench and 1st platoon when the flares burst above them. A grizzled old NVA senior sergeant leapt to his feet and with an angry growl and ordered his men forward with a yell that would make a banshee proud.

When gunfire opened up on both sides, Ruebal grabbed the handset back and requested additional illumination. He didn't want to order any HE or WP rounds, for by now the enemy was too close to his own men and as those two flares floated to the ground, gigantic shadows began to cover the muddy landscape.

The enemy had monstrous dark shadows of black, backed by a weird yellowish tint and then the brightness suddenly blinked out and the area was plunged into total darkness. A long 30 to 40 seconds would pass before the next flare was overhead, but more would soon follow.

But for now, only the flashes of rifles firing and their tracers provide the lighting as 2nd squad and the rest of 1st platoon sent out a massive wall of fire against the enemy. Campbell's M-79 HE round exploded in front of the NVA, throwing four men backwards as deadly shrapnel ripped through them. Two NVA trip over the bodies and they fall face forward into Matthew's line of fire. He didn't even blink twice or judge himself afterward, before he ended their lives with a burst of automatic fire. A third and then a fourth flare bring an eerie daylight over the scene, with hundreds of rounds crisscrossing the hillside. Then as suddenly as it began, the shooting stopped when the last NVA tumbled to his death and lay twisted in a heap only a few short feet from where John stood in his water-filled trench.

"Hold your position!" Campbell shouted, forgetting in the heat of battle of how the order should have come from Lt. Ruebal. He had gotten used to running the company and would need to break himself of that before he got himself into serious trouble.

A quick check of the men revealed how not one of the Americans was hit and had it not been for Campbell's hunch, it would have been a different story. Lt. Ruebal was man enough to acknowledge this and show how grateful he was, "Sergeant, you have my permission to offer advice when ever you feel it necessary. Thanks. You saved a lot of lives going with this... hunch of yours."

"Yes, sir." *Maybe this guy's smarter than I thought.*

29TH NVA

They had cleverly used the attack on 1st platoon as a diversion, while in the mean time had sent out a small 11-man force to silently work their way down the hill on a suicide mission. It was their assignment is to blow up the American's Command Post and for two hours they crawled, slithered and ran from point to point to get close enough to initiate their actual attack. Once in position, five-men split off from the others to begin harassment fire on the perimeter line as a further diversion. The remaining six soldiers, loaded down with satchel charges, split into two three-man teams.

The first team inched their way forward to draw within only a few yards from perimeter security. They lie there and smell the Americans by the stench of their mosquito repellant, C-ration chow and even one new guy, with only three-days in country, who was ignorant enough to show up with a heavy dose of after-shave on his chin.

The sapper force would wait until dawn before they would attack the CP in hopes of catching the most senior men inside the Command Post tent. The second team would also wait in hiding; they would carry out the mission if the first team failed. Matthew moved his way through the narrow trench to check on the men and he found Razor kneeling in a puddle and running his mouth- again, "Man, I couldn't see nothin', jus' pointed my old rifle up that hill an' shot off a burst. Yeah, I know I got one for sure…maybe two." Razor stopped bragging when he looked up and saw Matthew glaring down at him.

"Let me see your rifle," Matthew said with his right hand outstretched.

"Why…what you want it for?"

"Give it up," Matthew said, and he made the *come on* gesture with his right hand

Razor reluctantly handed up his rifle and Matthew jerked it away to check it over.

"Razor, this weapon hasn't even been fired. What kind of game are you trying to play," Matthew said with contempt, "All your big talk about how many men you were going to kill and you turn out to be a loud-mouthed coward."

Matthew tossed the rifle back and Razor barely caught it before it hit the water. The trench was already seven to eight inches deep and still rising.

"How'd you ever make Airborne?" Matthew turned his back and locked eyes with John, "You talk to him, I'm liable to hand him over to the enemy."

"Why, because I'm black," John shot back with an icy glare.

"Well, I keep hearing all this bro' stuff an' all that black power crap."

John tensed up, but then he worked to relax some, "Take it easy, Matt, that's not you talkin'."

Matthew looked hard at John for a moment, but then lowered his gaze and gently touched John's arm in friendship, "No, you're right. You don't deserve that from me. Cowards come in all colors, but I'm real surprised they ever got him to jump out of a plane."

"Maybe they gave 'im a shove, who knows. Firefights make people act weird an' so what if he froze his first time. Maybe next time he'll do a Sgt. Rock an' surprise us both."

Campbell appeared at Matthew's side, "Between us, I'm surprised he's the only one who froze. That was a pretty hairy thing the way those guys came down the hill. Reminded me of all the stories I heard about Japanese bonsai charges to intimidate the enemy. Only thing lacking was the bugles." Campbell began to turn away, but then turned back and added, "Those were some brave men we just killed."

"Any orders, sarge?" Matthew asked as he pulled out his canteen and took a sip before handing it to John.

"Check ammo...and get some salt tabs down those new guys. Sanders looks like he's about to pass out."

29th NVA

At 0610 hours and under the cover of sporadic sniper fire, the first sapper rushed C Company's perimeter. He carried a large lunch-boxed size satchel charge in his right hand and when he sprang up from behind a large boulder, he took off running like he had a charging water buffalo behind him. Though unarmed with the exception of ten pounds of explosives, his whole focus was to make it to the CP and detonate his charge before the Americans could stop him.

CHARLIE COMPANY

On a 50-50 watch since 0600 hours, two members of C Company sat in a foxhole along the perimeter line. One, the guy who won the coin toss, had just dropped off to sleep, while the other man continued to keep watch. A new lieutenant, flown in only the day before to take over a platoon, had allowed the men to assume a 50-50 watch at precisely 0600 hours and he was about to learn a hard lesson about battlefield conditions: stay alert when it's still dark or people die.

The NVA sapper, breathing hard from running as hard as he can, passed by the Americans before they knew what was happening. The blur of a dark shadow dashing by him, the young soldier was startled and seconds pass before he has the presence of mind to yell out a warning, "Sergeant, someone just ran through the line!"

With only 50 yards to go, the sapper reached up and pulled on the primer cord that started the fuse burning. In 15 seconds, the charge was going to explode and nobody can do anything to stop it now.

Hearing the soldier's call, a bleary-eyed captain yelled out, "Enemy inside the perimeter…alert-alert!", as he struggled to stand up. The sapper had then jumped over him as the officer lay beside a tree stump.

"There he is!" A PFC shouted and he brought his rifle up, but there were too many trees and friendlies in the way to get a clear shot off. Unfortunately, there were others who weren't so cautious and several men opened up.

A squad leader from C Company's 2nd platoon, a 22-year old sergeant from Boise, Idaho, was ambling his way over to the perimeter with three canteens full of hot coffee for his men. He stopped abruptly when a lone figure swerved around a stand of trees and headed straight at him, while bullets struck the ground and trees around them. There wasn't time to unsling his rifle, so the sergeant over-handed a full canteen fastball right at the sapper and caught him right in the face with the canteen. The sapper was knocked backwards to the ground, where he lay unconscious and bleeding from a broken nose.

With some degree of experience, the young sergeant realized the man was carrying a satchel charge and he quickly removed the explosives from the man's hand and threw it into an unoccupied trench. He yelled out, "Take cover! And then he shouted, "Grenade", several times so people understood what was about to happen.

A bright blaring flash and a loud blast, almost powerful enough to be compared with a sonic boom, lifted several surprised men off their feet and they landed flat on their backsides. One man was hurled into a tent, another was somersaulted backwards a half-dozen times and he landed in a trench on top of a startled corporal. One man was caught by the concussion wave and he was later found unconscious up in a tree and two small tents were ripped from their stakes and sent flying. The sergeant who removed the satchel from the unconscious sapper was temporarily blinded from the intense bright flash. But with the exception of the sapper, who also suffered numerous broken teeth and a fractured jaw, no one else was seriously hurt from that explosion.

A second sapper, who carried a four-inch knife, hung around his neck by a grass cord, offered up his final prayer to Buddha and began his mad dash. But the young NVA corporal was cut down by M-60 fire before he could cover five yards.

Seeing his comrade fall so abruptly, the third sapper launched himself from behind a Banyan tree. With the speed of a frightened teenager with his girlfriend's father in pursuit, he made it through the perimeter before coming face to face with a terrified administrative clerk from the CP. Frozen in place by coming face to face with an enemy soldier, especially one armed with an explosive charge the young PFC doesn't even remember firing his gun. He looked down upon the body of the dying sapper and was grateful when a major quickly ran up to remove the charge before the sapper could pull the primer cord.

2ND SQUAD

At 0630 hours, the artillery bombardment of the summit began with 155mm and 175mm howitzers and it lasted for ninety minutes. The men of 2nd Squad kept hands over their ears as the explosive sounds of impact carry down the mountain. Each man prayed the artillery boys didn't land one short and as it was, the American forces were actually within the dangerous zone for such heavy artillery fire.

At 0800 hours, Air Force, Navy and Marine F-4 Phantoms and A1-E fighters strafe and bomb the pot-marked summit with deadly accuracy.

Campbell sat in 6-inches of muddy water at the bottom of a trench, alternating between keeping his hands clamped over his ears and bailing water out with his helmet. To worsen matters, with each series of explosions, debris would rain down upon the men in baseball-sized clumps of earth. One man from 1st squad was knocked unconscious when a large rock landed on top of his head. If not for his helmet, the guy would be dead. As it was, he was going to have a very serious headache when he woke up.

A nearby explosion threw Matthew against the trench wall and knocked his helmet off. John was bounced against the trench wall and thrown face first into the trench water, with Monroe landing on top of him with a loud grunt.

"Stop it--Stop it--Stop it!" One of the new men hollered and he tried to climb out of the trench, but others nearby grab his legs and pull him back down as the earth continued to rumble and explode from under the intense bombardment.

"Pretty rough way to break new guys in," Matthew said. John, whose face was dripping, nodded his head in agreement when he stood up and braced himself against the trench wall. With the next nearby explosion, he fought to keep from biting his tongue.

For two hours they experienced the fire and brimstone of the U.S. Military's might and Matthew can't help wonder how if any of the NVA could survive such Hell fire. Then his thoughts are busy with other matters when the mountain began to fight back. The earth gave way and small avalanches of mud swept down upon the men of A, B and D Companies. Like an incoming tide and just as unstoppable, waves of slop pour into some of the more forward holes like fresh cement out of a mixer. Men were forced to abandon their positions; either that or risk being buried alive under tons of brown goop.

At 0830 hours, artillery and air support ceases, leaving the hillside smothered under clouds of smoke, the pungent odor of war and that same eerie silence as the air became still.

Matthew opened his eyes, ringed in filth and slowly pulled his hands away from his ears. The near total silence made him wonder, *Am I deaf?* Then gradually the sounds began to return and only then does he let out a sigh of relief. One by one the men of 2nd squad pull themselves up, each checking the other for wounds. It appeared the only injury suffered by 2nd squad is a few brain-rattling headaches.

Using his binoculars, Campbell confirmed the NVA trench above them was utterly destroyed by several direct hits and it frightens him to know how close his own artillery had come to Uncle Sam sending a life insurance check home to his parents.

Satisfied there is no immediate threat for the moment, he reported his squad's condition to Lt. Ruebal. From the lieutenant he also learned how several men in the company had suffered minor concussions and one man sustained a broken leg when a tree rolled down the hill and nailed him. The more serious cases were taken down the hill, while minor cases were given band-aids and Aspirin.

Matthew found Razor holding his jaw and there was blood on his lips, "What happened to you?"

Before Razor could reply, Habib pointed at him and said, "That idiot tried to take off during the barrage and I had to…umm, restrain him." Habib gave Razor a look of disgust.

"He probably saved your life, Razor," Matthew said bitterly. "Snipers are makin' it pretty rough on Charlie Company. They'd have nailed you for sure…but I still can't figure how you made it through Airborne. Your pop some big shot or somethin'?"

"Quit messin' with me, Kendal." Razor, who was shorter than Matthew, now resembled a cornered ten-year old.

"Mister, I ain't even started. You slack off or bug out could get one of my guys killed. So get your gear ready, hero because we're movin' out soon an' I want you up front with me."

"Hey Matt, Monroe's hit," John said. He was knelt down beside Monroe.

Bleeding from an open wound to the left cheek, Monroe lay in the bottom of the trench with a strange wild look to his eyes.

"You hit anywhere else?" John asked.

"Don't know, but ah feel dizzy-like."

While Matthew watched, John examined Monroe and discovered a piece of shrapnel in the back of Monroe's neck. "Angels workin' overtime on you, boy."

Using his knife, John removed a two-inch sliver from Monroe's neck and the man's eyes cleared up immediately. Another piece of shrapnel was pulled from Monroe's cheek, about the size of a .22 bullet.

"They call this friendly fire," Campbell said as he looked over John's work.

"Nothin' friendly 'bout this, Sarge," Monroe replied.

"You ready to stand up?" John asked, after he had bandaged Monroe's wounds.

"Yeah, ah feels a whole lot better. Thanks."

"Hey, lookee there." Sanders pointed downhill at a squad of men climbing the hill. They looked like beasts of burden because each man was hunkered over with the weight of a dozen flak-vests.

"Why'd they wait so long before issuin' 'em?" Campbell asked Lt. Ruebal, when the vests arrived.

"I'm not sure, Sergeant, but as they like to say...all too often in the Army, 'better late than never'." Ruebal pulled one of the vests on and wasn't sure he was all that happy with the weight of it.

Matthew put his on, *Cumbersome, heavy an' hot.* But he left it on so he could get used to it. "This might come in handy up here."

Campbell walked up and called the squad together, "We move out in 30 minutes an' like before, we're going' for the top...oh yeah, we got point."

"Great." Matthew replied. *I'll put Razor up in front.*

"Sergeant Campbell!" Lt. Ruebal shouted a few minutes later.

"Yes, sir." Campbell hustled over to where Ruebal stood.

"Change of orders, D Company is to hold here while C Company moves up. They'll take our position in the attack, while we're in reserve."

Campbell was dumbstruck. He looked back at Ruebal with his jaw hanging open, as if he didn't understand the orders. Even Matthew, who was reluctant to take point, had trouble accepting the new orders and muttered under his breath, "Why should C Company take our place?"

Campbell was upset and he complained, "Sir, that ain't right, we've been fighting for this accursed hill for the last ten days and now that we're just about to take the top an' they want to pull us out? They can't do that!"

"Sergeant Campbell, those are the orders. Tell your men that we'll remain here until C Company arrives. Captain Louis wants you to brief their CO on what's directly above us. Understand…Sergeant?"

"Yes, sir, but it still ain't right." Campbell turned away and walked over to the far side of the trench. Ripping off his new flak-vest, he threw it down on the edge of the trench and stared up the hill.

Matthew understood how Campbell felt. As stupid as it might sound, D Company deserved the right to be in on this final attack. "It just ain't right to bring them up now, we're too close."

The replacements didn't understand either, but not for the same reason. They couldn't understand why Campbell and Matthew felt so strongly about wanting to be in on another attack, when they could sit back here and let someone else risk their necks for awhile. Especially Razor, who sounded off with, "Let C Company play hero."

With a hard jerk, John yanked Razor around to face him, "Keep your mouth shut, Bro' or you end up eatin' mah steel." John emphasized his remark by placing his hand on his bayonet.

Razor saw how serious John was and he sunk back down into the trench. He couldn't understand why everyone disliked him so. He was a draftee, forced to go to Viet Nam and had only gone through Airborne school for the extra money it promised. Of course every jump someone had to force him through the door of the plane, but they had kept that quiet because of the new move to get more Afro-Americans and other minorities into the Airborne. Unfortunately, the new policy had allowed at least this one coward into their illustrious ranks.

D COMPANY

The rumblings of discontent concerned Captain Louis, especially rumors circulating that he was a coward who had requested another company enter the action instead of D Company. He didn't have time to explain things to his company, of how D Company was still at only 70% of its strength and C Company, which stood at 85%, had fresh troops. Battalion wanted the hill hit hard and they felt D Company, whittled down to two-platoons, was hurting too bad to make the attempt.

When C Company arrived, Campbell briefed their CO on what he knew. Eyeing the hillside above them, the new CO didn't like what he heard. Not that it mattered; he was given an assignment and C Company would attack at 1000 hours.

When the order was given, over 2,000 men from four-battalions and support elements assaulted Hamburger Hill and within minutes, the heavens opened to greet them with a torrential rainfall.

SUMMIT OF HAMBURGER HILL, 29TH NVA, MAY 19TH, 1969, 1000 HOURS

During the massive bombardment, Que was tossed around the tunnel like a toy doll and he collided with one frightened soldier after another. A lot of men died, some simply disappeared and a crater left where they once stood. Tunnels collapsed as the earth shook, closing off all avenue of escape for dozens of entrapped soldiers. During the attack, Que was struck by a large chunk of rock and knocked to the ground. He woke up with blood dribbling down his cheeks and a sharp pain from the wound. Taking one of the rags from his pouch, he bandaged his head and went back to helping the wounded.

A few moments later, an officer placed a soldier's helmet in Que's hands, "Use this, the one who owned it doesn't require it anymore." Que was thankful for the officer's act of kindness. Medics normally wore only a soft fatigue hat and the soldier's helmet he had traded for had been lost several days earlier. The bright red star on the front of the helmet helped Que feel closer to the men he helped and it made him feel stronger.

When the barrage finally ended, the surviving soldiers poured out of their tunnels to fill the trenches and bunkers. Meanwhile the men took up their positions, awaiting the American's attack, Que continued to search for the wounded and treat them the best he could. He carried no more bandages, had no water or even a single ball of rice, all he could do at this point was provide a strong back to carry the wounded back inside and out of harm's way. Several times he had used the men's own uniforms, tearing them up into bandages and wrapping their many wounds. But mostly it was his courage and strong back that had saved many of the men. With tunnel access no longer available to escape to Laos, the wounded were being carried down the opposite side of the mountain by fellow soldiers and taken across the border only three-miles away.

Looking out over the desolate hillside, Que knew it was only a matter of hours before the barbaric Americans would reach the summit. *Will they make me a prisoner or shoot me down as the leaders have told us? Can I die bravely...can I? Can I be as strong as the men I have held in my arms while they breathe a final breath? What of my dream to be a doctor?* Que reached down, grasped a handful of dirt and examined it closely, "This is such poor soil, why have so many men died for such a terrible place?"

18 – COUNTERATTACK!

As the exhausted men from Alpha Company moved through the first and second bunker lines, searching the soaked rubble for snipers, the die-hards of Bravo Company plowed upward on their bellies through six-inches of slop. Due to the costly efforts of D Company, Charlie Company was now above the bunkers and now approaching the enemy's final line of defense; lines of trenches below the crest of the summit's rim.

Blackjack was now airborne and with his right hand trembling from a nervous twitch, he watched his battalion's final assault from inside his Huey. His entire flight crew felt the CO's anxiety, while they flew in slow circles high above Hill # 937.

This was rotten weather to be flying, the helicopter's windshield was pelted with heavy rain and the hilltop was still protected by NVA heavy .51 mm machine guns. But through the rain, Blackjack studied the Battalion's ragged line of advance and took note of how several of the units were falling behind due to the deep slippery mud, while others surged on ahead.

On the other side of the mountain, 1st and 2nd Battalions had the farthest to climb and they were now facing fresh NVA troops, who as of yet haven't fired a shot. Yet to everyone's surprise, the NVA offered up no resistance, while the mud-covered and weary Americans draw closer to the summit and this gave the veterans an eerie feeling. One sergeant whispered to his assistant squad leader he felt as if they were the fly about to enter onto a spider's web.

Then it happened. At exactly 1035 hours the NVA were given the order to open fire and the hillside came alive. They caught the over confident 1st and 2nd Battalions by surprise in a deadly crossfire from light and heavy machine guns. One moment the mountain appeared to be asleep, as if the *crouching beast* was healing from the harm caused by the heavy bombardment. Then all too abruptly, the silence was shattered when the NVA ring the mountain with a heavy concentration of automatic fire. One man described the scene as a whirling buzz saw cutting into the stunned American force.

Charlie Company ran right smack into in to a wall of hot lead and within a few short moments, the rest of 3rd Battalion's advance was halted when casualties began to mount up. From overhead, Blackjack realized the NVA were going to make his men bleed for every inch of ground and Hamburger Hill was rapidly becoming a blood bath before his eyes. Sadly, the worst was yet to come.

By late afternoon, C Company had engaged the next line of trenches and with reluctance they obeyed the orders and left their wounded where they lie. When the sun began its slow drop below the horizon, C Company was locked in a hand-to- hand struggle of life or death with their NVA counterparts. But they battled their way upward while firing at point-blank range or using their knives, bayonets and butt of their rifle to silence their adversary.

The battle soon took on the sounds of a major riot, as angry men yell and shout, and painful cries burst forth from American and North Vietnamese alike. The wounded fall and the victor fought on.

Once a trench is secured C Company advanced, but with fewer troops for the fight ahead. Some of the wounded Americans fell to all fours, but they continued to struggle on with the wounded NVA and only the survivors pull themselves over the top of bodies. Steel clashed with steel, a knife fight in the most savage form, while other combatants club at each other with rifle butts and bare knuckles.

The Montegnard people had another name for Hill # 937; it was known to them as the *Mountain of the Crouching Beast* and for the last ten-days the beast had awakened to take a deadly toll from the two warring armies.

The rain and oncoming darkness made it difficult for Blackjack to follow the battle below and he ordered his pilot to fly closer to the summit. The pilot, a lowly captain, was reluctant to say the least to take his ship closer with tracers filling the sky all around him, but he obeyed and descended another 50 feet. Most of the Americans had their helmets off by now; either knocked off or used as a weapon during the melee. But they keep their flak-vests on; these thick padded vests protect their backsides from the long NVA knives.

Alpha Company made their way through the burned out bunkers and trenches now lined with the dead and soon came within sight of the summit and a man yelled out, "I can see the top!" His shout became a rallying cry, which gave the men a morale boost when they needed it most. They push on and climbed the hillside inch-by-inch and foot-by-foot. Some slipped back, but they were caught by their buddies and they continued to move ahead. By now it was hard to tell the men from the hillsides, the mud covered them so completely they had gained a natural camouflage and it even confused some of the NVA riflemen.

For several hours Bravo Company remained locked in a stalemate with an unforgiving enemy, then suddenly they're through the bunker line. But only to come face-to-face with a series of seven trenches filled with angry NVA riflemen. It didn't look as if B Company was going any where for a while.

On the other side of the mountain, 1st and 2nd Battalions, now joined by the ARVN battalion, pushed along by their American advisors, have engaged the 29th NVA. Here, fresh enemy troops have waited for over a week for a shot at the American devils and even more so an ARVN troop. The enemy had hidden from American artillery and aerial bombing and they now had a chance to shoot back. But with Cobra Gun ships providing assistance to the Americans and South Vietnamese troops, the 1st and 2nd Battalions continued to advance.

Now encircled by four battalions, the NVA began to panic and the Americans route of the enemy began when the lead elements of the 1st Battalion pressed in hard and a squad of NVA privates saw their sergeant seemingly disappear in front of them. The man was killed by a grenade blast. The assistant squad leader was already wounded and left behind in a trench, which now meant the men were unsupervised and they began a retreat.

Next, an NVA corporal ordered the remains of his platoon to fall back, unable to defend his position any longer against the hellish fire of the Cobra gun ships. Once others saw this happening, trenches and bunkers were quickly abandoned. NVA officers ordered their men to make a stand and they promised reinforcements, but they are either ignored or trampled upon when suddenly a mass retreat was in progress. With the Americans now so close, the officers have no choice but to fall back to the summit's fortifications. If they were unable to hold, they still had hopes of escaping through one of the many tunnels inside Hamburger Hill.

Then foul weather moved in and black clouds heavy laden with rain descended upon the top half of the hill. This prevented further air support and even forced an angry Blackjack and his airborne command post to land.

By 1800 hours, the viciousness of the battle scene and the resulting carnage resembled a scene from *Dante's Inferno*. Under heavy rain, scantly clad men, covered in blood, brutally attacked one another with an assortment of lethal weaponry. Snarling like rabid dogs and bearing their fangs of steel, they lashed out viciously in a fight where no quarter was given.

Boys, who were surfing the waves of California or skateboarding the sidewalks of Detroit only a few months ago, had been turned into enraged beasts because of this barbaric war. A young man who had walked in peace rallies and waved an anti-war sign, was now struggling to stay alive by snuffing out the life of another soldier locked in his grasp. Innocence was lost and for the young man who survived this brutality, he would be forever haunted by nightmares of this single night forever.

With the weather as an ally, the NVA held their position against C Company and pushed hard to force the dog-tired men of Charlie Company back down the hill in a deadly game of King of the Mountain. A valiant but all too costly game was being fought by young kids, a few inexperienced officers and a couple dozen grizzly old tough sergeants who refused to give up.

3RD BATTALION COMMAND POST

While the battle continued above, the second sapper force prepared to launch their attack on the CP. They put their plan into operation when they assumed the downtrodden posture of three worn out NVA soldiers who wanted to surrender. They wore ragged uniforms and with hands held high they left their place of concealment to gradually make their way forward. Each man had his hands raised over his head in a sign of surrender, but surrender isn't in their plan and they sincerely hoped the Americans didn't shoot them outright.

New replacements from Firebase Blaze had taken over perimeter security. For the moment they are under the command of a 36-year old supply officer, who is nervously waiting for an experienced officer to arrive and assume responsibilities for the guard duties.

The NVA soldier who walked in front held a white piece of cloth in his right hand and began to shout out in broken English, "Give up, no shoot! Give up, no shoot!" He waved the cloth frantically and smiled, he wanted to make the Americans understand they had surrendered.

"Sarge, we got three gooks coming in ta give themselves up!" A young PFC from Newport, California shouted out, while his rifle was pointed at the three NVA.

"Then bring 'em in!" Sergeant Elton shouted back. He had his boots off while changing his soaked socks for dry ones and figured even a couple of new guys could handle three surrendering gooks.

When the three NVA draw near, the PFC and his partner jump out of their hole and rushed forward to meet them. The two of them stop a few feet in front of the prisoners and gesture with their rifles for the three to stop. The young PFC from California trembled with adrenaline rush and his voice squeaked from a bad case of *new guy nerves*, when he yelled, "Keep those hands up, you move too fast an' you're dog meat."

The NVA with the white flag stepped forward and whispered over his shoulder an order to the other two in his own language, "Now."

The two men on the outside quickly brought one arm down behind their head and jerked up a thin grass cord wrapped around their necks. At the end of the cord was a tight loop holding two-pineapple grenades they had hung behind their backs. Suddenly these timid looking Vietnamese had become treacherous snakes. They had used a flag of surrender to entrap the Americans. The grenades were now lives and seconds were ticking off.

While the two new guys stood there with stunned expressions on their faces, the three NVA made a suicidal dash for their assigned target. The man with the white flag shoved past the two startled Americans, which allowed one of the men with grenades to drop one grenade into a trench full of startled young privates.

"Grenade!" Sgt. Elton shouted in panic. He tried to stand up while fumbling with his boot and clumsily fell to the ground with a grunt.

The double-grenade exploded, wounding five men who didn't react fast enough and suddenly this portion of perimeter was in absolute chaos as the three NVA are mistaken for a major counter-attack.

The first sapper, died under a hail of fire within seconds of tossing his first grenade. The second NVA went down as he was in mid-throw, but the explosion of the grenade wounded a young lieutenant and a medic. But it was the third sapper who was the most dangerous, for under his soiled shirt he had carried a ten-pound charge and right now he was on the run to reach the CP.

Sergeant Hovers from Seattle, Washington, wounded the previous day with RPG shrapnel to the left arm, was on his way to the latrine when he spotted the third sapper. Forgetting his own injury, the sergeant brought up his combat knife and let fly from over twenty feet away. The sapper had a surprised look on his face when he fell to the ground, the knife sticking out of his right shoulder. Yet the primer cord has been pulled and only a few seconds later the eardrum breaking blast knocked Hovers to the ground with a serious concussion that wounded three others.

The shout of, "Medic-Medic!" could be heard throughout the area and pandemonium broke out along the perimeter. Men were shooting at anything they suspected might be the enemy or a place a sniper could be concealed. MSgt. Riggs ran out of the CP and yelled out an order to ceasefire that was eventually echoed down the line.

"Everyone stay at your position!" Riggs shouted only seconds before he spotted an officer running through the trees toward him, making him a great target for an overexcited young kid on the battlefield for the first time. As the man approached at a dead run, his eyes wide with fear, Riggs tackled the second lieutenant about the knees and drove him to the ground. Pulling the startled young officer to his feet and brushing him off some, Riggs advised him of how close he came to getting shot.

"My apologies, lieutenant, but if you were to keep running like that...well sir, someone was liable to blow your stupid head right off...sir."

The startled lieutenant could only stare at Riggs with a blank expression on his face and a slow nod of understanding. He then stood there and watched as Riggs went off to check on the other positions.

In a large canvas tent positioned beside the CP tent, a visiting newsman picked up a black Underwood manual Typewriter and studied with keen interest the bullet hole in the side of it. He checked the other side and saw how the bullet had traveled clean through it. His typewriter, which had traveled with him since the second month of the Korean War, was a victim to friendly fire. When he realized how close he came to being shot by one of his fellow Americans, the man fumbled with a pack of cigarettes and quietly wandered outside for some fresh air and a smoke in the rain.

D COMPANY

With a constant deluge hammering at them from above, the men of D Company were forced to sit on their thumbs. Replacements might have reconciled with the order to stand fast, but it was a different matter for the veterans. They're chewing on their lips in frustration, disgusted with the order to remain on reserve. These men wanted back into the fight.

2ND SQUAD

While he listened to the fighting from above, Campbell pounded his fist against the side of his trench with a *splat*. A wayward bullet might strike the ground, but otherwise for the moment the war seemed to have left him behind. Campbell was so angry his whole body shook and everyone knew to stay out of his way and this included a very intimidated platoon commander. Campbell felt like a star lineman told to sit out during his senior year Homecoming Game and he was about to explode.

Several times Campbell looked as if he was going to jump out of the trench to follow C Company, but his responsibility to his squad held him back--reluctantly.

Through his binoculars, Campbell saw how the NVA had whittled C Company's numbers down and how their wounded now covered the hillside. In the upper trenches he saw mobs of men clash against each other like great ocean breakers striking rock cliffs, but at this point Campbell can't tell which army stood like the rock and which man was the wave that broke the rock down. He could not see their faces and the mud left all the soldiers from both armies looking the same. He could only hope C Company held the trench when the fighting was over.

CHARLIE COMPANY

After ten days of fighting it finally happened, 1st squad of C Company's 1st platoon forced its way over the edge and broke through the outer edges of the summit. But they have no time to celebrate, nor the man power to hold the position. Four surviving Americans now faced a rush of over twenty very angry and screaming NVA riflemen.

"Get more men up here, we can't hold?" The squad leader shouted to the positions below. He then turned around in time to block a lunging AK-47 bayonet and plunge his bayonet into the man's stomach. Beside him, a 19-year old boy from Phoenix, Arizona, swung his empty rifle in a sweeping motion like a baseball bat and knocked aside another bayonet tipped rifle and the NVA soldier fell on top of him. The fight was on, barehanded and no holds barred. But before they can get help, the four men were soon bowed over by the enemy's sheer weight in numbers.

"Fight your way through!" the platoon leader ordered. He soon reached the position and grabbed one of the NVA by the hair and kicked him in the stomach.

"Second Platoon, move up!" The Company Commander ordered in a loud shout and then he pointed to 3rd platoon, "Third Platoon, guide to your right in support of 1st platoon!"

Then just as it appeared as if the Americans might have secured a foothold on the summit, additional NVA troops arrived to reinforce their ranks. These are soldiers from other units who had retreated up the other side of the hill as the advancing battalions made their climb.

Most of the NVA are young men and they are terrified by the numbers of enemy making their way up the mountain and when they make their way back to the summit they find most of the tunnels now buried and now their only option is to make a stand of it. Surrender was not an option for them, they were not Viet Cong but North Vietnamese Army Regulars and they had been told over and over again of how Americans treated their prisoners in brutal and horrific ways.

C Company, exhausted from its struggle to break through was now facing a wall of fresh troops and they were extremely frightened young men. The NVA outnumber the Americans by better than four to one and the lieutenant can do nothing but order, "Retreat!" Wounded by a bayonet, his face battered by the butt of an AK-47, the lieutenant dragged his useless leg behind him and pleaded to God that he might survive this day.

"Grab all the wounded!" A squad leader yelled.

"Help me! Don't leave me here..." A wounded man shouted as his voice faded into unconsciousness.

"We got' ta hold here, Lieutenant. We can't leave our men behind to be butchered." A sergeant pleaded with his officer before he emptied a magazine into a mass of NVA.

"Grenade!" A man shouted, immediately followed by another man's warning, as explosions rock the crest of the hill and another American is wounded by shrapnel.

Chaos then breaks out when C Company's 2nd platoon moved upward in support of 1st platoon, but all they do is block 1st platoon's retreat. 3rd platoon remained alone for a brief moment, but when they attempted to flank the enemy's charge they end up walking into a hornet's nest.

"Retreat--Retreat!" The order was given when the frightened platoon commander for 3rd platoon suddenly locked eyes with an aged NVA major, who led a company-sized force of NVA against 3rd platoon with an actual Japanese sword in is hands. The young officer saw that sword more frightening than the AK-47's the riflemen were carrying.

Charlie Company's Commander had lost control of his command momentarily, while his platoon leaders and their RTOs were battling it out for survival and unable to even take a moment to give their CO an appraisal of the situation.

Having no other choice, the Company Commander ordered his men to withdraw, but most of them were already jumping down the hill to escape the enemy blistering hail of fire. Above them, the NVA soldiers now line the crest of the summit and fire down upon them. A couple of the wounded men were left on the summit and the NVA ruthlessly finish them off with bayonets and then toss them down the hill. No mercy was given the wounded in a battle such as this.

3RD BATTALION

With the NVA in a withdrawal in mass from the advance of 1st and 2nd Battalions, 3rd Battalion's Alpha and Bravo Companies were meeting up with stiff resistance. Command knew it was only a matter of minutes, before the NVA were ordered to overrun 3rd Battalion in hopes they could escape into the jungle.

Blackjack grabbed his radio handset and made contact with Captain Louis. He ordered Dog Company in to reinforce Charlie Company immediately.

D COMPANY

Captain Louis sent his 1st platoon in first, specifically tasking Campbell's 2nd squad to lead the way. Without even waiting for Lt. Ruebal's order, Campbell eyed his men, provided an animal-like snarl and growled, "Second squad, move out." When he climbed out of the trench, Campbell turned and shouted in a triumphant shout, "D Company, fix bayonets!"

Lt. Ruebal didn't say a word. He simply pulled out his bayonet and attached it to the end of his M-16. Campbell waved his right arm over him in a gesture of *follow me*, secured his shotgun in his left hand and gave the order to move out. "This is our day, D Company, let's mow 'em down and take this damn hill!"

Though spirited on by Campbell's gestures and words, 1st Platoon almost immediately found them selves in a hairy shooting war with the NVA riflemen firing down from the ridge line.

"Keep moving up, Campbell! Don't stop for anything!" Ruebal yelled out. He knew this was a bad spot to be caught in because there was so little cover. Lt. Ruebal glanced back down the hill and spotted Lt. Roberts leading 2nd platoon up the hill. Both officers shared a quick look and shared a thought; they both knew this climb was no simple task.

A man had to keep his weapon clear of the mud and grab a handful of mud with his free hand and struggle to pull himself up. But with every foot forward a man could slide two feet back if he wasn't careful. A man had to stop briefly, raise his rifle and fire before he resumed his climb, and the mud was still getting into their mouths, their eyes and often jamming their weapons. Spitting, coughing and wiping their eyes, they climbed or the ground could give way from underneath them and the next man below might be covered by a wave of mud, or a boot in their face from a man who lost his footing.

2ND SQUAD

Between the darkness and rain, all Matthew can make out is the muzzle flashes and explosions up ahead. Bullets continued to impact all around him and when they stuck the mud it made a strange sound that he compared to a fly being swatted on a mattress. He even felt a jerk when one round grazed the top of his vest. But still he held his fire in fear of hitting one of men from C Company. There was no talking as they labored to climb, only the grunt of sheer exhaustion or a burst of profanity to help quell the fear that rose up to choke each and every man. Yet they climbed.

Bright miniature suns burst overhead when the flares begin to illuminate the hillside and Matthew feared it was only making them better targets for the NVA. But still the mortar units down below fired off the flares as rapid as the men can load them. They had drilled and drilled and now they were putting their training to use and every man was exerting himself to the point of exhaustion and the low ceiling didn't help any. But then the cloud cover began to rise and now more than a dozen flares illuminated the summit crest area of Hamburger Hill. They created a false daylight, which gave the battle scene an even more eerie appearance of false colors and gigantic shadows.

*Dear Lord…*was all Matthew can think of when he sees what lay ahead.

Campbell doesn't care. Nothing was going to stop him from reaching that mountaintop and he waved his men onward again and again. The steepness of the grade had him on all fours, his shotgun slung around on his back, he crawled upward. He kept his M-79 clutched tightly in his right hand, the large barrel facing downward to keep mud out of it and his towel wrapped around the loading breach. They used some of the dead enemy as ladders, anything to help them get closer to the objective.

CHARLIE COMPANY

When the Commanding Officer of C Company received word D Company was on its way up, he turned to one of his platoon leaders and said, "We hold here…We have to cover their advance…Your men must hold."

"With what, sir?" The lieutenant asked. "In another few minutes we'll be down to throwing rocks at them, they outnumber us and what few men I got left is ready to shoot me if I order them to hold." The frightened lieutenant shot back.

The CO looked at him with an icy glare and in a low whisper only the lieutenant could hear, said, "With ever it takes, Lieutenant. You will hold here, even if that means I have to shoot the first man who disobeys my order and tries to run. You got me, *mister?*"

"Yessir!" The lieutenant was now more afraid of his CO than he was the men under him and knew the threat was very real.

2ND SQUAD

By 2220 hours, Campbell and his men had made it through a vicious gauntlet of enemy fire to finally join up with C Company. When Campbell reached up with a sweaty and mud covered hand and he was panting for breath from such a steep climb, he was surprised to find the hand grasping his to that of a grateful Company Commander.

"Glad you made it," The CO said. He was unsure of Campbell's rank due to the condition of his uniform and right now it really didn't matter.

"Mind if we talk later, sir. I don't want to stop my momentum."

"I've ordered my men to hold here…" The CO stopped in mid-sentence when Campbell simply shook his head and gently shoved the officer aside. He kept on going through the C Company's ranks with an exhausted squad of men right behind him.

It was while passing through C Company that PFC Sanders was shot in the back. Though painful, the wound wasn't fatal and a shot of morphine delivered him into a world of blue mist. *Yeah…this ain't so bad…cool.*

A driven man, Campbell doesn't stop to talk with anyone and with his shotgun at the ready and his M-79 slung over his shoulder, he charged through Charlie Company's position like an NFL All-Pro running back. Behind him, Matthew, John, Monroe and the rest of 2nd squad fight to keep up with him.

Man, I feel like I'm the shoulder section of a centipede and Campbell is the head, can't stop until he does and it doesn't look like he plans to stop until we take that summit. The thought raced through Matthew's tired brain, but he still continued to climb and watch for snipers who might try to stop Campbell.

Without waiting for orders and without saying a word to anyone, Campbell had taken it upon his own to launch a company-sized counter-attack. He was doing his impression of a 220-ton steam locomotive and it looked like there was actually steam emanating off Campbell's shoulder. He appeared to be unstoppable, not even a break to rest his legs and his courage and determination was unmatched, which inspired the men of C Company.

They saw him burst through their lines and without orders, the weary grunts turned to join with Lt. Ruebal's 1st platoon. Like the fairy tale Pied Piper, they began to follow that crazy sergeant right back up the hill. The tide had suddenly turned and the NVA had no idea what was coming their way.

"Don't stop!" Campbell yelled over his shoulder. He was panting now, but he wouldn't slow down. "Keep goin', don't stop for nothing!"

Even with this relentless rain, he refused to slow down and seemed to display an almost super human strength. With Campbell's bravado as an example, the men of 3rd Battalion began to issue forth strange yells of encouragement. A few rebel yells were recognizable from the men of the south, some profanity directed toward the enemy and even several declarations to the Lord. Men forget about their exhaustion, they ignored their pains and charged over the ridgeline like an unstoppable juggernaut.

They hit the NVA with quick bursts of rifle fire, supported by M-60s lugged up the hill by two-man teams and shotgun blasts. Grenades were thrown, RPG's shot off and then it was suddenly two companies of weary men who crashed against the NVA like two ragging bulls.

At first it's a stalemate. Neither side can move forward while point units battle it out up front in a full-fledged East LA street fight. Moments passed by, but slowly the Americans begin to drive the NVA back from the rim. This match-up was no longer two armies in a duel for ownership of Hamburger Hill. No, this had become a simple case of survival. Live or die. No time to think, no time to consider options or choose who your next opponent was. This was the cruelest part of warfare, where a man's savagery comes forth in its purest sense. Here, soldiers strike out quickly in a place where there are no rules.

Driving the attack on, Campbell felt the vengeance burning down deep inside him and he pumped shotgun rounds out one after another in quick succession until he was out of ammo. Much like an enraged water buffalo, he continued on, unrelenting and wreaking forth with a beast-like behavior. His shotgun now empty, he began to swing the weapon like a baseball bat and tonight, *Babe Ruth* was batting all home runs.

Screams of pain, a grunt, a yell or an animal-like snarl, these are the only sounds coming from the men. It's a massive braw in progress and everyone, including the officers, wanted a piece of this action.

These men had grown up with tales told to them of how the Marines on Iwo Jima and the Army at Omaha Beach had won out against overwhelming odds, and now came their turn on the summit of Hamburger Hill. It was a battle scene that would be told for a hundred years or more, of the courageous men of the 101st went hand-to-hand with the NVA for ownership of Hill # 937.

With barely enough time to bring his rifle up, Matthew dropped one soldier less than three feet away. Then caught up in the midst of all this mayhem, Matthew struggled to keep his footing in the tangle of bodies beneath him, while he brought up the butt of his rifle and used it as a club.

To his left, John shot from the hip to wound one man in the legs and then thrust forward with his bayonet to impale a growling NVA sergeant swinging a long knife intended for John's chest.

Swinging to his left, Campbell smacked two men in the face with the barrel end of his shotgun; the pistol grip was now shattered. To his right, Monroe fired into a squad of NVA only seconds before ducking underneath the swing of a large enemy sword. John moved in to assist Monroe and drove his rifle butt into the stomach of the officer holding the sword, following through with a blow to the back of the head.

Side by side the men of 2nd squad stood; Campbell to the far left, Matthew, John, and Monroe in the middle and Habib holding down the right flank. They moved forward like an offensive line.

The NVA are completely stunned by the sheer fierceness of the American's counter-attack and fall before their onslaught. Rather than face Campbell, several NVA run to escape this mad man who wields his shattered shotgun like a knight's battleaxe.

Habib, clutching his M-60 in a two-hand grip, swings the heavy weapon in a wide arc like a huge broadsword and leveled one man with a head blow. Then a second NVA crashed to the ground with a bent skull. With such barbaric actions and the Americans utter ferociousness, the NVA are unable to make a stand against them.

Out of ammo, Ruebal dropped to one knee, pulled out his pistol and fired his .45 at the enemy. After he emptied his magazine, he then ripped an AK-47 away from one wounded enemy soldier and used it to drop three NVA before reaching Campbell's side.

Matthew, now bleeding from a scalp wound and a minor scrape to his side by an enemy bayonet, glanced up in time to see John use his M-16 to club an NVA to the ground with repeated swings. Then Matthew was shoved roughly to the side and he spun around in time to bring his rifle up to fire, only to realize he was already out of ammo.

An NVA soldier attempted to fire his rifle, but the aged SKS rifle jammed and he lunged at Matthew with his 18-inch bayonet. Matthew parried the thrust with his own rifle and the two men are now locked rifle against rifle in a battle of strength. They shoved against each other, hoping for the upper hand and Matthew was able to use his height as an advantage. He drove the man to the ground and then knocked him unconscious with a quick blow to the side of the head. When the man fell to the ground, Matt heard a warning shout and turned around in time to block a rifle butt aimed at his head. Unbalanced, a quick second blow drove Matthew to the ground and a third blow might have taken him out of the picture completely if Monroe hadn't stepped in with his own rifle butt in to knock the man out with a vicious rap to the jaw.

"Why didn't you shoot him?" Matthew asked as he fought for air.

"No ammo," Monroe replied.

No time to rest, Matthew got back on his feet and stepped forward. Then the mass of humanity in front of him separated and he found himself facing a crazed looking man who waved a long sword about like an Arabian warrior might do with a scimitar. The NVA sergeant was bleeding from at least two wounds, but he still swung his weapon in wide arcs as he stepped forward and it seemed the man sincerely desired to cut Matthew's head right off. Not wanting to be separated from his noggin, Matthew grabbed the barrel of his M-16 and threw the rifle overhand at the man. He was surprised that he had actually nailed the guy in the chin with a disabling blow.

PFC Razor was pierced in the side by a bayonet and he let out a pitched scream, fell to his knees and clutched his side. He backed away from his attacker and barely holding his rifle, he fired off a three round burst into the man's foot and crippled the enemy soldier. Tossing his rifle aside, Razor began to drag himself away from the fight but soon passed out from a loss of blood. A moment later, Captain Louis's reserve platoon arrived to trample over the top of Razor in their quest to follow Campbell. With the arrival of new men, the front elements of C and D Companies fight on with a new vitality and they drive the enemy back into the middle of the summit.

3RD BATTALION

Alpha and Bravo Companies reached the rim and they immediately enter into the battle for the summit. Blackjack was back in the air and from his point of view, he can't tell the Americans from the North Vietnamese.

"My god, they're fighting it out with everything from fists, feet, knives, bayonets, rifle butts, rocks and whatever else they can lay their hands on," Blackjack said into his intercom, "One guy down there is actually using a tree branch to club 'em down with. I've never seen such..." He stopped talking and picked up his binoculars, "One man's now using his flak-vest to beat a man down..." Blackjack lowered his binoculars and didn't know what else to say. The unimaginable and grizzly scene below had rendered him speechless.

2ND SQUAD

Campbell was covered in blood, but none of it his own. He had remained untouched with the exception of a few minor cuts and scratches. He stood atop one body and delivered a wild roundhouse punch to knock cold a young NVA Corporal. And still he continued to press in. Behind him by only a couple feet now, Lt. Ruebal tried to stay clear of Campbell's bar brawling and head busting style of fighting.

Monroe got knocked to the ground by a good old fashion body block and he rolled to his side to avoid an NVA bayonet that missed Monroe's backside by mere inches. He came up with his survival knife and ended the face-off with stab to the man's hip and pushed him away as others crowded in.

Having delivered a disabling hand-chop to a man's throat, Matthew turned in time to see John, unarmed except for a bayonet in his hand, in a standoff with two NVA. Both men, armed with long knives, were circling him.

338

Running toward John, Matthew got tangled up with a very large NVA sergeant. They're on the ground rolling around and the man has his hands lodged around Matthew's throat in hopes of choking the life out him. But Matthew was able to break the hold and roll aside as another NVA lunged forward with a bayonet. The man ends up sticking his own sergeant in the chest. The startled NVA private was staring into the dying eyes of his sergeant when Matthew delivered a hard chop to the back of the man's neck and continued on toward John.

The taller of the two NVA stepped in with his knife and nicked John in the ribs, while the second man drew John off balance with a swing to the head. But an opening presented itself and John lashed out with his bayonet to slice the taller one's knife hand. John was an experienced knife fighter, having survived a lot of back alley duels from the old neighborhood. But he wasn't ready to take on three men at once. While facing the other two, a third NVA came charging up and jumped on to John's back and that's all it took. Under the weight of the third man and worn to a frazil from the longest rumble he'd ever been involved in, John finally collapsed to the ground, while the enemy slashed at him with their knives and bayonets.

Still unable to help John, Matthew was cut off by an NVA, an older soldier who desired to end Matthew's army career with a bayonet thrust. Matthew knocked the rifle aside, grabbed the man by his uniform shirt, rolled on to his back in a Judo flip and the man followed right over the top of him. Matthew jerked the rifle free from the man's grasp and delivered a hard blow to the man's forehead with the side of the weapon. He then jumped free in time to see John buried under the enemy's attack.

Screaming at the top of his lungs, Matthew charged and knocked the three NVA off his friend. Enraged and pumping adrenaline, he moved in a blur of speed, wrestled one of the long knives away from one man and slashed his throat. He then used a hard backstroke and plunged the tip of the weapon into another one's stomach. But before he could engage the third, the terrified man had run off to escape Matthew's vengeance.

Before Matthew can check on his friend's condition, which he knew had to be serious another soldier appeared behind Matthew and plunged his bayonet deep into Matthew's right side. Matthew bit off most of the scream as he fell forward, but he rolled to his uninjured side and stared back at his attacker, who was now moving in for the kill.

At that very moment, Matthew remembered he still carried Jose's .45 pistol and as the man began his downward plunge, Matthew rolled onto his back, did his best to ignore the piercing pain and brought his left leg up to protect himself. In doing so, he pulled the pistol from under his shirt and shot the man in the chest twice. But he wasn't fast enough.

Matthew screamed an ear piercing shriek when the man's bayonet entered through his kneecap and exited through his upper thigh. In near shock, Matthew stared at the weapon sticking out of his leg. Strange enough, the deepness of the wound kept the rifle suspended in mid-air. But his enemy was now dead. Matthew flopped over on his side and tried to use his right foot to push the bayonet back out, but white-hot pain burst through his brain and was followed immediately by darkness.

Wounded and left for dead, Matthew lay on the battlefield with a bayonet lodged in his leg and bleeding from a second wound to his side. There are no dreams and time meant little when a man hangs over death's door.

Fighting to breathe, his mind on fire, Matthew awakened to the sounds of fighting all around him. His leg burned and he knows that he has to pull that bayonet clear to live. The weight of the rifle prevented him from crawling off and he was losing his strength fast. Only the occasional moan escaped his lips because he wanted the enemy to think he was dead or he would be. *I have to live…Have to fight…I have to live…to live…to live. Help me, God!*

Building up his courage, Matthew held his breath while he bent over at the waist and with an excruciating yank, he was able to rip the bayonet free. But it took a lot of his hide and muscle with it. He woke back up a few moments later; pain and a fading determination to live was the only thing to keep him alive at the moment.

"Got' ta stop the blood," Matthew whispered. But he was too weak to go looking for a battle dressing and all of his were gone.

Time to die…We're all dead…Jose an' John…No more time. Matthew was ready to give up, but an inner voice kept telling him to fight on. If he was going to survive he needed to drag himself over to that nearby trench. *Got' ta try…got' ta try…got' ta try Oh, God give me strength!*

With what little strength he had left, Matthew dragged himself over ten feet to the edge of a rifle trench. Slowly and all too painfully, he pulled himself over the lip and with a painful jolt from the drop he now laid face first at the bottom. He thought he might drown for the trench was nearly eight-inches deep in murky water. He spat out the foul tasting water and lifted himself up by using his good leg to brace against the interior wall of the trench.

Matthew realized he wasn't alone, a small NVA soldier stood at the other end of the trench with a bolt-action SKS rifle in his hands. Matthew, his eyes first locked on that rifle and then on the soldier, watched, in no shape to stop him if he wanted to, as the man brought the long cumbersome rifle up to his shoulder and aimed it at Matthew's head.

With Jose's .45 lying outside the trench, all Matthew could do was to offer up a look that said, *you win this one, buddy, but I don't really care.* He then waited for the shot to come.

When it didn't come right away, he stared at the man and whispered, "You jus' go ahead...I've killed enough...go ahead."

Medic Que looked down the long barrel of the rifle, his finger gently pressed against the trigger and his trembling arms struggling to hold the heavy rifle up. The sergeant had showed him how to shoot the SKS only a few hours earlier, after he removed it from a fallen comrade and loaded the rifle for Que.

Seconds slowly pass by while Que debated with himself over whether or not he could shoot this man. *I should kill you for the harm your country has caused, for all my comrades who have died here. For all the men I have treated down below and the bombs you have dropped on my people. For this you should die...But, I am not a killer.* Que slowly lowered the rifle and for a moment he watched the American and sensed this wounded man was praying to his god. For some strange unexplainable reason, Que felt as if only he and this American were all alone on this mountaintop and sharing a special moment. *I do not understand this...*

Matthew looked into the eyes of the soldier in front of him, at first they were full of hatred but now the man appeared confused as if he struggled with the idea of killing him. Matthew thought about praying for his life, maybe even begging to this enemy, but instead, he began to pray for all the men around him and even this very soldier who cradled Matthew's life in his small hands.

"I forgive you..." Matthew muttered and in response the man had lowered his rifle.

Que didn't understand what Matthew had said, but his desire to become a doctor was stronger than his desire to seek revenge. For a moment their bloodshot eyes are locked as they seem to communicate a mutual weariness.

Then the silence was broken when Que whispered in his language, "My name is Lin He Que and I am a medic, a respecter of life. If your god wants you dead than he can do it for I won't." Que took one last look at Matthew and climbed out of the trench. He rushed off to follow other NVA who now fled down the mountainside through hidden ravines to escape into Laos.

Matthew didn't understand, but somehow he was spared. A moment later, darkness once more took hold and for a brief time the pain seemed to subside as shock settled in.

Campbell knew the NVA were on the run, they were abandoning their positions by groups of ten and twenty. Under the cover of darkness and this constant rain, they fled down the hillside to simply vanish into the jungle floor.

As of 0105 hours; May 20th, 1969, Hill 937, *aka* Hamburger Hill, now belonged to the 101st Airborne Division. Campbell's initial feeling of triumph quickly faded when he looked across the summit and peered down the hill to observe all the dead and wounded lying there from both armies.

Picking up a handful of mud, he studied it for a moment with a blank look and then hurled it to the ground with a *splat*. "The price we paid was a bit high for such an insignificant speck of mud."

19 – LEAVING PARADISE WITHOUT BUYING EVEN A POST CARD

A SHAU VALLEY, SUMMIT OF HAMBURGER HILL, MAY 20TH, 1969, 0200 HOURS - *DAY 11*

The battle was finally over, but an uneasy calm continued to linger over the mountain. Rain, now reduced to only a steady drizzle, left the summit flooded in over the ankle deep mud. Prisoners, the ones who could walk, were herded together by a platoon of men from 2nd Battalion's Alpha Company. Off to one side, medics had set up an aid station under a canopy of canvas tents flown up by Huey's earlier and they were busy with the treatment of the wounded men from both armies. A priority system was installed and it was known as triage, not by rank or officer over enlisted, they were examined by one doctor who marked their priority and they were treated as space became available. Some cases, those ones that couldn't be worked on in the field, got first dibs for a quick helicopter ride to the nearest Evacuation Hospital. With so many wounded troops, nearly every Evac Unit in Vietnam was used for treatment. The more serious cases, once the patient was stabilized, were flown on to Hawaii or Japan, and eventually stateside.

Hundreds of bodies lay scattered about; some stacked two and three high, while squads of men examine each one to determine if they were American or NVA, and if they still might be alive. In a couple cases the dog tag chain had been ripped off in the battle royal, but they were later identified by squad mates and platoon commanders. Still, dental records would have to be checked before death notifications were made.

Due to the mud, some of the Americans of an ethnic minority, such as Hawaiian or oriental decent were first identified as NVA and mistakes were made, but corrected. It was also a grizzly task and several of the newcomers had upchucked. But though the majority of the dead are NVA, there are enough American corpses to keep Camp Eagle's morgue busy for quite a while.

2ND SQUAD

Campbell and Monroe stood together in silence, while they watched broken and shredded bodies carried over to a flat spot, now set up as an in examination area. There, Americans were placed in to body bags, while on the opposite side of the summit the NVA are stacked like cordwood for the time being and their weapons piled nearby for later destruction. Overhead, the thick layer of the monsoon rains prevented the sun from breaking through and the occasional flare was requested for lighting effect against the rain. But the false daylight of the spiraling flare gave the dead men such a fiendish coloring, it bothered several of the young troops who were forced to turn away.

For many of the young men, this was their first brush with the enemy and some of them had not even fired a shot in the battle. But their war still awaited them. There would be many more battles and mountains to climb before the Americans would finally go home.

"Sometime tomorrow a lot of mothers and fathers are going to get notified by the Department of the Army of how their sons had died valiantly in the service of our great country," Campbell whispered to Monroe. "But right now I'm just too tired to care much." He took one last look and then he grasped Monroe on the right shoulder, turned him around with a gentle shove and they both ambled off to find a place to relax before they both dropped from complete exhaustion. The adrenaline shakes had left them, now they were being held up by sheer force of will and they both hoped they might find somewhere to sit out of this dreadful mud.

Campbell sat down on a chunk of blackened log and took a moment to examine his own body. Though nearly every part of his body cried out in dull pain and for a man, who had almost single-handedly led the counter-attack, he was more than amazed to have only sustained one minor wound; a small slice on his left arm where an enemy bayonet grazed him. He reached up to scratch an itch above his right eye and came away with fresh blood on his right fingers. He asked Monroe to take a look.

Monroe reached over, moved Campbell head so he could see the wound from under the glow of a flare. He then set back down on his own piece of log, shrugged his shoulders and said, "Looks like you got popped, Sarge. Ain't nothin' bad."

Campbell then recalled he had caught a glancing blow from the butt of an AK-47. "Ah, I forgot about that little dude with the rifle, he nearly took my head off." Weariness began to overpower Campbell and he slid off the log into the mud. Monroe stood up over him and held a strange looking weapon in his hand, "Yuh dropped it back dere. T'ought yuh might want it."

Campbell reached up with a tired hand and grasped one end of his broken shotgun, or what was left of it. "Looks pretty useless now...might make a decent wall hanging for some art nut. Think of all the stories I can tell when my buddies see this thing." But both he and Monroe knew they'd probably never tell this story. Campbell felt few would ever believe it and for those who didn't share the experience, Campbell didn't think they deserved to know.

"Thanks, I appreciate it." Campbell wrestled his canteen free from its canvas holder and emptied the last few drops down his dry throat. He then dropped the canteen into the mud, closed his weary eyes and immediately dropped off to restless sleep.

With Campbell napping and several dozen troops standing around to keep his sergeant safe, Monroe walked off to begin looking through the casualties for John and Matthew's bodies. Most of the dead still remained where they fell in combat and in a few places, an American remained locked in a death embrace with his enemy.

He sure wasn't looking for him, but Monroe found PFC Razor unconscious and lying in a crater with three dead NVA on top of him. After he found a pulse, Monroe yelled for a medic, and once one had arrived, Monroe moved on and he soon came upon PFC Habib and PFC Williams. Both of them were sitting in a bomb crater, their shirts and flak-vests off to let the rain wash away the mud from their sweaty bodies. Though two of them bled from minor wounds, but they knew they were low on the priority list and decided they needed a bath more. The rain felt refreshing and their weariness beginning to fade with the knowledge this battle was finally over, they still had to struggle with the stench of the dead. No matter where they could go for the moment, there were dead men and the stench of mortal remains. It didn't help that at their feet were the bodies of four NVA. Their lifeless eyes stared back at them and PFC Habib questioned the strange expressions on their faces, to which Williams had no answer. When Monroe came up, PFC Habib asked him, "What were they thinking about when they died? They weren't scared, that's not the look of frightened men."

"Did yuh kill 'em?" Monroe asked.

"We did," Williams replied, but there was no satisfaction or celebration in his voice or his eyes.

Both Habib and Williams wore mournful expressions on their filthy faces, now streaked with the rain and their eyes bore evidence to the deep mental wounds they had suffered in this fight. Monroe knew; no one who had fought in this battle would ever be the same. The raw brutality, utter savagery and the extent of carnage would forever leave its mark on a man.

"Ah t'hink dey did thu bes' dey could. Dey wanted ta win, but dey know it was over an' wanted ta go out as soldiers. Thu way you'd want ta."

PFC Habib nodded his head in understanding. He then put his shirt back on, grabbed his flak vest and told Williams to follow him over to where Campbell was resting. Before he left though, PFC Habib glanced over his shoulder at those four dead NVA, nodded his head once and turned away. He sincerely hoped this would be a short war, for he didn't want to go through another fight like this ever again.

Fifteen minutes or so had passed when Monroe spotted a pair of full American boots underneath two dead NVA. He dragged the bodies aside and Monroe recoiled in horror when he realized he had found John's remains and saw what the NVA had done to his friend's face. But with the amount of blood on John's ripped and shredded uniform and the damages done to upper body with the NVA's long knives, Monroe doesn't expect to find a pulse. Yet, he was compelled to check before he called for the soldiers who were given the sad duty of lugging the Americans bodies out of the battlefield.

Monroe knelt down, placed two fingers on John's neck and then he broke into a big teethe smile when he felt the ever so slow heartbeat of John's heart. He then jumped to his feet and started yelling for a medic. "O'va here quick! Medic--Medic, mah frien's alive!"

John was first bandaged up by a medic and then carefully loaded on to a stretcher by four-men. He was then carried over to the aid station, where a doctor was ready for him. Mercifully, he was still unconscious when the medic had placed a cut-down battle dressing over his bloody face. He had also placed other bandages over numerous stab wounds to his upper body and got an IV line running into John's arm before he was even moved. "This one's a priority case. Tell Doc he might want to leave my face bandage in place and we need to get him over to the LZ fast, his vision is at risk from knife wounds," the medic told the stretcher bearers. He had filled out the medical tag quickly and attached it to John's upper right shirt pocket.

Monroe found Campbell awake and gave him the good news about how he had found John.

"Great, Monroe," Campbell said. "But any sign of Kendal...or Lieutenant Ruebal?" Campbell asked.

"Still lookin', Sarge," Monroe said. "But we keep uh findin' wounded under thu dead." Monroe glanced around at those dead men around the summit and mentioned to Campbell, "Sure hope we'se gone bu'fore dat sun dun break thru dose clouds an' hits dose bodies."

"Yeah, but we did it, Monroe. We took Hamburger Hill away from them."

"Why'd we want it, sarge?" Monroe asked, and by his tone, Campbell knew he really wanted to know.

"Ask me later, I'm too tired to talk politics and the strategies of warfare."

They found Lt. Ruebal alive, but suffering from a fractured skull. All he could remember was seeing a blur of something to his right and then nothing. Next thing he knew was waking up with a medic wrapping his head in gauze and a force ten headache to beat the band. A shot of morphine helped a bit, but the bells were still ringing between his ears.

It was only by sheer luck or the Lord's blessing, depending on whom you talked to of how Monroe found Matthew. But if you asked Monroe it was from the Good Lord who gave him divine providence in locating his friend. He was about to turn away from yet another empty trench when by a hunch, he looked again and in the shadows of an overhead flare he found Matthew's crumpled up body beneath an NVA soldier.

"Matt!" Monroe screamed out when he saw Matthew's chest rise and fall. Monroe was ecstatic and began shouting out, "Halleluiah--halleluiah, praise-be duh Lord!" But when he saw how badly wounded Matthew was, he stopped praising so much and began yelling for the nearest medic.

"That you, Monroe? Can't...can't see too well...can't move nothin' either... jus' too weak."

"Yuh is one messed up dude, Matt, but ah got us a medic comin'." Monroe had knelt back down beside his friend in the trench. He had to remove the dead NVA first, but that chore was done.

"Been fightin' to stay awake," Matthew whispered. "Did you find John's body?"

"John ain't dead, Matt. He a real mess't up for sure, but thu medics work't on 'im an' dey got 'im over to the LZ. Looks like yuh'll be a joinin' 'im real soon." Monroe looked up to see the first medic arrive, followed by a second medic who rushed up to assist. With four battalions in the area, they finally had an ample supply of medics to go around and it was a good thing with the amount of wounded men they had to deal with.

"Move out of the way, give me room to work," The first medic said. He then jumped into the trench and straddled Matthew, giving Monroe barely enough time to leap out of the way.

When the second medic showed up, the first one began spouting off with the results of his initial survey.

"Got a real nasty wound to the left leg, looks like a puncture at the kneecap thru- and thru with an exit wound up his left thigh." He shook his head in wonder, "This man's got another major wound to the back and dozens of minor wounds to his upper body, both legs." He yanked another battle dressing out of his medic pack and began doubling up on the knee wound. "Hard to believe this guy's still alive, he's lost a lot of blood and will need a blood right away. He's a priority for those first flights out."

"You can tell the Doc, but fill out the tag since you examined him and I'll stay here and keep lookin' for the wounded, while you go back with the stretcher."

"You got it."

"Hey, I can hear yuh, so talk to me," Matthew said in a whisper. "You...you act like I'm already dyin'.'" But the effort to talk nearly brought the darkness back.

"You are one lucky dude, mister." The 1st medic told him. "Why you ain't bled to death I'll never know. I'm markin' you a priority case and you should be off this hill within the next half-hour...so fight to stay awake."

"Angels, man. That's what kept our buddy alive- angels...I can't believe he's still alive," PFC Williams said. He stood behind Campbell, who had walked over with Monroe and the others to watch the medics lift Matthew out of the ditch. His pants leg was cut open to display the bloody bandages on the knee and upper thigh.

"Matt's a fighter, his type don't give up," Campbell said in such a matter-of-fact way.

Once an LZ was declared safe for the medivac birds to land on, Hueys began to arrive steadily for medivac-duty. Campbell and Monroe were hard pressed, but they were able to keep John and Matthew together for the flight out and they stood by them until they were both loaded on the 6th bird, and had lifted off. There were a lot of priority cases from this last battle. Monroe felt a strange loss when he watched the Huey vanish into the darkness, but he lowered his head and whispered a prayer for his two friends. Afterward, he wandered off to locate ammo for the squad. He was now the new assistant squad leader and he didn't want to have to wait for Campbell to assign him the task.

Campbell set on top that same blackened tree stump and watched as a grayish dawn began to make its appearance. He knew this wouldn't be his last battle, but he couldn't imagine there ever being a bloodier one. But then he saw the newsmen and camera crew move around the aid station. They stopped to photograph wounded soldiers, the doctors and medics working feverishly to save their lives and then to photograph the line of body bags. He couldn't help but wonder, *what will Joe citizen think about when the casualty report shows up in the morning paper? Will they wonder if this war was worth it? Wish I knew; might help me stomach my part in this bloodbath.*

Campbell felt much the same way as the other survivors who now wandered aimlessly through the battlefield like lost souls in a place called Hell. *Will the people back home hear our stories of bravery, the courageous acts committed by hundreds of men over the last eleven days? Will they take a moment out of their busy lives to honor the men who have fallen here or pass it off as an after thought before they ordered their next cup of coffee, or argued with another driver for that one last parking place?*

Campbell felt the wave of emotion rise up to choke the breath out of him. *Who will call these men heroes, who will applaud their sacrifice and will Hamburger Hill be remembered or forgotten.* Campbell reached up to wipe the tears from his eyes, only a moment before Monroe and Habib appeared with ammo, water and food.

"Ah took care of it, Sarge." Monroe had slid Jose's .45 under Matthew's good leg, after making sure it and the magazine were empty. He also threatened the medic on the helicopter, "Dat gun mean a lot to mah friend. He lose it--ah come lookin' fur yuh."

Campbell smiled, "Thanks, I'm sure he'll appreciate it."

"Think they'll let him keep it?" Habib asked.

"We'll probably never know." Campbell looked into Monroe's face, "Got bad news, Monroe, I guess we'd better report in to Captain Louis and see what glorious job they have for us next." Campbell knew he was going to miss Matthew and John, but 2nd squad would live on with men like Monroe and Habib to carry the load. After all, they were Airborne.

Intelligence reports showed that as a result of the battle for Hamburger Hill, the 101st Airborne had seized a large cache of light and heavy weapons, more than 75,000 rounds of ammo, hundreds of RPG and mortar rounds and ten tons of rice from the network of tunnels within Hill # 937. Casualty stats showed 70 Americans had died, 420 Americans wounded and 633 confirmed NVA dead.

On May 21st, 1969, 3rd Battalion was removed from Hill # 937 and flown back to Camp Eagle for a much deserved R&R. On June 5th, 1969, the mountain fortress was abandoned by the Americans and within hours reoccupied by the NVA returning from Laos.

In the later part of June1969, a second battle was fought on the hillsides of Hill # 937 in which an additional 18 Americans were killed. Later, it was again abandoned and again reoccupied by the North Vietnamese Army. The Mountain of the Crouching Beast continued to consume the lives of man, while the infamous A Shau Valley remained in the grasp of NVA and VC forces. Except for smaller excursions, this accursed area of Vietnam was ignored by ground troops up through the end of the war (Jan-1973), for it had proven too costly and the results not worthy of the lives lost. B-52s continued to bomb the A Shau, but as President Nixon withdrew the American fighting man from the war the various fire bases were closed down and the North Vietnamese in the A Shau Valley began their build-up for the coming invasion of all South Vietnam. In 1975, South Vietnam fell to the North Vietnamese and reverted back to one country--all communist and allied to Russia and China.

95TH EVAC HOSPITAL, DANANG AIR FORCE BASE, SOUTH VIET NAM, MAY 27TH, 1969 1640 HOURS

Everything was still a bit blurry, but one thing for sure, Matthew knew he wasn't on Hamburger Hill anymore. Directly overhead was a real ceiling light that shined bright enough to be annoying and it wasn't raining on him. When he attempted to move, a jolt of extreme pain shot through him and he was forced to clench his teeth to bite off a scream, though a loud grunt sound still escaped him.

So presently, all he could do was stare at that ceiling light, the upper part of a blank wall and two stretches of curtain. But after 11-days on Hamburger he thought he could handle the boredom.

He dozed off for a moment, but was jerked awake by a humdinger of a nightmare; a flashback to that last attack and the bayonet sticking out of his leg. Awake, he decided to conduct a survey of his body and began with his right leg. Sore, but the pain was manageable. *Odd, I thought I got stuck in my right leg.* His attempt to move his left leg resulted in a strange tingling feeling, almost a numbness of sorts. But lifting his head was out of the question for the moment, the pain to his back wouldn't allow much movement.

My leg must be messed up pretty bad, they probably shot me full of something to keep me from screaming...like those shots they give women when they go in to deliver babies. Matthew gave up on his self-examination, it was tiring and within a few moments he had dozed off again. His last thoughts were, *wonder where John is?*

Two beds over, John awakened to his own intense pain, which radiated through his face and down all over the rest of his body. His depth perception seemed to be off and it took him a moment to figure out he was lying on his stomach and these were clean white sheets he was on. *Man, dat's a clean floor.* But like Matthew a jolt of pain ended any plan to move about.

"Ahh, Mr. Adams, you're awake. Very good, we were all hoping you might awaken today. So, how do you feel?"

John could hear the female voice and it sounded real nice but he couldn't see who was talking. "Hurts," John grumbled.

"Good, pain is a good sign you're alive. If you didn't hurt, then we'd be concerned. I'll give you something for your discomfort."

John never heard another word, his world sunk into a dark hole as the nurse injected another 10cc of morphine into his IV line. "Go to sleep, Mr. Adams. You need all the rest you can get."

Opening one eye at a time, his vision clearer today, Matthew could easily make out the ceiling tiles overhead.

"And how do you feel today, Mr. Kendal?" Lt. Rogers asked in a pleasant voice.

Matthew looked toward the direction of the voice and was surprised to see a very attractive nurse standing nearby. She wore her red hair in a tight bun and had large brown eyes to go with her full red lips. *She's beautiful!* Then her perfume hit him and it reminded him of his mother's flower garden. "Feel weak an' my left leg…it feels real weird. Hurts…"

"I need to check your eyes, so please hold still."

"No problem, don't have the juice to budge."

"Do you know what day this is?" Rogers asked as she waved her pen light in front of his eyes.

"I was going to ask you," Matthew replied.

"May 27th and this is Saturday."

"We lost track of dates and days since we got on the mountain. How long have I been here?"

"Seven days."

"I've been out for a whole week?" Matthew asked in disbelief.

"Yes. Now in answer to your next question, you are in the surgical recovery wing of the 95th Evac Hospital, Danang Air Force Base. We should be sending you to Hawaii for additional rest in two to three days, but the doctors wanted to make sure you're stabilized and pretty much disease free before the long flight."

"Can you tell me if there is a Spec 4 John Adams here?"

"Yes he is, exactly two beds over and sleeping. He'll probably be on the same flight."

"Is he all right?"

"Yes, but we didn't think so for awhile. Now I want you to rest, the doctor will be by to see you later in the day."

When John woke up, his first thought was to roll over, but severe pain vetoed that idea. "Now where's dat women who was talkin' ta me b'fore?"

A moment later, "About time you woke up, Mister Adams," Lieutenant Jackie Rogers said pleasantly.

"Ma'm, cun yuh come 'round here so ah can see yuh?" John asked.

"In a moment, I'm hanging up another IV bottle." Walking around the bed, she knelt down to look into John's one good eye, "Hi John, I'm Lieutenant Rogers but when we're alone you can call me Jackie."

"Mah head feels like someone's tryin' ta get out, dey're usin' a pick an' shovel."

"John you've suffered twenty-two stab wounds to your body, but the doctor will be by to explain everything to you. The good news is that you'll be flying home pretty soon and I bet you have a girl waiting for you?"

"Yuh lose...No girl, no family...no one!" John shot back. But his minor outburst drained him.

"I'm sorry, John."

"How long?" He asked in a whisper.

"You've been asleep for seven days and your friend is right over there." She pointed to the curtains that separated John and Matthew.

"Friend?"

"SPEC 4 Matthew Kendal, he's two-beds over. He told me you were buddies."

"Matt!" John shouted out with the last of his energy. But he couldn't believe Matthew was right here. Still, his outburst got him a stern, "Shhhhh" from Rogers.

"I'm over hear, John," Matthew said in a loud whisper. "Looks like we both made it out."

"What happen?" John asked in a feint voice that Matthew could barely hear.

"Thought you was dead for sure...Saw three of them jump you and I got two of those dudes off you before another one came out of nowhere and stuck me good. So you owe me big, buddy."

"Makes us even, Matt," John said. "Don't yuh forget Dong Agai. Yuh owe me, ah owe yuh, who cares. But what 'bout thu squad?" John asked.

Nurse Rogers couldn't believe the conversation; not the content, for she had been here at Danang for some time, but where these two soldiers were seemingly building their energy off one another. Almost always, these two men would be back asleep by now or speechless because of weariness. But not these two.

"Don't know, but Campbell an' Monroe made it."

"All right you two heroes, you'll have time to visit later. Now it's time to rest before the doctor comes by." Lt. Rogers continued on with her bed checks, a clipboard in hand. The hospital was full to the max with the wounded men from the battle for Hamburger Hill and still more needed to be seen. As soon as the current patients were considered transportable, the wounded were then flown on to either Hawaii, the Philippines or all the way to stateside hospitals. Japan was already full from the first wounded cases from the previous nine-days on Hamburger Hill.

By late afternoon the team of surgeons was making a check of the wards to talk with the patients and check their charts. A medical evac unit wasn't run like a civilian hospital where doctors visited everyday. Here the nurses did nearly all of the care, while doctors stayed busy in nearly non-stop surgery.

Lifting up the metal clipboard hanging from Matthew's bed frame, the middle-aged doctor with twin colonel's eagles pinned to the collars of his whites took a gander at Matthew's records. By the look on his face, the man was amazed with his patient's progress. Finished, he looked up and smiled at Matthew, "Hello, young man. I am Colonel Brisby, Chief Surgeon and part-time rat catcher around here. I'm also the doctor who spent nearly nine hours on my feet patching you up last week." Col. Brisby reached down, grasped Matthew's wrist and checked his pulse. "I've got to say I'm real pleased with how well you're doing. Nurses report barely any wound infection to speak of- a good sign I did my job right. Your medical records will show you were in a coma, but I like to think of it as a healing nap. Let the body do its job. So, how do you feel, Matthew?"

"Hurt some, sir, but my left leg feels really weird."

Col. Brisby exhaled a deep sigh, there was no getting around what he had to say and knew he might as well deliver it hard and fast, "I'm sorry, son but I had to remove your left leg from just above the knee. Right at the point where the exit wound was."

"What? Why?" Matthew was shocked. He didn't know what else to say.

"The object, I gather it was either a bayonet or one of those NVA long knives, shattered the bone as it entered and in the process destroyed all the nerves, tendons and just about everything that made your leg function. There was simply no way for me to have saved it and it's our main goal here to prevent an infection from setting in that might have killed you. To put it bluntly, it was either remove the leg or you would have died. I must also say the medics did a superb job of keeping you alive in the battlefield." No matter how many times he'd given this same speech, it never ceased to bring any comfort to the patient. "We also sewed up your back, Matthew. Whoever stuck you barely missed a couple of your vital organs and that includes your heart."

"I wish he'd have killed me," Matthew said in anger.

"You say that now, but you will learn to live with it in time." Brisby moved forward and gently touched Matthew on his shoulder, "We're going to send you home to get fitted with a new leg, one that only you will know the difference, I promise you. Right now I'm going to give you something to help you sleep."

Unable to speak, Mathew clutched his bed sheet tightly and stared up at the ceiling tiles. He wept until the medication brought sleep and the nightmares began again.

"John, I'm going to turn you over. I won't lie to you, this is gonna hurt so tell me when you're ready." Col, Brisby had his arms around John's shoulders and was assisted by Nurse Rogers and another nurse stood ready at John's feet.

John gritted his teeth and then nodded to give them the go-ahead and he almost immediately cut loose with an ear-piercing scream when they moved him. It only took them a couple of seconds and once he was on his back, braced by several pillows, the pain began to subside with the help of an additional dosage of morphine.

"Okay Colonel, ah heard what yuh tol' mah buddy. What yuh gots fur me?"

"My colleges and I spent over 13-hours on our feet with you, young sir. Twenty-two stab wounds, a hospital record I might add and we used up a lot of thread sewing you up. I had to remove one kidney, but you should be able to get by with the other one. Your liver got sliced, but I think my superb sewing job took care of it. From knees to chin you look like a mummy with all the tape and gauze we used on you but now cometh the kicker. And John, I had to remove your right eye." Doc Brisby didn't hesitate, but hit it head on.

"Mah eye?"

"You have a deep slash across the brow and the blade slid across your eye ball, slicing it wide open. There was nothing I or my colleges could do to save it." Brisby hesitated as he saw John's good eye tear up. "Now listen up, troop, the Army will teach your friend to walk with a new leg and they'll show you how to live with one eye. By all standards you two should both be dead, but for some unknown reason and it probably has a lot to do with God's blessing, you're both here and alive."

Brisby looked to Nurse Rogers, "Administer another 10cc of morphine in one hour. If he needs more, give it to him as you see fit, but wait at least three hours between doses. Make sure you log it down and if the pain persists, find me or another doctor. I don't want to send these boys home as dope addicts because we got sloppy, but I want them as comfortable as possible, too."

After shift, Colonel Brisby got himself very drunk at the Danang Officer's Club. Being one of the few bird colonels in the club, no one was about to say anything concerning his over-indulgence, even thought this was an unusual occurrence for the good doctor. But after three wars of repairing wounded men and crying over the dead ones, he was glad this was his last year in the service. He couldn't take it anymore and looked forward to retirement. The Battle for Hamburger Hill had tasked the last of his mental reserves and he had put in for reassignment to Hawaii, where he could spend his last year dealing with the ailments of retired veterans.

Two days later they prepped John, Matthew and three others for the flight to Hawaii. Before they could leave though, word came down that some big brass was coming by to see them.

Lying in bed all decked out in clean gowns and braced up by pillows, Matthew and John were surprised to see Blackjack enter the ward with an unknown three-star general in tow. The general was followed by an entourage of lower ranking officers, plus an enlisted man who carried a large camera with a flash attachment.

"Sergeant Kendal, you look like something my dog might've dragged in from the back yard," Blackjack said. He was dressed in clean and highly pressed green jungle fatigues, and smiled like an appreciative father as he approached the bed and gently patted Matthew on the shoulder with a thick paw of a hand. "Look smart, kid, we got big brass here today." Blackjack moved aside as General Morely, Divisional Commander, moved up to stand beside Matthew's bed. He smiled first at Matthew and then over at John.

"I've been informed by the hospital commander that you're both about to leave here in a few moments for Hawaii...so I will keep this short," General Morely said in a friendly manner. But then his voice took on a more serious tone, "Sergeant Kendal, Sergeant Adams, I've read the statement of your Company's CO and talked with both your squad and platoon leader. From what they say, I strongly believe our final victory over the enemy was greatly due to the courageous acts and spirited actions you both displayed upon Hill # 937.

"I personally visited the hillside where your squad spearheaded the counter-attack, an act of gallantry denoting the very espirit de corps of the 101st Airborne." General Morley gestured to his aide and was handed a small blue presentation case containing the five-pointed Silver Star medal. "It is with great honor I award you, Sergeant Kendal, this Silver Star for Valor." General Morely carefully pinned the medal to Matthew's gown and shook his hand. "The formal citation will be forwarded to you, but I wanted you to have this and your Purple Heart before you left. You did your country a great honor, son. Get well soon."

That was the cue for the photographer to move in and snap a couple shots of the two senior officers standing on each side of Matthew's bed. Once the pleasantries were over, the party moved over to John's bed where he also received the Silver Star and Purple Heart and more photos were taken.

But in John's case most of his face was still bandaged and he closely resembled a mummy from the waist up.

Before leaving, Blackjack stopped by Matthew's bed and placed a rubber band wrapped bundle of mail beside him, "Mail call, Sergeant Kendal."

"But, sir I'm not a sergeant," Matthew said.

"Promotion came with the medal, son," Blackjack said. "Oh, just so you know, if your sergeant would have had his way you both would have received the Medal of Honor. Man thinks pretty highly of you both. Good luck to both of you."

Matthew was all teary-eyed as he watched Blackjack leave the ward. He also thought of Campbell and wondered if he would ever see him again?

Picking up the stack of mail, Matthew looked at the raised sheet supported by a wire frame above his stump and remembered back to the day they received Luke's Silver Star in the mail. He didn't think of it as much of a trade, a chunk of shiny metal for his brother. He didn't think so now either.

He ripped the medal off his gown and held it in front of him, "A Silver Star for a man's life and another Silver Star for a leg…looks like I got a better deal than my brother." Matthew threw the medal across the room, forgetting the wound to his back and he let out another scream. That display of emotion nearly ripped a dozen stitches off his back and brought tears to his eyes.

Nurse Rogers walked over and retrieved the medal. She placed it back into the presentation case and gave Matthew a friendly blink before inserting the case into his Red Cross provided AWOL travel bag.

"Matt, we'se alive. Nothin' else madder," John said.

"Yeah, right." Matthew picked up the letters, but before he got a chance to open even one, the ambulance crew arrived.

"Time to go, men," Nurse Rogers said. She took the letters and shoved them into the bag.

"Oh, I forgot to tell you. Word came down that this belongs to you," Lt. Rogers pulled Jose's .45 from out of the bag. "I had a friend clean it all up, it's unloaded and the magazine is in the bag too." She placed the weapon into a pillowcase and wrapped it up before replacing it back into the bag. "You take good care of yourself, Matthew." Lt. Rogers zipped the bag closed and instructed the medic to make sure the bag accompanied Matthew on to the plane and was not opened.

"Thank you, Lieutenant," Matthew said, as he presented her with his best crisp salute and tried to hide his wince.

"You take it easy too, John."

"T'anks fur everythin', Jackie. Didn't know yuh officers could be so nice."

"Get out of here, I need the beds." Jackie Rogers watched as the men were transported out of the ward. She saw them come and saw them go, often wondering how they ended up when got home? *They'll make it. They may be angry now and they got a right to be, but those two…they're survivors.*

After a bumpy and painful ride to the flight line, the patients were loaded onto a medivac jet. Forty-five minutes later they are airborne, "Next stop; Hawaii," the pilot advised them over the aircraft's intercom. For the men who could, a small cheer went out while others simply smiled or let out a sigh of relief. Their time in Hell was over, they were headed home.

THE WORLD, UPLAND, CALIFORNIA, MAY 28TH, 1969 1600 HOURS

The phone call came late in the afternoon and Jean Kendal was the one to answer it. Over a lousy connection, a Sergeant Rickles informed Jean how Matthew had been wounded in combat and was en route to Hickam Air Force Base, Hawaii for rest and recovery. "Ma'm, you'll be notified if and when a new destination is known. But I have no other information at this time."

"How badly injured…" Jean started to ask but the man cut her off, "Ma'm, I'm only a clerk making notifications for the 101st Airborne. That's all I know."

With tears flowing, Jean thanked Sergeant Rickles before hanging up. Immediately afterward, she called Walter at his office and he raced home to be with his wife. They held each other in a tight embrace as tears flowed down their cheeks. Walter and Jean then dropped to their knees in the living room and asked the Lord to bless their son with a speedy and a thorough healing. With an "Amen" they looked into each other's watery eyes and knew they had a visit to make.

OSBORNE RESIDENCE

Driving home from college, Kathy Lee looked forward to a nice hot bath. Grabbing an arm full of books, she slammed the car door closed with her right foot and headed for the front door. Walking into the living room, she stopped in mid-stride when she saw her father standing with Pastor Kendal. Sitting on the couch in front of them, her mother and Mrs. Kendal showed signs they'd been crying.

"He's dead! He's dead…isn't he?" Kathy Lee's knees buckled and she began to fall to the floor. Her father and then Walter rushed forward to catch her before she hit the rug and they placed her on the couch. When she opened her eyes, she found her head nestled in her mother's lap and Kathy Lee could feel the tears welling up when she looked up into her mother's bloodshot eyes.

"Matthew isn't dead, sweetheart, but he has been wounded. Jean received a call today from the Army. He's being flown to Hawaii for a period of rest and recovery. I'm sure he will call as soon as possible. He knows you'll be worried. *Not to mention his parents and a couple of perspective in-laws.*

"Oh, Matthew...." Kathy Lee hugged her mother tightly as she wondered what might have happened to her young man. *You shouldn't have been over there, honey. You didn't belong there...Please call, Matthew...oh, please--please call.*

20 – ACCEPTANCE DOESN'T COME EASY

AMPUTEE WARD, HICKAM AIR FORCE BASE HOSPITAL, HAWAII, MAY 29TH, 1969 0918 HOURS

Dear Matthew,

I wanted you to know I attended one of those anti-war demonstrations on campus yesterday and there were several hundred students in attendance. Things got out of hand and the campus was closed when a whole lot of police showed up. Matthew, I read one of those newsletters put out by an organization called the SDS (Students for a Democratic Society), it left me speechless to say the least and sad to think you may be involved in such atrocities.

Matthew, I want you to know I could never be with a man who was guilty of any of the crimes described in those articles. I couldn't marry a man who has turned into some kind of ruthless killer, a murderer or a rapist. I'd be unable to let you hold me, knowing your hands were stained with innocent blood.

Matthew lay in his hospital bed, his hands trembling, when he let go of Kathy Lee's letter and it floated to the floor. *She's accusing me of war crimes? Not wanting to be with me--to let me hold her! Why's she doing this?* Matthew grew angry, he was unable to understand why she felt this way and then he remembered how her first letter was so full of love, as she talked about their dreams and then three days later she wanted to label him a killer. *I don't believe it, what's happened to her. Why is she telling me this?* Angry, he crumbled up the remainder of the unopened letters and threw them to the floor. Sweat beaded up on his forehead from the exertion and he stared down at his bandaged stump, gritted his teeth and then released a mournful cry of anguish. "Nooooo..." Matthew reached up to grab the hand bar hanging above his head and with noticeable effort he jerked himself up and worked his way to the side of the bed.

"I'm getting out of here...I've had it." Matthew slid off his bed and landed hard on the polished linoleum floors of the hospital ward. His movement ripped an IV line out of his arm, a drain tube was yanked out of his stump and a mixture of the blow and the intense pain knocked him unconscious.

Summoned by another patient, a nurse hurried in and yelled for assistance to return Matthew to his bed. It was over two hours later when Matthew awakened to a few new pains, some added bruising and his body now in restraints. An unhappy Air Force doctor ordered the restraints; a locked belt around Matthew's stomach and another strap holding his good leg down to the mattress.

The doctor had seen the pile of ripped up mail on the floor and knew the signs, "Poor kid probably got a *Dear John*. We'll put him on a suicide watch for the next 12 hours."

Disgusted with his life, Matthew pounded the mattress with his fist in frustration. He was then surprised when someone called to him. "Take it easy, man. You'll just hurt yourself and they'll keep you in restraints even longer."

"What'll you care?" Matthew growled."

"I like it peaceful, man an' you're makin' it rough to catch up on my Zs." The man two beds over wore his black hair long, over the shoulder and he sported a bushy moustache. Matthew also noticed the guy was also missing both legs from the hip down and it looked as if he'd been here a while.

"You sure looked silly floppin' down there on the floor, thought you might've hurt yourself. Had to call the nurse before you messed up the shine, janitors here take a real pride in keepin' these floors shiny."

"You should of let me bleed, maybe I would've died."

"You wanna die that badly after surviving Nam? No woman's worth that!"

Matthew eyed the man suspiciously, "Did you read my mail?"

"Yeah, I walked over to your bed and read your mail while you were knocked out. Get a grip! Doc mentioned you probably got a Dear John when he ordered the restraints."

Annoyed, Matthew couldn't think of anything else to say but, "Why don't you mind your own business."

"Hey, dude, I can take a hint. But if you wanna talk later, my name's Brad...Brad Railsback...formally a crew chief with the 1st Air Cav out of Danang."

With patients having little else to do but read, talk with one another or wait for their therapy appointments, Matthew was quickly bored. John was in a different ward and Matthew learned from the nurse this was due to patients being separated by their injuries. Matthew was in the ward for those patients who had lost a limb or more, while John was in a ward for those who suffered a loss of sight and those needed facial repair.

So, weary of counting ceiling tiles and dwelling on his problems, Matthew looked over at Brad and thought any conversation was better than staring at the blank military walls. *Didn't anyone think of murals or wall hangings to help improve the morale of the troops? Maybe some plants...this place would drive my Mom crazy.*

"Listen, Brad...That's your name right, Brad?" Matthew asked.

Lowering a thick paperback book, Brad answered, "You got the name right, what do'yuh want now? Can't you see I'm tryin' to solve the secrets of the universe?"

"Sorry for sounding off, guess I was wrapped up in my pity trip. My name's Matthew Kendal. I served with the 101st Airborne."

"Yeah, I know. I asked the nurse when they brought you in. You were pretty out of it from the all the pain meds they shot you up with for the flight from Nam. They had me in la-la land for two or three days myself. Stuff made me sick to my stomach when I woke up."

"How come we're the only ones in here?" Matthew counted eight empty beds.

"Amputee Ward, they come an' go," Brad said. "That's why I was hoping you'd wanna talk. Your bed's been empty for a week. Most cases go stateside right off, but a few of us end up here in cold storage why the paper shufflers figure out what to do with us." Brad pointed to a bed by the door, "That's where Mr. Happy lives, he's a Marine. You'll meet him later. They hauled him off to Pearl Harbor for some mental mumbo-jumbo. Guess Air Force head docs ain't good enough for Marines."

"Where'd you get hit?" Matthew asked.

"My bird went down outside Marble Mountain...near Danang. Got myself trapped and it took 'em a while to pull me clear. They had ta cut 'em off," Brad pointed to his legs, "...but at least I'm alive. Rest of the crew...they...my buds, they didn't make it." Brad looked toward the wall for a moment, while he fought to compose himself,

"Real good bunch of guys too. Hard dudes, got the job dones...didn't deserve to go out that way."

"How long have you been here?" Matthew wanted to get him off the crash, he could hear how it was rebuilding in him and right now he didn't need to nurse another guy's meltdown.

"Two months next Tuesday. I picked up a weird wound infection and they want to clear it up before they ship me home." Brad moved around a bit to get into a more comfortable position and then asked, "So, how about you, Matt, where'd you get it?"

"Hill # 937, but we called the place Hamburger Hill. I got it on the last day."

"Heard about it, they say some real heavy-duty fighting went down there."

"My nurse in Danang said over 400 men were wounded and nearly 70 KIA. I know my company sure got shot up. My squad leader became Company Commander, I got made squad leader and only three of us made it out of the original squad." Thinking about the squad, Matthew suddenly remembered John and wondered if they'd be allowed to see each other soon.

"I came here with another guy by the name of John Adams. Do you know where the ward is for guys who lost their sight?"

"If he isn't an amputee case, he could be anywhere. This place is huge. You'll see when they start cartin' you off for therapy. What happened to him?"

"Lost an eye an' got stabbed twenty-two times."

"And this dude is still alive? That's one tough dude."

"Yeah, he is one tough dude," Matthew said. He was growing weary and had to stop talking. Brad understood, he remembered how whipped he was for that first couple of weeks.

THERAPY

Therapy began the next morning and it was an extremely painful experience for Matthew to endure. Following a long ride on a raised gurney down a mile of drab hallways, Matthew was carefully lowered into a hot whirlpool bath. Afterward, he was tortured with an hour of physical therapy. Exhausted, he fell right to sleep when he finally got back to bed and when he woke up, Brad was eating lunch and the aroma was overpowering for a guy who hasn't eaten anything solid in nearly ten days.

"'Bout time you woke up, but it'll be like that for the next few days or more. First week is worse and the second week…not much better. Your body will take some time to get back to normal."

"That's really encouraging, thanks."

"Give the nurse a call an' she'll bring your lunch. Not bad today, fried chicken an' mashed potatoes with gravy. I imagine it'll taste a whole lot better than those nasty C-rats you'd been eatin'."

Matthew glanced at the chicken leg in Brad's hand, could feel his mouth salivating and he pulled the cord to summon the nurse. When she arrived, Matthew was dismayed to hear he was restricted to clear liquids. "For lunch you will receive chicken broth, a bowl of cherry Jell-O and if you're real nice and finish that off, a grape Popsicle."

362

"Not much of a menu. I thought the Air Force served better food."

"You've been getting your food by IV for the last week or so, we're not about to throw you a bone to chew on so quickly. Let's see how you do with the clear liquids first."

Lunch was depressing, but his spirits picked up when he got his first visitor, "Hey, Matt."

"John!"

Riding in a wheelchair, a large black Air Force orderly with the three stripes of buck sergeant on his arms, pushed John across the ward and positioned him beside Matthew's bed.

"Nice ride, does it come in any other colors?" Matthew asked. "I was wondering when I'd see you." His grin showed how happy he was to see his best friend and John was smiling right back at him. The two men had endured Hell together and it had only increased their bond of friendship.

"This big dude's name is John too, a real cool guy. He sneaked me out 'a mah ward so ah could check on yuh. Ain't got long, mah nurse, a captain, is a real sticker for rules...but a good looker."

Matthew shook hands with Big John and then introduced both of them to Brad, "I've been baby-sittin' this clown since boot camp, Brad, an' we ended up getting sliced an' diced together. You can't get much closer than that." Matthew then admired John's extensive bandage job to his face. "What are they gonna do?"

"Talkin' 'bout plastic surgery," John said. He wanted to change the subject, the thought of going back under a blade made him mighty uncomfortable. So he asked about Matthew's restraints, "Do dey t'ink you'se gonna run off, Matt?"

Matthew's smile disappeared. He'd fought hard not to think about Kathy Lee. "Kathy Lee's made some new friends, John. She mailed me one of those *Dear John letters,* guess I don't match up with all those smart college boys." Matthew choked up and then he continued on, "Doc put me in restraints, I tried to leave."

The news hit John hard. Kathy Lee had been a hot topic of conversation between them since they met at Boot Camp. "Ah'm sorreee, Matt. Real sorreee..." John didn't know what else to say.

"Hey, cut that downer stuff. It's depressing enough around here without bringin' up old girl friends," Brad said. "My girl friend did the escape act too, didn't want to spend the rest of her life with a stump, but hey, I don't blame her. I caught a rough ride and she bailed, maybe she wasn't so hot anyway.

"You got a girl, John?" Brad asked. He didn't want to think about the old girlfriend anymore.

"No...nev'a had thu time for one girl. Ah was a lover, then a fighter... now I gots to find me a woman ta settle down wit'."

"You will, John. There's a lot of nice ladies out there who really go for us disabled vets...war heroes, who have a steady income with benefits." Brad then turned to Matthew, "Maybe you should try to win her back, talk it out some. Sounds like you two have been together for a while."

"Right now I just wanna get through this and go home to my folks." Matthew stopped when he saw the ward doors open and another orderly come wheeling in with a patient.

"Ahh, Mr. Happy is back," Brad said.

The man in the wheelchair, who wore an angry expression on his face, was pushed up to the nearest bed. "Hey Big John, give me a hand," The orderly asked. Big John made sure John's wheelchair brakes were in place and then hustled over to help lift the patient on to the bed. Without a word of thanks, the man rolled over on his side and showed his back to the others.

"What happened to him Brad?" Matthew asked in a low voice.

"All I know is he stepped on a mine, somewhere south of Saigon. Supposedly he was left for dead and abandoned by his men. Another patrol found him, but he won't talk...we'll he does yell a lot an' growls at everyone."

"Time to go, guys," Big John said. He released the wheelchair brakes and began to push John out of the ward.

"I shall return!" John yelled as he flashed Matthew and Brad the two-finger V for victory sign and passed through the double doors.

Matthew tossed John a casual wave and noticed that Mr. Happy had rolled over to face him. "You an' that black boy sound down right friendly. Is he your boy friend?" Mr. Happy asked.

"Don't even get started, 'Mr. Death before Dishonor'," Matthew said in a threatening tone and Mr. Happy rolled back over. But not before he flashed the single digit insult with his right hand.

"Hearts an' flowers, he just can't help it. Can you, Mr. Happy?" Brad asked, but the man remained silent and Matthew thought he might have heard a whimper coming from the man.

Following a week of daily therapy, Matthew was allowed to spend a couple hours each evening in the hospital recreation room. There, Matthew, Brad and John play a little cards and watched some television. Westerns or comedy shows are the favorites and no one in the rec' room wanted to watch war movies or nighttime soap operas. They already had enough realism in their lives.

After one lengthy therapy session, Matthew returned to the ward to find another guest waiting for him. "Sergeant Campbell...excuse me, I mean Lieutenant Campbell...Wow!" Matthew was surprised to see the gold bars on Campbell's shirt collar.

"I don't believe it...Sir. How'd you get out of Nam, Lieutenant-Sir?"

"Drop the *sir* stuff, Matt. Call me Bob. I'm not too use to these things yet." Campbell pointed to the gold bars and then glanced down at Matthew's stump, as the orderly helped him on to his bed.

"Sorry about the leg, Matt."

"Forget it. At least like John says, 'We're alive'. So, how'd you get the gold bar?"

"The brass had this big awards ceremony at Camp Eagle. Monroe got the Silver Star like you guys did and promotion to SPEC 4, but you should have seen the big grin on his face when the Colonel pinned the medal on." Campbell broke into a smile, "Monroe forgot to return the Colonel's salute, he just kept grinning away and Lt. Ruebal nearly burst out laughing himself when the Colonel smiled right back at him. PFC Habib was awarded a Bronze Star and they tossed out the most Purple Hearts I'd ever seen awarded at one time."

"What about the gold bars, sir." Matthew was relentless.

"Oh, they must've been short of officers because the Colonel handed me a battlefield promotion an' sent me here for a seven-day R & R. And you being such a nice Christian boy, I won't tell you what I've been doing to pass the time."

Matthew laughed and then asked, "Any word on the others?"

"I checked, but no one seems to know where Walstein, Andrews, Baxley and Razor went to. I recommended decorations for all of 'em, but Razor, so hopefully the paperwork will catch up with them eventually."

"I notice a new ribbon on your chest too, isn't that the Distinguished Service Cross?"

Campbell wasn't the type to blush, but he nodded and then passed it off, "Yeah, they made a big thing of it. With it and ten cents I can buy a cup of coffee."

"You sure deserved it, Bob. You took D Company on when everyone else was shot up an' you carried us up that hill on your back. I'd be proud to serve under you, anytime-anywhere."

"Thanks, Matt. That really means a lot."

"Oh, and thank you for making sure I got Jose's pistol. It saved my life."

"Well, he would've wanted you to have it." Campbell's gaze dropped as he remembered the little bandito. "Hey, I gotta go. I'll check on John before leaving, but I gotta date with a luscious blonde tonight who really loves war heroes."

"Women always go for officers, especially ones with medals on their chests."

"Right you are and with only seven-days, I'll take whatever advantage I can get. Hey, in case I miss you, don't forget about me trompin' through the boonies while you relax on the beach back home."

"Yeah, I'll think of you…probably like for the rest of my life. You take care of yourself…Lieutenant, Sir."

Campbell looked at Matthew for a moment before he bent over and carefully embraced him, "You take care too, Matt. I'll miss you." Campbell whispered before he pulled away and walked out of the ward.

Matthew was teary eyed as he watched the big man leave, it surprised him how warmly he felt and it made him wonder; *Is it that way with all men who've experienced combat together?*

Days pass by slowly for Matthew and John as they struggled through painful therapy, but their conditions continued to improve. Forty-eight-hours after John's surgery, he was allowed to see his face for the first time, "Ah look a bit like a black Frankenstein, Doc."

"John, the swelling will go down and the incisions will eventually become thin scars." the Air Force doctor said. He then presented him with a black eye patch, "Add a gold earring and you'll be this generation's first black pirate, John."

"I'd rather be a lover, but wit' dis face ah'm sure not going to attract thu ladies."

DAD ARRIVES

On their 17th day in the hospital, Matthew looked up from reading a local news paper to see a familiar face, "Dad? Dad! What are you doing here!?"

Walter walked forward and embraced his son about the shoulders, "I'm so glad you're alive, son. You had your mother and I pretty worried."

"Oh, dad…" Matthew burst into tears as father and son share a quiet moment.

Brad watched from his bed and wished his dad could've made it over from the mainland, but there wasn't enough money for a trip like that.

Walter had waited nearly a week for some news or a phone call, but when none came he began making calls of his own. When the decision was made, he flew to Hawaii and Jean stayed home--with extreme reluctance.

Walter wiped his eyes with a clean handkerchief and while doing so he gave his son a good looking over. "You look a bit on the thin side, son."

"I've put on ten pounds since I got here, Dad."

"You didn't call and the Army didn't seem to know anything except to say you were here in recovery."

"How's mom handling this?"

"I'm the only one who knows about the seriousness of your wounds. I talked with your doctor a moment ago and he filled me in. It's a miracle you survived."

"They keep tellin' me I'll get a new leg when my stump's toughened up enough to handle it. I'll probably end up at the V.A. Hospital in San Fernando. The Army will try to get us as close to home as possible."

"Why didn't you contact us?"

"I'm sorry I didn't write, but I just didn't know what to say."

"They do have this invention called a telephone, I happened to notice several of them in the hallway when I entered the hospital." Walter gave Matthew a father's raised eyebrow, "You should've called. You have a lot of people praying for you, son and Kathy Lee is about to drive us all crazy."

"Kathy Lee?" Matthew's look of confusion concerned his father.

"Of course Kathy Lee!" Walter exclaimed and then his voice softened, "It took both her father and me to keep her at home, or she would've been over here on the first airplane. It's only the fact that you'll be needing the money to live on once you two get married that convinced her to stay home."

"Dad, I don't understand. Her last letter...I thought she was done with me."

"I know about that letter; it was mailed by mistake when Kathy Lee was delirious with fever. She wrote you right afterwards, explaining what happened."

"Once I read that letter, I tore up the rest of 'em and I haven't received any more mail since I got here."

"She fainted at school from some flu bug and it really made her sick. This happened right after the demonstration at Chaffey and she wrote the letter after reading some SDS propaganda flyer. Once she learned the letter had been mailed, she immediately wrote you an explanation." Walter gave his son a thoughtful look, "You got a girl back home waiting to become Mrs. Matthew Kendal."

"What about that?" Matthew asked and he pointed a finger at his stump.

"I won't lie to you, Matthew, it's gonna be tough on her. But it won't change anything. She loves you too much to ever let you go. You got one headstrong lady there...reminds me of your mother."

Matthew's eyes are all watery again, hearing that his Kathy Lee was still there for him produced a big grin.

Now I understand from your doctor how you were decorated. So, I think now is a good time to tell your father what happened over there."

Over the next hour, Matthew told his story and Walter listened without comment. He was saddened to hear how Jose was killed saving his son's life, but delighted with Matthew's account of the squad's amazing counter-attack. Hearing the events surrounding Matthew's strange encounter with the enemy soldier in the closing moments of battle left Walter shaking his head in wonder. Concluding his story, Matthew showed his father Jose's .45, his Silver Star and finally, his Purple Heart. "I forgot to duck." Matthew said in jest.

"If you let me, I'll take these home and place them beside Luke's medals?"

"Sure, Dad. I think Jose would like that we had his pistol on display and beside Luke's photograph. It makes him part of our family's history."

Matthew, letting his dad push the wheelchair, led his father over to John's ward and the two of them finally met. When they acted like two long lost friends, Matthew knew it was due to all the letters he wrote home and his parents had written to him. John had learned about Matthew's father and Walter heard all the funny stories about John.

Three days later, Walter flew home. The hotel rates were too high and Walter still had a church to run. Not too surprisingly, Walter spent a few hours with Mr. Happy, who's real name was James Bishop. This happened while Matthew was in therapy. At first rebuffed and even threatened, Walter continued to press in until Bishop's barrier of hostility finally collapsed and he burst into tears as Walter held him. He shared of his terrified hours alone in the minefield, not knowing whether he was going to live or die and the feeling of abandonment by being left to die by his buddies. With Walter's counseling and prayer, James Bishops inner healing took its first steps on a long journey.

The night Walter left, Bishop asked if he could join the others in the recreation room. Matthew smiled and said, "Welcome back to the land of the living."

"Thanks."

TIME TO LEAVE

The notifications came right after breakfast: Matthew and John were going home to a VA hospital for further treatment. Eventually, they would be given medical discharges rating them at 100% disabled and entitled to full veterans' benefits.

With some doings on the part of a hard working clerical staff, John was allowed to accompany Matthew to the V.A. Hospital in San Fernando instead of being flown back to Washington D.C.

On Jun 30th, both men said their goodbyes to the hospital staff, to Brad, Big John and Bishop, and fly by military jet to Norton Air Force Base in sunny Southern California. From there, the two men were transported by Air Force bus to their new home- San Fernando V.A. Hospital.

When they passed by his hometown of Upland, Matthew began to wonder if he was prepared to see Kathy Lee? "John, it feels so strange. We're passin' by my home an' Kathy Lee's only a mile away from here. Yet, I feel like such a stranger. Do you think we'll ever feel at home again?"

"Ah jus' don't know. We'se been through a lot an' we'se still got us a lot of healin' ta do."

"I'm scared, John. Scared to see her, scared I won't be able to walk. Maybe marrying' a one-legged man is too much to ask of her?" Matthew stared out the bus window and watched the familiar sights pass by, while the bus lumbered down the highway. "Same stuff, but everything feels so different. Have I changed that much?"

REUNION TIME

On the drive to the hospital to see Matthew for the first time, Kathy Lee's nervous stomach caused Walter to pull to the side of the road more than once. "Good thing we're getting close to the hospital. You keep this up and you'll need a bed there too." Walter complained.

"Drive, Walter. You men just don't understand these things." Jean said as she comforted her future daughter-in-law.

On the other hand, Matthew was handling the upcoming reunion quite well. Only falling out of bed once this morning, he sat holding a mirror for 20 minutes, while he combed his hair in four different ways and tried on three different shirts. The two shirts he didn't like were tossed to the floor, along with one pair of gray sweat pants.

John watched as his friend broke a shoelace. "It's only Kathy Lee, Matt. Loosen up 'fore your blood pressure jumps an' the Doc sends 'em away."

They wouldn't do that, would they?"

"Jus' calm down, buddy." John tossed him a new shoelace and walked over to look out the window. "You're gonna save a lot of money on shoe laces." John said it in jest, but Matthew only frowned.

"Sorry, bad joke." John apologized and then breached an unpopular subject, "Yuh know ah'll be leavin' here pretty soon." They rarely talked about his leaving since John received the news from his doctor. His wounds had healed and there wasn't much the hospital could do for him under in-patient status.

"Don't remind me. I'm not sure what I'll do around here without you." Matthew glanced over and studied his friend for a moment as John continued to gaze out the window. "You still haven't told me what your plans are."

"Don't know. California is a one big place, so maybe ah'll spen' some time checkin' it out. See thu sights…Hey, I got mah disability pay to live on an' a few hundred saved up from Nam. That should hold me for a bit. Anyway, ah hav'ta come back here ev'a two weeks for check-ups."

"I'm really gonna miss hanging around with you…You're as close to me as my own brother was."

"Hey, knock it off. Kathy Lee will be here soon, so get your head together."

Matthew picked up his hand mirror and admired himself, "Does my hair look all right?"

"It'd better be," John said and he pointed out the window and down toward the parking lot. "Looks like a real fine lady walkin' dis way from thu parkin' lot an' dat's your dad wit' her."

"Oh God…I'd need to change my shirt." Matthew began to unbutton his shirt, but John moved in to stop him.

"You only got four shirts an' you've already wrinkled up three of 'em. Now chill out, it's show time, dude."

When the ward door opened a moment later, Matthew was awestruck with her beauty. Kathy Lee; his Kathy Lee, stood there and the two of them gazed deeply into each other's eyes from across the room. *She's real…an' so beautiful.* Sitting in his wheelchair, he remained in place as he admired every inch of her. *Her hair's a bit longer an' she's lost some weight…probably from worrying about me.* Wearing a blue denim dress, nearly a mini in style and brown suede calf-length boots, Kathy Lee was stunning. A couple of other patients let loose with a pair of wolf whistles, but Matthew didn't mind one bit.

Behind Kathy Lee stood Walter and Jean, who remained in place as they allowed these two to have this special moment between them, not that Jean Kendal didn't consider pushing Kathy Lee aside and running up to embrace her son. But she fought the urge down.

Unable to wait any longer, Kathy Lee dropped her purse and dashed across the room to wrap her arms around Matthew and present him with a very long kiss. The room broke out with applause as other patients added in their admiration for this romantic reunion.

Whispers of love were shared until Kathy Lee was forced to give way to Jean. A mother could wait only so long. In tears, a mother leaned down to place her trembling hands on Matthew's cheeks. Unable to speak, Jean smiled as Matthew gently wiped her tears away with his handkerchief. "It's okay, mom...I'm home."

John, felt a bit uncomfortable and stood off to one side in his desire not to interfere with their reunion and was utterly taken by surprise when Kathy Lee walked up to him, hugged him affectionately and placed a gentle kiss on his cheek. "Thank you, John. Thank you for bringing him home to me." Kathy Lee had recognized John from his photograph.

Incapable of speech from embarrassment, John was saved when Walter walked up to shake his hand, "Very nice to see you again, John. You look very well. They must be taking good care of you here."

"Yes, sir," John said. "Good doc's... friendly people."

"John, this is my mother, Jean Kendal," Matthew said as he presented his mother to his best friend.

"Welcome home, John. I am so pleased to finally meet you." Jean first gestured to shake hands, but she couldn't help herself and hugged John around the neck. "Thank you for being his friend and saving his life," She whispered to John.

Not sure what to say, he finally said, "We...uh saved each other's lifes over an' over. Way it was."

After introductions, the five of them spent the next few hours having lunch in the hospital's cafeteria and making a casual inspection of the grounds. Kathy Lee pushed Matthew, while John walked with the parents a good 15 feet back to allow the couple some privacy. But the hospital grounds were quite crowded and privacy was hard to come by as hundreds of people rushed about. Not that Matthew or Kathy Lee ever noticed them. They were in a private world by themselves.

Knowing they only had another hour before having to leave, Walter ushered his wife and John off to allow his son and Kathy Lee some time alone. Leaving them by a stand of Elms, the others returned to the cafeteria for some coffee.

With his new eye patch and his facial scarring, John reminded Walter of a rogue-like character from the 18th century. Six long scars cut across his forehead and upper cheek and during their coffee several of the nurses stopped by their table to say how "Dashing" John looked. John knew they were tying to encourage him and he deeply appreciated it.

As the nurses left, John commented to Walter on how things had changed, "Ah really used ta hate white people, t'inkin' dey was always lookin' down on mah people. Your son changed all dat an' then thu Lord came into mah life. Now ah see people as...people. Color don't seem so important... 'Cept ah wanna see..." John was having trouble explaining what he was feeling deep down, but Walter and Jean waited. "Ah wanna try ta get what ah feel to mah people back home." John looked to Walter, "You understand what ah'm sayin', sir."

"Yes, John I do. I got an idea that might help. Why don't you come stay with us? We have an extra room and I know Matthew would want this. You'll be close enough to come back here for your re-checks and you can pop by to see Matthew."

Stunned by his suggestion, John didn't know what to say. He glanced at Jean and she was smiling, nodding her head in agreement and then she said, "You're very welcome in our home, John. Please consider it."

When it was time to gather up the lovebirds, John walked up to Matthew and asked, "Hey Bro, okay if I use your room? Feel kina funny usin' your brother's."

"What?"

"Your Dad and Mom ask't me ta come stay at your house. You okay wit' it?"

"Hey, that's great! Maybe after a while I can get you to lose some of that weird east coast accent, turn you into a Californian."

"What weird eas' coas' accen'?" The next two months are tough for Matthew as he learned how to walk with an artificial leg. First comes the toddler stage, falling down and pulling himself back up to try again. His stump grows raw and painful, but eventually it toughens up and he can use the hard plastic leg with little discomfort.

COMING HOME

On September 14, 1969, Matthew came home to a large party of friends. Sadly, during the closing moments of the party Matthew learned of John's problems with trying to find employment in the area. "Matt, no one wants ta hire a one-eyed Black Viet Nam vet with a eas' coas' accen'."

Walter hoped to find him a job through some of the men in his congregation, but oddly enough there didn't seem to be any openings and Walter struggled with judgment of his friend's truthfulness and came close to slapping one of his oldest friends when he said, "Maybe this young man would be happier with his own people."

"We are his own people, Mark. Maybe you should spend it bit more time in the Word and less time..." Walter stopped when he saw Jean shaking her head. He knew what she was thinking, *I know, you can't change how people think with anger. But it appears I need to spend a few more Sundays speaking on racial equality and how our Lord died for all of us. So many people still have an image of Jesus being some white kid with blue eyes. My god, excuse me lord, but you were Hebrew!*

Added to the pressure of being the only Black man in Walter's church, he was stopped three times by the local police when he got edgy and decided on taking a walk at night. By the end of the week though, all the policemen knew who John was and left him alone. Then things changed and in a way John would have never suspected.

THE CAMPUS LIFE RALLY

Kathy Lee, Matthew and a very depressed John drove to Pomona to attend a special rally at Cal Poly, a small college on the outskirts of Pomona that hosted some 2500 plus students. It was good location for a rally because more than ten-high schools were within a 15-mile drive.

When Kathy Lee pulled into the parking lot, the number of young people entering the gym amazed them. Still having a minor problem with balance, Matthew used a wooden cane to walk with. John was growing his Afro out and sported a short beard to go with his eye patch and expand on his roguish look.

Entering the rally, they were handed literature concerning tonight's rally and the guest speaker was a Nicky Cruz. "He's a former warlord for some New York street gang. Found salvation through a gutsy young street pastor and now he travels around the country giving talks," Kathy Lee said.

"Yeah?" John said a bit too half-heartedly. He really didn't want to be here, but finally gave in to Matthew's repeated requests.

"The pastor's name is David Wilkerson, their story was written in a book called "*The Cross and The Switchblade*," Matthew said as they made their way through the crowd to find a seat in the stands.

Once the music began the people began finding their seats and the rally kicked in as over 500 young adults began to worship a new style of beat called Christian contemporary music. Rock guitars and drums were now involved in the praising of God, which was a challenge to many of the older pastors and certain denominations who thought electric guitars and drum sets had to be the tools of the devil.

Once the worship music ended, a longhaired guitarist spoke on the goals behind Campus Life Ministries and then introduced Nicky Cruz. Right from the start, Matthew couldn't help but notice the transformation that occurred in John. His friend was riveted to his seat and hanging off Nicky's every word. At the end of his message, Nicky offered up an alter call and dozens of people came forward to be directed to a side room where prayer volunteers waited. A final song and the rally ended.

"Hey, can you guys give me a few minutes. Ah'd like to talk wit' that guy," John said. He then stood up and began making his way forward through the crowd.

While Matthew watched, John patiently waited his turn and was soon introduced to Nicky Cruz. After a few minutes of conversation, Nicky escorted John over to where several older men were standing together.

Wonder what that's about? Matthew wondered.

After shaking John's hand, Nicky resumed talking with others as John introduced himself to the group of men. For nearly thirty minutes they talked before they shook hands and John returned to Matthew and Kathy Lee.

"Okay, Bro, what's going on?" Matthew asked when John plopped down beside him.

"Jus' foun' me a job, my man. Got an interview dis Friday wit' thu director of some drug rehab...he called it *Reach Out*."

"Oh, John that is so cool," Kathy Lee said as she reached across Matthew and laid her hand on John's.

"They use thu Lord's Word ta fight gangs an' beat drugs. They knows your dad too, I use't him as a reference. Funny, mah lack of education don't seem ta matter none, they said somethin' 'bout life experience bein' its own value. Smart guys!"

"You blow my mind. I didn't know you wanted to work with kids," Matthew said.

"Been talkin' 'bout it wit' your dad. Said ta ask God for a direction, must be why I came here tonight."

John walked out of the gym that night a new person. He had a direction to take and the support of his friends to see it through. He wondered if maybe tonight the nightmares wouldn't come and he could finally sleep a whole night through. Like Matthew, John would later be diagnosed with Post Traumatic Stress Disorder (PTSD) and in former wars it was often referred to as battle fatigue. From what Matthew could learn through his out-patient counseling, a lot of the combat veterans coming home from Vietnam suffered from varying degrees of PTSD and this concerned him. He continued to lift his nightmares up to God in hopes they would end and he could lay to rest the faces of all those men he had killed in Vietnam.

TIME PASSES BY

Once John was hired on as a counselor it wasn't long before he was traveling around Southern California. He visited Watts and other parts of Los Angeles every chance he got, but most of his nights he spent with drug addicts and gang-bangers.

He spoke at rallies, participated in community-action center programs and the Lord continued to bring out a hidden talent in John for public speaking. His appearance got his foot through the doors with several of the young black gangs and his experiences from D.C. and Vietnam got them to listen. With every talk John threw in a few scriptures and before long the questions started flying about God, and what could this almighty dude do for them?

John began taking courses at Cal Poly and he was shocked to find out he had a brain between his ears. He eventually obtained a Bachelor's Degree in Social Work in three years and as Reach Out grew he traveled to Fresno, San Diego and San Francisco.

But it was during a visit to Watts that John met a Miss Denise Summers. She was a 20-year old black woman and former gang member. A high school dropout, Denise raised her younger brother when their parents died. But then a caring social worker placed the younger brother into a drug rehab program when police found him semi-conscious on the floor of a utility room inside an apartment building. They also found heroin in his pocket and a hype kit strapped to his leg underneath his pants.

Denise Summers was a looker. She was 5'7", 125 pounds, and wore a large Afro style down over her shoulders. She also had very large brown eyes that seemed to swallow John right up. But through all her beauty, John recognized the look of a young woman who had seen too much on the streets that said *I've been there and I've done that. So don't mess with me.*

Then there was the obstacle of faith, Denise was a Muslim and was still carried on the unofficial rolls of a local gang. Yet, John felt drawn to her and they began dating. After four weeks of sporadic dates, he decided it was time for Denise to meet his family.

With all his traveling, John maintained a small one-bedroom apartment in Pomona, but he slept at the Kendal house usually once or twice a week. So when John bypassed the Pomona exits and continued heading east on the freeway into White man's land, Denise asked, "Where we goin'?"

"Upland, dat's where mah family live."

Confused, Denise knew Upland was nearly an entirely white middle-class community with a couple neighborhoods of Hispanic people. So when John pulled his 1967 Pontiac into the Kendal's driveway, Denise couldn't help but notice the nice house appeared to be a bit pricey for whom she thought John was and then she noticed the two cars parked in front of the garage. She remembered how John had told her about his family being in the minister business, but the wealth she saw before her was not like any ministers she knew of and she was puzzled. She'd always heard how ministers were all poor, having to live off the scraps of the people in their churches. A moment later, she was introduced to Walter and Jean and now she was really confused.

They're white!

For a moment there, John thought Denise was going to walk right out of the house and his life, but seeing her startled and uneasy expression, Jean moved in and within minutes she had Denise sitting on the couch with a glass of iced tea in her hands. Relaxing a bit, she soon learned of how the Kendals had become John's family.

John knew from her statements that Denise was quite bigoted and it had come from the Watts riots where her father was beat up by over zealous white National Guardsman. But Jean's kindness seemed to be doing the trick to help Denise relax as Jean told her stories about Matthew and John's strange relationship.

Coming in from a walk, Matthew and Kathy Lee were introduced to Denise. Sitting together in the living room, it was John and Matthew's turn to tell stories and for the first time Denise was able to hear about some of John's experiences in Vietnam. By the end of the evening, Denise felt strangely comfortable with John's family. Not surprisingly, they were the first white family she'd taken the time to get to know.

Following dinner, Denise listened in awe as John and Matthew shared about how Jose had died, which explained to her why a .45 caliber pistol was displayed in a glass cabinet over the fireplace mantel. Over the next few weeks, the four of them, John and Denise, and Matthew and Kathy Lee, checked out several of the restaurants in the area and set through several movies from their various cultures. They did indeed encounter several stares and some people had a hard time seeing white and black couples together, but they ignored them and enjoyed each other's company. The times were a changing and both Matthew and John decided people needed to catch up.

The dictates of Bible College didn't prevent Matthew from marrying his special lady and Pastor Walter Kendal conducted the service. John stood as Best Man and Denise surprised quite a few attendees when she walked down the aisle as Made of Honor.

But typically, Kathy Lee's father kept complaining through the reception, "This is going to put me in the poor house!" And each time she heard him complain his wife would thump him in the chest and tell him to be quiet.

It was during a Campus Life Rally, where John was one of the guest speakers, that Denise responded to the alter call and gave her life to the Lord Jesus Christ. They were married shortly afterward and this time the roles were reversed with Matthew pulling down the Best Man duties and Kathy Lee walking in before Denise as the Maid of Honor.

This wedding ceremony was also held in Walter's church and the reception was held in the Watts Community Center. Over 800 people stopped in to offer their blessing to the couple, which included a clean younger brother who was now holding down a full time job and taking night school to obtain his GED. Some of the locals were a bit stunned when John introduced his family as they stood in the reception line.

But Walter couldn't help but notice though that the Afro-Americans attending the wedding were somewhat more accepting of this arrangement than the Whites of his church family and it saddened him. But this also gave him a lot to pray about for the weeks, months and years ahead.

It wasn't long before the Lord blessed John and Denise with a baby girl. She arrived at 7 lbs and 12-ounces and was a bubbling joy to behold. During the christening, John was speechless when Walter blessed Roberta Lee Adams and to no one's surprise, Matthew and Kathy Lee become her godparents.

Anthony Jose Kendal made his presence known a year later, though the parents had hoped to hold off on children until Matthew was a working church pastor. But God apparently had other plans and an 8 lb and 7-ounce boy of screaming delight arrived at 4:12 a.m. on a wintery morning. During the christening he promptly spit up all over his grandfather and of course, John and Denise were named as godparents.

WILLIAM CASSELMAN

EPILOGUE: OLD ACQUAINTANCES AND UNVEILINGS

VIETNAM MEMORIAL, WASHINGTON D.C., NOVEMBER 13TH, 1982 1333 HOURS

A cool crisp wind welcomed a large crowd of gathers who are on hand for the unveiling and dedication of the Vietnam Memorial. Several of the local citizens look skyward as they catch a whiff of snow in the air, announcing the end of fall and the coming of winter. One of the TV newscasters, his coat collar turned up to emphasize the cold, continued his live report, "Even with the mercury dropping, thousands of people have come out today to participate in this memorable event." What he didn't mention was the near endless line of long-winded speeches the crowd was forced to listen to before the unveiling could occur.

Outside the National Mall area another type of festivity was in progress. Several dozen booths were set up for the sale of goods and wares, and a few of the more reputable ones provided educational literature for veterans; among them representatives from the American Legion and Veterans of Foreign Wars. Yet others are present too- the *shysters,* conmen who passed themselves off as Vietnam veterans in hope of making a quick buck, but most of these people had never worn the uniform of their country. Still, more than half the peddlers were dressed in camouflage shirts, selling *authentic* Vietnam memorabilia to any passerby. "I got your MIA-POW patches right here. I've got miniature American flags to put by the Wall for your fallen loved one and I have..." A shaggy looking character waved a handful of flags in the faces of perspective customers and shouted out his wares and prices to compete against the next guy.

A man in a wheel chair holds up a South Vietnamese flag and shouts, "Five dollars for a genuine South Vietnamese flag, a real collector's item! No more being made, once these sell that's it...just like South Vietnam. C'mon folks, only a pittance, just $5.00 to help support a disabled veteran," the man yelled in hopes he could be heard over all the other conversations and sales goings on.

A New York sweatshop produced the man's flag and others by the gross and the *disabled* veteran, he would load the wheelchair into his car trunk before running around to the driver's door and *jumping* into his car for the ride home. He saw this opportunity as a way to make his car

379

payments and he saw no harm in it. But there were dozens of others out there in wheelchairs, disabled by the wounds they received fighting an unpopular war and now some of them worked to supplement their disability pay by hawking everything from Purple Heart Medals, various ashtrays made from brass artillery shell casings and bottle openers transformed from .50 caliber machine gun casing, a necklace of M-16 bullets and the ever popular boonie hats. And for entertainment, disabled veterans and a few guys too young to have ever fought in that war, play their guitars and sing for small change. For a donation, they'll offer up a song from the Viet Nam era and one of the most common requests is a song recorded by Barry Sadler; *Ballad of the Green Beret.* Some would even tell you a war story, usually pure fiction, but keep tossing in that change and you could hear of their heroic feats, or how they lost their best friend in a terrible firefight.

But between the actors, a few real to life veterans are making their way through the crowds of people in on push-boards. A few have lost limbs or use of them and most carry the weight of having lost their innocence when they were far too young to have done so. It's in their eyes. A passer-by, usually a fellow vet, could see into those tortured eyes and visualize the lost soul of a fellow veteran and more times than not he can often recognize the pain as his own. Change or cash would be dropped in a hat or jar in the front of the push board, thanks were offered and the disabled vet moved along.

Yet, with even all this commercialization and stark realism of seeing the horrible results of the war, no one can take away from the moment. It is time for the *Wall* to be unveiled and thousands grow silent as the massive covering is pulled away to reveal the engraved names of over 58,000 men and women killed in Vietnam.

For several moments a hush hangs over the crowd as a silent vigil takes place in respect for fallen comrades, brothers, sisters, fathers, sons and daughters. Engraved names identify men and women from all over the United States; blacks, whites, browns, yellows and reds; boys and girls from small towns and large cities, and from the East Coast to the West and onto the Hawaiian Islands. On this Wall ethnic background and one's faith no longer matters. These are simply the Americans who gave the greatest sacrifice in a war their country hated.

But now isn't the time to argue whether Vietnam was right or wrong. No, now is the time to honor the dead and hopefully, a time for healing to begin for those who still suffered the horrific nightmares.

A lone bugler played taps as veterans from Vietnam and other wars salute the fallen. As the tune played, a strange feeling of warmth seemed to carry through the crowd as the masses remember the men and women who went with those names. It is a very solemn moment. This would be a moment that would continue for generations to come, for of all the monuments in Washington DC, the Wall would carry the emotion of a very confused nation during a time when unrest and chaos seemed to be the centered around a loss of youth and their innocence, of betrayal and distrust, but still our nation carried on.

Far back in the crowd and holding his youngest son on his shoulders, Matthew's eyes began to water. He remembers again each and every man who died fighting beside him and knew their names were now engraved upon this memorial. Men like Jack Waterford, Isaac Washington, Captain Sampson and Jose Martinez.

With grief exploding in his chest, Matthew trembled ever so slightly as he imagined the face of his brother, Luke Kendal, staring back at him from the black marble surface of the memorial. He lowered his two-year old son John to the ground and looked to Kathy Lee for reassurance. She was holding their six-month old daughter Rachel in her arms, a bottle of breast milk in her mouth.

"You sure it's not too cold for her out here?" Matthew asked as he wiped away the tears.

"She's bundled up, my worrisome husband."

Pastor Matthew Kendal smiled at his wife before glancing over at his best friend. John Adams was hugging his wife Denise, while beside them, their daughter, Roberta huddled against Anthony. She was using him as a wind block.

"Where's Curtis?" Matthew asked. Curtis was John's youngest son and at 4-years old he was displaying an annoying ability to slip away undetected. Looking around, Matthew spotted Curtis's red cap between two people and grabbed him before he could get away. "Not this time, Curtis."

John made his way over to Matthew and picked his son up. Placing him on his shoulders, John didn't see when Curtis stuck his tongue out at Matthew.

"Matt, so what do you think of my home town?" John asked. With all of his public speaking on the West Coast, John had finally lost most of his East Coast accent.

"That drive through your old neighborhood yesterday was pretty interesting. I wasn't sure we were gonna make it out alive. There's a lot of hostility there, worse than I've seen in L.A."

"I've been thinking 'bout comin' back there, Matt. I want to open a community center like we have in California. Denise doesn't like the idea much, but she knows we have to go where the Lord directs."

"We'll talk more about it later, looks like they're going to let us get close enough to read the names. There's supposed to be some kind of guidebook up front to help locate the names we want to see."

"You grab your kids up an' I'll grab mine," John said. "Who would believe it, thirteen years ago we're lying on top of Hamburger an' now we're here with our families?"

"I often wonder what Jose might be doing now...if he'd survived?" Matthew asked as he directed his family toward the Wall. They were making their way along with thousands of others shoving their way forward.

"Knowing Jose as we did, he'd probably have become a police officer. He liked action an' liked to see the little guy win out against the bad guys. Yeah, he would have made a great cop." John grabbed Curtis's hand as the boy reached out for another man's hat.

For a brief moment the two men stopped and with tow of their kids on their shoulders, they reached out to each other as they remembered their old buddy. Of course both Curtis and Little John thought it was time for games and the two boys started swatting at each other.

"Mom, dad an' Uncle John are cryin'. Why they cryin', mom?" Little John asked as the men pulled then troublesome two apart.

"Their just sad, honey. Mourning the friend they lost in the war," Kathy Lee said. She and Denise walked up to embrace their husbands and this wasn't an isolated display of affection. All around them people were hugging each other as they remembered the ones who had died. People were coming to terms with feelings they had kept bottled up for years and right now emotions were running wild.

Looking around, Kathy Lee realized how this memorial was in fact a healing medicine for so many. Old wounds were being healed on the spot, especially for those who spent their lives feeling their country didn't care about them. She knew, deep in her heart, how thousands more would be coming here and for each one it would stir their feelings and more healings would occur.

Pointing to the spot on the Wall where they found Jose's name, Matthew lifted Anthony up so the boy could touch the name of the man who saved his father's life. A moment Matthew hoped Anthony would never forget. Working their way down the wall, Matthew was able to find the engraving of Luke's name and he took a photograph of it too. He had promised to make copies for his parents, who were now retired.

Placed along the strip of grass below the Wall were bouquets of flowers, POW/MIA miniature flags, POW bracelets, assorted medals and ribbons, and letters to the men whose names were listed above.

In front of the Wall stood men clad in expensive three-piece suits, embracing longhaired bikers dressed in leathers. For a brief moment, all barriers seemed to have fallen as men shared a common past and memories of old friends.

One of the caretakers, an old gentleman employed by the National Park Service, waited patiently for the crowds to disperse so he could clean up the debris. He turned to his associate, "I haven't seen this much hoorah displayed since the anti-war demonstration of '69."

"Makes it kind of fitting then, that rally wasn't held too far from this very spot."

The two workers watched as yet another veteran fell to his knees before the Wall, and the one said to his work partner, "This place's gonna have a powerful effect on a lot of people for years to come."

"I wish they'd just clean up their mess before they left."

"Think of it as job security, my man...just job security."

Curtis had taken off again and two sets of frantic parents were moving through the crowds to find him, a difficult task for someone who only stood three feet tall. It was Little John who spotted him though. Curtis was standing with several other small children in front of a life-size bronze sculpture of three soldiers. Standing side-by-side, these three bronze men were the second part of the memorial. The soldier in front appeared to be a white man wearing a flak-vest, the soldier to his left resembled a black man and the third soldier, he was a man who could be of any race because he wore a *boonie* hat to hide his features and he carried an M-60 over his shoulder.

Kneeling down to have a few choice words with his son, John glanced up at the sculpture and his eyes locked on the three soldiers. It caught Matthew off guard too. He was stunned by the similarities and was speechless. Matthew and John turned to look at each other and it was John's oldest daughter, who first commented, "Mom, those metal guys look just like dad, Uncle Matt an' their friend Jose."

Wiping Curtis's face, he was drooling again Denise looked up and blinked several times. "John, she's right it does look like you two and that sure looks like that picture we have of Jose." Denise turned to look at her husband, moving toward him when she saw the tear running down his cheek. "Oh, Baby..." Denise wrapped her arms around her husband's neck as John holds Curtis tightly against his leg.

"It's like they encased Jose in bronze...I can't believe how close the artist came to capturing us," Matthew said as he pulled out his camera and began taking pictures.

"The three caballeros," Kathy Lee said and the three others adults nod in agreement, as they all remember a certain photo of Matthew, Jose and John upon completion of Jump School.

Before leaving the memorial, Matthew walked up to the wall by himself and laid his hand upon his brother's name, "I love you, Luke. Thanks for leading the way."

Wiping a clean handkerchief over Luke's name, Matthew walked toward the families and passed by dozens of others who reached out to touch a loved one's name.

VACATION

Once a year the two families come together for a week long vacation at an agreed upon location. With John now running a drug rehabilitation center and also a community center in D.C., and Matthew pastoring his father's church in Upland, it becomes the only time for them to see each other. During this one-week they celebrated all the birthdays and holidays rolled into one big night of sharing. Gifts were sent during the year of course, but this time was allotted for stories about each other and a prize was awarded for the most humorous.

This year the sight chosen for the annual getaway was Yellowstone Park and while unloading the cars, Matthew hits John with an idea he'd been tossing around in his head.

"I'm thinking about taking some Christian Nam vets over with me to Hanoi?"

"Hanoi...as in Hanoi, Vietnam? Are you crazy?"

"The President has opened the door for trade with Vietnam and several small groups have already gone over with some real positive results. They say it's like getting new memories to cancel out the old ones." Matthew pulled out two-sleeping bags and tossed them to his youngest. "Give those to mom."

"So, why Vietnam for a mission trip and why now," John asked. He leaned against the car and waited for Matthew's reply.

"I want to visit some of the hospitals, see what we can do to help and just maybe see about helping out with an underground church or two. I've heard there are dozens of them operating throughout Vietnam and they are in need of Bibles."

"Good way to end up in prison, buddy. Communists still run that place and Christianity is forbidden."

"So, you wanna go?"

384

"It's been twenty-five years, Matt...an' I've got my center to run. If you're not a gay organization or an AIDS research group, it's nearly impossible to obtain grant funds anymore. Those kids need the center, for some it's their only safe place to hang out."

"Last time we talked you said you were having no trouble in finding help." Matthew gripped a hold of the family tent and pulled it out of the Suburban, "Give me a hand, will yuh?"

John grabbed one end of the large tent and helped Matthew carry it over to a clearing. Dropping it to the ground, John eyed his friend for a moment as he gave Matthew's idea a thought. "Who's going?"

"You only know one of them, a certain former PFC Baxley from 2nd squad."

"Really? When did you run into him...an' how is he?"

"We ran into each other at the V.A. hospital in Los Angeles. I was getting my leg worked on and there we were sharing an elevator. He's paralyzed from the waist and uses a motorized wheelchair. We have to take a converter over to keep his battery charged. Anyway, we had lunch together and I found out he was saved after a few years of boozing it up and taking the long ride down pity lane. Now he works in L.A. as a paralegal for the city."

"So he went along with your idea?"

"He loved it."

"Is there any new word on any of the old guys?" John asked as he knelt down to help un-wrap Matthew's tent.

"Monroe dropped me a line to say he's out on retirement and took over his dad's gas station. He was the one who told me about Walstein's suicide back in 1988, but I already sent you a note on that."

"Yeah, I thought about sending a letter to his folks, but I didn't want to open an old wound."

"Campbell's doing all right. He called me last week to brag about his new sporting goods store. Said to say hello to you and your family and hopes to make it to DC in the near future...Can you believe that guy, retired as a Lt. Colonel, has a beautiful wife and two wonderful kids and he's complaining to me about the hardships of running a business. Maybe next year we can take our vacation in Idaho and spend some time with him and Lucy."

"Sounds cool...but Matt, I don't know 'bout that trip to Nam. I'll let you know though. When you thinkin' 'bout going?"

"Next fall," Matthew said. "There will be ten men including you and I. Cost about $3,000 each for travel and another $1,000 for incidentals."

"I'll let you know…Now do you now how to put this tent up?"

"Sure I do…Kathy Lee, I need you!" Matthew shouted and then smiled at his friend.

The two oldest children were absent this year. Roberta Adams was off to college in Arizona and Anthony Jose Kendal was in his first year at San Diego State. This left Curtis, Little John and Rachel, three teenagers to terrorize the adults during this-years camp out.

HANOI, VIETNAM, JULY 9TH, 1995

Disembarking the Air France jet, Matthew stretched out his arms and one good leg to get some blood flowing again and led nine nervous men into Hanoi's busy air terminal. After a 23-hour flight the men were grateful to be on solid ground again and find a restroom larger than a broom closet. While unloading Baxley's wheelchair from the back of the aircraft, John pointed to several Vietnamese MiGs parked on the tarmac and said, "Those look like some pretty fast fighters, wonder what they top out at?"

"You was a grunt, what do you care how fast some jet jockey goes," Baxley said as they lowered him into his chair.

"I notice for a grunt you seem to be moving along at a good pace," Matthew said.

"Wheels, Matt…no jets," Baxley responded with.

John led Matthew and the others toward the customs counter and what should have lasted only an hour, the men from America were forced to endure over six hours of red tape. They waited as uniformed officers tore apart their baggage and reviewed their paperwork several times. Tape recorders were disassembled, items of clothing strewn about and one rather nice camera was seized as contraband because it was made in Japan.

Everything changed once they were outside the airport though. The Vietnamese people seemed genuine friendly and several teenage boys came running up shouting, "Americans numba-one!"

A sour faced young man was assigned to their group as a tour guide. He spoke fluent English and half-heartedly said, "I take you all sights. You safe wit' me. You call me Nuq Le Wan, or Mr. Lee. Okay?"

After finding all their rooms bugged and searched daily, the group began to relax and enjoy the scenery. Lee was constantly with them from morning to night, leading them through countless war memorials, government museums, government culture centers and other selected points of interest--but all owned or run by the government.

This wasn't what Matthew wanted to see. He came here to see the hospitals and hopefully a few orphanages. Places where his church could help, either with funds directly or helping in the education of medical workers. For three days he stressed this desire to Lee, but the young guide continued to take them to yet another cultural center where communist propaganda was shoved down their throats.

Matthew knew the man was under orders, so one night he brought he team together and they prayed for breakthrough. Then with only three days left in their trip, the guide suddenly changed directions one morning and they ended up in front of one of the largest hospitals in Hanoi. Delighted by the surprise, Matthew entered the hospital and with Lee acting as interpreter, was introduced to the supervising team of doctors and several administrative personnel. They showed the Americans the advancements made in Vietnamese medicine since the end of the war and visited one of the children's wards.

"Lee, I understand this is one of your best hospitals, but what about clinics in the hamlets and trained medical people for the villages?"

"No questions, time to go," Lee said and he began to usher the men out.

Then a strange event took place that both Matthew and John would never forget, or for that matter anyone on their team. As they were on their way out of the hospital, the group ran into the hospital's Chief Surgeon. Surprised to see so many foreigners, he asked to be introduced and Lee reluctantly obliged him. Curious by the lightweight structure of Baxley's wheelchair, the doctor asked Lee to interpret several questions he had for Baxley about the chair.

I know this man…but how? Matthew wondered, while he watched the middle-aged physician closely examine the chair.

Trying not to be offensive, Matthew knelt down beside the doctor and looked into his eyes. A bit uncomfortable by Matthew's closeness, the man turned to him as they both stood and then backed away in surprise. That's all it took. Matthew remembered the eyes. *It's him!*

"I can't believe this."

"What's the matter, Matt?" Baxley asked.

"John, it's him!"

"It's who?" John answered back, confused by his friend's conduct.

"The guy I told you about, the soldier who let me live on top of Hamburger Hill." Matthew pointed to the doctor who began to slowly back away in some confusion.

"That's him!"

By now Lee is becoming worried because one of the Americans was behaving improperly toward a very respected senior member of the hospital staff. "We must leave now!" Lee ordered, but Matthew refused to budge.

"Please, Mr. Lee...I mean no disrespect, but please ask him if he remembers me? We met on a dark night in May of 1969. On the summit of a place we called Hamburger Hill and he allowed me to live when he could have easily taken my life."

Lee hesitated, but then shrugged and asked the question. The doctor, Dr. Lin He Que, responded in Vietnamese and Lee in turn spoke Que's words in English, "Dr. Que not wish to talk about a time...many bad memories for him. We go now!"

Matthew wasn't about to leave, "Please sir, I offer no offense. I only wish to know if you are this man who spared my life?"

"Too many questions. Go now!" Lee was growing concerned, a complaint by the hospital staff would mean him losing this job and maybe worse.

Then to the American's surprise, Dr. Que waved Lee aside and addressed Matthew in perfect English, "Yes, I remember you. Our eyes, they never grow old and we once shared a deep...umm moment...Yes, a deep moment during a very bad time in our young lives. I see your god allowed you to live, but you misunderstand...I was not a soldier, but a medic. Had I been a soldier, then it would have been my duty to kill you."

"Praise God!" Matthew exclaimed, completely forgetting he was in a Communist country that still imprisoned Christians. "I thank the Lord for bringing us together again, allowing me to thank you face to face for sparing my life."

"I see by your words and actions that you have repaid your god by becoming a minister, maybe?"

"Dr. Que, my father was a church pastor and three years ago he retired. I now serve in his place as senior pastor. These men with me are all Christians and three of us served together in that same battle." Matthew pointed to John and then Baxley.

"Your friends suffered great injuries, but I see you have healed well."

Matthew reached down and knocked his knuckle against his artificial leg, "I lost my leg, but those times are behind us. We've come to Hanoi to see how we can help the Vietnamese people? Not charity, but sincere hands across the water assistance to bring our two countries closer together and heal the wounds of both."

"You men lost so much at the hands of my people, why would you want to help your old enemy?"

"Sir, I lost my brother here in 1968 and I came over here in 1969 to avenge his death. One of my best friends sacrificed his life so that I may live during that battle, but my Lord, Jesus Christ teaches us forgiveness and I have forgiven the people of Vietnam for what happened to me." Matthew hesitated, wanting to make sure his words come out properly, "Now, I ask you, Dr. Que...as a representative of your people, to forgive me for the harm I caused your countrymen."

Lin He Que was stunned by Matthew's admission and even more so by his request for forgiveness. He was speechless as the others stepped forward to echo Matthew's request and poor Mr. Lee was growing frantic with all this talk of Christianity. He knew he was headed for jail unless he could break this up.

"I am troubled by this, Mister...what was your name please?"

"Pastor Matthew Kendal, Dr. Que and I am so pleased to meet you, but forgive me for interrupting you, please go on."

"Mr. Kendal, why is it then so important to you whether or not I choose to forgive you. If you had not seen me today, who would you have asked?"

"I am not sure how to answer you, sir...except I feel very strongly that my Lord brought us together today." Matthew looked to John, who was nodding his head in agreement.

"Then it is most fortunate you came today, for I was visiting my family outside the city for the last four days. Had you come earlier, we would have missed each other." Dr. Que studied the smile on Matthew's face, wondering if there was a story within a story and then addressed Lee in Vietnamese.

Hesitating at first, Lee lowered his head in respect and turned to leave. Only stopping long enough to tell Matthew he would be waiting outside for them.

After Lee was out of earshot, Dr. Que relaxed some, "I have heard of this Jesus Christ for many years and I know of some who pray to him." His admission to knowing of an underground church surprised Matthew and then he knew, *Lord's at work here.*

"You may be right, either a strange wind of destiny or your even stranger god has brought us together. Now we will sit and talk and have some tea." Dr. Que led the party through a maze of hallways until they entered upon a large open room with a beautiful garden setting in the center.

"We will have tea." Dr. Que gave an order in Vietnamese and one of the staff members departed.

While they wait, the Americans learn three of the other doctors speak English, "It is a necessary tool to read American medical books left after the war." Other medical books were received from *other* channels and Matthew suspected through the ever popular Black Market. Besides English, Dr. Que spoke Japanese and French and was now learning some of the Chinese dialects. "I wish to be prepared in the event war should ever come between us and our northern cousins."

For the next three days, Americans and Vietnamese spend their time in the private garden area. This was one of few places Que felt they're free of surveillance devices. During this time Lee was forced to spend his time outside the hospital, chain-smoking cigarettes in fear he was going to end up before the police or worse the military. It was only out of fear he didn't report the goings-on to the authorities, fear of being questioned on why he allowed the Americans in the hospital in the first place. A question he continued to wrestle with, "Why did I take them here?"

GOING HOME AGAIN

When the aircraft lifted off from Hanoi, Matthew, John and the others left behind several new friends and a few small bibles they had smuggled into Viet Nam inside the bottom of Baxley's wheelchair seat.

Flying out over the China Sea, Matthew felt a real satisfaction in knowing he was leaving behind a new underground church. Without looking to John, Matthew released a soft sigh and said, "Feels pretty good doesn't it, buddy."

"Matt, I got a confession to make…when I came on this trip I was getting close to burn out. Mah oil lamp was running' dry an' ah wasn't hearin' from the Lord anymore. Lot's of money problems. The city wants to tear the community center down to build another parking lot and the gangs continue to grow in number. You know what I mean?"

"I've been there a couple of times," Matthew admitted.

"Well, I got a real Holy Spirit shot in the arm when I saw you an' Dr. Que prayin' together. When he accepted the Lord, I got so recharged and on fire an' I'm ready to take those city politicians on. Felt like that time on Firebase Blaze…you know when I asked the Lord into mah life. Got all energized an' I'm ready for the battle."

"John, I've helped a lot of people open their hearts to Jesus, but this was a first for me. This man was my enemy, a guy who aimed a rifle at me and had my life in his hands and now he's my brother. Yeah, I feel real energized myself. It's time to take names an' kick butt, as my youth pastor often likes to say."

Resting his had back on a small airplane pillow; Mathew continued talking after he closed his eyes, "Last time we flew into Viet Nam we came with rifles to wage war. This time though, we brought in the word of God for a far more important battle."

"Ah think I can finally put some nightmares to rest." John then looked to his friend and placed his hand on top of Matthew's arm, "Thanks for invitin' me, Matt."

"You're most very welcome." Matthew settled back as he thought over the events of the last three days and he couldn't wait to get home and tell Kathy Lee.

Several of the men on his team had promised to come back, hoping to raise funds from their local churches to purchase hospital equipment and Bibles written in Vietnamese. Dr. Que promised in turn to make the arrangements necessary for the equipment and especially the Bibles to bypass government inspection, and both Matthew and John believed he was a man capable of getting this dangerous task done.

As the Air France 747 headed toward home, two middle-aged men dropped off to well-needed sleep. For them the war was finally over.

THE END

Thank you for reading Apache Snow.
If you enjoyed this book, please consider posting a review.
The author and publisher would greatly appreciate it.

ABOUT THE AUTHOR

William Casselman was raised in Southern California and he enlisted in the U.S. Air Force in 1971 to become a Law Enforcement Specialist/Military Working Dog Handler. He served the next ten years in the military and met his lovely wife, Mona Sue, at Eielson AFB, Alaska.

A Vietnam veteran, he left the service to become a police officer in Dillingham, Alaska and spent the next twenty years in Alaskan police work. From patrolman to investigator, he has worked with four police departments and became Public Safety Director for the City of Whittier during the tragic Exxon Oil Spill of Prince William Sound in 1989.

William, a 32-year Christian, retired as Senior Investigator for the State of Alaska gaming program. With 35 years in Alaska, six children and 13 grandchildren, William and Mona Sue now live in rural Alaska.

Other Titles from

ALASKA DREAMS PUBLISHING

My Life In The Wilderness

A Coming Storm

Ghost Cave Mountain

Inside the Circle

The Silver Horn of Robin Hood

Alaskan Troll Eggs

Through My Eyes

The Professional Ghost Investigator

The Adventures of Jason and Bo

Please visit www.alaskadp.com and sign up for the ADP mailing list to be notified of future titles by Alaska Dreams Publishing.

www.ingramcontent.com/pod-product-compliance
Lightning Source LLC
Chambersburg PA
CBHW071149020726
47502CB00002B/342